How (Not) to Have an Arranged Marriage

Dr Amir Khan

How (Not) to Have an Arranged Marriage

MACMILLAN

First published 2023 by Macmillan
an imprint of Pan Macmillan
The Smithson, 6 Briset Street, London EC1M 5NR
EU representative: Macmillan Publishers Ireland Limited, 1st Floor,
The Liffey Trust Centre, 117–126 Sheriff Street Upper,
Dublin 1, D01 YC43
Associated companies throughout the world
www.panmacmillan.com

ISBN 978-1-0350-0822-3 HB
ISBN 978-1-0350-0823-0 TPB

1 3 5 7 9 8 6 4 2

A CIP catalogue record for this book is available from the British Library.

Typeset by Palimpsest Book Production Ltd, Falkirk, Stirlingshire
Printed and bound by CPI Group (UK) Ltd, Croydon, CR0 4YY

Visit **www.panmacmillan.com** to read more about all our books
and to buy them. You will also find features, author interviews and
news of any author events, and you can sign up for e-newsletters
so that you're always first to hear about our new releases.

To my Boo, this is for you

Prologue

THE CLASSROOM FELT LIKE the inside of an oven. The combination of an exceptionally dry summer and the explosion of traffic around the school over the last few years had thickened the air, making learning a rather uncomfortable experience. Feroza fanned herself with the end of her dupatta, wishing, not for the first time, that her parents could afford to send her to a school with air conditioning. She tried her best to concentrate. History was her favourite subject; she wanted to give it her full attention.

Miss Akram had brought in a large map of South Asia from home. She had unrolled it onto her table at the start of the lesson and pinned down its corners with cups from the canteen. They all stood huddled around as she explained how the 1971 war with India and East Pakistan eventually led to the formation of Bangladesh.

'East Pakistan was very different to the Pakistan we know now,' she explained, looking up at the class. 'We live in an area that was once called West Pakistan. Now we just call it Pakistan because East Pakistan eventually became Bangladesh and there were no longer two Pakistans.' She scanned the students. 'Can anybody tell me about the key differences between East and West Pakistan at the time?'

Feroza looked at the other girls, waiting for one of them to answer. Nobody raised their hand. Good, she thought, another opportunity for her to show Miss Akram she was still the cleverest girl in class. She put up her hand. Miss Akram nodded at her.

'Miss, they both shared a dominant religion of Islam, but were very different in terms of language, ethnicity and culture.' She looked around smugly. 'The East Pakistanis voted for a political party that advocated autonomy for the East but were blocked by the government in the West, which led to mass protests and eventually war.'

'Very good, Feroza.' Miss Akram looked impressed.

Feroza beamed with pride. 'Thank you, miss.'

'*Teacher's pet*,' Sania hissed in her ear.

'You're just jealous,' Feroza whispered back.

The thing Feroza loved most about history was learning about Pakistan. She knew it was still a relatively young country, one which had a lot to do before it would catch up with the rest of the world, but they had just had a female prime minister, Benazir Bhutto, who had finished a second term in office only last year. That was progress. She often wondered what it would have been like being alive and living here before the British came, before the partition of 1947 when India had been hastily and brutally carved up by the Raj. She imagined the people from all backgrounds, cultures and religions living seemingly peacefully side by side. The bell rang, marking the end of class. She gathered up her things.

'Did you have to embarrass the rest of us like that?' Sania asked as they made their way to the school gates.

'Sania, it's not my fault you don't do the reading before class.' Feroza shrugged. 'Maybe if you spent more time studying, you would know the answers too.' She stopped to wipe the sweat from her forehead. 'It's so hot,' she complained. 'Can't we take a rickshaw home?'

'And who is going to pay for that?' Sania demanded. 'Do you have the money?'

Feroza shook her head.

'Then we are walking.' Sania grabbed Feroza's hand. 'Come on, Azeem will be waiting.'

Azeem was Sania's brother. He came from helping his dad out at the market each day to walk the two of them home. Sania lived two streets away from Feroza and their parents knew each other. Feroza's dad bought meat from Sania's dad's market stall, so she was allowed to walk home with them.

Sania spotted her brother and headed towards him. 'Salaam,' she said to him, handing him her school bag. He gestured for Feroza to do the same.

'It's okay, I can carry my own things,' Feroza said. It was the same thing she told him every day.

He shook his head. 'Give it to me. I will carry your bag for you,' Azeem said quietly.

Feroza handed him her bag. 'Thank you,' she said. He nodded.

Azeem led the way. The streets of North Nazimabad were heavy with traffic. They had to navigate a busy roundabout where several lanes of traffic came at them haphazardly. People on mopeds whizzed passed, honking the horns. Brightly coloured buses inched out from the roads, not waiting for other vehicles to give way. Azeem cautioned them as they walked past a stray dog who was nursing her pups on the side of the road. All Feroza could think about was getting home and lying underneath the ceiling fan in her bedroom.

They eventually got to Feroza's street.

'You can leave me here, if you want,' she said to Sania. 'You don't have to walk me to the door, it's too hot.'

'Are you sure?' Sania asked.

'Yes. I'll be fine.'

'Okay, Azeem. Let's go,' Sania said to her brother.

Azeem shook his head. 'No, we will walk you all the way home,' he said to Feroza.

'But Azeem, it's *so hot!*' Sania complained. 'She said she will be fine. I can see her house from here.'

But Azeem had already started down the street. Feroza looked at Sania, shrugged and followed. They got to her house. Azeem handed her back her school bag.

'Thank you,' she said. 'See you tomorrow.' Azeem nodded and headed back up the street, Sania in tow.

Sania wasn't in school the next day. She had come down with a kidney infection and the doctor had advised a few days of rest. Feroza planned to get a rickshaw home that afternoon. She would get the money to pay for it from her mum; she knew her parents would prefer that to her walking home on her own. It was another hot day. She came out of the school gates and headed towards the main road in the hopes of flagging down a rickshaw.

'Feroza! Salaam,' a voice called from behind her. She turned to look. It was Azeem.

'Salaam, Azeem. What are you doing here?' she asked, confused.

'I've come to walk you home, same as always,' Azeem said. 'Shall I take your bag?'

'But I thought with Sania off—'

'I walk you both home,' he said. 'Dad said I should make sure you get home safely too.'

Feroza stared at him. Was she allowed to walk home alone with a boy? She wasn't sure. If his dad knew about it and her dad had previously approved, then she supposed it wouldn't do any harm. And besides, it would save her parents the rickshaw fare.

'Okay, well, let's go then,' she said.

'I'll take your bag.' Azeem held out his hand. Feroza gave him her bag and they set off.

'How is Sania?' she asked.

'Not well. The doctors gave her an injection of antibiotics and want to see her again today,' Azeem replied. 'Careful,' he said, pointing at some excrement on the road. Feroza side-stepped it just in time.

They walked in silence for a few minutes.

'Be careful here,' Azeem said. 'Aunty Sajda's goat has got loose again. She can be very dangerous.'

They all knew about Aunty Sajda's goat, Pasanti. She was old and probably a bit senile, and only gave a little milk each day. Really she ought to be slaughtered for meat, but after Uncle Mohnis died, Sajda only had the goat to keep her company.

'I'll be careful,' Feroza said. She had heard of Pasanti running at strangers if she felt cornered.

They got to Feroza's house.

'Thank you,' she said, taking back her bag. 'Do you think Sania will be back tomorrow?'

'I'm not sure,' Azeem replied. 'I'll walk you home either way.' He turned and walked off.

Her mum was in the kitchen, preparing dinner.

'Assalamualaikum, Mum,' she said.

Her mum looked at her and then the clock. 'Walaikum salam,' she said. 'You're late.'

'Sania is ill, she has an infection,' Feroza explained. 'I was going to get a rickshaw home, but Azeem came anyway to walk me home.'

Her mum furrowed her eyebrows. 'Alone?' she asked.

Feroza nodded. 'I suppose he wanted to make sure I got home safely.'

Her mum looked at her. 'So why are you late?'

'My last class ran over time,' Feroza lied. She could see that her mum wouldn't be happy if she knew she had not only been

walking home with a boy, unaccompanied, but taking her time
with it.

There was a pause as her mum looked at her.

'Go wash your hands and help me with the rotis,' she eventually said. 'Your father and brothers will be home soon.'

Sania still wasn't in school the next day. Azeem waited for
Feroza at the gates. She handed him her bag and off they set.
The street vendors were setting up their stalls, hoping to entice
people with the smell of their food and repetitive calls.

'Do you like gol gappay?' he said.

'Gol gappay?' Feroza asked, confused by the question.

'Yes, gol gappay,' Azeem repeated. 'You do know what they
are, don't you?'

'Of course I do,' Feroza replied.

'Well, that vendor over there does the best gol gappay in all
of North Nazimabad.' Azeem pointed at a man who was busy
frying crispy puris in oil. 'You should try them.'

'Maybe one day,' Feroza replied. She watched as the puris
puffed out into hollow balls in the hot oil. The man pulled
them out, placing them carefully inside a glass box. She knew
she didn't have enough money to waste it on street food.

'Why not now?' Azeem said, excitedly. 'I haven't eaten
anything all day.'

'I should get home . . .' Feroza said. Her mum would worry
if she was late again. 'And I don't have any money.'

'It's only a few rupees, and besides, we sold out on lamb at
the market today so Dad gave me a bit extra.' He looked at
her. 'Come on.'

'Azeem, I don't want to be late.'

'We will eat fast.' Azeem was already at the vendor. 'Give me
two portions, and don't be stingy on the size!' he said. The
vendor nodded, plating up several of the gol gappay, filling

them with the mix of potato, onions and chickpeas and finally pouring in some spicy water. 'You have to eat them fresh and all in one go.' He opened his mouth and placed one of the filled balls inside, laughing as some of the water escaped and rolled down his chin.

'You are making a mess,' Feroza said. 'Let me show you how to do it properly.' She took one of the gol gappay, placing it inside of her mouth. It tasted delicious but was too big to eat all at once, so some of the water and chickpeas escaped. Azeem burst into fits of laughter.

'Show me how it's done, eh?' he said. They tried several times to eat a whole one in one go, but neither succeeded. 'Right, come on,' Azeem said. 'We don't want to worry your mum.'

He walked her to her door and handed her back her school bag. She thanked him and rushed inside.

For the first time since she could remember, Feroza found herself looking forward to the end of school. The clock seemed to tick along slowly all day. Eventually the end-of-school bell rang, so she quickly gathered up her things and rushed out to the gates. He was there.

'Sania tells me you like history,' Azeem enquired.

Had he been talking about her with his sister? Feroza felt something inside of her she hadn't felt before. She didn't know how to describe it but it felt good – jittery, but good. 'Yes, it's my favourite subject,' she replied. 'I like learning about our culture, where it came from, how it has been shaped over the years. Usually by outside influences.'

'What is it about our culture you like so much?' Azeem said as they walked past a cow that was tethered to an iron gate.

'I don't know,' Feroza mused. 'I suppose I like how it has stood the test of time. So many things have changed over the years, especially with British rule, but we have held on to our values. The things that make us Pakistani.'

'And what is it that makes us Pakistani?' he asked, suddenly stopping to look at her.

His stare felt simultaneously uncomfortable and pleasant. She looked away. 'I don't know. Everything, I suppose. Our religion, food, dress, country, language, values – so many things. But things that are easily lost if not looked after.'

Azeem nodded. 'You are very clever,' he said, smiling at her.

Feroza felt herself blushing. They got to her door.

'I bought you this,' Azeem said, handing her over a plastic bag.

'What is it?' Feroza asked, taking the bag and peering inside.

'Chicken thighs, freshly slaughtered this morning. They will make a good karahi. Thighs have the best flavour.'

'Thank you,' Feroza said. He was staring at her intensely. 'I'd better go in.'

He nodded. 'See you tomorrow.'

'Assalamualaikum,' she said to her mum, who was sitting on the sofa sewing. 'Azeem gave us this, says it's fresh from this morning.'

'What is it?' her mum asked.

'Chicken thighs.'

Her mum took the bag and looked inside. 'Feroza, we can't afford all of these thighs.'

'He doesn't want any money, Mum,' Feroza said. 'I think it is a gift.'

Her mum looked confused. 'A gift for what?'

Feroza shrugged. 'I don't know, but he didn't want paying, so I took them.'

Her mum stood up and went to the kitchen. She placed the thighs in the fridge. 'Feroza?' she said.

'Yes.'

'Don't tell your dad about these thighs.'

'Why not? He loves chicken,' Feroza replied.

'Yes, but you don't want him getting the wrong idea about why they were given to you,' her mum explained.

'What do you mean?' Feroza said. 'They were from Azeem. Dad knows the family.'

'Just listen to me, okay. Don't tell him,' her mum said sternly. Feroza nodded.

'We will have them for dinner tomorrow. I'll tell your father I got them cheap from a street merchant. Now go get changed out of your uniform, we have to get dinner ready.'

Poor Sania was off for the next two weeks with her kidney infection. Azeem would wait for Feroza each afternoon at the gate.

'Here,' he said, handing her a book. 'I found this at the book stall at the market, I thought you would like it.'

'What is it?' she asked.

'A book, silly!' He laughed.

'I know that. But what kind of book?'

'A book about Pakistani heritage,' he replied. 'My reading isn't so good, but Pervais who owns the stall says it's all the different kinds of people in Pakistan and where they came from.'

Feroza took the book out of the paper bag and stared at it. She had never been given such a thoughtful gift before.

'Don't you like it?' Azeem asked.

'I do,' she said slowly.

'Good. Pervais says it covers all the ethnic groups of our great country: Punjabis, Pashtuns, Sindhis, Kashmiris, Uzbeks. He even says there is a chapter on the Afghans in the North.'

Feroza nodded, turning the book over in her hands. 'Thank you. You didn't have to spend your money on me.'

'That's okay. I don't read as many books as you, but I know

Pakistani culture is made up of many different things and many different people.' Azeem started walking again. 'We'd better hurry, or we will be late.'

Feroza pushed the front door open. Her mum was waiting for her inside.

'Is Sania back yet?' she asked.

'No, not yet. Azeem says she is getting better and might be back next week.'

Her mum nodded. 'Did he walk you home again?'

Feroza also nodded. She didn't like the tone of her mother's voice.

'Did anyone see you?' her mum asked.

'What do you mean?'

'The neighbours. Did anyone see you alone with that boy?' her mum demanded.

'I don't know. We weren't doing anything, just walking. So what if they saw us?' Feroza was confused.

'Get changed before your father gets home,' her mum replied.

The last class of the day was science, and Feroza took notes as the teacher explained how to balance out chemical equations. She looked at the clock. Only half an hour to go before she would see Azeem again. When the bell went, she rushed to the bathroom, took her hair out of its usual plait and brushed out the waves until it was smooth. She had put some of her mum's lipstick in her bag that morning and she quickly applied it before heading to the gates. There was the usual rush of students and parents milling around. She looked at the spot where Azeem usually waited. He wasn't there. *He must be late*, she thought. She hurried over so she could wait for him.

Eventually the number of people started to dwindle as parents took their children home.

'Salaam, Feroza,' a voice called from behind her.

She turned to look. It was her father.

'Walaikum salam, Abu,' she said, looking to see if Azeem was anywhere.

'Who are you looking for?' her dad asked.

'Sania's brother Azeem. He usually walks the two of us home,' Feroza said. Her dad knew this.

'I will be walking you home from now on,' her dad replied. 'Come on.'

'What about your work?' Feroza enquired.

'I have made arrangements. Hurry.'

Feroza obeyed. Where was Azeem? Why was her father here? She struggled to keep up with her heavy bag of books. They eventually arrived home. Her dad stood at the door. 'Go inside, I have to go back to work. I will see you tonight.'

She went inside. Her mum was chopping onions in the kitchen.

'Mum, why did Abu come and collect me from school today?' she asked.

Her mum put her knife down and walked over to her daughter. Without saying anything, she took Feroza's bag and emptied the contents onto the floor. The lipstick rolled across the tiles, coming to a halt by the table. Her mum went to pick it up.

'Why did you take this?' she asked.

Feroza didn't say anything. Her mum pursed her lips and nodded.

'Go get changed, we need to prepare dinner.'

Feroza didn't answer. She picked her things up off the floor, putting them back in her bag, and went to her room.

After she had finished making the rotis, Feroza set the table. Her dad returned home from the office. Her brother was still at the shop and would eat later. Her mum brought over the daal she had been preparing.

'Feroza, could you get me a glass of water?' her dad asked. She got up and went to the kitchen to fill a jug. Returning to the table, she poured her father a glass. 'Feroza, how old are you now?' he asked.

She looked at him, puzzled. He knew how old she was. 'Eighteen,' she replied.

'I was speaking to Uncle Rehman today. You know his son, Abdul?'

Feroza shook her head. She didn't know Abdul.

'He is a good boy with a good job. He has plans to go and work in England.'

Feroza didn't say anything.

'I think he will be a good match for you,' her dad said. 'He will look after you.'

'But Abu—' she said, trying to protest.

'I have spoken to your mother and she thinks it is a good idea too.'

Feroza looked at her mum.

'England, beta,' she said. 'Such a good opportunity.'

Feroza finished her daal quietly.

'Can I finish college first?' she eventually asked.

'You can continue with college until the wedding,' her dad said. 'After that, it's up to your husband.'

Feroza nodded, trying her best not to cry.

'Good, that's settled then,' her dad said proudly. 'I'll ring Rehman tomorrow to tell them the good news.'

Feroza helped clear the table after dinner, and then went to her room. She could hear her parents talking in the living room. She took out the book Azeem had given her. She flicked through the pages, stopping every so often to read a paragraph. She probably wouldn't have any need for it now, she thought. She would be moving to England; what use was Pakistani culture there? She'd be leaving it all behind – her family, her culture, the traditions she loved so much. She held tightly to the book. She would take it with her, she thought. An act of defiance, a reminder of who she was and where she came from. She stopped flicking through and went back to the beginning, chapter one. She wanted to know everything.

Part One

London, Twenty-Five Years Later

Chapter One

Yousef

YOUSEF WAS STANDING ON the sidelines watching his girlfriend play football while rehearsing different ways to break her heart. He was also trying not to get sauce on his white shirt as he ate his cheeseburger. But every time he took a bite, the meat slipped further back in the bun which increased the threat level to his shirt. He decided enough was enough – on both food and his internal monologuing – and stuffed the rest of the burger in his mouth, wiping his hands on the cheap paper napkins the takeaway had provided.

Jess's football team were practising for their final game of the year. They'd had a good season, and if they won their next game, they could top the National University League table. The stakes were high but for Yousef they felt insurmountable.

The whistle blew for the end of training, pulling Yousef out of his thoughts. Jessica ran over to him. Her hair was tied in a ponytail and she wore a blue headband to stop stray strands falling in her face as she darted across the pitch. She gave him a kiss on the lips. The taste of her strawberry lip balm mixed with the salt of her sweat flooded Yousef's senses.

'You taste like burger,' she said, taking a sip from her water bottle. Yousef didn't say anything. 'Everything okay?' Jess asked,

handing him her water bottle so that she could pull her ponytail tighter.

'Yeah, fine, just feeling guilty for not having got you one,'
Yousef said.

'It's okay, I'm going out for dinner with the girls tonight,
remember?' Jess gestured to her teammates who were heading
back to the changing rooms. 'But I'll come over after if you're
still going to be awake?'

'Yeah, sounds good.' He kissed her again before she ran to
catch up with the rest of her team. He heard her laughing
loudly as they all disappeared into the old sports hall.

Yousef could have kicked himself. She had been standing right
there. He should have told her but he had bottled it again. He
had resolved to tell her today, right after the football practice, but
as soon as she had kissed him he knew it had been a futile trip.
He screwed the burger wrapper into a ball and, taking aim, he
threw it into the litter bin half a metre away. He missed. It wasn't
his day. He picked it up and placed it inside of the bin, looking
around to see if anyone had seen his failed effort. He was alone.
Throwing his backpack over his shoulder, he went home.

'So did you tell her?' Rohit asked as Yousef entered the house.

'No, she was busy . . . it wasn't the right time,' Yousef said,
dropping his rucksack on the floor.

'There's never going to be a right time. Just bloody get on
and do it.'

Rohit was Yousef's housemate as well as being his best friend.
They'd met on the first day of university, five years before.
Yousef's parents had dropped him off and helped him unpack.
Like most of the freshers, he'd chosen to spend his first year
in the shared university dormitories rather than individual flats.
Yousef figured that by sharing a kitchen and bathroom he would
make more friends.

'It's not very clean, is it?' Yousef's mum had said back then when she'd inspected the shower. 'There is mould on the ceiling.'

'It'll be fine, Mum,' Yousef had said quietly, looking around to make sure none of the other students could see them.

Yousef's parents always wore traditional Pakistani clothing. When they were home in Birmingham it was fine, but here he felt they stuck out like a sore thumb. The other parents, who were mostly white, were wearing toned-down dresses or smart shirts. Unfortunately, there didn't appear to be a 'toned-down' version of Pakistani clothing. His mother wore a powder-blue kameez emblazoned with a large floral print and, despite the rain, sandals that were covered in glass jewels. His more conservative father wore the traditional Pakistani kurta, which was essentially a very long green shirt and billowy white trousers. Yousef had looked around furtively, hoping nobody would see them as they headed towards the kitchen.

'Look at that cooker, it's still got last year's food on it,' his mum had said, grimacing.

'Do you want me to make a complaint to the university?' his dad had asked.

'No, Dad. I will just use the microwave,' Yousef had said, ushering them out of the kitchen.

'Beta, you should have gone to Birmingham University, that way you could have stayed at home where it is nice and clean,' his mum had said.

'I told you, Mum, I didn't get in. With medicine you just go where you get a place.' Yousef had lied. He'd been offered a place at Birmingham Medical School but he had torn up the letter as soon as it arrived. He'd wanted to get away from Birmingham, away from his parents who governed his every move. Besides, London wasn't a million miles away. It had still felt like a compromise to Yousef, who would have been happy to go as far as possible if needed.

'Well then, they are silly for turning my boy down,' his mum had said, squeezing his cheek. 'You are going to make a fantastic surgeon.'

'Thanks, Mum,' Yousef had said. He'd had no idea if he wanted to be a surgeon. 'I think that's everything. I'll be fine from here.'

'Make sure you focus on your work,' his father had said as he walked them out.

'I will, Dad.'

'And don't forget to put the meals I made you in the freezer. There is enough for two weeks,' his mum had said. 'I will send more once you have eaten that.'

'Yes, Mum.' He had no intention of putting them in the freezer. He hadn't wanted to be known as the boy who smelled of curries on his first week. They had gone straight in the bin. He'd waved his parents goodbye and went back to his room.

He had been keen for them to leave immediately so he could get on with starting university life, but the minute they left he'd felt suddenly alone. He hadn't known how to 'start' his university life. Was he just supposed to wander around and hope to be accepted into a clique of some sort? He had laid down on his bed wishing his parents had stayed a bit longer. He could hear the chatter of the other new students and their parents through the door. He'd wanted to go home.

Eventually Yousef had forced himself to get up and put some music on. He'd chosen the music he played carefully, conscious that everyone outside could probably hear it. He'd picked a hip hop artist who wasn't too mainstream to be considered a sell-out but also not too underground so nobody had heard of him. He'd propped his door open deliberately so the music resonated down the corridor.

'Love this tune, mate.' A boy had stood in the doorway. 'Have you heard the remix?'

'Yeah, I have it here,' Yousef had said, pointing to his collection of vinyl.

'Whoa, are those proper records? That's sick,' the boy had said. 'Can I see them?'

Yousef had gestured for the boy to come in. 'I'm Yousef.'

'Rohit.' The boy still had his eyes focused on Yousef's record collection. 'You got some seriously good stuff here.'

'What are you studying, Rohit?' Yousef had asked.

'Accountancy, you?'

'Medicine,' Yousef had replied.

'My parents would have loved it if I'd wanted to study medicine. I think that's every Asian parent's dream,' Rohit had said, sitting on the end of the bed.

'I actually wanted to be a vet, but my mum wouldn't let me.'

'Nah, you don't get many Indian vets.' Rohit had laughed.

'You get even fewer Pakistani ones!' Yousef had said, laughing too. 'Do you know what she said when I told her I was going to apply for veterinary school?'

'What?'

'Son, why do you want to be a vet? When the white folk kick us out of this country, nobody has pets in Pakistan. You will be jobless, on the streets.' Yousef had done his best impression of his mother. 'Be a doctor, it will be easy to get you married then.'

They had both fallen into fits of laughter.

'What did you tell her?' Rohit had asked.

'Well, I'm studying medicine, so she got her way.'

'She sounds like a bit of a traditionalist,' Rohit had said.

'You have no idea. Mind you, with Brexit she might be right.' Rohit laughed.

Yousef had met Jessica at the freshers' ball. It hadn't really been a 'ball' – none of the boys wore suits and none of the girls were in posh frocks. It had been no different to any of the student nights at the student guild, it just had a different name. Yousef had never had a girlfriend before. In fact, his parents had strictly forbidden him from talking to girls.

'You are going to university to become a doctor, don't mess around with girls. They will distract you,' his mother had said. 'I will find you a nice girl to marry after you qualify.'

He'd paid the barman for his drinks and headed back towards Rohit who was sitting at a table with Steve, another student who lived on their corridor. He'd handed them their beers and taken a sip of his drink.

'What's that you're drinking?' Steve had asked, gesturing to Yousef's drink.

'Coke.'

'Don't you drink?'

'No, I'm Muslim, we don't drink,' Yousef had said. He felt suddenly out of place, with everyone laughing loudly and drinking shots or pints.

'But Rohit's drinking,' Steve had said as Rohit took a huge gulp of his beer.

'I'm Hindu, mate. We can drink as much as we want.' Rohit had downed his pint to emphasize his point. 'You want another one?' he'd said to Steve.

'Yeah, go on.'

Rohit had disappeared, leaving Yousef with Steve.

'So you've never had a drink?' Steve had asked. Yousef had shaken his head. 'Wow.'

Before Yousef had been able to answer, three girls had laughed loudly behind him.

'Is anyone sitting there?' one of them had said. She'd pointed at Rohit's chair. The girl had brown hair that fell softly over her shoulders and the softest-looking lips Yousef had ever seen.

'Actually there i—' Steve had said.

'No, it's free,' Yousef had cut in. 'You can sit down.'

'Great, thanks.' The girl had picked the chair up and taken it to another table where other girls were sitting. Yousef had watched as she tossed her head back and laughed with the other girls. He hadn't been able to hear what they were saying but he'd had a sudden urge to know what it was.

'Hey, where's my chair gone?' Rohit had stood holding three drinks, looking confused.

'Yousef gave it away,' Steve had said, pointing at the group of girls, 'to that girl over there.'

Rohit had looked to see where Steve was pointing and noticed Yousef was staring in the same direction.

'Just go and talk to her, mate,' Steve had said, placing a hand on Yousef's shoulder.

'Nah, she isn't my type.' Yousef had laughed.

He'd lied, he'd been nervous. The truth was, he hadn't known how to simply go up and start a conversation with a girl who was clearly out of his league. As a result of his mum constantly telling him about the perils of the opposite sex, Yousef had feared talking to all girls. They had been an enigma, to be wary of in case they jeopardized any chance he had of becoming the surgeon he didn't know he wanted to be. He had simply expected one to be handed to him on a plate when the time came for him to be married, and his parents would make sure that happened.

There was something different about this girl. Yousef felt as if he was in a trance. Every one of her movements seemed like a beautiful dance in motion. He noticed how she pulled her earlobe ever so slightly when she was listening intently to what her friends were saying and when she laughed Yousef felt his heart tug. This had been a new feeling; none of the girls he'd come across before made him feel this way. She'd noticed him staring at her, and he'd quickly looked away.

It would be the following week before Yousef saw the girl from the freshers' ball again. Yousef was sitting in the lecture theatre; he had arrived early. It was his first medical school lecture. The previous week had been filled with joining various university clubs and societies but now it was time to work.

The lecture theatre felt huge and steeped in history. In the corridor outside were pictures of the medical school deans from years gone by. Yousef wondered how many doctors had started sitting right there, the same as him. It was set out like an auditorium and Yousef sat himself down in the third row. It felt like a safe bet. He'd wanted to sit in the front row but didn't want to appear too keen and the second row already had people on it. So, the third row it was.

Professor Moore had given the lecture and he'd joked that he was a vascular surgeon in his 'spare time' but preferred teaching. He'd been wearing a pair of jeans and a white shirt that hung loose, making it look as though he had carefully planned his casual look.

I'm a professor and a surgeon, but I am also hip and cool, like you guys.

Yousef had got out his laptop to take notes. To his disappointment, the lecture had contained very little medical information. Professor Moore had begun by saying how privileged they all were for getting into medicine and embarking on a 'trusted and noble' profession. Yousef had heard all of this before. In fact, he'd used these same words during his interview to get into medical school. He'd closed his computer and allowed his mind to drift. He hadn't made any friends on the course yet. Neither Rohit nor Steve were studying medicine. He needed to find a group he could talk shop with.

The front row had been full of students who were hanging off Professor Moore's every word. Technically, everyone at medical school was a bit of a geek. You had to work hard and get top grades to get in. They also liked it if you excelled in an outside interest – something that said you were a 'fully rounded individual'. Yousef had briefly taken up ballroom dancing in order to beef up his application form; when his offer for a place at medical school came through, he never attended another class.

He had decided the crowd at the front of the lecture theatre looked too 'fully rounded' for his liking.

He had turned his attention to the second row – a group of students were sitting there that appeared to know each other. They had been whispering things and smiling as Professor Moore talked. Yousef had noted that most of them looked like they hadn't washed anytime recently – they had a very earthy, hippy vibe about them. They wore loose baggy trousers bearing elephant prints that Yousef had only ever seen worn by people on television who belonged to a commune, and they had corduroy jackets and backpacks that bore environmental symbols. Yousef was all for saving the environment, but this group had looked a bit too hardcore for him. And besides, he had tried to go vegan once for a biology project but was immediately derailed by his mother who refused to cook separate meals for him or buy anything other than cow's milk.

'You think I have time to cook two dinners?' she had said firmly to him. 'You eat what we eat, or you go to Asda yourself and buy your own food. I'm not your slave.' Yousef didn't have the funds to buy his own food from Asda, so he did what he always did: succumbed to his mother's will.

To his left had been the religious groups who had clearly found each other during freshers' week: the Muslim boys and girls, who sat separate from each other. The Jewish students, who were paying very close attention, and a group of neatly dressed Christians. No, none of them had been for Yousef.

Yousef had looked at a group of black students who were sitting to his right but hesitated. He'd joined the Afro-Caribbean society during freshers' week, his only point of reference being that he liked R'n'B music. They had welcomed him with open arms and told him about the activities they ran. Although he wasn't black, he felt a kinship with anyone from a minority background. A connection that was there but didn't have a name. He couldn't see any familiar faces so decided he'd keep them in reserve in case he couldn't find another group of friends. Not far from them were the Malaysian and Chinese students – an impossible group to penetrate, Yousef told himself.

He'd turned around and taken a quick glance at the back row, which tired-looking boys in caps and girls in tracksuits dominated. In any other situation the current group on the back row would be considered geeks or swots, but now they were in a room where everyone needed top grades to even be there so these lot were simply the least geeky and swotty and were now the 'cool' crowd. Yousef felt slightly intimidated by them, so he'd decided he would also keep them on the reserve list too.

'Is anyone sitting here?' a voice had said, bringing Yousef out of his thoughts. He looked up. It had been the girl from the freshers' ball, the one that Yousef had not been able to stop thinking about. He'd quickly grabbed his bag from the seat and gestured for her to sit down.

'No, it's free,' he'd said, trying to sound as casual as possible.

The girl had smiled at him and sat down. Professor Moore had broken his 'cool' persona to give them a pointed look which simultaneously reprimanded the girl for being late and also sent out a message for them to shut up.

Yousef had kept chancing sideways glances at the girl. Her hair had been tied loosely in a bun and she'd worn a grey T-shirt with a pair of jeans. Yousef had thought she looked even more beautiful that day than when he had first met her. She must have felt as though she was being watched as her eyes had darted over in his direction, and he'd quickly looked away, hoping she hadn't seen him staring at her.

'My final words to you all are: remember to treat the patient, not just the disease,' Professor Moore had said proudly as he finished off the lecture, staring triumphantly into the crowd. There had been an awkward silence where Yousef thought Professor Moore had expected applause. Clearly one of the Jewish students had the same thought and had started clapping slowly. Nobody else joined in.

'Oh no, you don't have to clap,' Professor Moore had said, not in the least bit embarrassed.

'What a wanker,' the girl had muttered under her breath. Yousef had snorted, trying to suppress a laugh. She'd looked at him and smiled.

'That's the second time you have asked for my seat,' he'd said to her.

'Sorry?' She had looked confused.

'Oh, you probably don't remember but you asked to borrow a chair from our table at the freshers' ball,' he'd said, trying his best to keep the conversation going.

'I can't really remember much from that night, sorry,' she'd said. 'It was a heavy night with the football girls.'

'You play football?' Yousef had looked surprised. The girl hadn't matched up to his idea of what football girls looked like.

'Don't look so surprised, girls play football too.' She'd laughed. 'Usually better than men.' She'd winked at him. He hadn't known what to say. 'I'm Jess.' She'd held out her hand.

'Yousef,' he'd said, shaking it.

'Nice to meet you, Yousef,' she'd said as she stuffed her notebook back into her rucksack.

'Jess, do you fancy maybe going for a coffee?' Yousef had chanced it.

'What, now?' She'd looked surprised.

'Unless you're busy?' He'd felt his face heating up. One of the advantages to having brown skin was not blushing but it didn't stop the heat rising into his face.

'Sure, go on then, and you can fill me in on whether I missed anything at the start of this lecture.'

'Well, I can tell you that now: you didn't.' They'd both laughed.

Yousef and Jessica sat together in every lecture that week. He looked forward to seeing her each day. She asked a lot of questions. In the past when white folk had asked about his culture Yousef felt as though they were mocking him or getting him to justify something they had read that no longer applied to his religion. It was always 'What, you're a Muslim? So that means you can have four wives, right?' or, 'Is it true women are forced to cover themselves in your religion?' Yousef found himself inadvertently becoming the spokesperson for modern-day Muslims. But Jess was different, she would ask genuine, gentle and open questions about him and his culture. It wasn't morbid curiosity but interest in *him*.

The more he learned about her, the more fascinated he became. She had a joy for life. Everything was something to be enthusiastic about, even the small things Yousef took for granted. They had been having lunch in a park and a butterfly had landed on a dandelion nearby. It hadn't even registered with Yousef, but Jess had made it sound like the most wonderful thing on the planet. She talked of the patterns on the wings of the butterfly being unique to just that one insect and they had got up close so they could see its long tongue drinking from the dandelion.

'That's its proboscis,' she'd said. 'Isn't it fascinating?'

Yousef hadn't been looking at the butterfly any more, but at Jess. 'Yes. Yes, it is.'

They had their first kiss a month after meeting. Jessica had initiated it – Yousef had been too nervous. He had never kissed a girl before. He had, of course, seen kisses on television when his mum wasn't in the room. The first time he had seen it, he couldn't believe people put their tongues into other people's mouths – that was so gross. But the thought of Jess's tongue made him slightly dizzy. She caught him watching her lips one day whilst she was talking.

'You're looking at my mouth.' She smiled. His heart skipped a beat.

'No, I wasn't,' he protested.

'Yes, Yousef, you were. It's okay.' She smiled again and looked him in his eyes. The scents of the flowers around them suddenly became more vivid. 'Do you want to kiss me?'

'Yes,' he whispered. 'Very much.'

She waited. He didn't know what to do. She must have guessed. 'Let me show you.' She took his hand and their fingers interlocked. She tilted her head and moved her face towards his. Her lips were as soft as the ripest of strawberries, and he could taste her breath. He pushed his lips against hers, taking charge. He felt the flicker of her tongue inside his mouth; he did the same to her. Then their tongues met and it wasn't gross at all. It was wonderful. Yousef didn't want to stop. After a few seconds she pulled away.

'Not bad for your first time,' she said.

'That was . . . amazing,' he said, dazed. She laughed and they kissed again.

They officially became boyfriend and girlfriend a few days later. It was new territory for both of them. Jess had had boyfriends before but nobody as serious as Yousef. Their first night together had been awkwardly magical. They were both nervous but it felt right. Yousef knew what he was supposed to do, but still felt woefully unprepared. They took it slow, and the night culminated in a wonderful moment for the both of them. Yousef told Jess he loved her the following morning, and she said the same. They went out for coffee and scrambled eggs. It had been perfect.

'So, when do I get to meet your parents?' Jessica said to him one morning as they were lying in bed.

'Sorry, what?' Yousef's voice came out much higher than he had wanted it to. The question had caught him off guard.

'Your parents, when are you going to introduce me to them?' She gave his hand a squeeze.

The thought of introducing Jessica to his parents had never occurred to Yousef. He had always intended to keep his university life very separate from his family life. In his head, the two would never meet.

'Why would you want to meet my parents?' he asked. Jessica untangled herself from his arms and sat up in the bed.

'Because that's what couples do.'

'Well, I haven't met your parents.'

'They're coming up to visit in a couple of weeks. They want to take us both out for dinner to meet you.' She ran her hand through his hair. 'Mum says you look handsome in the photos I've sent them.'

'You've sent them photos?' Yousef felt like he was being blindsided.

'Of course I did, I tell my mum everything,' she said. 'Obviously Dad will do the whole "make sure you treat my daughter right" thing, but he's a pussycat really.' She laughed.

'Your dad knows about me too?' he said, his mouth becoming dry.

'Yes.' Jessica stopped playing with his hair. 'Yousef, what did your mum say when you told her about me?'

Yousef stared at the ceiling. It had always surprised him that Jessica was friends with her parents. She called them up every other day and he could hear her chatting to them in turn, laughing and going into the details of her day. He had even heard her casually swear whilst talking to them and they hadn't told her off.

He had a very different relationship with his parents. He might speak to them every day – at his mother's insistence – but the conversation revolved around what he had eaten, whether he was studying hard and who exactly he had spoken to that day. It was more interrogation than conversation. He had definitely not told his mum about Jessica. It would confirm her worst nightmares.

Also, he feared for Jessica's safety if his mum found out about them.

'Yousef?' Jessica said, more firmly this time.

'I haven't told her about us yet,' Yousef said quietly.

'What?'

'There just hasn't been a good moment.' He sat up to meet her gaze.

'Yousef, it's been eight months,' Jessica said flatly. 'Why haven't you told your family about us?'

'It's complicated,' he said, getting out of bed. 'You wouldn't understand.'

Jessica stood up. 'Try explaining it to me then! Whenever we talk about your family, you just change the subject or go quiet, so how am I going to understand?' She got dressed.

'Hey, listen, don't go,' Yousef said. 'I'll make us breakfast.'

'I'm happy to stay if you want to talk about your family with me.' She looked at him. Yousef stayed silent. Jessica sighed and left.

Yousef sat on the bed. He thought about what Jessica had said. As naive as it sounded, he had hoped to keep Jessica a secret from his parents for ever. He didn't have an endgame, he just assumed that the relationship would have fizzled out by now, but instead he had developed feelings towards Jessica and now missed her every time she left the room. Being away from his family meant he had the freedom to explore these feelings and he had never felt better.

When he returned home during the Christmas break, he resumed his role as the dutiful son, getting the meat from the halal butcher's, going to the mosque with his dad and arguing with his sister over the television remote. Jessica was separate from this life, she didn't fit in. He had told her that the phone reception was poor where they lived so he couldn't ring her every day but would text.

'You are always on that bloody phone,' his mum said as they sat watching one of her favourite Indian dramas. 'Who keeps messaging you?'

'Just Rohit, Mum. It's nothing,' he said.

She had given him a knowing look. 'As long as it is just Rohit and not some girl.' Luckily, her drama show had begun so she wasn't giving him her full attention. He looked at his dad to see if he was listening. He had nodded off in his chair.

He had come back to university in January and his other life picked up where it had left off. He and Jessica were spending more time together and things just felt right. He was happy as long as the two parts of his life remained distinct. The way he saw it, nobody was losing out.

He was wrong.

Chapter Two

Feroza

FEROZA KNEADED THE DOUGH for her chapattis with tightly clenched fists. She was anxious. Yousef was getting his final results and she had been praying for good news all day. To add to her prayers, she had also kept a fast in return for what she hoped would be positive news. The sight of the soft dough was making her hungry, but it would all be worth it if her son passed his last medical school exams. To be honest, she expected him to pass with honours.

She set the dough to one side and looked at her phone. It was almost five o'clock and Yousef still hadn't rung. Perhaps it was bad news and he was working up the courage to tell her. Feroza wanted to be one of those mothers she saw on British television who were supportive even if their child wasn't exceptional but she knew it wasn't her.

Feroza and her family were the first of their friends to own a giant flatscreen television. Abdul had to call the neighbour over to help bring down the big chest of drawers from their bedroom so they could mount the television on something. It looked magnificent. Feroza polished the screen every day and showed it off to all of her friends, who made all the appreciative noises she hoped they would. She could tell they were envious and she savoured the moment.

Feroza loved the new television. She watched it every day whilst Abdul was at work. Being a seamstress, she was able to work from home, so she laid out all of her fabrics and threads, got the sewing machine ready and made her alterations whilst keeping one eye on the television. At first Feroza's English wasn't very good so she didn't understand all that was being said on the programmes she watched, but she enjoyed them nevertheless.

When they had been in Pakistan, Abdul would go to the cinema with his friends to watch the latest Bollywood movies, but she wasn't allowed to go. He said it wasn't 'a place for women'. She had really wanted to go. The posters for the movies looked so colourful and dramatic; they were painted rather than being photographs, which added to the allure. She looked at them longingly as she passed them on the way to the meat markets. The women looked incredibly glamorous and the men so handsome. Watching television all day, Feroza felt she was making up for lost time. Though the women on British television didn't seem as glamorous as the actresses on the Bollywood posters – in fact, they looked a lot like the women she saw each week in the supermarket – Feroza learned much about British culture whilst watching television. The thing that surprised her more than anything was that the actors and actresses were allowed to kiss on screen. When she saw it happen she couldn't quite believe it. Surely the actor and actress in the soap were not married in real life? She had asked her neighbour, Mavis, about it, who had laughed and said it was 'just acting'. Feroza was shocked, only married people should kiss like that, but the shock wasn't enough to put her off watching every day.

When Yousef and Rehana were old enough to watch television – after they'd finished any homework, of course – she was always on standby to change the channel should anything resembling a kiss present itself. She didn't want her children to be corrupted by such obscene images. She would watch the shows they watched – often comedies imported from America, different to the British comedies she had enjoyed when they got their first television. She noticed the parents on these shows were far more open with their children and would talk to them about things Feroza deemed inappropriate, but it was often too late to change the channel by the time she realized what was going on. She also noticed the parents didn't seem to mind if their child failed an exam or was not top of their class. What rubbish, she thought, surely every parent wanted their child to do well at school? Why were these programmes suggesting otherwise? So when those TV mums said things like, 'Don't worry, son, I know you tried your best and that's all that matters,' she chortled to herself.

The words didn't sit right with her. Feroza had worked hard to ensure both of her children could go on to university. She had arrived in the UK from Pakistan with Abdul in 1992. Abdul had come first and got a job driving trains, and when he had saved enough money to rent a bedsit for the two of them she had come over. She became pregnant soon afterwards with Yousef and then Rehana a year later. She loved both of her children, but Yousef was her favourite. He was polite, clever and so handsome. She knew as soon as he was born that he would become a doctor. Education was free here in the UK and she intended to make the most of it for both of her children.

Rehana was not the daughter Feroza had hoped for, not quite as pretty or dainty as she would have wanted. Feroza would carefully plait her hair each night so that it wouldn't tangle as she slept, but Rehana was a restless sleeper, kicking out and turning over in her sleep. She had a rebellious side. She didn't always listen to her mother and got away with murder, being the apple of her father's eye. Well, today was not about Rehana. Feroza was focusing all of her energy on Yousef.

She had woken up early that morning and got out her prayer mat. She had been to the mosque the day before and asked the imam for a set of special prayers that would aid Yousef in passing his exam. She had also made a rather generous donation to the mosque in Yousef's name.

'It's a bit late to be praying now,' Rehana had said when she asked her what she was doing. 'He did the exam weeks ago.'

'You don't think God can help at any time, Rehana?' Feroza had asked of her daughter. Rehana had stopped praying years ago. It was an ever-present thorn in Feroza's side and one she constantly reminded Rehana of.

'Mum, Yousef is going to pass, he always passes,' Rehana said, rolling her eyes.

'Say inshallah, Rehana,' Feroza said firmly. 'We don't want to put the evil eye on him.'

'Inshallah!' Rehana said loudly, leaving the room and Feroza in peace.

Rehana was right, Feroza already had a list of friends she was going to call after Yousef told her he had passed his exams. She relished the thought of phoning them up one by one to tell them the news. They would pretend to be happy but she knew inside they would be seething with envy. None of her friends' children had become doctors. Yousef would be the first. Every time he came home for the holidays, she insisted on parading him around at dinner parties and weddings like the sultan that he was.

Feroza didn't bother taking Rehana with her on these rounds. She would leave her sitting with her father. Feroza had tried to get Rehana interested in a career in pharmacy but had failed. It didn't help that Abdul never supported her when it came to their daughter. Abdul infuriated her sometimes. Rehana ended up studying English Literature at university. Feroza had warned her she wouldn't get a job with such a degree but Rehana did not listen. Feroza had been right, Rehana struggled to find work after finishing university. Not that it bothered her. She seemed quite happy to sit on the sofa scrolling through her phone. No, Feroza could not boast about her daughter's English degree, but she would certainly make the most of her son's medical one.

Chapter Three

Rohit

ROHIT HAD AGREED TO wait with Yousef until he knew the outcome of his exam results. To be honest, he was just glad to get away from home for a bit. He knew Yousef was anxious. His mum had rung six times in the last hour to see if the results were out and each time Yousef had become more agitated. At one point, Yousef's mum threatened to call up the medical school directly if the exam results were not released soon.

'Don't they know how stressful this wait is for me?' she had asked Yousef. 'It is setting off my migraines.' Yousef promised to call her the minute the results came out.

Rohit had finished university a couple of years ago. His course was shorter than Yousef's and he was already a qualified accountant. He didn't recall being this stressed about his final results but then again, he didn't have the pressure Yousef's mum seemed to place upon him.

Rohit had been close to both of his parents, but after his dad's death, his relationship with his mum had taken a different turn. Watching Yousef talk to his parents reminded him of the day his dad had died. He had been at work and had several missed calls on his phone from his brother. He had just started his new job so dared not answer in case his boss saw. Rohit had been keen to make a good impression. He'd wanted to progress to chartered accounting, which would bring him one step closer to his dream job of investment banking.

Rohit had watched the phone light up silently, and each time he'd pressed the 'decline' button. Whatever his brother wanted would have to wait. He'd told his family to only call him at work in emergencies, but that rule had been completely ignored. During his first few weeks at his new job, his mum had called about the colour of her new curtains and his dad to ask where the code for the Wi-Fi was written down. It was at that point that Rohit had decided his family were unable to tell the difference between an emergency phone call and a routine one.

By the time he had got round to ringing Amit back, several hours had passed.

'Why aren't you answering your phone?' Amit had hissed.

'I was at work, you know I can't answer my phone at work.' Rohit had arrived at the bus stop and put his bag down on the bench.

'You should have answered. Dad's been taken into hospital. You need to come home. They're saying he's had a heart attack.' Amit's voice had cracked as he finished his sentence.

'What? How serious is it?' Rohit had asked, feeling his legs go weak.

'Serious, he's not conscious. Just come home, please.' Amit had sounded desperate. Rohit had got the message.

'I have to go, the doctors are here to speak to us. Just come home. We're at the hospital.' Amit had hung up.

Rohit had been hit by a sudden wave of nausea. Even if he had got on a train now, it would take at least two hours to get back to Manchester and then he would have to get a taxi to the hospital, which would take another thirty minutes. A sense of panic had erupted. He had felt his heart beating in his chest and he'd suddenly felt short of breath.

He'd quickly sat down on the bus shelter bench beside his

bag, closed his eyes and slowed his breathing down. His coun-
sellor had taught him how to manage his panic attacks. He
pushed down the overwhelming feeling to run home and lock
himself in his bedroom until all of this went away. They were
the same feelings he used to get when his mum took him
shopping to Manchester city centre – the crowds, the worry of
losing his parents and being left alone. These feelings were now
fighting for dominance in his head. Surely his father wouldn't
leave him now?

'Breathe slowly and focus on what you can do, not on what
is out of your control,' she'd said. Rohit opened his eyes. He
had to get to the train station and the quickest way was to
walk. He picked up his bag and took his first step.

By the time Rohit had arrived at the hospital, it had been
too late. Amit had been comforting his mother in the corridor
outside the room in which his dad now lay. Rohit had felt his
stomach lurch. He'd gone to hug his mum but one of the nurses
had appeared from the room and asked him if he wanted to
see his dad. He'd nodded.

Rohit's dad lay bare-chested on the hospital trolley, one of
his arms dangling off the side. The sheet covering him had
been haphazardly placed to conserve his modesty, but had left
his feet exposed. His dad had always complained about his feet
being cold and even wore two pairs of socks in the winter. A
tube had come out of his mouth but wasn't attached to anything.
He had a cannula in the back of each of his hands and the
stickers from the heart machine had still been on his chest.
He'd looked like he was the star of a macabre hospital-themed
play. The machine next to him had been beeping and the nurse
had gone to switch it off.

'We tried for nearly an hour to get him back,' she'd said,
eventually unplugging the machine after the buttons she'd
pressed failed to stop the noise it was making. 'They were
resuscitating him in the ambulance on the way here too.' She'd

carefully placed his father's dangling hand back on the bed. 'There, that's better.'

Rohit had watched as she removed the stickers from his chest, taking some of his dad's chest hair with each one. He would have hated that. His mum was always telling his dad he was too hairy and joking about how he should shave his chest, but he'd refused.

'It is a sign of my virility, my dear!' he'd exclaimed. Rohit smiled at the memory.

'We let your mum watch some of the resuscitation process,' the nurse had carried on, moving on to the stickers on his ankles. 'It's important she knows we did everything we could.' Rohit had nodded. 'I will give you a few minutes alone. When you're ready, we'll move him to the mortuary.' She'd left.

Rohit had stood at the end of the bed looking at his father. They had only spoken on the phone a couple of days before. Rohit had rung home to speak with his mother but his dad had answered and they had chatted about how Rohit was getting on at his new job and what he was having for dinner that evening. It hadn't seemed like an important conversation at the time, but now it was the most important conversation in the world. Rohit had gone to hold his dad's hand but stopped short. He had never seen a dead body before and there had been something unsettling about being in the same room as one. He had heard dead bodies felt cold and he hadn't wanted to remember his dad's hand that way; he'd wanted to hold on to the memory of his dad's hand when they crossed roads, and how it had felt warm and comforting.

He had gone to pull the sheet over his ankles, and as he'd got closer he had been able to smell his dad's aftershave. It wasn't an expensive brand – he had hated wasting money on things like that. Rohit and his brother had once got their father an expensive aftershave gift set for Diwali, but he had never worn it. They'd found it months after his death, in the back of his cupboard. Rohit had imagined his dad getting showered and dressed this morning as if it would have been a normal day. He had looked at the pile of clothes that now lay on the hospital floor. Yousef had once told him they cut you out of your clothes in a medical emergency using scissors. He'd picked the clothes up. There were tiny splatters of blood on the sleeves from when the ambulance crew had taken blood. Rohit's tears had fallen silently onto his dad's clothes.

Rohit had heard his mum's cries from behind the door. He'd known he should probably go out and see how she was but he hadn't felt he could leave his dad. Rohit had been overcome with guilt. He should have answered the phone earlier, he should have been there in his dad's last moments. The feelings had clawed at him, making it difficult for him to breathe. He had known his mother would be thinking the same: he'd been too far away when his parents needed him and now it was too late.

Neither Rohit nor his brother had organized a funeral before and they had relied on advice from the elders in the community to guide them. The cremation itself had been relatively easy to arrange once they had the paperwork from the registrar. The catering, however, was a sticking point. Everybody had an opinion.

'Just go for something simple. I have the number of a good caterer,' one of the uncles had said.

'No, no, people will expect to be fed properly after spending all day at a funeral,' another had replied, 'and make sure you get meat and vegetarian options.'

The brothers had decided to go for something in the middle, ordering one meat and one vegetarian curry but no starters or dessert. After the funeral, Rohit had felt he had a bit more breathing space. He'd been so preoccupied with making sure

everything went smoothly and his mother wasn't troubled by
any of it that he'd not had the chance to grieve the loss of his
father.

He'd gone to his room and shut the door. With all the visitors they had, it had been the first time he'd been alone. He
had thought of his father, all the things he would never see
him achieve. A few minutes later there had been a knock on
his bedroom door. It had been one of his mum's friends.

'What are you doing up here?' she'd said sharply. 'You should
be downstairs with your guests. They have all come to pay
their respects. It is rude to stay up here on your own.'

Rohit had quickly wiped away his tears, feeling slightly
embarrassed at the sudden intrusion. 'I'll be down in five
minutes, Aunty,' he'd said as she'd glared at him through eyes
heavily coated in eyeliner.

'Don't be too long. Your poor brother is having to look after
everyone on his own. You are the man of the house now,' she'd
said, adjusting the scarf on her head and disappearing downstairs. He hadn't quite understood the last comment. Amit was
the older of the two, surely he was now the man of the house?
The whole idea of a 'man of the house' had felt archaic to Rohit.
He hadn't wanted to be in charge of anything; organizing the
funeral had been bad enough. They hadn't been able to ask
their mum for money so Rohit and his brother had split the
cost. It had been expensive, and Rohit was still a junior member
of staff at his work and his pay reflected that. He couldn't afford
much else other than his rent, let alone pay for any more of
his parents' expenses.

Rohit knew his mum had found comfort from the endless
stream of people who were arriving at the house. It was a Hindu
tradition to come and pay your respects in person. It had been
nearly a week since they had buried his dad and the well-
wishers kept coming. Each new arrival had expected a cup of
tea and at least a plate of biscuits.

The women, his mum's friends, had been in the kitchen alternating between cooking and consoling his mum, who had seemed to renew her loud sobs each time a new guest arrived. It had been like each new arrival reopened a wound inside of her and just as they had managed to stem the bleeding a new person would turn up.

Everyone had wanted to know the same things. How did it happen? What had the doctors said? Didn't we see it coming? Rohit had wondered if any of the guests knew how inappropriate the questions were or whether they just didn't have anything else to say. Each time he'd finished telling the story, it had been met with variations of the same response:

'When it is your time, it is your time.'

The same solemn look had accompanied all the variations of this line. It had been a nothing sentence providing no comfort. All he had wanted was for everyone to go home so he could just have a few moments to himself, but each time it had felt like the numbers were dwindling, the doorbell had rung again.

After that first week, Rohit had been more than ready to go back to London. He'd told his mum he was needed at work but would be back soon.

'You should stay for another week,' Amit had said when he'd told him he was leaving.

'I've got work to do,' Rohit had said feebly.

'Bullshit, you can't wait to get away. You barely visited after you left for university. You know Dad was hoping you would get a job back here in Manchester, but you got that posh job in London instead.'

That had hurt. Rohit's dad had always encouraged him to do whatever it took to get into banking.

'Amit, that's not fair. It's not like you live at home.'

'I'm married, it's different. I didn't gallivant off to London at the first chance I got, I stayed and studied here in Manchester.

Besides, I only live ten minutes away and visit every week. Not like you.'

Amit had been right. Rohit had been desperate to leave home and hadn't thought twice about what that might mean for his parents. He'd ordered a taxi and made his way back to London, feeling ashamed of the relief he had felt when he finally left the house.

After a few weeks it had become clear that his mum wasn't going to cope without his dad in the house. His dad used to drive his mum everywhere; she now had to rely on taxis or Amit coming to pick her up. She hadn't been able to pay the first set of bills when they arrived and there had been a mountain of paperwork and phone calls to be made in order to sort out what little money his dad had left behind.

Rohit had needed to call his brother.

'I think it's best if she moves in with you and Priya,' Rohit had said. 'We can't leave her by herself in the house without Dad.'

Initially, Amit had agreed but after speaking to his wife, he'd changed his mind.

'Look, it's just Priya doesn't think she can live with Mum,' Amit had explained to Rohit on the phone. 'Priya likes her obviously, and feels terrible about what has happened to Dad, but she says Mum is too interfering.'

'What are we supposed to do?' Rohit had asked. 'She can't live with me here in London, I share with two other blokes.'

'No, that won't work either,' Amit had said. 'Unless . . .'

'Unless what?'

'Unless you move home,' Amit had replied. 'Then we won't have to worry about Mum being on her own.'

'Amit, what do you mean? I have a job here in London. I can't just leave.' Rohit had been taken aback at the suggestion.

'Well, Priya is adamant we can't have her here. You know what they say, you can't have two queen bees in one hive, they end up killing each other.'

Rohit had felt Amit had practised that line.

'Is that what Priya told you to say?' he had retorted.

'Rohit, be fair. I didn't go away to university like you did. I stayed at home until I got married. You've had your time away, now it's time for you to come home.' Amit had sounded resolute.

'But what about my job? My career?'

'Family is more important than any job,' Amit had said. 'Look, Priya said we can have Mum come and stay with us whilst you work your notice period then she can move back home with you.'

'What? So, you and Priya have already discussed this?' Rohit had said, surprised.

'Rohit, you're an accountant. There are plenty of jobs here in Manchester for an accountant. I don't understand why you're resisting this so much.'

If Amit and Priya had decided they weren't going to have Mum long term, then he knew he couldn't change their minds. Once Priya had decided something, Amit always agreed and that was the end of the discussion.

'I'll think about it,' he'd told Amit.

But Rohit had known he had no choice. The anxiety he had fought so hard to keep at bay began to seep insidiously back into his thoughts. All Rohit had wanted was to prove to people he was just as good as them. He had come to accept, being from an Indian background, that he had to work especially hard to get a seat at the coveted corporate table. After getting a first in his accountancy degree, he had finally managed to get a job at an international accounting firm. But it hadn't been what he had expected. The constant need to prove himself at work had been exhausting, but he'd felt grateful to have this job. He wasn't at the table yet, but at least he was in the same building. Most of his contemporaries were white – nothing unusual there, Rohit told himself. But as time went on, he'd noticed they were given larger accounts whilst he was kept in the audit office. Rohit knew his limitations, he knew he didn't have it in him to challenge the unfairness of the situation, so instead he'd worked harder to prove he could complete his financial audits quicker and more efficiently than anyone else. He would get emails back from his bosses saying how impressed they were at the quality and speed of his work, but that was where they'd stopped short. There was no mention of career progression or a raise, but Rohit had felt he had to be grateful for the recognition, so he'd carried on. He'd accepted it as a fact of life: people like him had to work harder and prove themselves over and over simply to achieve the same things white people got by virtue of their potential alone.

Rohit had resented his brother, but the thing he felt most ashamed of was that he resented his dad for dying. Rohit hadn't wanted to move home; it meant that all those months of being a 'yes man' at work had been for nothing. His dad had died and that was it, he had to leave his job and move back to Manchester. It just hadn't seemed fair. The following week he had handed in his notice, his boss's secretary acknowledged receipt of his resignation, and he'd left one Wednesday without any sort of fanfare.

The Manchester accountancy market was competitive. There were fewer jobs and more people applying for them. He had eventually taken a job at a small accountancy firm. It didn't have the prospects his job in London had but it would give him the experience he needed, and besides, he'd just wanted to be out of the house.

When Yousef rang to see if he wanted to come down to London for a few days until his results came out, Rohit had jumped at the chance. His new boss was quite flexible and happy to give him holidays at short notice, and he'd booked his train early enough to get a cheap ticket. Going back to the house he once shared with Yousef and Steve felt great. They had been out to all their old bars and played Xbox all day. Now Rohit sat on the sofa watching Yousef refresh the university webpage for the millionth time.

'Oh shit, the results are out,' Yousef whispered, staring at the screen.

'Well, did you pass?' Rohit said, unable to read his best friend's face.

Chapter Four

Rehana

REHANA WAS LYING ON her bed, her headphones turned up to maximum volume. Her mum was downstairs on tenterhooks waiting for Yousef's exam results and she wanted nothing to do with it. Her dad was pretending not to care by reading the paper, but his facade dropped each time her mum rang Yousef for an update.

'Well?' he would ask.

'Still waiting,' her mum would say. 'My nerves can't take much more.'

'Don't be so dramatic, Mum,' Rehana had said.

'You shut up, Rehana. And turn that television down, I am trying to concentrate on my prayers.' Her mum had finally got up and switched the television off.

'Mum, I was watching that!' Rehana had protested.

'You can watch it later, I need silence for my prayers. Abdul, why are you sitting there so quietly, huh? Tell your daughter.'

'Rehana, just leave it today. Can't you see your mum is worried about your brother?' her dad had said from behind his paper.

'Fine, I'll just go up to my room then, shall I?' She'd waited for an answer. Silence. Sighing loudly, she'd stomped upstairs.

She didn't remember either of her parents ringing her to see if she had passed her final exams. She had watched as all her friends had got phone calls from their parents, whilst her phone had remained silent. Some of them were even happy when they heard their child had got a 2:2 in their degree. Rehana had got a first, something she was very proud of. She knew her parents were not happy that she had taken up an arts course; her mum had always said she wanted her to study pharmacy. She kept telling her that being a pharmacist was a 'good job for a good girl'. Rehana had no interest in becoming a pharmacist, or a 'good girl'. She loved reading. Ever since she was a child she would immerse herself in storybooks. She dreamed of becoming a writer in some faraway city, of having affairs and leaving a trail of broken hearts in her wake. Sadly, none of that had materialized. The furthest she was allowed to go was Leeds and the boys there had been complete dicks. The only heart that had been broken was her own.

On her results day, after waiting several hours, she'd decided to ring her parents herself.

'I passed, Mum. I got a first,' she had said excitedly when her mum answered the phone.

'Oh, is that today? That's very good, Rehana,' her mum had replied with much less enthusiasm. 'Will getting a first mean it will be easier for you to get a job?'

'Well, I'm not really thinking about that right now, Mum. I'm just going to enjoy this moment,' she'd said, determined not to let her mum ruin this for her.

'I hope that doesn't mean you are going out partying? Here, your father wants to talk to you,' her mum had said before Rehana could say anything.

'Hello, Rehana? I knew your results day was soon, but couldn't remember the exact day, sorry,' her dad had said. She didn't mind that her father had forgotten, he wasn't very good at keeping on top of such things.

'Dad, I got a first class honours degree,' she'd said.

'Mashallah, that is very good. I knew you would make us proud.' She thought her dad sounded genuinely delighted. 'Does this mean you are moving home soon?'

Rehana had been dreading this question. She had fought so hard to go away to university, she wasn't in a hurry to move back. Her mum, rather predictably, had been vehemently against it, arguing they couldn't afford to pay her fees and rent. Rehana had pleaded with both of her parents. She felt constantly under surveillance at home. Her mum even listened in on her phone conversations just in case she was talking to a boy. Rehana wasn't stupid enough to let a boy call her at home. In the end her dad had caved and convinced her mum that she could go away to university on the proviso that she return home after her degree.

'I thought I would stay and try to find a job here. Leeds has a great art scene.' Her dad was her best bet at being able to stay, she just had to convince him.

'Rehana, we had an understanding,' her dad had said firmly. Rehana had known not to argue.

'Yes, Dad. My rent is paid until the end of July, so I guess I'll come home after that,' she'd said sullenly.

'Good girl. I really am proud of you, and so is your mum. She will be ringing her friends telling them what a clever daughter we have.' Rehana had known he was lying but she wasn't in the mood to call bullshit. This was her day and she was going to go out and celebrate.

Now she was home, university seemed like a distant memory. She had struggled to find work related to her English Literature degree. The problem was, she wasn't exactly sure what she wanted to do. She tried writing but every time she sat down at her computer she couldn't think of how to start. She had spent so long studying other people's work, she just didn't believe she could produce anything that would stand up to the same level of scrutiny. Her lack of self-belief became so overwhelming she eventually stopped trying to write and decided she would take the equivalent of a gap year and start afresh the following summer.

Sadly, the Pakistani version of a gap year didn't involve travelling the world (on your parents' dollar), getting braids and not shaving your armpits. For Rehana, it meant watching Netflix, making endless cups of tea for her father and informing her mother of her exact whereabouts at all times. As her Eat, Pray, Love days failed to materialize, Rehana gave in to her mum's nagging and applied for a teacher training course. She didn't dislike the idea of teaching English, she just didn't like the fact it was her mum's idea. But she had no money and was out of options.

Being at home aged twenty-one was much worse than when she had been a teenager. She had grown up watching her mum and dad play out stereotypical gender roles. When she didn't know any better, she assumed this was normal. But going to university had opened her eyes to a whole new world. Most of her college tutors were women who had inspired her to consider writing. One of them was even Pakistani and married with children; this had literally blown Rehana's mind. Here was a woman who looked like her – albeit with much better clothes – who taught on gender roles in nineteenth-century literature. She wondered if this woman ever went home and cooked dinner for her husband, but she bet he cooked dinner for her. Rehana had studied women in literature and knew exactly the kind of woman she wanted to be. In her mind she was going to be a trailblazer for Pakistani girls everywhere. She was going to be a queen.

The problem was, whenever her parents were around she forgot she was a queen. When she moved home, and without her friends to encourage her, she found she no longer had the confidence she once had. Her mood began to slip and she eventually gave up looking for work altogether. Instead, she would stay in bed for as long as possible in the hope of avoiding her mum. But the house was small and there was no getting away from her.

'Nobody will want to marry you if you lie in bed all day. Get up, I am going to teach you how to make rotis.' Her mum had clearly had enough of her staying in bed until lunchtime. 'Look at you, Rehana, it is nearly eleven o'clock and you are still asleep. It is embarrassing.'

'Mum, I was up late looking for jobs online,' Rehana lied as she buried herself underneath the duvet. She had been up all night watching Netflix.

'Get up!' her mum said, snatching the duvet off the bed. 'Have a shower and come downstairs.'

Rehana couldn't think of anything worse than spending the day learning how to make chapattis. Queens had rotis made for them, they didn't make them themselves. But her mum was not taking no for an answer. In the past, Rehana would have put up more of a fight, but these days she felt she had less and less motivation to resist. Her mother had tried numerous times over the past months to teach her to cook. In theory, Rehana liked the idea of traditional recipes being passed down from generation to generation; she just didn't understand why each member of these generations had to be female.

As expected, the cooking lessons had not gone well. After watching her mum make perfectly round rotis all her life, she assumed it must be easy. It wasn't. Her dough kept sticking to the rolling pin and each time she put one on the pan, it failed to fluff up as it should have. It didn't help that her mum was not the most patient of teachers.

'You have put too much water in your dough, that's why it's sticking,' she scolded. 'You have not rolled that thin enough, we are making rotis, not naan.'

Rehana watched as her mum tossed her perfectly rolled roti

onto the flatbread frying pan. She didn't even use tongs to flip it over after the first side was cooked, she simply got an edge of it between her finger and thumb and casually turned it over. It was a wonder she didn't burn herself.

'You know, I went to Aunty Rubina's house for dinner last week,' her mum told her after she had decided that was enough roti making for one day. 'And her daughter, Lubna, made the most perfect rotis. They were delicious. Very fluffy and light.'

'Yes, Mum, you told me that the minute you got home from their house,' Rehana said, rolling her eyes.

'I am just saying, Aunty Rubina doesn't have to even cook any more. Lubna makes dinner for them all every day. It must be such a relief for Rubina, knowing her daughter can make full Pakistani dinner.' Her mum sighed.

'Well, Lubna doesn't have a degree, does she, Mum?' Rehana retorted. 'She has probably spent her whole life learning how to make perfectly round rotis.' Rehana knew that Lubna wasn't as perfect as she liked all the aunties to believe. They had some mutual friends on Facebook, and much as Lubna liked to think there were no dodgy social media photos of her on nights out, she couldn't quite police everyone's page. A few rogue shots of her at parties with boys had briefly appeared online before being swiftly deleted.

'And yet you have a degree and no job. You laugh at Lubna and her rotis, but those are the kinds of things boys consider when they are looking for a girl to marry,' her mum said, giving her a sharp look.

'Mum, I don't want a boy who wants to marry me because I can make perfectly round rotis!' Rehana said, louder than she had expected. Her mum didn't break stride.

'Neither do they want a girl who stays in bed all day feeling sorry for herself. I guess it will be up to me to find you a nice boy to marry. You couldn't even manage that at university.' Her mum looked at her triumphantly.

Rehana was rather taken aback at the last comment. 'Mum, you told me I wasn't allowed to even talk to boys. You said it would bring shame on us and nobody would speak to us again.'

'I meant English boys. You could have found yourself a nice Muslim boy whilst you were wasting your time there and we might be preparing for your wedding now.'

Rehana decided this was not the right time to call out racism. In truth, she had spoken to many boys during her time at university, of all nationalities and religions. But she couldn't tell her mother that. In fact, she had got to know some of them rather well, but none of them would have been appropriate to bring home to meet her parents.

'Mum, if we've finished making rotis, I'm going out for a walk.'

'And who is going to clean up this mess you made?' her mum said, gesturing to the worktop that was now covered in flour and sticky pieces of dough.

'I'll do it when I come back,' Rehana said, swiftly moving past her mother towards the door. She could hear her mum chuntering to herself as she put on her jacket. Rehana knew she wasn't suffering from depression, but she simply wasn't happy any more. She couldn't tell her parents about it, they wouldn't understand. Mental health wasn't really a thing you talked about in Pakistani culture, it was best kept firmly under the carpet. All those campaigns Rehana had seen about talking about your feelings were all well and good, but they didn't have her family in mind. The walks helped with her mood, and she made sure she went on at least one a day.

Sadly for Rehana, that wasn't the end of the cooking lessons. Her mum was insistent on teaching her what she called the 'basics'. Chicken biryani, kofta, bindi, saag. It was difficult. Rehana never seemed to chop the onions fine enough or put enough oil in the pan. It didn't help that her mother refused

to use any form of measurements when teaching her how to
cook. Everything seemed to involve a 'little bit of this', or 'a
few of those'.

'Mum, how am I supposed to learn how to make any of this
stuff when you can't tell me how much of everything goes in?'

'What do you mean?' her mum had said. 'I am showing you
how much to put in.'

'Yes, but Mum, you just grab a handful of things and toss
them into the pan,' Rehana said, sounding exasperated.

'Well, that is how you cook. I don't have time to measure
anything out, I just know what to put in.' Her mum looked at
her, eyebrows furrowed.

'Yes, but I don't know, do I?' Rehana had decided to write
down all of her mum's recipes in a large pad she had purchased.
If she was going to learn how to cook, she might as well do
it properly. And besides, she had been surprised to discover
that she didn't hate learning how to cook any more. 'I need
to know specific measurements, so I can recreate these dishes
in the future.'

'We are not making a cake, Rehana. We don't have time to
measure ingredients,' her mum said. 'This is how my mother
taught me and this how I am going to teach you. Stop writing
in that book and pay attention.'

Rehana gave up. She would just have to guess at quantities
and hope for the best.

After a while, Rehana seemed to get the hang of cooking.
Her rotis were getting rounder and her curries were beginning
to taste more and more like her mum's. Her dad said he couldn't
tell the difference between the aloo saag she had made that day
and her mother's. She was embarrassed to admit it, but she
had felt proud. It was strange, because the last thing she wanted
to be was a 'good housewife', but the cooking had given a new
purpose to her long days at home, and whilst she was waiting
for her teaching course to begin, there was something quite

romantic about learning recipes that had been handed down from previous generations of her family.

One afternoon, Rehana was being supervised by her mother making palak paneer when she was caught off guard.

'Aunty Rubina rang today. Lubna is getting married,' her mum said abruptly, observing her for a reaction.

'Good for Lubna,' Rehana said. She liked Lubna, but if she was being honest, she was a bit of a goody two shoes. They had grown up together and were the same age and inevitably the comparisons had started at an early age. Yousef and Rehana called her 'Miss Perfect' and would watch with envy as the aunties gushed over how gorgeous she looked in her shalwar kameez and conversed with them in flawless Urdu. Rehana's Urdu was the Pakistani equivalent of Spanglish. When the aunties spoke to her in Urdu, she would attempt to reply back in the same language but eventually gave up and reverted back to English.

'A boy from right here in Manchester and from a good family, isn't that lucky? It is so hard to find nice boys with good families these days,' her mum said wistfully.

'I wouldn't know,' Rehana muttered. 'I think this palak paneer is done now. It just needs to simmer for a few minutes.'

'You know, I think it is time you got married too.'

'What?' Rehana said, turning to look at her mum. 'I don't think so. I want to complete my teacher training course first.'

'Rehana, you are nearly twenty-two, that is the right age to get married. I was seventeen when I got married. Your dad and I were talking about it and we want to start looking for you. You can still finish your course whilst we look.' Her mum had clearly given this a lot of thought.

'Mum, you can't just decide it's time for me to get married.' Rehana couldn't quite believe what she was hearing.

'Calm down, Rehana, we are not going to force you to marry anyone, we are simply going to introduce you to suitable boys.

You know, ones with good families and good values,' her mum
said in as much of a soothing voice as she could muster. 'Think
of them as pre-approved. You can choose the one you like the
most and marry that one.'

'And where are you going to find these suitable boys?' Rehana
laughed. This was beginning to sound more and more ridiculous.

'I will speak to a few of my friends about you, they may
know someone who is eligible. I wonder how Aunty Rubina
found such a good match for her daughter, Lubna.' Her mum
lifted up the lid of the pan with the palak paneer in, peered
in and turned off the hob. 'It is cooked now.'

'Mum, you know, I think I'll find my own husband if that's
okay,' Rehana said, worried that her mum was being serious.

'What, you mean, like a love marriage?' It was her mum's
turn to look shocked. 'What would everybody think if you had
a love marriage? Shame, shame. Love marriages never work.
Remember Saif and Anum? They had a love marriage and
divorced after just three years, now their parents can't show
their faces anywhere.'

Rehana found the concept of love marriages versus arranged
marriages difficult. To her parents, the gold standard was
marrying a relative stranger who was deemed appropriate. It
didn't matter that you didn't know them that well. If your
families got along, it was assumed you would too. The idea
was, you would have enough in common to agree to marriage
and then you would fall in love later. The fact that they called
what others would deem a normal marriage a 'love' marriage
had always amused Rehana. Asian parents didn't trust their
children to find someone for themselves, and they certainly
didn't like the idea of love before marriage. Whenever a couple
who had had a love marriage got divorced, her mum would
look at her dad and say:

'See, divorced. It was love marriage.' Her dad would nod in
agreement.

'Maybe I want a love marriage, Mum. Would that be so bad?' she said, attempting to shock her mother.

Rehana's mum laughed. 'Well, if you find a suitable boy yourself, that is fine. But you never leave the house, how are you going to find anyone, huh?' She was right, Rehana's love life was non-existent. Even if she did want a love marriage, there was the slight issue of not having anyone she actually loved. 'I tell you what,' her mum continued. 'We both start looking. If you find someone before we do, and they are suitable, we will consider it.'

Rehana thought about the offer. She had nothing to lose. Her parents were simply suggesting they were going to introduce her to a string of men who had been carefully selected for her. If she didn't like them, she would refuse their advances and if she did, she would go on dates with them to see if they were compatible. To be honest, she didn't have a great deal of other things going on in her life right now. And when she thought about it, she had always wanted to leave a string of broken hearts behind on her gap year. This wasn't the way she had envisaged that happening, but she had to be flexible.

'Okay, well, let's see who comes up trumps first then, shall we?' she said, to her mum's delight.

'Fantastic, I will make phone calls. Your dad will be very happy.' Her mum left the kitchen, presumably to start on her calls.

Rehana wondered if she had just made a huge mistake allowing her mum to take control of her love life.

As she lay on her bed listening to her music, she thought about the kind of man she would want. He would have to be understanding of her career obviously, though she recognized she had yet to start any kind of career. She wanted him to be kind but, most of all, she recognized that getting married to any kind of man was her ticket out of the house she shared with her parents. And that alone would be worth it.

'Rehana, come quick.' Her mum's shrill voice coincided with the end of one of her songs. 'It's your brother, his results are out!'

Rehana plucked her headphones from inside her ears and made her way downstairs.

Chapter Five

Jessica

JESSICA LAY ON HER back staring at the ceiling. The exam results were supposed to have been out an hour ago and they still hadn't been published. Her friend Kate lay on the bed with her. She had her laptop open and every few minutes would check to see if their results had finally been released.

'Why are they doing this to us?' Kate whined. 'Don't they know we have a bottle of prosecco in the fridge that needs drinking?'

'Kate, you have nothing to worry about. You're the cleverest person I know. It's me who should be worried,' Jess said.

'Don't jinx it for me, Jess. We will both pass and we will both get pissed tonight!' Kate refreshed the page once more. Nothing. She let out a dramatic sigh and turned onto her back. 'Wankers.'

Jess had wanted to get her results with Yousef, but he had said with Rohit and Steve around, having her there as well would be too much pressure. She knew he was lying – he was nervous in case he failed. Not because of her or Rohit or Steve but because of his mother.

Yousef's mum had sent down a large flask of water which she had been praying on. She wanted Yousef to drink a glass each day in the hope that it would somehow influence his exam results. Jessica thought it was stupid, but she knew better than to say so. Technically, Jessica was Catholic and knew all about holy water, as she had spent her entire youth being dragged to church by her mother each Sunday and made to listen to sermons and sing hymns. She hadn't minded so much when she was a child, when she'd found the stories from the Old Testament interesting if a little unbelievable. But as she got older she began to question some of her mother's religious beliefs. At first her mum had tried to explain away some of the inconsistencies but Jessica asked so many questions loudly in church that her mum eventually decided not to take her any more, and this suited Jessica fine. To Jess, religion didn't seem to align with her own developing beliefs. According to her Church, people who Jessica knew to be good, decent people would not get a place in heaven. Gay people, those who followed another religion, or those who had no religion at all could dedicate their lives to good causes but not be rewarded in heaven in the same way that those who did nothing but go to church and read the Bible all day would.

No, Jess had decided, aged fifteen, that religion was not for her. She sought comfort and understanding in science. Things made sense there. The break from the Church actually improved Jess's relationship with her mother. Now Jess no longer spent her time quizzing her mum about her religious beliefs. Instead, they could talk about other things.

When she had met Yousef five years ago, she thought he was similar. When they had spoken about religion, Yousef had said that although he believed in God, he didn't agree with everything that he had learned about Islam growing up. Jess had learned about Islam in school and tried her very best to be open-minded, but she was embarrassed to say that even for her the word 'Muslim' conjured up images of terrorist attacks and soldiers in faraway countries dressed in black and holding rifles. Even the Muslim girls in her year were a bit of an enigma.

She had a small group teaching session with one of them, Bushra, and was surprised to find out she was completely normal. In fact, Bushra was funny, articulate, clever and despite her headscarf wore very tight jeans and figure-hugging tops. When she had told Yousef this, he had laughed at her calling Bushra 'normal'. He also told her the headscarf was not really required by Islamic law and that girls were expected to dress 'modestly' which had been interpreted by some as covering up their hair.

'Sounds like another act of historical patriarchy to me,' Jess had told him.

'Maybe, I don't know. But if girls choose to wear them, that's cool by me,' he had said. 'If they don't, that's also cool.'

'Yeah, but who interpreted "modest" as wearing a headscarf?' she continued. 'I bet it was a man.'

'Leave it out, Jess. Women cover their hair in loads of religions. Nuns, Hindus before they go into a temple . . . It's just something that's been done for ages,' he said, sounding pissed off. 'Besides, do you think someone like Bushra would wear a headscarf if she didn't want to?'

Yousef had a point; Bushra wasn't the kind of girl to put up with anyone's nonsense. She had told one of the boys in their group to go fuck himself when he said something about how good her legs looked in her jeans. But her conversation with Yousef left Jess wondering, was she a racist? She didn't have any friends at home who were not white, but that was because there was nobody in her school from a non-white background, so that wasn't her fault. She had, of course, seen non-white people on the television, she just hadn't interacted with many in real life. There was Shelley in the football team – she was half Chinese and two years older than Jess, but they were not really friends. Jessica thought Shelley was a bit of a bully on the pitch. The only non-white people Jess had known growing up were Daniel and Ana, who owned the pharmacy in the centre of her village. She was shocked when one of the girls at school had told her their real names were Deepak and Anampum.

'Yeah, they changed them when they moved here,' the girl had said. 'You know, to fit in.'

When Jessica had come to university she had been delighted by the variety of people on her course. They all went by their real names, and they fitted in perfectly. She had been excited to come to London and it was living up to her expectations. Finally, she felt she was living in the real world, away from the picturesque village in Somerset that had shackled her for so long.

Part of Yousef's allure had been his dark eyes and caramel skin. But Jess felt bad even thinking that – did that make her racist? Was she allowed to be attracted to someone because of the colour of their skin if she wasn't allowed to be repelled by someone for the same reason? It was all very confusing. Jess read many books on anti-racism, and while some said it was racist to be attracted to someone because of their ethnic background, others said it was a completely different argument. She took comfort in the fact that Yousef's outward appearance, as lovely as it was, was not the only thing she was attracted to. He was kind and generous and funny. No, she was not a racist, she decided. She had just discovered she preferred Asian men, that's all. Or one particular Asian man. Surely that was the opposite of racism?

When Jess had told her parents about Yousef, she had braced herself for an unpleasant reaction, but instead they had surprised her by being supportive of the relationship.

'Gosh, he's very handsome, isn't he?' her mum had said after she had sent her a photo of him. 'Look at those eyes and all that thick hair. I can see why you like him.'

'He does have lovely eyes,' Jess had said proudly. 'He's funny too,' she had added quickly in case her mum thought she only liked him for his dark eyes.

'And he's a good lad?' her dad had asked. 'Treats you right?'
'Honestly, Dad, you have nothing to worry about,' Jess had
told her father. She had smiled at his questions. She was an
only child and he had always been protective over her.

Jess learned early on that Yousef was very guarded when it
came to talking about his own family. Every time she brought
them up, he would look anxious and find ways to change the
subject. It became exhausting. She would tell him everything
about her parents and in return he would divulge very little.
Even when his mum rang, he would take the call in another
room or attempt to speak in Urdu. Yousef's Urdu was not good
and was peppered with English words, meaning Jess could
eavesdrop and follow the gist of their calls. The conversations
all seemed pretty mundane. He told his mum what he had
done at university that day and what he had for dinner and,
if it was cold, he would tell her that yes, he was wearing a
jumper.

It felt to her like Yousef was being interrogated rather than
involved in a two-way exchange of equal parts. His mum would
ring every day, which by anyone's standards was excessive. He
would become anxious when the phone went. If he was busy
and didn't answer, his mum would leave a voicemail demanding
to know where he was and saying that he should call her back
immediately. His whole relationship with his mum was weird.

Yousef's refusal to tell his family about her put strain on the
relationship. He kept telling her the time wasn't right and his
parents simply wouldn't understand.

'Look, they're really worried about me being distracted by
girls whilst I'm studying,' he had tried to explain to her. 'Once
we get through university, that won't matter any more and I'll
tell them.'

'Get through university?' Jess had said. 'It's a five-year
course. Am I supposed to wait five years for you to grow a
pair of balls?'

She knew him not telling them about her was a red flag and had once given him an ultimatum. That had shocked him and as a compromise he agreed to tell his younger sister about the two of them. It was a start, Jess had thought. Rehana had been perfectly understanding about them being together. She was at university too and by the sounds of things was having the time of her life.

'See, that wasn't so hard,' Jess told him, feeling guilty about having had to give him an ultimatum. 'I'm sure your mum will be just as understanding about it.' Yousef had kept quiet and they had ended up having sex, which drew a line under the matter for the time being. But the feeling niggled at her. What if he didn't tell them at the end of the course? They had planned what they were going to do once they had completed medical school. Yousef needed to be near his family so they agreed they would apply to the West Midlands medical deanery; that way they would spend their first two years out of university working in the cluster of hospitals around Yousef's parents' house in and around Birmingham. All of her friends were either applying for jobs in London or near their own parents' homes. Jess was taking a huge risk so she could be with Yousef; he had to tell his parents about her. Once they had completed their first two years as junior doctors, they would have to choose a speciality to train in. She hoped to be embedded in Yousef's family by that stage. She knew she could win his mum over if only she was allowed to meet her. Jess had her heart set on becoming an emergency medicine doctor as she'd loved her time in the accident and emergency department last year. The consultant who had been overseeing her had just finished training to be a helicopter medic so she could go out to emergencies in remote locations, and she had inspired Jess. She knew Yousef's mum wanted him to be a heart surgeon, but she wasn't sure Yousef had enjoyed his surgical placement, and she had seen his stitch work in the lab – it was terrible.

Jess learned if she didn't mention his family, their relationship was good. And part of the problem was she loved him so much, some days she could pass away the time just staring at him as he studied. Being with Yousef felt easy; he made her laugh and her friends liked him. In those moments she felt lucky. And besides, each new year brought them closer to the end of their course, the time Yousef had promised to tell his parents about her. She just had to stick it out.

As Jess lay on her bed waiting for the results to come, she felt nervous. Not so much for the exam results; no, because the day they had talked about for so long was finally here. The day Yousef would finally tell his parents about her. All they had to do was pass. She was confident. The two of them had worked hard, and they had not missed a single day on their hospital placements, often staying late speaking to patients and logging the cases they had encountered. They had gone to the library straight after their placement days and studied hard. They deserved to pass.

'Jess,' Kate whispered, staring at the computer screen. 'The results are out.'

Jess sat up in bed and opened up the laptop, typing in her password as quickly as possible. As she did, Kate shrieked, 'Oh fuck, I've passed!' She sounded elated.

Jess was pleased for her. 'Amazing. That's amazing, Kate.'

'Well, what about you?' Kate said.

Jess logged on to the university website and held her breath as the page opened up.

She had passed. She let out a gasp. 'I've passed,' she said, not quite believing it was true.

'YES! Let's crack open that bottle of fucking prosecco!' Kate said, jumping on the bed, making Jess laugh. 'Fucking hell, Jess, we're doctors,' Kate said, suddenly still. 'Can you believe it?'

'I certainly can, Dr Hamilton,' Jess said, getting up so she too was standing on the bed.

'Well, thank you, Dr Pritchard,' Kate said in an exaggerated posh voice. They both laughed and began jumping on the bed screaming.

'Go get the prosecco, I'm a thirsty bitch,' Jess commanded, out of breath from the jumping and laughter.

'Jess, I don't think you understand what a thirsty bitch is,' Kate laughed. 'I have some vodka too, we can do shots.' Kate climbed out of bed and ran out of the door screaming. Jessica smiled. She couldn't wait to tell her parents. She stared at her phone. Yousef would have his results by now. She would wait for him to call before she rang her parents, as she knew they would ask after him too. Kate returned with two shot glasses filled to the brim with vodka.

'Vodka shots first,' she said, trying not to spill any of the precious contents. 'Just like old times. Then we can pretend we're sophisticated doctors and drink prosecco.' She handed Jess a glass.

'To becoming sophisticated doctors, darling!' Jess shouted, raising the shot glass in the air.

'Yes, darling!' Kate repeated. They both downed their shots.

Chapter Six

Yousef

YOUSEF REFRESHED THE PAGE just to be absolutely sure. His eyes flicked from the left side of the screen where his name was to the right where the result was posted. He realized he was holding his breath and let out a deep sigh.

The first thing he thought of his was his mother. She had been praying all day. Rehana had sent him a picture of their mum with her scarf over her head, eyes closed deep in prayer.

Mum never did this for me, the text that accompanied the picture said. **Anyway, good luck!**

Despite how overbearing his mother was, he knew he owed a lot of what he had achieved to her. As a child, Yousef had never been the cleverest person in his class. His mother had pushed him to work harder, even at the subjects she didn't deem important.

In fact, he recalled the very first day she told him he was going to be a surgeon. It was the September before his fifth birthday. She sat him down and told him how lucky he was to be getting a free education, something she had never had. She told him if he worked hard, he could be a surgeon and that was the best job in the world.

Rather than buying a school uniform, his mum had sewn

him a pale blue shirt and navy trousers from fabric she had left over from a client. They were both too big for him.

'You will grow into them,' she said as she tightened the belt around the trousers to stop them from falling down. She then packed some of last night's aloo behngan into some Tupperware with a chapatti and placed them carefully into one of his dad's rucksacks which had the logo of the bus company his dad worked for on it. After breakfast, Yousef was instructed to put on his jacket and shoes. His mum walked him to school with Rehana where a gaggle of children the same age as him were waiting anxiously with their parents in the school playground. Yousef looked at their uniforms; they looked different to his. Most of the children had the school logo on the front of their shirts and rucksacks with the same logo on. Yousef looked again at his dad's old work bag. He had been proud to take it to school with him when they left the house; now he wanted desperately to hide it.

One of the other mums came up to Yousef and his mum and said something in a language he didn't understand. His mum replied in the same language. He had heard her speak this exotic-sounding language before, mainly when talking to the milkman or Mrs Peel from next door. Now it felt like he could hear this language being spoken all around him. He felt suddenly afraid. He tightened his grip on his mum's hand. He wanted to go home.

A lady came out of the school door and said something that made all the parents hug their children and leave them in a line at the entrance of the building.

'That is your teacher,' Yousef's mum said to him. 'And the other lady there is the teaching assistant. Make sure you listen to everything they say and work hard. Eat all your food and I will pick you up at home time.' She gave him a hug and kissed him on the forehead, walked him to the line that was forming outside the building and then she was gone, pulling Rehana along in her wake.

Yousef stood with the other children, completely bewildered. One of them started to cry. Yousef could feel his own eyes welling up and he let out a sob. The teaching assistant came up to him and started making sounds that he didn't understand.

'I want to go home,' he said, crying. 'I want to go home to my mummy.' The teaching assistant looked a bit taken aback at what he had just said and started talking to him in that funny language again. This just made him cry more. The assistant went to talk to the teacher. He could see them gesturing at him. The teaching assistant then went inside and came back out with another lady.

'Hello, Yousef,' the lady said. 'My name is Mrs Malik, I am one of the teaching assistants here. Shall we go inside?' Yousef was relieved to find someone who wasn't speaking in those funny sounds. He allowed Mrs Malik to take his hand and walk him inside.

Mrs Malik told Yousef that the other teachers and children in his class spoke a language called *English* and that he would pick it up in no time. She took Yousef over to the corner where the toys were. He found one where he had to match up numbers. His dad had bought him something similar from the market a few months ago. He picked it up and began putting the numbered shapes into their corresponding holes.

'Aren't you clever!' Mrs Malik said. Another child came over to see what the fuss was about and tried to help Yousef. The child picked up some of the shapes and tried to force them into the wrong holes. Yousef looked at him, horrified, and pulled the toy away.

'No, you are doing it wrong!' he said. The boy looked at him blankly.

'He doesn't understand you yet, Yousef,' Mrs Malik said gently. 'But why don't you show him how to do it?' Yousef spent the rest of the morning trying to instruct the boy to put the numbered squares into the right holes. Although they were speaking different languages, the boy was able to follow Yousef's instructions. When it came to lunchtime, they were instructed to get their bags from the hooks they were hung on and return to their tables. Mrs Malik helped Yousef find his.

'Have you brought a packed lunch with you, Yousef?' Mrs Malik said, looking a bit worried. Yousef nodded and Mrs Malik's face flooded with relief. He pulled out his Tupperware and opened the lid. The smell of his mum's food comforted him as he unfolded the chapatti his mum had packed to eat the aloo bengan with. He tore off a piece of chapatti, scooped up some of the curry and stuffed it into his mouth. It was delicious even though it was cold. The boy who he had been playing with earlier was staring at him. He said something to the girl opposite and they both laughed and pinched their noses, talking loudly. The gesture seemed to spread through the class and more and more children began pinching their noses and laughing. Yousef looked confused. He looked at Mrs Malik for help.

'It's okay, Yousef; they have a different lunch to yours. Their mums have packed sandwiches for them.' She turned to the class and said something so sternly to the children that they all immediately took their fingers off their noses and started to eat their lunches quietly. 'Perhaps you can ask your mum to make you sandwiches tomorrow, Yousef?' she said. He nodded, his mouth full of curried aubergine.

The rest of the day involved Yousef playing on his own. Whatever had happened over lunchtime meant none of the other children wanted anything to do with him. Yousef was relieved when home time came. He could see his mum outside of the window with his sister. He waved excitedly at her, and she saw him and waved back. It struck Yousef even at that age that his mum looked different to the other parents who came to collect their children. She wore different clothes.

Mrs Malik took Yousef to the front door. 'Have you got

everything, Yousef?' she asked. He nodded. His form teacher, who Mrs Malik had told him was called Mrs Burrows, was also waiting by the door. Yousef ran to greet his mum, who gave him a big hug.

'My beta,' she said, beaming. 'How was your first day?'

'Good, Ma. But the other children don't like me,' he told her.

Mrs Burrows came over and said something to his mum. Mrs Malik was standing next to her and gestured for them all to move into the far corner of the room. Yousef was sent to play with the same toys he had been playing with all day, this time with his little sister in tow, whilst the grown-ups discussed something. Eventually his mum came over to get them and said they were going home. She didn't seem very happy.

When he got home, both he and Rehana were sent upstairs whilst his mum spoke with his father.

'His teacher, *Mrs Burrows*, was talking to me in that slow and loud way that English people always do when they think I can't understand them. I told her I wasn't deaf or stupid,' he overheard his mum saying to his dad.

'I am sure she doesn't think you are either of those things,' his dad said.

'You were not there, Abdul. They kept asking me why I hadn't taught Yousef any English.'

'What did you say?' his dad asked.

'I told them that was *their* job,' his mum said. 'Our boy can speak, read and write in Urdu – which other children can do that at age five, huh? I don't want him or Rehana growing up like Ayesha and Mahmood's children, only speaking English, thinking they are white. Shame, shame.' Yousef heard his dad try to interject, but he was swiftly cut off by his mum. 'You know, I tried to converse with them in Urdu and they didn't understand a single word, *not one single word*.'

'Feroza, calm down. It will be fine. Yousef will pick up English quickly, children learn fast.'

'I know he will, my son is very clever,' his mum said quietly. 'They also said I should make him cheese sandwiches for lunch. So that he will fit in better with the class.'

'Let's do that then,' his dad said. 'Sandwiches are easy to make.'

'Easy but tasteless,' his mum said stubbornly.

Abdul was right, Yousef picked up English quickly. To his mother's dismay, he began speaking English at home with Rehana, who also learned quickly, and by the time she started school a year later, she was fluent. Their parents would talk to them in Urdu and the children would reply in English. It was something that would continue for years, until it got to a point where Yousef and Rehana could only speak broken Urdu and only then when forced to do so. They had become just like Ayesha and Mahmood's children. An embarrassment.

'Yousef? Don't you need to phone your mum?' Rohit said, his voice cutting through Yousef's thoughts.

'What?' he said, still taking in his exam results.

'Your mum, she's been ringing all day. Phone her now. Tell her.' Rohit gestured to his phone.

'Oh, yeah.' Yousef picked up his phone. His hands were shaking as he scrolled through his list of contacts, getting to 'home'. He pressed dial.

'Hello?' his mum answered.

'Salaam, Mum, it's me,' he said. 'My exam results are out.'

'Wait, wait, let me get your father.' He heard her place the phone down on the small cabinet it was kept on in their hallway and shout for his dad and sister. 'Abdul! Rehana! Come now, Yousef is on the phone, his results are out. Abdul, bring me my thasbi, it is on the back of my chair.' His mum's thasbi was her equivalent to rosary beads. She would use them to help count her prayers.

Yousef waited for his family to congregate.

'Hello, Yousef, it is your dad here.' His dad's voice came through.

'Hi, Dad, my results are out.'

'Stop! Don't tell us yet.' His mum was on the phone again. 'I have to say one more prayer.' Yousef could hear his mum praying loudly on the phone.

'Mum, prayers won't change anything now,' he heard Rehana say.

'Shut up, Rehana. If only you would pray more, maybe you would have passed your exams,' his mum scolded his sister.

'I did pass my exams, Mum,' Rehana shot back. 'I got a first.' She was ignored.

'Okay, Yousef, we are ready now,' his dad said.

There was a moment of silence.

'I passed,' he said, not being able to hide the smile in his voice.

'You passed?' his dad asked.

'Yes, Dad, I PASSED!' Yousef shouted down the phone.

'Mashallah, we knew you would,' his dad said proudly. Yousef could hear his mum praying loudly again in the background. 'Your mum is giving thanks to God,' his dad told him. 'She will want to speak with you in a minute.'

'Well done, bro,' Rehana said. Then to her parents, 'Is it okay for me to go back upstairs now?'

'Rehana, give me the phone and move out of the way,' his mum said. 'Yousef, well done, make sure you do thank-you prayers to God tonight,' she said. 'I am so proud of you, beta.'

'Thanks, Mum,' Yousef said.

'Shabaash, you are my good boy.' Yousef could tell she was tearing up.

'When does your job start?' his father asked.

'In just over four weeks,' Yousef replied, a sudden sense of dread creeping in.

'I can't wait to have you back home!' his mum said. 'You have been away too long.'

They talked for a few more minutes.

'Don't forget your prayers!' his mum said again.

'And don't stay out too late tonight!' his dad said. Yousef hung up and looked at Rohit. 'Dude, I passed,' he whispered.

Rohit looked at him firmly. 'That's great and I don't want to rain on your parade or anything, Yous, but don't you also need to call Jess?' Rohit asked. Yousef knew this conversation was coming. Rohit had been on at him for months about being honest with Jessica.

Jessica would be waiting for his call. They had agreed to call each other the minute the results were out, but his family had taken priority as they always did. He knew she was waiting for his call, but he couldn't bring himself to dial her number. As much as he had been waiting for this day for so long, in many ways he wished it would never have come.

'I think I'll go over and see her,' Yousef told Rohit.

Rohit nodded. 'I'll be here waiting.'

Yousef put on his jacket and headed out the front door.

Chapter Seven

Feroza

FEROZA WAS EUPHORIC. SHE couldn't quite collect her thoughts. She needed some space, so she told Abdul she was getting something from the kitchen and quickly scuttled off. She closed the door and let out a shriek. For Feroza, all the hardships in her life had been leading to this one moment. She'd had to endure so much when she first came to this country – the comments about her clothing, the looks in the supermarket when she struggled to converse with the checkout lady, the racist comments from those girls at the bus stop as she trailed bags of clothing to her customers' homes. She had pretended that none of it mattered, but it did. The comments had lingered inside of her and festered, becoming something darker and more sinister. She wanted to go back and tell all those people that her son was now a doctor and that commanded respect. To Feroza, this was the pinnacle of all occupations. He would now be doing an invaluable service to the same country that had mocked her all these years. They would be grateful to her for producing a son who would be saving the lives of their parents and children. For the first time in almost twenty-five years she felt she truly deserved her place here in England.

She collected her thoughts and went back out to see Abdul.

'Are you okay?' he asked. 'You were making funny noises in there.'

'What noises? Don't be silly,' Feroza said. 'I needed a glass of water, I had a dry throat.' She knew he didn't believe her, but it didn't matter. 'Abdul, don't just stand there staring at me, you need to go to the sweet shop and get boxes of mithai.'

It was a Pakistani tradition to give out sweets on the receipt of good news. They had done it when both of their children had been born, but for Feroza this day was more important.

'Now? I was thinking we should ring my parents in Pakistan,' Abdul protested.

'Abdul, it is the middle of the night in Pakistan, we can do that tomorrow. If you don't go now, the shops will close.' Feroza handed him his jacket and ushered him towards the door. 'Get plenty of boxes, we have so many people to tell.'

When Abdul finally left, Feroza was torn. She knew she should get back on her prayer mat and say some thank-you prayers, but she so desperately wanted to ring her friends and tell them about Yousef becoming a doctor.

Anyone could have children, Feroza thought, but not everybody could raise their child to be a doctor. Feroza had trumped them all, and that was worth celebrating. She thought of how Musarat from down the street had come over when her daughter had got her law degree.

'Zara has completed her law degree, we are all so proud,' Musarat had said as they sat in the living room. Feroza had made the tea after Rehana refused to come down from her bedroom. 'She got a 2:1,' Musarat said, taking a loud slurp of tea from her cup.

'That is so nice,' Feroza said, trying her best to smile. 'What a clever girl.'

'Yes, she worked hard and, of course, keeping her at home rather than letting her go off to a faraway university played a big part,' Musarat continued. 'It is so important that children understand our traditional values.' Then, 'How is Rehana getting on?'

Feroza didn't let her smile falter. 'Oh, perfectly fine. She got a first, you know . . .'

'In English, though, yes?'

'She's an artist, you know, always doing a bit of this and a bit of that.'

'Won't she come down to say salaam?' Musarat quizzed, raising one judgemental eyebrow.

'She is not feeling so well,' Feroza lied, smoothing out her kameez.

'I see. Has she found a job yet?' Musarat said, not breaking her stride.

'No, not yet, but I am sure it won't be long now. Not with her first class degree.' Feroza took a bite of the ladoos Musarat had brought with her. They were dry. 'These ladoos are delicious,' she said.

'Well, only the best for my daughter. You know, Zara already has a job at KPMG. Have you heard of it?' Musarat enquired. Feroza shook her head. 'It's right here in the city. Her dad can drop her off at work in the morning and pick her up afterwards.' Musarat took a bite of her ladoo. 'Oh wow, these really are delicious. Well, you must not worry about Rehana. If she does not find a job, I am sure we can find her a man instead. Then she will not have to work.' Musarat took one final slug of her tea. 'Anyway, I must go, so many more people to distribute mithai to. You know how it is.'

That was a deliberate dig. Musarat knew that Feroza had not distributed any mithai after Rehana had passed her degree. They had already spent enough money on Rehana's rent at university, she wasn't going to waste any more on mithai. She thanked Musarat for stopping by and walked her to the door.

'It's important not to let children sit idle for too long,' Musarat said as she put on her coat. 'Best get them married before they do something . . . unsavoury.'

Feroza decided she would do her thank-you prayers later. She made herself a cup of tea and got cosy by the phone. Feroza still used a landline for most of her calls. Abdul had got her a mobile a few months ago; she was only just beginning to get used to it. But for important calls like these, she trusted the landline more than her new mobile. She sat on the sofa, placing the mug down on the side table. She wanted to savour this moment; she had worked so hard for it. She dialled her first number.

'Salaam, Musarat?' she said. 'It's Feroza, how are you?'

'Walaikum salam, Feroza. I am very well, just busy with things, you know how it is. How are you?' Musarat said.

Feroza didn't want to hear about how busy Musarat was, this day wasn't about her. It was all about Feroza. She was suddenly overcome with a hunger to tell Musarat. She resisted it. 'Oh, we are all busy these days, aren't we?' she said, determined not to let Musarat interrupt. 'It's been a momentous day in our household, I have just now managed to sit down.'

'Really? It has been like a circus in our house too. I was meaning to ring you—'

Feroza cut her off. 'Well, I rang you. We have had excellent news.' Feroza paused, waiting for Musarat to pick up the cue.

'What kind of excellent news?' Musarat said slowly.

'It's about Yousef.' Feroza was dragging it out deliberately. 'I have just this minute sent Abdul out for some mithai.'

'What are you celebrating?' Musarat asked. Feroza was listening for hints of envy in her voice. She heard nothing.

'Yousef passed his final university exams. He is now officially a doctor!' It was the first time Feroza had said it out loud and she couldn't contain her excitement. She waited for Musarat to respond.

'Feroza, that is wonderful news,' Musarat said. 'A doctor, what an achievement.'

Feroza was disappointed she couldn't sense any bitterness in Musarat's voice. In fact, Musarat seemed fairly nonchalant. She decided to lay it on thick.

'I can't take all the credit, of course,' Feroza continued. 'It really is by the grace of God that Yousef turned out to be such a good boy and now a doctor. I don't know of any other children in our community who have become doctors, do you?'

'No, I believe Yousef is the first,' Musarat said.

Feroza was annoyed that Musarat wasn't taking the bait. 'Well, you know they say it takes a village to raise a child, and I think that is true for Yousef. Everybody had a hand in looking after him when I was working, even you. So in a way his success is a product of all our efforts.' This was a lie. The one time Feroza had asked Musarat to look after Yousef whilst she delivered some clothing to a customer, Musarat had said she was going out.

'Well, that is very kind of you to say,' Musarat said slowly and deliberately. 'I suppose I must then congratulate you for the hand you played in raising Zara. We too have good news to share.'

Feroza felt her stomach lurch. What possible good news could Musarat have that could not wait for another day?

'Really, what good news?' Feroza said, trying to sound chipper.

'We have agreed her marriage. As you can imagine, we are all over the moon. I too have sent Wasim out to get mithai. He should be dropping a box off at yours later.' Now Feroza could hear the emotion in Musarat's voice. It wasn't envy, it was triumph.

'Oh mashallah, that is good news,' she said. 'We will all be eating mithai for days to come.'

'Well, you can imagine, it has been a hectic few hours trying to arrange a date for the engagement party. Their family has just left. Zara is so excited; she is already looking at wedding venues online. Her father has told her no expense will be spared.' Musarat was now in full swing. 'The boy is a lawyer, just like Zara. He is training to be a barrister. I mean, jobs don't come much better than that, do they?'

'I don't know, Yousef is going to be a surgeon,' Feroza said, but her heart wasn't in it.

'I know, and that is simply lovely. But a barrister, I don't suppose there are any barristers in our community yet either. He will be the first.'

'Musarat, I must go. Abdul is back with the boxes of mithai, he will need a hand,' Feroza lied. She had had enough of this conversation.

'Oh, that's a shame, I wanted to tell you about his family. His parents are lovely, and he has only one sister. She is married with two children, lives in her own house.' Feroza could tell Musarat was relishing this conversation.

'Well, you must fill me in on the details another time.' Feroza hung up. She was furious. Her chest was heaving and she could hear herself panting. This was her day and Musarat had ruined it. It turned out there was something better than having a son qualify as a doctor after all, and that was having one of your children wed. She didn't feel like ringing anyone else; all her joy had fizzled out. She sat staring at the wall, trying to calm down. She heard the key turn in the front door. Abdul walked in carrying two bags that looked full to bursting.

'I have the mithai. Who shall we give it to first?' Abdul looked at her. 'Feroza, what's wrong?' he asked.

'We have to get our children married,' she replied.

Chapter Eight

Jessica

JESSICA WAS DRUNK. KATE had opened up a second bottle of prosecco and insisted they had to finish it before they went out. Jess didn't argue with her; she felt like drinking.

She checked her phone again. Nothing.

'For fuck's sake, Jess, just ring him.' Kate pulled on a dress that she had been saving for tonight. 'Can you do the honours?' she asked, turning around. Jess zipped her in. 'I can't look at your sad face any longer. We should be celebrating!'

'No, he said he would ring me as soon as the results came out.' Jess took another swig of prosecco. She knew she wouldn't be the first person Yousef would call after his results, that honour would always go to his precious mother, but she had expected a call by now. It had been nearly two hours. She was concerned. What if he hadn't passed? As angry as Jess was with Yousef for not calling her, her overriding emotion was worry. She checked her phone again. Nothing. Her parents had been thrilled when she'd finally called to give them her news, but she hadn't been able to get them off the phone again fast enough just in case Yousef tried to call.

Jess didn't quite understand why Yousef didn't just tell his mother that she was suffocating him with all the phone calls and prayer books she sent in the post to him. Yousef told Jess that his family had only just invested in Sky television and his mother had discovered a selection of religious channels, including some Islamic ones. On them were Muslim scholars who would take calls from people who wanted particular problems solved and the scholars gave them specific prayers to recite depending on what the issue was. Yousef's mum had rung up and told the scholar she was worried her son wasn't working hard enough at university and would fail his exams. The scholar had given Yousef's mum a prayer that Yousef had to recite in the run-up to his exams.

'What?' Yousef had said when Jess questioned him. 'It's just a prayer, and who knows, it might work?'

Jess would not admit this to anyone, but she felt as though Yousef never prioritized her over his family. Whenever they had plans to do something, she would always have to factor in Yousef's daily phone call to his mother. If Yousef had any important news to share, he would ring his family before he rang her. She told herself that in every relationship came compromises, that it was a cultural thing that she did not quite understand, but the more it happened, the more annoyed she became.

'Right, that's it. Stop checking your phone, Jess, and get ready. We're going out!' Kate said whilst refilling her glass. 'Looking at your phone won't make him call any sooner. We're now late, everybody will already be there.'

Kate was right, fuck Yousef. Jess wasn't going to let him spoil their evening. She put her phone on the bedside cabinet and picked up her glass. 'Okay, Kate, let's do this!'

Once they were satisfied with their appearances they headed out of their flat to the lift. Jess checked her phone one last time before putting it in her bag. Nothing.

'The Uber is on its way,' Kate said as they called the lift, 'and I have this for the journey.' She pulled out another bottle of prosecco from her bag with two plastic champagne flutes.

'Though I think you need it more than me.' She winked at Jess.

Despite it being summer, it was raining outside. They looked out of the glass door for their taxi, trying to match up every car's licence plate to the one on Kate's app. They didn't want to be outside in the rain a second longer than they needed to be.

'There it is,' Kate said, pointing to a car parked at the end of the road. 'Let's just make a run for it.' Neither of them had brought a jacket. Kate held her handbag over her head in an effort to protect her hair. 'Ready?' she said.

'Ready.' They ran towards the taxi. Jess opened the door and ushered Kate in, who wriggled over to the far side of the car. She was about to get in when she heard Yousef's voice.

'Jess, wait!' She turned to the voice. He was standing on the pavement.

'Yousef, what are you doing here?' Jess said. They had agreed he would ring her, then they would meet in town. Had he walked here? He was soaked through; large drops of rain ran off his hair onto his face.

'Can we talk?' he said.

'What, now?' Jess could feel the rain running down her back, a sensation she normally didn't mind when playing football, but today it felt icy cold. 'We're heading out. You were supposed to call me.'

'I know, but I had to see you. Please can we talk?'

'Yousef, did you pass?' Jess was hit by a sudden wave of anxiety.

'I passed. Did you?' he asked. She nodded. He passed and hadn't called. Something felt off to Jess. Why hadn't he called? And why wasn't Yousef out with Rohit and Steve celebrating his exam results and instead insisting on talking out here in the middle of the street in the rain?

'Please can we go inside?' he asked.

'Hey, Yousef.' Kate got out of the car. 'As you can see, we're on our way out. I don't know what's going on with you, but don't piss on the vibe, okay?'

'Jess, please?' Yousef ignored Kate.

Jess sighed. 'Kate, you go ahead. I'll meet you in town later.'

'You sure, babe?' Kate said, not taking her eyes off Yousef.

'I'm sure, go ahead,' Jess said, turning towards her friend. 'I'll see you later.' Kate looked at her for a beat then got back in the taxi. Jess shut the door and headed back to her flat. Yousef followed in silence.

'Well done on passing your exams,' Yousef said once they were inside. 'I knew you would.'

'What's going on, Yous?' Jess knew he wasn't there to talk about their exams. 'What are you doing here?' Yousef didn't say anything. 'Yous?'

'Just give me a minute, okay!' he snapped. She recoiled. Yousef had never raised his voice at her before. She took a step back. 'I'm sorry, I'm just thinking.'

'Thinking about what, Yousef?' Jess was regretting all the booze she had drunk. She could feel a headache coming on. She went to the sink and poured herself a glass of water. 'Thinking about what, Yousef?' she repeated.

'Thinking about us,' Yousef said quietly.

Jess didn't say anything. She took her glass of water and sat down.

'Jess, these last few weeks I . . . Well, we're finished at university now, we start our jobs as doctors in less than a month, everything is, I don't know . . . changing.' Yousef came to sit next to her.

'None of this is news, Yousef. What are you trying to say?' She picked at the hem of her dress – one of the threads had come loose. She thought about her nails, how perfect they looked. She had had them manicured earlier that day to keep her mind off the exam results.

'I don't know what I'm trying to say, it's so fucking hard,' Yousef said.

'Just say it, Yousef,' she said, her voice emotionless.

'We're so different, Jess. You're so brave, nothing seems to faze you, and I wish I was like that but I'm not.' Yousef tried to look at her but she couldn't bring herself to meet his gaze. 'I thought some of your fearlessness would rub off on me. That my feelings for you would carry us through . . .'

'Carry us through what? Have your feelings changed?' The room suddenly felt shaky. Jess didn't know if it was the alcohol or Yousef.

'No, no, I love you. God knows, I love you.'

'What is it then?' she asked. This was good, he still loved her.

'I'm just not brave enough to carry this on. To carry us on.'

Jess's heart broke in that instant. She felt it, a sudden pain right in the middle of her chest. She hadn't expected heartbreak to be a physical pain, but it was. For a moment the pain swallowed her. It took her down a dark hole where it was just her and the pain. She wanted to scream so someone could hear her but that needed strength and she had none.

'My family,' Yousef continued. 'I really thought I would be able to tell them about us, but I don't think I can. My mum wouldn't accept it, our relationship would break her. You have no idea how many times I've tried, but I just can't do it.'

And there it was. Yousef choosing his family over her again. Her pain subsided for a moment as rage crept in.

'Yousef, we had a plan. You were going to tell them about us after our exam results. We talked about this.' Her words came out fast. 'It's been five years, you have been telling me for five years that you would tell them when today came.'

'I know, but I can't. You don't understand, my family are deeply religious. They care so much about what other people think, and me being with you . . .'

'Would shame them.' Jess finished his sentence. She felt sick.

'No, but it would be difficult for them to accept.'

'Accept what, Yousef? The fact that I'm white or that I'm not Muslim? Because that's fucking racist,' Jess said, turning to look at him. She wanted him to feel uncomfortable about this question. She had tiptoed around conversations about his culture and religion for years, not wanting to offend or say the wrong thing. It had been such a minefield. Now it was his turn.

'Both,' Yousef said. 'I just thought I would be able to tell them. I love you so much, but I can't do that to them.'

'And what about what you're doing to me?' Jess shouted. 'You say you love me, but you don't give a shit about me.'

'I do love you, it's just that when it comes to my family it's so complicated. It's hard to explain.'

It seemed fairly simple to Jess. Yousef loved his family more than he loved her. 'You had me believing in a fairy tale. You made me think you would tell your family about me when the time was right. Yeah, they would be upset for a short period of time, but then they would come round.' Jess could see the scenario in her head. 'But you had no intention of telling them, did you? You're a liar.'

'I did, Jess, I really did. I thought I would have the strength to do it, but I just don't have it in me.' Yousef was crying. 'I'm sorry.'

'I'm not interested in your apologies, Yousef.' Jess was suddenly going through all the people in her head who she would have to tell about this break-up. All the people who told her to stay well clear of a 'Pakistani lad'. She hadn't believed them. The pain in her chest started to get stronger. 'How long have you known about this, Yous?'

'What do you mean?'

'How long have you known that you were going to end it with me?'

'I don't know, I was hoping things might change—'

'How long?' she screamed.

'Maybe a few months, I don't know,' Yousef said quickly.

'A few months?' Jess countered. 'We applied to the same deanery for our jobs, I'm moving to a whole other part of the country to be with you.' Jess was panicking. She was moving to Birmingham in a few weeks to start her new job. She didn't know Birmingham at all; all her friends were staying in the south. But Yousef had reassured her they would be there together.

'I know, I wish I had told you earlier but every time I tried, I lost my nerve.'

'Lost your nerve? Jesus Christ. Yousef, I'm moving to Birmingham. We're going to be working at the same hospital. What the fuck am I supposed to do?' Jess could feel herself becoming short of breath. 'Yousef, please don't do this.'

'I'm sorry, Jess, I don't know what else to do.'

'But I love you, surely we can work this out? Maybe we don't have to tell your parents straight away?' She hated herself for saying it, but panic was setting in.

'I love you too, but that's not enough,' Yousef said. He took her hand. 'I am so sorry.'

Jess looked at him. She hated him in that moment; real violent hatred ran through her. But she hated herself too, because deep down she knew. She had always known but hoped that it might be different. He didn't love her in the way she loved him. She pulled her hand out of his. 'You need to leave.'

'Jess, we should talk.'

'Just leave. Please,' she said firmly. Yousef stood still for a second, then picked up his coat and headed towards the door.

'I am truly very sorry, Jess,' he said. 'And for what it's worth, I do love you.'

Jess remained silent as the door closed behind him. She went to the bathroom and grabbed a flannel and started scrubbing furiously until all her make-up was smeared over her face. She

needed to feel something. She ran the cold tap and filled up
the sink. Plunging her face into the icy water, she let out a
silent scream.

She took off her dress and put on her dressing gown, sat on
the sofa and picked up her phone. She had several missed calls
from Kate and a text message: **Babes, you ok? We are at The 911,
meet us there.**

She texted back, knowing Kate would worry. **Not coming.
Yous just broke up with me.**

She put her phone down and stared at the ceiling. What was
she going to do? She was embarrassed to tell her parents. They
had asked if she had been sure about Yousef when she told
them she was applying to work in Birmingham with him. Her
phone beeped. It was a text from Kate. **On my way home. See
you soon.**

A sense of relief washed over her. She felt bad for making
Kate come home, but she didn't want to be alone. She needed
someone on her side right now. Jess closed her eyes and waited
to be rescued by her friend.

Chapter Nine

Rohit

ROHIT WAS ROYALLY PISSED off. He had come down to London to escape the stress he faced at home, and instead he was caught up in an even worse drama. He wanted to go out, meet the rest of the gang and get drunk. But he was stuck in his old student living room with Yousef. Yousef sat on the sofa opposite, replaying the conversation he had had with Jess over and over. Rohit found it difficult to summon up any genuine sympathy for his friend.

Yousef had told Rohit about the dilemma he had with Jess two years ago. Initially Yousef would tell Rohit that he would tell his family about his relationship with Jess, but it became increasingly obvious to him that Yousef wasn't ever going to tell them. He'd encouraged his friend to do the right thing and tell Jess the truth. Yousef would claim he was going to do it, then inevitably come up with an excuse as to why he couldn't.

He looked at Yousef, slumped on the sofa feeling sorry for himself. Rohit had always been envious of Yousef. He was exceptionally good-looking, lean and muscular without so much as going to the gym and, up until this evening, he'd had an incredibly beautiful girlfriend. When they had first met, Rohit couldn't quite believe that Yousef wanted to be his friend, and then when he was introduced by him to Jess and her friends, for the first time in his life, Rohit felt popular. Rohit had always been on the outside looking in, but finally by complete chance he was now in the inner circle.

'You understand why I had to break it off with her, don't you, Ro?' Yousef asked. It was the fourth time he had asked the same question of Rohit.

'Yes, Yousef, I do.' He sighed. 'But you should have done it before she applied to work in the same hospital as you.'

'I know, I know. But at that point I felt like I would be able to tell my parents about her,' Yousef tried to explain. 'The truth is, they would never accept it.'

'Look, Yousef, far be it for me to tell you what to do in this situation. I've moved back to live with my mother and taken up a shitty job due to family pressure. But your situation is different. You really love Jess. Are you sure you're doing the right thing?' If Jess had been Rohit's girlfriend, he would never have broken up with her. There was always a part of Rohit that was envious of Yousef's relationship. He would watch them together around the house, laughing and being affectionate, and then when she left, Yousef would tell him how difficult it was balancing his life with Jess with that of his family. Was Yousef really that insensitive? Could he not see that Rohit couldn't even score himself a snog on a night out, let alone a proper girlfriend? He didn't know how good he had it.

'It doesn't feel like the right thing now, but with me moving back home in a few weeks, it was my only option,' Yousef replied.

'And you're sure it wasn't simply the easiest option?' Rohit had to be honest. To him, it felt like Yousef had taken the coward's way out. Being Asian meant you lived with a certain degree of family pressure but there came a point in your life when you had to man up and make a decision in your own best interest.

'Fucking hell, Ro, do you think that was easy? Because let me tell you, it really wasn't.'

'That's not what I meant. Of course it was hard, but it would have been harder for you to tell your family about Jess. So, in a way it was the easier of the two options.'

Yousef didn't say anything.

'Do you think you may be underestimating your parents, Yous? Maybe they would be more understanding than you think.'

'You don't know my mother,' Yousef spat out. 'People assume these things are like in the movies: my parents will get all upset to begin with but then they will see how happy Jess makes me and after she has been through a few ups and downs with my mother they will realize they both want the same thing – to see me happy.' Yousef looked at Rohit. 'And everything will end with a happily ever after, right?'

'Right. In time, they'll probably come round . . .' Rohit felt he was being led into a trap.

'Yeah, and maybe for most normal families that would be true, but not my family,' Yousef said. 'My mother isn't a character in a movie who learns the errors of her ways, Ro. Do you know what she did after Rehana told her she was applying to study English Literature at university?'

'What?' Rohit asked, not really wanting to know the answer.

'She said she had chest pain and took herself to A&E,' Yousef answered. 'After they sent her home, she told Rehana that if she died, it would be all her fault.'

'Jesus,' Rohit said.

'And she still hasn't forgiven her for not wanting to be a pharmacist. She never gets over things.'

'But this is different. You have done everything she has asked of you up until this point. You applied to study medicine when you wanted to be a vet. Surely she needs to compromise too?' Rohit thought someone just needed to take a stand against Yousef's mum. But to be honest, he had met her and would never dare to do so himself.

'It would kill her. She wouldn't be faking chest pains, it would be the real thing,' Yousef said glumly. 'Best just skip that part and move on.'

'Move on to what?' Rohit asked.

'I don't know, whatever she has lined up for me.'

They stayed silent for a while. Then Rohit addressed the elephant in the room. 'Mate, I don't want to state the obvious but isn't it going to be weird working in the same hospital as Jess?'

'That won't be until my second foundation year in twelve months' time. She may feel differently then . . .' Yousef said, but it was more of a hopeful question than a statement. Although they had both applied to work in the West Midlands, they had been given jobs in different hospitals during their first year. Yousef would be at the Sandwell General Hospital, whilst Jess would be spending her first foundation year as a newly qualified doctor at New Cross Hospital. When they had found out they would be at different hospitals, Jess had been worried she wouldn't know anyone, but Yousef had assured her it would be okay, they would support each other. Now he was glad they would have at least a year apart before rotating into the Queen Elizabeth Hospital for their second foundation year training.

Rohit shook his head. He was thinking about how he was in the same situation, albeit for different reasons. Their perfect university lives had come to an end. He hadn't found a girl-friend, but he'd had a far better university experience than he ever dared to hope. Perhaps he had got greedy by trying to prolong it by staying in London. He had responsibilities at home. It was hard. They had flirted with what life might be like without the restraints of their parents and the expectations of their communities. He imagined it was the same for Yousef. Maybe they should just be grateful for the experiences they'd had, and it was now time to close that chapter. But it didn't seem fair to Rohit; he wanted more. 'So, what now?' he asked Yousef.

'Now I pack up and go home,' Yousef said, staring at the floor.

Strangely, Rohit felt a moment of pleasure knowing that Yousef was now in the same boat as him. He didn't feel as lonely. If it could happen to someone like perfect Yousef, then what chance did Rohit have? There was a sense of inevitability.

'Just like that? All over,' he pondered, more to himself than to Yousef.

'Just like that,' Yousef replied. 'All over.'

Part Two

Twelve months
later

Chapter Ten

Feroza

FEROZA STUDIED HERSELF IN the mirror. She decided she would go for the pale pink lipstick. It complemented her yellow kameez better than the red one did. Once satisfied, she carefully took out her jewellery box from the drawer. She hid the box under folded bed sheets and yards of fabric that she hadn't yet had the time to sew into clothing. Feroza lived in constant fear of the house being burgled and her jewels being discovered by the thief. She didn't have a large collection, but what she did have meant everything to her. Her own mother had given her the gold bangles and matching necklace on the day she and Abdul were married. Feroza's wedding had taken place in her family home in Pakistan. Abdul lived just a few streets away and had arrived on foot with the rest of his family. The imam from the local mosque had married them and the women of the family had cooked the food. She recalled having to stay up the night before her wedding helping her mum and aunties chop the onions and cook the lamb. Lamb was expensive, but she was her parents' only daughter. She had cried as she walked back to Abdul's house. She had only met him twice before the wedding, and although he had been handsome and had seemed kind, she hadn't wanted to leave her family.

She was finally ready.

'Rehana, come here, let me see what you are wearing!' she shouted for her daughter. 'Yousef! Abdul! Hurry, we don't want to be late!'

Rehana came in looking sullen.

'Mum, do I have to go?' she said. 'I won't know anyone there.'

'Don't be silly, Rehana, you will know everyone there. Come here, let me have a look at you.' She dragged Rehana to the mirror and inspected her. When she tried, her daughter did really look quite beautiful. It was a shame she did it so infrequently.

Feroza had made a green lengha for Rehana to wear especially for today. 'Here, put these bangles on, they match your lengha perfectly.' She handed Rehana a box. 'And you need more make-up. We are going to a wedding, not a funeral.' Rehana scowled at her and returned to her room. Feroza loved the process of getting ready for weddings and it bothered her that her daughter didn't. She had put oil on her hair the night before to ensure it was especially glossy for today. She wanted to do the same for Rehana, but her offer had been stubbornly rebuked. She knew she had to pick her battles with Rehana and getting her to agree to wear the lengha was enough for today. A quick spritz of perfume and she made her way downstairs.

Abdul and Yousef had been ready for some time and were now watching television. They both looked wonderful in their matching kurtas.

'Did you go to the cash point?' she asked of Abdul.

'Yes,' Abdul said. 'I have put fifty pounds inside the card and signed it from all of us.'

How times had changed, Feroza thought. She used to be able to go to the local Woolworths to buy a kettle for every new couple, but now every invite to Pakistani weddings came with clear instructions: no boxed gifts, please. This was a polite way of saying cash only.

They all gathered in the hallway as Feroza gave them one final look.

'Dad, can you bring the car round to the front of the house,' Rehana said. 'I don't want to walk down the street looking like this.'

'Like what, Rehana, huh?' Feroza said sharply.

'Like a typical Pakistani,' Yousef joked, laughing. 'She's embarrassed.'

'Piss off, Yousef,' Rehana said.

'Rehana, don't talk to your brother that way. And we don't have time for your dad to bring the car round, we are late.' She ushered everyone out of the house and locked the door, checking it twice.

The car was parked at the end of the road. It was the only free space left when Abdul had returned from work last night. Yousef was checking his hair in the window of a neighbour's car and Rehana stood, arms folded, next to him. Feroza sighed. Were they incapable of doing anything without her instruction?

'Move!' she said firmly to the pair of them. She led them towards the car.

'Oh shit, there's Aunty Angie,' Rehana hissed, nodding towards one of their neighbours who was coming out of her home. She was accompanied by her daughter, Lottie.

Rehana and Yousef increased their pace, pushing past Feroza in a desperate attempt to get to the car. It vexed Feroza that her children were ashamed to be seen in their cultural outfits. She, however, was not.

'Angie, hi!' she called out.

'Oh my, don't you all look gorgeous!' Angie shouted from across the street. 'Where are you off to?'

'To a wedding,' Feroza replied. 'Musarat's daughter, Zara, is getting married today.'

'That explains all the noise we heard this morning, doesn't it, Lottie?' Angie turned to her daughter. 'They had someone playing the drums out in the street. I thought there was a carnival going on.'

'Yes, we saw the dhol player too. Such a wonderful sound. Reminds me of weddings back in Pakistan.'

Angie turned her attention to Rehana and Yousef, who had hurriedly got into the back of the car. 'Look at you two, so grown-up.'

'Rehana, Yousef, get out of the car so Aunty Angie can see your clothes,' Feroza said, still smiling at Angie.

'I thought we were late, Mum?' Yousef said, putting on his seat belt.

'Yeah, Mum, we'd better go,' Rehana said, trying to avoid eye contact with her mother. Feroza opened the car door and demanded they both get out. 'Out. Abdul, you too.' She watched proudly as Angie admired her family.

'It's like something out of one of those Bollywood movies,' Angie said.

'How would you know, Mum? You've never watched a Bollywood movie,' Lottie said, showing no interest whatsoever. *What a rude girl*, Feroza thought.

'True, but they have Indian people in *Coronation Street* and sometimes they get dressed up in saris and they look stunning. I could never pull one off myself,' Angie said, looking at Rehana's dress.

'Oh, that's not a sari, it's a lengha. Quite different. Saris are worn mainly by Indian people. We are Pakistani,' Feroza corrected her neighbour. 'I made it myself.'

'I didn't know there was a difference,' Angie said. 'No offence, love,' she said to Rehana.

'None taken,' Rehana said. 'It's a bit like comparing British people's clothes to that of the French. They're both groups of white people, only the French dress better.'

'Rehana, get in the car,' Feroza hissed. 'Don't the boys look handsome?' she asked.

'Very handsome. Reminds me of our trip to Sharm El Sheikh last summer, doesn't it, Lottie?' Angie said. 'Mubarak, the fella in charge of the camels, was wearing something similar. He looked like the Prince of Persia.'

Lottie rolled her eyes. 'Different continent, Mum.'

Angie laughed. 'Whoops, I've never been much good at geography. Anyway, you look wonderful.'

'Thank you, Angie,' Abdul interjected. 'It was lovely seeing you. Pop over for a cup of tea sometime.' He ushered Feroza into the car.

'Have a great time at the wedding,' Angie said, waving them off.

The wedding was being held in the town hall. With it being in the town centre, there was no designated parking, so they'd had to pay to park.

'What kind of wedding doesn't have parking?' Feroza said, annoyed. 'Now we have to walk through town to get there. It's not how I would plan a wedding.'

Feroza had endured the last year listening to Musarat talk about her daughter's wedding. She had to pretend to be interested when she had told her about how the jeweller had measured Zara's ring finger, exclaiming he had never seen such dainty hands. She had smiled through the time Musarat told them they had to taste the food of six different catering companies before the couple-to-be were finally happy with the wedding menu. She had nodded and agreed when Musarat had told her Zara had cried because they couldn't find a wedding dress to her taste here in the UK, so they were having to take an emergency trip to Pakistan. She was expecting big things from this wedding, and she would be taking notes.

The town hall looked beautiful. Rows of tables were tastefully decorated with arrangements of pink and white roses, each chair had a soft white cover, tied back with the palest of pink bows, and the guests were given a flute of mango juice as they arrived. A string quartet was playing classic Bollywood songs in one corner and a DJ was setting up his booth in another. At the far end was the stage. It was decorated with pillars topped with more flowers and the centrepiece was two thrones, where the bride and groom would eventually sit. Feroza was disappointed. So far she could not find anything to fault.

'We are on table eighteen,' Abdul said, returning with fresh juice for them all.

'A table plan? What is this, a gora wedding?' Feroza muttered under her breath. Rather annoyingly, their table was towards the back of the room and behind a large pillar which obstructed their view of the stage. Feroza did a quick sweep of the other names on the table. 'Yousef, you come and sit next to me,' she said, swapping his name with Rehana's. 'Rehana, can you at least look a little bit pleased to be here?' Her daughter sat slumped in her newly appointed chair.

Feroza scanned the room. People were milling around chatting and admiring each other's outfits. There were lots of people present she knew, but Feroza wasn't interested in them. With her children now of age, weddings were no longer about socializing with her friends; they were prime hunting grounds for potential partners for Yousef and Rehana. She and Abdul had spent the last year making phone calls to their friends to see if there were any suitable partners for their children, but so far that had yielded nothing. No, she needed new blood and the scent of it was thick in the air. The problem was, Feroza's contemporaries all had children of a similar age to her two and would be thinking the same thing. It was a competitive market. Feroza would have to act quick if she wanted to secure the best suitors. All she needed to do was meet the right people.

'Salaam, Feroza, so nice we are on the same table together,' a voice said. She turned to see Zareen and her husband Adil taking their seats. 'Though we can't see much of the stage from here.'

'Walaikum salam, Zareen,' Feroza said, also taking a seat. 'Yes, I thought we'd be on a better table given we are neighbours of the bride.' Feroza liked Zareen. Maybe she would take a small break from her mission of seeking out new families to talk to her. Abdul and Adil immediately began discussing the politics of Pakistan. She couldn't understand her husband's obsession with it, they had left that country nearly twenty-five years ago, but he still insisted on talking about how it was run whenever he got the chance. Abdul occasionally talked about returning 'home' to Pakistan once their children were settled in their own lives. She humoured him but had no intention of leaving her children, or Birmingham for that matter.

There was a sudden commotion at the entrance to the hall and the sound of the traditional Punjabi dhol sounded through the room. The groom and his family had arrived. Everybody stood up to go outside and get a better look. This was Feroza's favourite part. She rushed to the front. The dhol players led the procession wearing traditional Punjabi shirts and decorative turbans. The groom's family arrived in a pair of yellow Lamborghinis – hired, no doubt. How tacky, Feroza thought. They were followed by a string of Range Rovers and BMWs, all adorned with the obligatory wedding ribbons on the bonnets. Feroza didn't understand this new generation's obsession with hiring flash cars for weddings. It was such a waste of money. Better to spend it on saving for a house the whole family could live in. She arched her neck, trying to get a glimpse of the groom. He emerged from one of the Lamborghinis. He was tall. Feroza felt a pang of bitterness – tall Pakistani men were hard to come by. The groom appeared nervous, looking at his dad, who gave him a gentle nod of support. He wore a custom-made deep blue sherwani with gold embroidery and a matching pagri on his head. His dad encouraged him to join a group of other men who had begun dancing. There was lots of raucousness as they coaxed others into the dancing, many of whom put up a faux show of resistance, only to succumb to the music and the bhangra. Soon the whole of the groom's party began dancing their way into the hall.

Musarat's family and closest friends lined the walkway to the stage, clapping and throwing confetti at the dancing arrivals as they made their way forward. Feroza assessed each one of the dancing men and counted two that could be potential suitors for Rehana. She made a mental note to follow this up. Once at the front of the hall, the groom and his parents climbed the stairs to the stage and stood proudly looking out at the other guests. Feroza was overcome with a sudden wave of jealousy. She so wished that this was Rehana's wedding and it was her and Abdul who were waiting at the end of the walkway to receive the groom and his family. She kept smiling and clapping. She just had to wait for her turn.

'Hope you're practising your bhangra, Yous,' Rehana laughed. 'That'll be you next.'

'Or you, sis,' Yousef retorted.

'It will be both of you soon, inshallah,' Feroza said. Abdul nodded.

'Musarat has done very well for herself marrying Zara into that family,' Zareen said to her after they were sat down again. 'Apparently they have a very big house in Sutton Coldfield.'

Sutton Coldfield was an area Feroza could only dream of living in. It was a far cry from her modest terraced home. She hoped that Yousef would one day buy a house there and she and Abdul would move in.

'What a lucky girl Zara is,' she replied. 'I only hope one day my Rehana will be so lucky.'

Rehana made a face at her.

'Are you looking for someone for her?' Zareen asked. She was looking at Rehana as if it was the first time she had seen her. 'How old are you now, Rehana?'

'I didn't think you could ask a lady that question,' Rehana said flatly.

'She is twenty-three,' Feroza said quickly. 'The perfect age to find a husband.' She gave Rehana a stern look. 'She has had a number of offers but we haven't found the right match, you know how it is,' Feroza lied.

'She won't catch the attention of any of the boys here if she sits in that chair all night on her phone,' Zareen said, turning her attention to Yousef. 'And I should think we need to find you a nice girl to marry, Yousef. I imagine they are breaking down your door.'

Yousef smiled and Feroza's heart melted. He had the most radiant smile. 'That's very kind, Aunty Zareen, but I have been so busy working shifts at the hospital, I haven't had time to look.' Rehana pretended to vomit and Feroza kicked her underneath the table.

'You don't need to worry, that's what us aunties are for,' Zareen said to Yousef. 'We will find you the perfect wife.'

They were interrupted by the DJ making an announcement for everyone to be on their feet. The bride was about to enter.

Zara was breathtaking as she glided down the walkway guided by her father to rapturous applause. She wore a dark green lengha, decorated with ruby-red stonework and floral patterns, her dupatta was draped behind her back over her arms rather than over her head, freshly applied henna adorned her hands, and her jewellery caught the light with her every movement. There was something about seeing a young Pakistani girl getting married that made Feroza feel proud. Her generation had worked hard so their children could prosper here in Britain and there was always a worry their culture and heritage would be diluted somehow, but seeing Zara dressed like this as she was marrying a man who was also in traditional clothes was a comforting feeling. Their culture still flourished, even all these miles away from their homeland.

'Beautiful,' Feroza said to herself.

Despite all the fuss around the entrance of the bride and groom, Feroza knew that a Pakistani wedding is judged by the quality of the food that is served. The starters were adequate, she thought. Not enough options for her liking. The mains were served hot, but the karahi chicken had too much oil, hardly worth all the effort Musarat had told her they had gone to find the right standard of caterer. But even Feroza had to admit the dessert of coconut ice cream served with baked caramelized pineapple was delicious.

As the tea was served, Feroza thought it was time to go and mingle. She had spent far too much time talking to Zareen. She made her way to where the groom's family were sitting.

'Assalamualaikum,' she said to the lady who she knew to be the groom's mother. 'I'm Feroza, Musarat's neighbour and best friend.'

'Walaikum salam. I am Zaitoon,' the lady said, smiling. 'Best friend, you say? I didn't see you at any of the ceremonies this week?'

Feroza ignored the question. 'Beautiful wedding. You must be so proud.'

'Oh yes, Zara is a wonderful girl. I know she will make my Asad very happy.' She looked fondly at her new daughter-in-law, who was busy taking photos with her friends.

'I am sure she will. Does Asad have any brothers or sisters?' Feroza asked.

'Yes, two brothers.'

Feroza's interest was piqued. Two brothers, that doubled her chances for Rehana. 'You have three boys, mashallah. Such a blessing.'

'Indeed. And Asad is the last to be married, so I can finally rest now. Enjoy being old.' She laughed. 'Spend more time with my grandchildren.'

'And the boys who were dancing with your son, were they his university friends?' Feroza quizzed.

'Yes, such good boys,' Zaitoon said, looking at Feroza. 'All married.'

'That's wonderful,' Feroza said, bitterly disappointed. 'Well, it was lovely to meet you.' But Zaitoon was already being dragged away by her family for more photos.

What a waste of time, Feroza thought, returning to her seat. Yousef had left to talk to some of his old school friends and Rehana was still on her phone.

'Is she nice, the groom's mother?' Zareen asked.

'I suppose,' Feroza said. 'Asad, the groom, was the last of her children to get married. No wonder she looks so happy.'

'That is all any parent wants,' Zareen replied wistfully.

'Zareen, how did Zara and Asad meet?' Feroza said, suddenly aware that she had no idea how this union had come about. 'Who introduced Musarat to their family?'

'You don't know?' Zareen asked, sounding surprised.

'No, why?'

'It was through a matchmaker. Apparently Musarat had been looking for a husband for Zara for a long time and it wasn't until she was put in touch with a woman who specializes in Muslim matchmaking that she found someone.' Zareen looked positively ecstatic to be able to give this news to Feroza.

'A matchmaker?' Feroza marvelled. She hadn't thought of that, but it made perfect sense. Professional matchmakers were commonplace in Pakistan. In fact, it was a booming business. Parents would give the details of their children to these people and they would suggest possible matches for them. It made sense that there were similar professionals here too.

'Yes, and I hear she is very good,' Zareen said.

'Zareen, do you have this matchmaker's number?' Feroza asked.

'I will send it to you right now,' Zareen said, getting out her phone.

Chapter Eleven

Rehana

REHANA READ THROUGH HER finished essay one last time. Finally satisfied, she pressed send and closed her laptop. Her postgraduate diploma was unbelievably dull; she'd had no idea when she embarked on her teaching course that it would involve so much reflection on learning methods. She just wanted to get into a classroom and get kids excited about the classics. If she couldn't float around the globe reading books and admiring art, then she could inspire some other young girl to do so. Someone who didn't have the same restrictions put upon them that she had. But this was the last essay she would need to do for a while, as the teaching element was due to begin the next day. And, even better, she was going to get paid for this part of the course, which would mean no longer having to beg her dad for money.

She went to the bathroom to brush her teeth. She wanted an early night. Tomorrow was her first day on placement at the local school as a teaching assistant, so she wanted to be well rested.

The truth was, she would be glad to be able to get out of the house. Since her brother had returned home her mum had become even more unbearable to be around. Rehana had always known he was a prince as far as her mother was concerned, but Yousef becoming a doctor seemed to have taken the level of adulation to stratospheric heights. Every time he returned home from the hospital, the two of them would sit at the dinner table and he would recount what he had seen and done that day. Her mum sat enraptured. It was as if he was single-handedly performing lifesaving miracles every day. One time he had arrived home still wearing his stethoscope around his neck. *What a twat*, she had thought, but her mum had literally swooned. Rehana wasn't stupid, she knew what junior doctors did in hospitals: exactly as they were told by their seniors. They wrote out prescriptions, chased up investigations and completed any of the other jobs the rest of the team couldn't be bothered to do. She wondered if her mother would be so enthusiastic to know how her first day at the school went tomorrow.

'Look at you two, going to work. So grown-up,' her father said, coming into the kitchen as they ate breakfast. 'Rehana, I need to leave in ten minutes. If you want a lift, make sure you are ready.'

'I'm ready, Dad,' Rehana said, taking her dishes to the sink. 'You know, now that I'm working you could buy me a car like you did Yousef.'

'It's a placement, Rehana, not real work,' her mother said. 'Besides, Yousef works shifts, we can't have him getting the bus in the middle of the night.' She ruffled Yousef's hair. Rehana ignored them; she wasn't going to let her mother ruin her first day at work. She would be getting the bus home, a fact that her mum seemed perfectly fine with.

'I will just go get my things, Dad, then I'm good to go.'

'Have a great first day, sis,' Yousef said. Rehana looked at him – he was genuine. She smiled.

Rehana studied herself in the bathroom mirror. To her surprise, her mother had offered to tie her hair back in a French plait earlier that morning.

'You don't want it falling in your face whilst you are on placement,' she had said.

Rehana was nervous. This was her first stab at independence since she had moved home. She had borrowed money from her parents to buy a navy-blue tunic dress and white shirt. She had teamed it with a pair of tights and the shoes she had bought for her graduation. She looked smart, she thought, if a bit boring. She couldn't decide whether or not to paint her nails last night and in the end had decided against it. Now she wished she had. Painted nails in the workplace gave an air of confidence, Rehana thought. Feminine whilst still being a feminist. It was important that she succeeded in making a good impression today. She desperately wanted to be good at something. She loathed herself for feeling this way, but she wanted her mother to feel proud of something she had achieved. She knew that wasn't a particularly feminist thought, but it was the way she felt.

One last look in the mirror and she grabbed her rucksack and headed down the stairs. Her mum was waiting at the bottom.

'Rehana, you look—'

'Don't say it, Mum. Whatever you're going to say, don't say it,' Rehana cut in.

'I was going to say you look beautiful,' her mum said, sounding wounded. 'Here, I have packed your lunch for you.' She handed her a Tupperware container.

'Oh, thanks, Mum,' Rehana said, surprised.

'I have put in some almonds, they are good for your brain.' She looked at Yousef for his expert confirmation, who just smirked. 'Make sure you eat them all.'

There was an awkward moment where the three of them just stared at each other. 'Okay, well, you'd better go, your dad is waiting for you in the car.'

Rehana was met at reception by one of the secretaries, who introduced herself as Nicky. She took her to the staffroom.

'You can leave your stuff in here if you want. The lockers

are all occupied by the teaching staff,' Nicky said. 'Don't worry, it's perfectly secure.'

'Thanks,' Rehana said, looking around. It didn't look secure, so she decided to hold on to her belongings.

'Ms Hudson, whose class you will be joining, should be in soon.' Nicky left.

Rehana stood in the staffroom alone. She was deciding whether or not to sit down when a woman entered.

'Hi, are you Rehana Ahmed?' the lady said. She pronounced her name like most people did, incorrectly. Rehana was used to non-Asian folk saying her name like Rihanna, the singer. When you are brown you always have two ways of saying your name: the actual way it is supposed to be said, and the white way. She had put up with it at university because she thought it was cool, but now she was starting a new chapter in her life, she wanted people to say her name properly. And besides, she had the right to be called by her actual name, not by that of some pop star, no matter how fabulous they might be.

Correcting those older than you was seen as a mark of disrespect in the Pakistani culture. This lady looked to be a couple of years older than her. But they weren't at some Pakistani function, and she meant to start as she hoped to go on.

'Hi, yes I am. And it's actually pronounced Ray-haana,' she said, sounding it out.

'Sorry, Rehana,' the lady said, saying it properly this time. 'I'm Emma Hudson, you're joining me in my class.'

'Thanks, Emma.' Rehana smiled. 'I'm really looking forward to it.'

'You might change your mind when you meet the kids. Teenagers can be . . . tricky.' She winked at Rehana. 'Come on, let's go. Leave them alone too long and they either start shagging or fighting.'

Even though she was only observing, Rehana thoroughly enjoyed her morning. Emma seemed to have the students captivated by her interpretation of **Mrs Dalloway**, making sure even the quietest of them had some input. When one of them got too loud, she managed to quieten them down by getting them to voice their opinions on Richard Dalloway.

'Wow, you really know your stuff,' Rehana said to Emma after the first lesson.

'It's Virginia Woolf, Rehana. Everybody knows it,' Emma said, cleaning the whiteboard.

'I know, but the students seemed so interested, not like when I was at school.'

'This is A-level English Literature,' Emma said to her. 'The students have chosen to do the course and they know this book will most likely feature on their exam. Basically, if they don't pay attention, they'll fail.'

The next class arrived and this time it was *Lord of the Flies*.

The staffroom was busy when they arrived for lunch. Rehana realized that aside from the almonds, she had no idea what her mother had packed for her. She was pleasantly surprised to find tuna sandwiches wrapped in cling film and a mint Club. Emma sat next to her with her salad.

Rehana wondered if Emma had anything other than her salad. In Pakistani culture, salads, as delicious as they were, were always a side dish to a curry or rice dish. Even whilst at university, Rehana couldn't bring herself to make a salad the main event of any of her meals. It was a curious thing that white people seemed to do. She could imagine her mum's response if she told her she had just a salad for her main meal at dinner.

'So, Rehana, tell me about yourself,' Emma said, taking in a forkful of greens. 'We're going to spend the next term working together so best we get to know each other.'

Rehana didn't know what to say to such a broad question.

Nobody had asked her about herself in such a long time. In fact, nobody had taken an interest in anything she said or did in ages. 'What do you want to know?' she asked.

'Well, where did you go to university? Why do you want to become a teacher?'

'I studied English at Leeds and had the best time. Graduated last year. Now I live at home with my parents, not having the best time.' She laughed nervously. 'And I wanted to be a writer, but that didn't work out, so my mum suggested I become a teacher.' She looked up at Emma, who had stopped chewing her food.

'Well, that's a depressing story,' she said, resuming chewing.

'What about you?' Rehana asked, keen to move the conversation along.

'Love teaching, always have. Shit pay and shit conditions, but still I keep coming back for more.' She took a slurp of her juice. 'What do you do in your spare time?'

'Not much. I'm kind of learning to cook from my mum,' Rehana said, rather embarrassed.

'That sounds like fun. Does she make delicious food?'

'I suppose so. I'm only doing it to keep her off my back really. She tends to nag a lot when I sit on the sofa and watch Netflix all day.'

'Well, you'll have to bring some food in for the rest of us. Can't beat authentic Indian food,' Emma said.

'We're Pakistani, it'll be authentic Pakistani food,' Rehana said. She didn't understand why she felt the need to be so particular about her culture today, but it felt right.

'I'm asking genuinely here, and I don't want to offend you. But is there a difference?' Emma said, looking worried she had said the wrong thing.

'To be honest, I don't know,' Rehana said as she thought about it. 'They seem pretty similar and I'm not an expert on either culture!' They both laughed. 'Mum thinks it's a good idea I get a few staple dishes under my belt before I get married.'

'Oh, are you getting married?' Emma asked, looking very interested.

'No, but if my mum had her way, I'd be betrothed and with child by now!' Rehana said.

'She sounds like my mum.' Emma laughed. 'She's always asking me when I'm going to settle down and give her grand-children. Just ignore her.'

'Really?' Rehana said, wide-eyed. 'I thought it was only Asian mums who did that.'

'No, it's all mums,' Emma said, packing up her salad box. 'They don't think we can be happy without a man in our lives and children latched onto our tits. You should hear my nan; I think she thinks I'm a lesbian, I haven't brought a man home for that long.'

They laughed again.

'How does it work then? Does your mum find you a husband?' Emma said, taking out a packet of crisps from her bag.

'She's put the feelers out. I don't think she's had much success yet.' Rehana unwrapped her mint Club. 'To be honest, I'm hoping to find someone before she does.'

'And that'll be okay?'

'As long as they have a good job and are Muslim and Pakistani, I don't think she'll mind.'

'Wow, that's interesting,' Emma said, frowning.

'What do you mean?'

'Well, imagine if I said that I would only consider white Christian men as potential boyfriends, I'd be accused of all sorts of racism,' Emma said. 'I'm not judging, just putting it out there, that's all.'

Rehana considered what Emma said. She had never looked at it from this perspective before. She had always assumed her husband would be Muslim and Pakistani, even when she'd had boyfriends in the past who had not been. Deep down, she didn't put much importance on either religion or race, but knew her family did so went along with it.

'I suppose it's about preserving our culture in another country,' Rehana said, thinking out loud. 'And if you really think about it, most people do marry inside of their race, no matter what that might be; it's just they are less open about it than my mum is.'

'Hmm, maybe,' Emma said. 'As long nobody forces you to do something you don't want to do.'

'See, there's the issue. So many people who don't understand arranged marriages confuse them with forced marriages.' Even though Rehana wasn't a staunch believer in the arranged marriage process, she felt compelled to defend it. 'It's a bit like the British aristocracy: they marry other rich white people, usually approved by their parents, so that wealth remains in their families. It's simply an introduction to someone who comes from a family who has similar values to ours.'

'They don't all marry rich white people. Look at Harry and Meghan. She's not white,' Emma said.

'Yeah, and look at the crap they have to put up with,' Rehana replied. 'Plus, arranged marriages are all the rage now. Look at all the dating shows on the telly: Married at First Sight, Love is Blind . . . They should really be paying royalties to our ancestors, they had the idea first.'

'Sorry, I didn't mean to offend you,' Emma said. 'To be honest, I wish my mother would introduce me to a string of eligible bachelors. It would save me from the shits that are on Tinder.'

'Don't even talk to me about internet dating. I've spent the last few weeks sifting through some right bastards. It's all in a bid to get my mother off my back – I promised I would look for a husband myself too. And the sooner I get a husband, the sooner I can move out,' Rehana said.

'Can't you just rent a place and move out now?'

Rehana made a pretend shocked face. 'A single Pakistani girl, living on her own? The aunties would have a field day with that. No, I have to be married first. Those are the rules.'

'Well, you know what they say.' Emma leaned in, whispering now. 'Rules are made to be broken.'

'Don't let the kids hear you say that,' Rehana replied. They both laughed again and any tension that was in the air evaporated.

'Come on, we'd better get back to the classroom before all hell breaks loose.' Emma tossed her crisp packet into the bin and Rehana followed her out.

Emma had offered to give Rehana a lift home, but she had declined. The walk to the bus stop in the fresh air would do her some good and she wasn't in a hurry to get back. She had enjoyed the day and felt as though she had made a friend in Emma. Over the last year, Rehana had lost contact with most of her university friends. They all seemed to be doing so well for themselves, and she didn't have the heart to tell them she wasn't. She had missed having someone she could talk to. It reminded her of when she would stay up all night talking to her girlfriends.

It was a warm evening and the bus dropped her off at the end of her road. As she walked home, she wondered if she just might enjoy being a teacher. Emma made it look so worthwhile, though the pile of papers she had to take home to mark didn't seem so appealing. But overall, she thought perhaps she had made the right decision.

She thought about why she had felt so compelled to defend the concept of arranged marriages. In the past she had simply whitewashed over any conversations with her friends that mentioned arranged marriages, despite it being a cornerstone of her culture. They were always talked about in such negative ways, and usually assumed a decision that went against the wishes of the girl involved. As a brown girl, she had been asked whether or not she would be getting an arranged marriage several times before. It seemed to be a standard question when hanging out with a group of white people. She found it strange; she would never ask them, 'So will you be finding your own husband?' Often the question came out of the blue. One person would ask it while the others in the group would look simultaneously embarrassed and intrigued. She would have to explain the concept each time. It was simply an introduction, and many people went through several potential suitors before deciding on their life partners. And besides, was it really any different to Tinder? Instead of relying on complex algorithms to set her up with a partner, she was depending on her parents, and a few select people in her community. Surely that was a safer bet? And besides, as much as Rehana wanted to be a feminist, she didn't want to end up being single and arranged marriages almost guaranteed that would not happen.

'Hello, Rehana!' a voice called out.

She looked up. It was Aunty Angie.

'Hi, Aunty Angie, you okay?' Rehana said. She kept on walking, hoping that Angie would take the hint.

'How was the wedding? Bet it was gorgeous,' Angie said, stepping in front of Rehana so she couldn't get away.

'I suppose it was gorgeous, if you're into that kind of thing,' Rehana said.

'I'd love to come to an Asian wedding; I've heard the food is to die for.'

'We eat that kind of food all the time, Aunty Angie. So, it's no big deal to us,' Rehana replied. She didn't care too much for Asian wedding food; it was far too rich.

'A bit like us serving up a Sunday roast at one of our weddings,' Angie said, laughing. 'Hey, I suppose it'll be your turn soon?'

God, was there nobody left on the planet who wasn't obsessed with her getting married?

'Aunty Angie, I will get married when I choose to get married and not a moment sooner. It will be me who decides who I marry and then it will be me who decides who is and isn't invited to the wedding, so back off!' Rehana stared at Angie until she moved out of the way.

'Sorry, Rehana, I was only trying to make conversation,' Angie said, sounding hurt.

Rehana felt bad. Clearly Angie had meant no harm.

'Sorry, Aunty Angie. Tell you what, if I do get married, I'll make sure you're invited and then you can come and taste all that food for yourself.'

Angie smiled. 'Deal,' she said, turning the key in her door and stepping inside. Rehana smiled back and headed home.

'Ah, Rehana, you are home.' Her mum was waiting in the hallway. She must have been cooking – a spice-filled aroma wafted through. 'I was just about to call you to see where you were.'

'Sorry, Mum, I was just talking to Aunty Angie outside,' Rehana said, taking off her coat.

'She never stops talking, that woman. Come into the kitchen and tell me all about your day.'

Rehana frowned, confused. 'You want to hear all about my day?'

'Don't say it like that,' her mum replied. 'Of course I do. Come on, dinner will be ready soon.'

Chapter Twelve

Jessica

THE HOSPITAL WAS BUSY. The summer was supposed to be the quieter season, but someone had forgotten to tell the patients. The nurses said there was no longer a quiet time in the NHS, every season felt like winter now. Jess was the foundation year doctor on call, which meant she was the first person that many of the patients saw and spoke to on arrival at the hospital. The acute medical ward was full and the sister in charge was now having to place new patients on whichever ward they could find a bed.

Her shift was almost over and she was looking forward to the moment she could hand her bleep over to the night team and get to football practice. She checked her watch. Twenty minutes to handover – time to check on one last patient. Betty Munroe had been admitted by her GP after complaining of feeling short of breath. Her doctor had assessed her and found her to have an irregular heartbeat and low blood pressure. A year ago, managing a patient like Betty would have given Jess palpitations of her own, but she had seen this presentation so often now, she knew exactly what to do.

'Hello, Mrs Munroe, I'm Dr Pritchard,' Jess said, trying her best to muster up a smile after twelve gruelling hours on call.

'I'm sorry to have kept you waiting.' She drew the curtain around the bed.

'No problem, love,' Betty said. 'I can see you're all busy.'

Betty looked tired. Jess checked her list to see what time she had come in. Nearly nine hours ago. She had already changed into a hospital gown and was now lying propped up in bed attached to a heart monitor.

'Do you mind if I ask you a few questions?' Jess started; she did a quick assessment of Betty. Slim but not frail, her hair looked like it had been recently cut and curled and she wore freshly applied nail varnish. Not a woman who was used to being sick, Jess thought.

'If it means I can go home, you can ask me all the questions you like.' Betty smiled at her.

'Well, that decision is up to my seniors, I'm afraid,' Jess said, taking out a pen from her satchel. 'But I'll plead your case.' She winked at Betty.

Betty's symptoms had started the day before. She woke up feeling more tired than usual and then found she was unusually short of breath when she made her way to the bathroom. As the day progressed her symptoms got worse, so she rang her GP, who saw her that afternoon at the surgery. She'd been surprised to learn her blood pressure was dangerously low and heartbeat dangerously fast.

'That isn't a combination you want to have,' Betty said. 'Anyway, he said I needed to go straight to hospital, so here I am.'

'Who do you live with at home, Mrs Munroe?' Jess asked, making notes.

'My husband. He was here earlier but went home to feed the dog.'

'And do you work?' Jess had learned early not to assume anything when talking to patients; they always surprised you. Betty might be approaching eighty, but she could well still be working.

'Yes, part time. I'm a psychic,' she said.

Jess looked up. 'A psychic?'

'Yes, love. A psychic.' Betty smiled. 'Not what you were expecting?'

'In this job you come to expect the unexpected, Mrs Munroe. But I have to say, you're my first psychic.'

'I can see you don't believe in my abilities,' Betty said, sounding amused. 'It's okay, not many people who work in the medical profession do.'

Betty was right, Jess did not believe in the abilities of psychics. Her mum was a fan of attending evenings with psychics. She always returned home claiming some huge revelation had taken place. Jess just laughed cynically.

'I think I have all the information I need, Mrs Munroe,' Jess said, trying to change the subject. 'We're just waiting for your blood test results to come back from the lab and we'll have a better idea as to what caused this irregular heartbeat.'

'End of your shift, is it, love?' Betty asked.

Jess looked up, surprised.

Betty laughed. 'Don't worry, that wasn't information from the beyond. The nurse told me you would come see to me before you went home.'

'Oh right, okay,' Jess said, standing up. 'Actually, yes, it is the end of my shift. I'll be back tomorrow. In the meantime the night team will look after you. Hopefully, we can get you home soon.'

'Don't you want a reading?' Betty asked. 'The nurse who took my bloods did. I have time to kill. Sit down.' Betty patted the bed.

'I actually need to hand over to the next doctor on call, she'll probably be waiting.'

'Go on, love. I've been here for hours. Give an old lady something to do.' Betty looked at her expectantly. Jess took a moment to think. The night team would be waiting, and she didn't want to be late for football practice, but she could spare five minutes to humour Mrs Munroe.

'Okay, but I have to tell you, you were right about one thing, I'm a sceptic.' Jess sat down.

'That's okay, just play along. Here, give me your hands.' She took Jess's hands in hers. The fingers on her right hand were nicotine-stained. 'You have a cold aura,' she said, closing her eyes.

Charming, Jess thought. 'Usually, patients complain about my cold hands, not my cold aura.' Betty ignored her.

'You're close to your parents,' Betty said, eyes closed. *Who isn't?* Jess thought. 'And you have a sister?'

'Actually, I am an only child,' Jess said, rolling her eyes. She tried to pull her hands away, but Betty tightened her grip. 'Mrs Munroe, I really should be going.'

'Sorry, love, sometimes the messages become difficult to read when you have a cold aura. Stay for a minute.' She pulled Jess in.

'Okay, but enough about my cold aura,' Jess said.

'You're far away from your family now, though,' Betty continued. 'They miss you.'

'Everybody's family misses them.' Jess was unimpressed and presumed her accent might have given Betty a clue as to how far away from home she was.

'Your dad worries about you,' Betty whispered. 'He worries that you're on your own.'

Jess was quiet.

'He never says it, but he worries. Your mum wants you to ring her more often. You should phone her tonight.' Betty's voice trailed off at the end.

Jess knew she didn't ring her parents often enough; they had been so supportive after her break-up and helped her try to move deaneries so she wouldn't have to go to Birmingham. Her mum had got together a list of numbers for people who worked in the admin office, but none of them had been able to help.

'Whatever has happened, she wants you to let it go.'

This was too much. Jess had had enough. Her mother might have fallen for this broad, generic crap but she wasn't about to. 'Mrs Munroe, I really do need to go.' She pulled her hands free.

Betty opened her eyes. 'Sorry, love. Sometimes I forget that this isn't for everyone.'

'That's okay. Like I said, the night team will be looking after you now.'

'Dr Pritchard?' Betty said. Jess turned around. 'Heartbreak can be hard, but don't let it close you off to new possibilities. You will have some difficult choices to make. Go with your heart, not your head. And always forgive. Forgiveness is key to your happiness.'

'Right, well, thanks for that,' Jess said. 'I'll be back to check on you in the morning. Try to get some rest.' She pulled back the curtain and hurried out of the ward. *What a load of nonsense*, she thought.

Football practice had already started when she arrived.

'You're late, Pritchard,' Jonathan shouted as she pulled in.

'I know, sorry. My shift ran over.' She headed to the changing rooms. She was annoyed with herself on the drive in for letting Mrs Munroe get to her. She hadn't thought about Yousef for at least two days, a new record for her, but now she was back to wondering what he was doing and if he was thinking of her. They hadn't spoken since the day they broke up. Graduation had been awkward. She had tried to avoid him but he had come up to her after the ceremony. Thankfully she had been with Kate, who intercepted him and told him to fuck off. They were both now working in the West Midlands deanery, but so far had been placed at different hospitals, although that was about to end come August when their rotations would bring them together in the same hospital. Jess was dreading it. It had taken months for her to come to terms with their break-up. She had trained herself to not hate him but it had been difficult. The first few months were the worst, but now she had made new friends at work and joined a local women's football team, she felt more settled. When she was distracted she was okay, but she felt it impossible not to be angry with him in those moments when she was back in her flat, alone.

'Warm up with a couple of laps,' Jonathan said to her as she emerged, 'then come join the rest of us.'

Jess played in defence alongside another girl, Sandi. The team were practising ahead of a league game against another team in Wolverhampton that weekend. Jonathan was confident they could win it if they worked more cohesively. With the medics' football team at university, Jess had known all the girls from the course so it was easier to bond on the pitch. Here everybody had a life outside of football, and some of the team members had children they had to rush home to, which made getting to know them harder. Thankfully Sandi was just a couple of years older than her and, more importantly, she was single, which usually meant she didn't have to rush off anywhere after practice.

'You two played well today,' Jonathan said after they had finished. 'Keep that up on Saturday.'

'Yes, boss!' Sandi said, doing a mock salute.

'What she means is, thank you, Jonathan, and we will smash it on Saturday,' Jess said.

Sandi laughed. 'You joining your favourite two girls for a drink, Jonathan?'

'I shouldn't, I'm working tomorrow.'

'We're all working tomorrow,' Sandi said. 'Come on, it's just one drink. It doesn't have to be alcoholic.'

'Okay, fine. But just one,' Jonathan said, sighing dramatically.

★

Jess sipped on her Diet Coke. Jonathan was talking tactics for their upcoming game. She had heard it all before and allowed herself to zone out. Her mind kept going back to the conversation she had had with Mrs Munroe. She wasn't closed off to the idea of a new relationship. The problem was, she wasn't over her first one. She was no longer angry at Yousef. To be honest, she was angrier at herself. She had spent so long allowing Yousef to string her along; she should have put more pressure on him earlier on in their relationship to introduce her to his family. Perhaps if they had got that out of the way sooner, things would be different. Whenever she voiced these feelings to Kate on the phone, Kate would tell her off.

'Stop blaming yourself, Jess,' she would say angrily. 'Yousef was a prat, you can do much better.'

Jess didn't think she could do better. Whenever she told the story of her and Yousef to her friends and family, they would all say she could do better, but they didn't understand the relationship. They were not there when it was just the two of them in a room. It was perfect in those moments. She had been totally immersed in their love. Sometimes she had thought if she saw nobody else in the world, just Yousef, she would be happy. During the junior doctors' nights out, she had been asked out twice. Each time she had said no; she wasn't ready to expose herself in the way she had done with Yousef. She had made herself vulnerable to another person and they had taken a shit on her from a great height. No thanks, she didn't want to go through that again. Perhaps this was what Mrs Munroe meant when she had said Jess was closed off? Well, Mrs Munroe hadn't gone out with an absolute tosser of a mamma's boy.

'What do you reckon, Jess?' Jonathan said, staring at her expectantly.

'Sorry, what?'

'Do you want me to pick you up on the way to the match next week?' he asked. 'Sandi's driving in too, but she's coming from the other side of Birmingham. You're on my way.'

'Erm, sure, that would be great.'

'I tell you what, if we win, I'll buy you lunch on our way home.' Jonathan smiled. Jess didn't think she had seen him smile like that before. He was usually barking instructions at them from the side of the pitch.

'When we win, I hope you're going to buy lunch for the whole team!' Sandi interjected.

'Not sure my bank balance will stretch to that.' Jonathan laughed. 'How about a round of drinks instead?'

'Deal,' Sandi said.

'Do you fancy another drink?' Jonathan asked the two of them.

'Thought you were staying for just the one?' Sandi teased. 'Seriously, though, I have to go. I have an early start tomorrow.' She gave Jess a hug. 'Get home safe, don't stay out too late with this one.' She nodded at Jonathan.

'What? I'm a good boy!' he protested.

'Yeah, yeah. See you guys on Saturday.' Sandi grabbed her rucksack.

Jess went to grab her bag as well. 'I should be heading off too. I'm back at the hospital first thing.'

'I was being serious, you know, Jess,' Jonathan said, looking at her intently.

'Serious about what?' Jess said, putting on her jacket.

'About taking you out for lunch.' He looked her in the eye for a beat longer than felt comfortable. She looked away.

'Well, let's see if we win the game first, Jonathan.'

'No, I mean regardless of if we win. I would really like to take you out to lunch, so we can spend more time together.' Jess looked at him. His cheeks were flushing. She thought it was cute.

'Like on a date?' she asked, not quite sure what was going on.

'Yes, very much like a date,' he said, more confidently now.

Jess put down her bag. This was totally unexpected. She had always assumed Jonathan had a girlfriend, but now that she thought about it, he had never really talked much about his private life. She would be lying if she said he was her type, but there was no denying he was attractive. Lots of the girls on the football team thought so, they often joked about it in the dressing room. Playing football was the one thing that brought her a little bit of solace from thinking about Yousef, and she didn't want anything to spoil that. No, going on a date with Jonathan would only sour things with the team.

'Jonathan, don't you think it would make things weird for the team if we started dating?' she asked.

'It doesn't have to,' he said. 'It's just a date, they don't even have to know about it.'

He was smiling at her in the same way he had done a minute ago. It was cute, if a little crooked. She thought about it. Maybe it was time she let go of the spectre of her previous relationship. And one date wouldn't hurt.

'Yes, Jonathan. That would be lovely.'

'Yes? Really?' It was his turn to sound surprised.

'Yes.' She laughed. 'But not straight after the game on Saturday, I need to go home and get ready. How about dinner Saturday night?'

'That sounds great. Shall I pick you up?'

'No, just book somewhere nice and I'll meet you there.' She put on her jacket. 'I really need to go.'

'Sure,' he said, getting up so she could get out. 'See you on Saturday.'

She smiled. 'See you on Saturday.'

Jess walked to her car. She wasn't even sure if she liked

Jonathan in that way yet, but she was proud of herself for having agreed to the date. She couldn't wait to tell Kate. But first, maybe she would call her mother just to let her know everything was okay.

Chapter Thirteen

Abdul

ABDUL WAS WAITING DOWNSTAIRS for his wife. After being insistent he be ready on time, she was late. Typical. He would, of course, not say a word about it. He knew better than that.

'No shalwar kameez today,' she had said, whilst they were getting ready. 'We want to give the impression that we are modern parents.' He knew by 'modern' she meant Western. Feroza had gone to great lengths to secure a meeting with a local matchmaker. She kept telling him this woman was very sought after and only took on the very best Pakistani families, hence why he had to wear a shirt.

Abdul was not entirely convinced enlisting the help of a matchmaker was such a good idea. In Pakistan they would simply send word of any son or daughter who had come of age to family friends and wait until someone contacted them with a suitable rishta. He had hoped the process would be the same here in the UK, but this had not been the case. When they had put word out in the community, the replies were slow. Most of the families gave them the details of suitors their own children had rejected.

'My children won't be having anyone's cast-offs!' Feroza had exclaimed after Musarat had given her the numbers of three boys her own daughter had turned down. Abdul had suggested they at least meet the families, but Feroza was having none of it. 'Can you imagine Musarat's face if Rehana ends up marrying one of the boys Zara rejected? I wouldn't hear the end of it.' Things were much easier in Pakistan. There was a bigger pool of people to choose from and getting children married was everyone's business, not just that of an isolated matchmaker.

Abdul had been on the website belonging to the lady they were going to see. Much of the site was 'under construction' but the home page still worked. There was a stock picture of a happy-looking Muslim couple with the caption 'where your family's halal dreams come true'. The lack of community involvement worried Abdul. When a suitor came recommended from a trusted source, it was usually a safe bet. But Abdul recognized his world was changing, and whether he liked it or not, he had to move with the times. Feroza would not entertain the idea of considering anyone for either of their children who did not have a degree. She was also quite keen on the idea of Yousef marrying another doctor.

'We need someone on the same intellectual level as him,' she had said. 'And someone who understands how demanding the life of a heart surgeon is.'

'Yes, but won't that mean two people with very busy jobs? How will they find time to spend together?'

'We will see if there are any GPs available, they usually have lots of spare time,' she had replied.

Feroza appeared in the doorway. She was wearing a plain blue kurta and white pyjamas. It was as close to a western outfit as he had seen her wear; there was not an embroidered hem or decorative jewel in sight.

'Are you ready?' she asked. He nodded.

Rehana appeared behind her mother. 'So, you two are off to meet the professional busybody, are you?' she said, pushing past her mum into the kitchen. 'Doesn't Pakistan have its own

version of *Love Island* I can just go on? It'll save you the
trouble. Obviously, the rules would have to be changed. I'm
thinking no touching, no bikinis and definitely no hideaway.
Plus, there will have to be parents around to keep an eye on
things.'

'Rehana, what nonsense are you spouting now?' her mum
quizzed. 'Where is this island you are talking about?'

'No, Rehana, we are not going to meet a professional busybody, we are going to meet with a professional matchmaker,'
Abdul interjected. 'And you need to start taking this more
seriously. This person may be responsible for finding you a
husband.'

'I am taking it seriously, Dad, but you're making it sound
like a business deal. Are things really that desperate we need
to pay someone to find me a husband?' She put a slice of bread
in the toaster.

'We are not paying them to find you a husband. We make
a token payment in good faith,' Feroza said. 'It is like a charity,
a donation to say thank you.'

Rehana laughed. 'I bet the bigger the thank you, the more
chance you have of getting a match.'

'Rehana, these things are in the hands of God, you shouldn't
make jokes. It would do you good to pray every now and again,
it might improve your chances of finding a husband.' Feroza
turned to Abdul. 'Let's go, we don't want to be late.'

'Yoohoo, Feroza!' a voice called out from across the road as
they made their way to the car. It was Angie. 'Where are you
two off to?'

'Nowhere,' Abdul said quickly.

'It's not nowhere,' Feroza replied. 'We are going to see
someone about getting our children married.'

Angie looked interested. She hurried across the road to where
they stood. 'What do you mean, like a priest? I didn't know
your Rehana or Yousef were engaged.'

'No, not a priest. A matchmaker,' Feroza explained.

'Feroza, we should get going, we don't want to be late,' Abdul cut in.

'Just one minute,' his wife replied. She turned back to Angie. 'She has a catalogue of eligible single people and she is going to match our Rehana and Yousef up with the best ones.'

'I see, like a blind date, only you're getting married.' Angie nodded. 'Shouldn't Rehana and Yousef be going with you to help choose?'

'Of course not,' Feroza squawked. 'We elders decide who the most appropriate matches are, then they can choose to agree.'

'Right, well, good luck!' Angie said. 'And if there is anyone in that catalogue for me, let me know. I could do with an upgrade!'

Angie laughed, but Feroza only frowned. 'This is serious business, Angie, no laughing matter.'

Angie looked serious. 'Of course it is. Let me know how you get on.'

Feroza did a quick inspection of the car, making sure it was clean enough to go to a complete stranger's home. Once she was satisfied, she got in.

'We need to make sure this matchmaker understands how special our children are,' Feroza said. 'Any parent would be lucky to welcome them into their families.'

'We just want good, respectable families who will keep them both happy,' Abdul replied.

'Yes, of course, but remember Yousef is a doctor and Rehana can make full Pakistani dinner, so I won't be settling for any scraps left behind by other families.'

The house was quite ordinary. Abdul wasn't sure what he was expecting, possibly something a bit grander than a two up, two down. Perhaps the matchmaking business didn't pay as well as he had thought.

They were greeted at the door by a young girl who led them

to a living room and then quickly disappeared. Abdul had thought they would be discussing such serious matters in a more formal setting, some sort of office perhaps. There was an old television set in the corner and the sofa suite had been wrapped in plastic film to keep it from getting dirty.

'See, I told you we should have put plastic on our sofas,' Feroza said. 'Look how clean these are. Ours are covered in tea stains because of that clumsy Rehana.' Feroza shifted in her seat. The plastic squeaked.

The young girl came back in. 'Would you like some tea?' she asked quietly. 'My mum will be down soon.'

'Tea would be lovely,' Feroza said. 'Thank you.'

'Just water for me,' Abdul said. The girl nodded and disappeared again.

'Such a nice polite girl. And so slim,' Feroza said. 'I bet she will have no problem finding a husband.'

They sat in silence for a few minutes. Abdul was quite comfortable with silence. He knew his wife, however, was not. She sighed loudly. He ignored her. She sighed again.

'What is it, Feroza?' he asked.

'I am just worried about Rehana. What if even a matchmaker can't find her a husband?' She shifted on the sofa, making it squeak again. 'She can be . . . difficult.'

'Feroza, why do you keep putting her down? No wonder she has no confidence,' Abdul said. 'Have faith.'

'I'm not putting her down, I worry about her. You treat her like a baby.'

'Perhaps we should have brought Yousef and Rehana with us today. They could have told this matchmaker what kind of partners they are looking for themselves,' Abdul said.

'Don't be ridiculous,' Feroza said sharply. 'These are matters for adults. We start it off, and the children have their say later on.'

Before Abdul could answer, the young girl came back in.

Abdul had expected her to be carrying a tray of tea, but she came empty-handed.

'My mum is asking for the cash donation before she comes in,' the girl said, much more confident now.

'What, now, before we have even spoken to her?' Abdul said, surprised. 'What if she isn't able to help us?'

'We have had many people not pay in the past, so we now ask for full payment upfront,' the girl replied. 'No exceptions.'

'Before the tea even?' Feroza was shocked.

'Yes, before the tea and before any conversations take place.' The young girl had gone from being a timid young thing to a business tycoon.

'Abdul, pay her,' Feroza hissed, gesturing at her husband. Abdul got out his wallet and took out one hundred pounds in twenty-pound notes before handing them to the girl. The girl counted them carefully.

'You are here for two of your children, no?' she asked. Abdul nodded. 'It's one hundred pounds each.'

'Each?' Feroza exclaimed. 'But my son is a doctor – surely we should get a discount on him as he will be easier to marry? My daughter I understand.'

'Sorry,' the girl said, not sounding sorry at all. 'It is the same fee per person, regardless of their occupation.'

Abdul could see that putting Yousef in the same boat as everyone else would be a step too far for his wife, so he quickly interjected. 'It's okay, Feroza. I have the cash.' Abdul handed over another hundred pounds to the girl. She counted the notes again. Finally satisfied, she left.

'What a rude girl! I bet they will struggle to find her a husband.' Feroza scowled. 'And did you see her hair? Doesn't she own a brush?'

'Leave it,' Abdul whispered. 'Someone might hear you.'

'Let them hear me, I don't care.' Feroza sat back in her chair. They sat in silence again; Abdul could hear the rattling of cutlery coming from down the corridor. This might be the most expensive glass of water he had ever had. An older lady entered carrying a folder.

'Assalamualaikum,' she said, looking at them both. 'My name is Henna.'

'Walaikum salam,' Feroza said eagerly. 'Thank you for meeting with us.'

'Sorry to have kept you waiting.' Henna sat down. 'It is wedding season, so many phone calls. I always get invited to the weddings I set up. So very busy.'

'Weddings where you introduced the couples?' Feroza said in awe. Henna nodded smugly. 'Wow, very good.' Feroza looked at Abdul. He was less impressed.

'Where in Pakistan are you from?' Henna said, opening her folder.

'Karachi. Our parents were born in India but moved to Pakistan after partition. Such awful times,' Abdul said gravely. Abdul loved England for what it had given him and his family after they moved here, but he could never forgive this country for tearing apart his home nation and creating political divides that continued to lead to the death of many people. No, those scars ran deep and through many generations.

'Do you speak Urdu or Punjabi?' Henna was asking questions like this was a job interview. Also, where was his water?

'Urdu,' Feroza said. Abdul could detect a hint of pride in her voice. Urdu was considered slightly more upper class than Punjabi.

'So, tell me about your children,' Henna said, sitting back on the sofa. 'One of them is a doctor, no?'

'Yes, our son. Very handsome,' Feroza said. 'And such a good boy. Lives at home with us.'

'Height?' Henna pressed on, looking at Abdul.

'Um, about as tall as me, so six foot,' Abdul replied, unsure.

'He is six foot two inches,' Feroza said, giving Abdul a sharp look.

'That's good, a tall doctor should be fairly straightforward. I already have two or three families I am thinking of for him.' Henna was writing everything down. 'I presume you will want someone in the medical profession?'

'Yes, a GP ideally. Or a dermatologist. Someone with a medical degree who doesn't have to work long hours,' Feroza replied. 'He is going to be a surgeon, so will need someone who can look after him. That's why I think a GP will be perfect.'

Henna made a note on a piece of paper.

'How religious is he?' Henna asked. 'Does he pray regularly?'

Abdul wasn't sure how to answer this one. Yousef wasn't particularly religious at all. The only time he went to the mosque was twice a year on Eid, and only because his mum made him go.

'Oh, he is very good, prays five times,' Feroza said quickly. 'Very spiritual,' she added solemnly. 'He keeps saying he is going to take us all to Hajj, doesn't he, Abdul?' She looked at him. He gave her a confused look.

'And would he want a girl with a hijab or without?' Henna asked as casually as if she was asking about extra toppings on a pizza.

'I think he would prefer one without,' Feroza said, nodding.

Abdul knew his wife wanted a daughter-in-law she could parade around to parties and events, someone the other women would be jealous of. Feroza knew that for Yousef to become a heart surgeon he would have to schmooze at various hospital events and 'fit in' with the team. In her mind, having a wife who wore a hijab might hinder this process. It would be a step too far for some of the older, whiter surgeons.

'Good, well, that is all very straightforward,' Henna said, turning the page in her notebook over. 'Now tell me about your daughter.'

'Rehana is a lovely girl, any boy would be lucky to have her,' Abdul said. He wanted to get in before Feroza started with the negative aspects of their daughter's personality. 'Very family orientated.' Abdul had heard other fathers talk about their daughters, and the term 'family orientated' seemed to come up a lot. He had banked it in his head for use on days like today.

'That's good, and it said she was a teacher on her form?' Henna enquired.

'She has nearly completed her teacher training course,' Abdul said proudly. Nearly finished sounded better than halfway through, he thought.

'How tall is she?' Henna asked.

'Five foot six inches,' Feroza said. 'Perfect height for a girl, don't you agree?'

'It is a good height, mashallah. How would you describe her build?' Henna asked, not taking her eyes off her notebook.

'Build?' Abdul said, confused.

'Yes. Is she heavy set, medium or slim?' Henna looked at him. 'Perhaps your wife is better placed to answer this question.'

Feroza looked lost for words.

Henna sighed. 'Boys need to know these things,' she said. 'Don't worry, it's all very standard.'

'But you didn't ask the same of my son,' Abdul said.

'It is different for girls. Extremely competitive,' Henna said, unperturbed. 'I know some of these questions are difficult but believe me, they are important to avoid any disappointment. Please don't be offended.'

'She is slim,' Feroza said quickly, then thought about it. 'Well, maybe average build. Yes, average.'

Henna spoke with the authority of someone who had had many similar conversations in the past. 'I will put slim to average. Does she pray?'

'Yes, she is very good. Prays all the time.' Feroza gave a nervous laugh. 'Sometimes we have to say, Rehana put down the Qur'an, for goodness' sake, and come down for your dinner.'

She looked again at Abdul for confirmation. He stayed silent. 'Always praying, our Rehana.'

'What is her complexion like?' Henna asked, ignoring Feroza's anecdote.

'Complexion?' Abdul said. 'She has very clear skin.'

'No, I mean, does she have light skin or dark skin, or perhaps she is somewhere in the middle?' Henna looked at him. 'We call that wheatish.'

Abdul would like to think he was offended, but truth be told, he was well versed in the Pakistani mentality of beauty. Girls with fairer skin were deemed more beautiful; if they had lighter-coloured eyes and hair then they were often doted upon by the community. Abdul was embarrassed. One of the things that had attracted him to Feroza was her fair skin, but sadly their daughter had inherited his darker complexion.

It had always amused him when he was doing the late shift on the buses, how young white girls would apply tanning cream to make themselves look darker in order to be considered prettier. What a strange world we live in, he had thought. He felt sad for his daughter. She had to deal not only with the very real challenges of everyday racism in this country, but also the equally and often more overt challenge of colourism from her own community. What chance did she have?

'She is in the middle,' his wife finally said. 'I would describe her complexion as wheatish, as you say.'

'That's good, we can work with that,' Henna said. 'Now, would she be willing to give up work for her husband if necessary?'

'What? No!' Abdul said. He looked at his wife. She knew not to challenge him when he spoke like this.

The young girl appeared with their drinks. She looked around the room, sensing the tension. 'Sugar?' she asked Feroza, putting the tray on the coffee table.

'Three, please,' Feroza said. Abdul looked at the tray – no

biscuits. He thought for two hundred pounds they could have at least offered them a biscuit.

'Haleema, type up these notes, please,' Henna said to the girl. Haleema gave Abdul his water and took the folder from her mother.

'What happens next?' Feroza asked, slurping her tea.

'Well, we need the complete biodata for both of your children with up-to-date photographs. Profiles with photos are much more likely to get a match. Include as much detail as you can; the obvious things like exact height, build and skin tone are essential. Try to capture their personalities too,' Henna said. 'But remember, marriages are between families, not individuals, so include information on yourselves too: what kind of in-laws you will be, where in Pakistan you are from, what language you speak, your caste.'

'Caste?' Abdul enquired. 'Do people still care about that sort of thing?'

'Not everyone, but you never know,' Henna replied. 'I will get Haleema to email you a template to fill out, nothing too difficult. And then we can get started.' Henna stood up, signalling the meeting was over. Abdul had not had any of his water.

'How soon are we likely to find a potential match for our children?' Abdul said.

'The sooner I get the completed biodata profiles on your children, the sooner I can start making enquiries. It usually takes one to two weeks.'

'And you think you can find someone for them both?' Feroza asked.

'Look, I will find them several matches. What happens after that is up to you and, of course, God.'

'Yes, it is all in God's hands,' Feroza said, as if repeating a mantra.

'Well, I don't see God taking cash payments,' Abdul muttered under his breath. They were led to the front door.

'Can I give you some advice?' Henna said as they stood in the hallway. 'Try not to be too fussy. I see so many children decline matches based on petty things and before they know it, they are too old to get married.'

'How old is too old?' Feroza sounded worried.

'Above twenty-five it becomes much more difficult. Especially for girls. Boys, maybe thirty. Your job as parents is to guide your children and ensure they make the right decision.' She paused. 'And quickly.'

Feroza nodded obediently. 'Thank you, Henna baaji,' she said. 'We will make sure you have the biodata this week.'

Abdul had a feeling this entire process wasn't going to be as straightforward as he had hoped.

Chapter Fourteen

Yousef

'YOUSEF, REHANA, GET DOWN here NOW!' His mum summoned them down in a high-pitched voice she only reserved for emergencies. 'Here, we need to fill these out.' She thrust an application form at each of them. Their father made a quick exit, saying something about having to meet his friend, Naresh. Their mum ignored him, her attention fully focused on her children.

'Yousef, go get the photo albums from upstairs. Rehana, fetch two pens,' his mother continued. 'We have no time to waste.' She told them the matchmaker she had been to see the previous week had two potential suitors for both of them but needed their biodata forms completed along with photographs. She had printed them out and had them ready. Yousef had hoped Rehana would put up a fight, but to his surprise she seemed nonchalant about the situation.

'Why are you so chilled about this?' he whispered to her as they filled out their forms.

'Unless you haven't noticed, Yous, my love life is pretty non-existent. I am willing to give anything a go,' she hissed back at him. 'And who knows? I might find my Prince Charming.'

'Since when did you want a Prince Charming?' He sniggered.

'I thought you were part of some kind of independent sisterhood thing.'

'Independent girls don't have to be spinsters. They can be married as well, you know, even have kids,' she whispered back.

Yousef felt as if he was applying for a job. He had no idea what caste he was, or which part of Pakistan his grandparents originated from.

'Mum, what caste are we?' he asked, looking at the form. 'Do we even have castes any more?'

'Leave those parts blank, I will fill them in later,' his mother said, peering over his shoulder. 'Also, leave the mother's age segment blank too.'

The next section was about interests and hobbies. Since he had moved home, his life consisted of going to the hospital, coming home to relay the day's occurrences to his mother and finally resisting all urges to phone Jess. He simply wasn't interested in anything else. Every day he pretended, for the sake of his family, to engage in conversations and laugh along with their jokes. He had always been good at avoiding his feelings, but the truth was, he resented his mum and dad. There were days when he would watch his parents at breakfast time, filled with a dark rage. He still blamed them for making him break up with Jessica. Some days he hated his entire culture. If he wasn't brown, he would be free to make choices other people took for granted, like who they were allowed to love. But most of the time, he hated himself for being such a wet lettuce. And now he had to fill out a form to apply for an arranged marriage to some girl he had never even met. He wasn't interested.

'I don't have any hobbies, aside from work,' he said miserably.

'Sure you do,' Rehana said. 'Being a full-time mummy's boy. I'm sure every girl would find that really attractive.'

'Jealousy isn't a good look, Rehana,' Yousef countered. 'Just because you're nobody's favourite.'

'And what's wrong with being a mummy's boy, huh?' their mother cut in. 'Yousef is a good mummy's boy, like all sons should be.'

'You're right, that doesn't sound weird at all,' Rehana muttered.

'I'm being serious, I have no hobbies,' Yousef moaned.

'Just make some up,' Rehana said. 'Look, I've put down travelling, cinema and long walks in the countryside.' She showed Yousef her form. 'The truth is, I have only ever travelled to Pakistan to see Naana and Naani, I can't remember the last time I went to the cinema, and I couldn't give a toss about the countryside.'

'So basically, you're lying?' he said. 'What a great start to a marriage.'

'Everyone lies on application forms. It's standard. And besides, they're white lies. I would be happy to travel the world, go to the cinema and even go to the bloody boring countryside with the right man,' Rehana said triumphantly.

'Good girl, Rehana,' their mother said, inspecting her form. 'Yousef, just put something down, okay? Rehana is not lying, she is trying to entice a husband. Very normal.' It was one of the rare occasions when his mother sided with his sister. Yousef hated it. Surely after everything he had given up, the least his mother could do was always take his side. 'It doesn't matter, you are a doctor, we will find you a nice girl, no problem. Rehana, make sure you write you like spending time with your family. Every man wants a wife who is family orientated.'

'You mean, every man wants a wife who will get on with his mother?' Rehana said, adding 'family orientated' to her list.

His mother ignored her. 'And don't forget to add you can make full Pakistani dinner.'

Once they had filled out their application forms, they turned their attention to finding the perfect photograph.

'Can't I just use my graduation photo?' Yousef said, pointing to the one his mum had framed above the fireplace.

'No, you have a hat on, and I want everyone to see your thick hair,' his mum said. 'Here, look through this.' She thrust an album at him. 'There are some photos in there from Romana and Tariq's wedding, where you wore your blue suit.

'Oh, you look so handsome in this photo,' she added. 'But look at this one, and this one. You are so photogenic, so many to choose from. Any girl will be lucky to marry my little sultan.' She smiled at him. It only served to make Yousef resent her more. Rehana made a fake vomiting sound.

'Great, am I done then?' he said, getting up. The more time he spent with his mother, the more time he would sit in his room raging about all the things he wished he could say to her.

'No, we need to find a nice picture of your sister,' his mum said. 'Nobody is leaving this room until both application forms are complete. I want to get them back to Aunty Henna tomorrow so she can send me your matches.'

Yousuf sat back down, thoroughly pissed off.

'Mum, I've narrowed it down to these five. What do you think?' Rehana handed them over to their mum. Yousef looked at the photos, mildly interested now the attention had moved on from him.

His mother inspected the first one. 'Not this one, you look too dark. Henna said men like girls with fair skin.' She looked up. Both Rehana and Yousef looked horrified. 'What can I do?' their mother said, discarding the photo. 'Don't look at me like that, I told you to apply Fair and Lovely cream to your skin, but you didn't listen.'

'That's because I didn't want to end up looking like Michael bloody Jackson,' Rehana protested.

Feroza ignored her and moved on to the next photo. 'Rehana, you can't use this one, you are standing next to Tanveer. She is so pretty. Everybody will be looking at her, not you.' She tossed the photo onto the table.

'We can crop her out,' Rehana said. 'I like the peach kameez I'm wearing in that one.'

'People will think we are hiding something if we crop photos,' Feroza replied.

'We are hiding something,' Yousef said. 'Tanveer!'

'Piss off, Yousef,' Rehana said, throwing a cushion at him.

'Rehana, leave your brother alone. You should be taking this more seriously.'

Rehana rolled her eyes.

'Not this one either. Who taught you how to apply foundation, huh?' Feroza said angrily. 'Look at your face and your neck – two different colours.'

Yousef was about to laugh, but then caught his sister's eye. That one had hurt. He had often wondered if Rehana was really bad at putting on make-up, or whether she put it on in a bid to make herself look lighter skinned like him and their mother.

'And in this one, it looks like you have put some weight on. It must have been after your first year at university when you ate too much.' She discarded the photos and looked at Rehana's final offering. 'Didn't you wash your hair on this day? It looks so greasy.' She placed the photo on top of the other ones she had turned down.

Yousef suddenly realized why his father had made a quick getaway. When stressed, his mother turned nasty and, more often than not, she took it out on his sister. Except this time, even he knew she had gone too far.

'It's not my fault that I am so dark, greasy and fat!' Rehana yelled, getting up and storming out the door. His mum looked at him, bewildered.

'What did I say?' she said, genuinely puzzled.

'Sometimes, Mum, try to remember she's your daughter and an actual human being.' He left his mother and went to check on Rehana. Rehana was sitting in bed crying. He hadn't seen his sister cry in years.

'What do you want?' she said, quickly wiping away her tears.

'Just coming to see how you are,' he said, standing in the doorway.

'How do you think I am? Even my own mother thinks I'm a fat, ugly bitch, so what hope do I have of finding a husband?' She let out a sob.

'Mum doesn't think those things, she just wants the best photo possible of you so you can find the best possible husband,' Yousef said. He came in and sat on the end of the bed.

'Well, she could have been nicer about it.'

'Agreed.'

'What about you?' Rehana said, looking at him.

'What about me?'

'Come on, Yous, you forget that I actually met Jessica when I came down to visit you. Are you sure you want to go ahead with all of this?' She sat up in bed. 'I mean, that relationship was pretty serious.'

'We broke up last year, Rehana. She's probably moved on and I need to as well,' he said quietly.

'Isn't it going to be weird, seeing her again next week?' Rehana said, pulling at a loose thread on her pillow. Although they were brother and sister, it was unusual for them to talk about such private things. She avoided eye contact. 'I mean, you won't be able to avoid each other working at the same hospital.'

Yousef didn't say anything. He had tried not to think about his next rotation. The thought of bumping into Jessica again filled him with dread. He wondered if she was still angry with him. He wouldn't blame her if she was.

There was a knock on the door. It was their mum.

'Rehana, I just spoke with your Aunt Angie – her daughter Lottie knows someone who works at the make-up counter in John Lewis,' she said, looking sheepish. 'He will come over tomorrow and do your make-up nicely and we can take a photo of you in the garden wearing your gold lengha afterwards.'

Rehana looked at her mother, not saying anything.

'And I will curl your hair for you. You look nice with curly hair.' She left without waiting for a reply.

'I think that's her way of apologizing,' Yousef said.

'Worst apology in the history of apologies,' Rehana said. They both laughed. 'But I'm shit at putting make-up on, so she's doing me a favour really.'

'You believe this whole arranged marriage thing is going to work?' Yousef asked.

'I don't know. But it's been around for a really long time and that's got to count for something. Plus, all of these interfering aunties and uncles have been together for a really long time and they all had arranged marriages,' Rehana said, pondering the question.

'Yeah, I guess that's true.'

'And besides, have you tried dating these days? There's just a bunch of sex pests and weirdos out there.' They both laughed again.

'Speak for yourself, sis. I've been inundated with offers from the ladies at the hospital,' Yousef said. It was true. A couple of the female doctors had made their interest in him very clear.

'Gross,' Rehana replied.

'You're lucky, you know, Rehana.'

'Oh yeah, and how did you figure that? Is it my dazzling good looks?' she asked, snorting.

'Because when you get married, you get to move out of this shitty house and live your life. When I get married, I'm expected to stay here and look after Mum and Dad like all good sons do.'

'Yeah, that sucks. But think about your poor wife having to live with Mum,' Rehana said. 'And you never know, I might get stuck with some shitty in-laws too.'

'True,' Yousef said, getting up.

'And I was serious before, you know.'

'About what?'

'You and Jessica. Aside from anything else, it's a pretty shady thing to marry someone whilst you're still in love with someone else.' Rehana gave him a pointed look. 'Imagine if someone did that to me.'

'I am not still in love with Jess,' Yousef said. 'And besides, what choice do I have?' He left.

Yousef felt trapped, like he was on one of those moving walkways at an airport unable to get off, resigned to ending up in whatever destination his parents had decided on.

Chapter Fifteen

Rehana

To everyone's surprise, Aunty Henna had come through with the matches they had been promised.

The make-up session, on the other hand had been hellish, with Rehana's mum arguing with the make-up artist over which base foundation Rehana should wear.

'I like that one,' her mum had said, pointing to one that was clearly designed for someone with porcelain skin and red hair. 'Make her that colour.'

'I think this one is more appropriate,' Lottie's friend said, pulling one out of his bag that even Rehana thought was too dark. His name was Sean, and his own make-up was flawless. Rehana was mesmerized by his contouring and perfectly lined lips. How did he do it? Her mother, who would normally take issue with a man in make-up, had done a quick assessment of his smoky eyes and concluded that he was Rehana's best bet at getting a half-decent photo for her application form. And besides, they were on a tight schedule and there was no time to waste arguing.

Sean moonlighted as a drag artist and much to Rehana's dismay, mistook getting make-up done for an arranged wedding application form for getting ready for one of his performances.

'You are going to make the most gorgeous bride, isn't she,

Aunty?' he said to her mother. Clearly he had done make-up for other Pakistani women and knew the etiquette.

'We need to find her a husband first, then she can become a bride,' her mother said, now in cahoots with Sean. 'Do you think you can make her eyes look like yours?'

'I can do anything,' Sean said, looking at himself in the mirror. 'I subscribe to Asian Bride magazine – you've got to in this job. Anyway, I'll make her look like a cover girl.' He turned to Rehana. 'If we highlight her eyes like this and contour that kink out of her nose, we'll have no trouble finding her a hunky man!' Sean grabbed her mother's arm and they both giggled. Whose side was he on? 'There, that should do it.' He stepped aside so she could inspect herself in the mirror. She looked like a drag queen.

'Don't you think it's a bit too much?' she asked, inspecting the silvery blue eye shadow. 'I mean, it's just a photograph.'

'Darling, it's never too much. Think of it as stage make-up,' Sean exclaimed. 'Besides, you said yourself you never really wear make-up, so anything will feel like a lot to you.'

'I agree with Sean,' her mother beamed. 'You look beautiful. Sometimes it's nice to go a bit over the top.'

'I look like I'm going to my own wedding.' Rehana remained uncertain. 'Either that or I'm going to be a contestant on *RuPaul's Drag Race*.'

'Who is Paul, huh?' her mother said. 'I hope you are not talking to boys.'

'It's a beauty pageant show on the telly,' Sean cut in. 'Rehana could win it looking like that.' He admired his work.

'I don't want to win it,' Rehana muttered.

'You're giving the men a taste of what they can expect on the big day. You know what they say: dress for the job you want, not for the one you have,' Sean said, sounding slightly offended that Rehana wasn't loving his work.

'What a clever saying,' her mum replied. 'Sean, did you just come up with that?'

'I was hoping for something a little more subtle,' Rehana said, still staring at herself in the mirror.

'I mean, if you want to go back to being a plain Jane . . .'

'No, no, Sean, puthar. She just needs to get used to it,' her mother said. 'Now we can take a nice picture and get her a good husband.'

'Good luck!' Sean called as he left. 'I expect an invite to the wedding!'

When they got home, her mum curled her hair and took out her gold *lengha* for her. Her dad cleared up the back garden, shoving all the rubbish into one corner and moving the wheelie bins out of view so they could take a nice picture. After several attempts, her mum was finally happy. Rehana inspected the photograph. Not exactly Deepika Padukone, but it would have to do. It wasn't going to get any better. After her mother approved the completed application forms, her dad personally drove them over to Aunty Henna's house. A week later she phoned with a potential match for Rehana.

'Let me see the picture,' Rehana said excitedly, trying to grab her mother's phone. The best thing about this process was that the girl got to approve the bloke before he was even allowed to see a picture of her. In fact, it was highly unlikely that this boy had any idea that Rehana and her family were critiquing his profile right now. So Rehana had the power to say no to any matches Aunty Henna sent over and the bloke would be none the wiser. Only if she said yes to a meeting would her profile and picture get sent to his family. At that point, he had the opportunity to decline a meeting, but Rehana was hoping with Sean's magic make-up and her mum's nifty skills with a curling iron, no boy would be able to resist.

'Forget the picture, looks are not important,' her mother said, moving her phone out of reach. 'Let me read his profile. What job does he do?'

Poor Mum, Rehana thought. Looks were important, she wouldn't get married to anyone who she didn't fancy. She wasn't that desperate – yet.

'It says he works in recruitment,' her mother said, sounding confused. 'What does that mean? He finds other people jobs. Does that pay well?'

Rehana snatched the phone away from her mother, scrolling down until she saw his picture. He had a full head of hair, that was a start, and a nice smile. She scrolled up to check his height – five foot six inches. That was the same height as her. If they got married, she could never wear heels. That was a big commitment.

'He's a bit short,' Rehana said, deflated.

'You girls today, always worrying about looks. Do you think I would have married your father if it was just about looks alone?' her mother said.

'What?' Her father looked up from his paper.

'Never mind,' her mother said quickly. 'As long as he is a nice boy, from a nice family with a good job, you should meet him.' Rehana rolled her eyes. Her mother simply did not get it. 'And look,' Feroza continued, 'they are from the same part of Pakistan as we are!' She sounded delighted.

Rehana couldn't give a hoot about which part of Pakistan this boy was from, but she agreed to a meeting. Her mother rang Aunty Henna that night, who liaised with the family. After a tense forty-eight hours where Rehana did not know whether her profile had been rejected by his family, his mother rang and confirmed they too were interested in a meeting. Without any input from either Rehana or the as yet unnamed boy, it was agreed he and his family would come to see Rehana at home this Saturday.

★

They weren't arriving until the evening, but the preparations began straight after breakfast. Their mother summoned the entire family to the kitchen.

'Abdul, I need you to go and get the keema for the samosas. I have written a full list of what I need here,' her mum said, handing him a piece of paper. 'Yousef, make sure you look smart tonight, no jeans. And Rehana, you can help me in the kitchen.'

'Why can't Yousef help in the kitchen?' Rehana said. 'Why is his only job "no jeans"? That's hardly fair.'

'Leave him alone, he has been working hard all week. He needs a rest,' her mother scolded. Yousef made a face at her and then a quick exit. As usual, her dad did what he was told. He knew better than to argue with his wife on such an important occasion. 'I don't know how many people are coming, but we need to make enough samosas and seekh kebabs so that everybody has plenty.' Her mother was already donning her apron and tying the strings behind her back.

'What if they are vegetarian?' Rehana said. 'Shouldn't we have a vegetarian option?'

'You bloody modern kids, all turning vegetarian these days,' her mum said, annoyed. 'Making it so hard. Fine, we will make pakoras as well, in case somebody is "vegetarian".' She used air quotes for the word vegetarian, making Rehana laugh.

'Right, what should I do?' she asked, looking around.

'Chop the onions, roll the pastry for the samosas. Why do I have to tell you everything?'

Despite her tutorial with Sean, Rehana was still hopeless with putting on make-up so she had called Emma to help. Emma had been only too pleased to come over, claiming she was at a bit of a loose end herself.

'Wow, it smells delicious in here,' Emma said, when Rehana opened the door. 'Your visitors are really in for a treat.' Rehana hurried her upstairs before her mother saw her and asked her a million questions.

'I just want something simple,' Rehana said, laying out the make-up her mum had forced her to buy during their visit to John Lewis. 'Nothing too over the top.'

'Simple. Got it, babes.' They both sat at the end of the bed whilst Emma did her face. 'So, you don't even know this guy's name?' she asked.

'I know it sounds weird, but his name is the least important thing about him,' Rehana said, eyes closed as Emma applied eyeliner. 'Mum's more interested in his earning potential, but I'm a bit worried he's too short.'

'Rehana, take it from someone who has dated a lot of guys, don't focus on things like height,' Emma said. 'Tall, pretty boys always turn out to be knobheads, in my experience.' She put down the eyeliner and began work on Rehana's lips. 'You are better off finding yourself a nice guy who makes you laugh.'

'See, that's the problem with this whole arranged marriage thing. You have the luxury of getting the sexy knobheads out of your system.' Rehana opened her eyes. 'Us lot have to bypass that whole phase and go straight for the funny nice guys. It's not fair. I wouldn't mind a short stint with a handsome bastard.'

'Trust me, you're saving yourself a lot of trouble and trips down to the sexual health clinic,' Emma said. 'So, if your Aunty Henna has any boys going spare, send them my way.'

'It'll cost you,' Rehana said. 'Aunty Henna doesn't come cheap.'

'Probably less than what I'm paying for all my dating apps,' Emma said. 'Anyway, what happens at this meeting? Do you have to decide whether you have to marry the lad today?'

'God, no!' Rehana said quickly. 'If we both like each other, then I guess our parents arrange more meetings.'

'Your parents?' Emma put down the lip liner. 'Don't you get to see each other without your parents being present?'

'Well, of course, we'll have a few dates alone, but we keep all of that on the down-low. I can't very well have all the aunties thinking I'm a floozy now, can I?'

'Jesus, I'd tell the aunties to do one. I need to try before I buy!' Emma laughed.

'It's different for us, we have three or four dates max and then we need to make a decision.'

'After three dates, bloody hell.'

'Yep, any more then I'm a slag.' Rehana laughed.

'I hope you're good at making decisions.' She inspected Rehana. 'There, I think you're done.'

Rehana looked at herself in the mirror. She looked pretty. 'Thanks, Em. You should really get a job as a beautician.'

'Yeah, I'm wasted in teaching. Want me to curl your hair?'

After Emma left, Rehana put on the clothes her mother had put out for her. She had been instructed to stay upstairs when they arrived. Then, once a suitable amount of time had elapsed, she could come down and make an entrance. Her mother had tried to get her to come in with a tray of tea and biscuits to start the evening off, but Rehana had put her foot down.

'I'm hoping he's looking for a wife and not a maid,' Rehana had said. 'I don't want to give them the impression that I'll be waiting on them hand and foot after marriage.'

'Is it too much to ask to make your guests a cup of tea, Rehana?' her mother had countered. 'I make cups of tea for you and your brother, am I your maid?'

'Mum, that's different!' Rehana said. 'Anyway, don't stress me out before they come.'

'Fine, I will call you when it is time to come down,' she said before leaving.

Rehana was scrolling through Instagram when the doorbell went. She rushed to the window, being careful to hide behind the curtain so she wouldn't be seen. She counted four people waiting outside her house. She could only see the tops of their heads but was relieved to see the boy did, in fact, have a full head of hair. He was holding a bunch of flowers. *Good start*, she thought. Her dad opened the door, and they disappeared inside.

She carefully opened her bedroom door and made her way onto the landing. Everybody was saying salaam to each other and Yousef offered to take their coats – all very polite. She was feeling nervous, but more than that, she was excited. She could potentially meet her future husband today; he could be in her home right now. She looked at her feet. Shit, she hadn't had a pedicure in ages. Ugly feet were such a turn-off. Did she have time to do a quick one now? Probably not a full one. Should she wear socks? No that wouldn't work with her outfit. She decided she would give her toenails a quick once-over with some red nail varnish, which wouldn't take long.

She was almost finished when her mother came into the room without knocking. 'What are you doing?' she said, looking at Rehana trying to paint her toenails. 'It's time to come down.'

'I'm almost done,' Rehana said, quickly doing her last two toes. She gave them a quick blow. 'Ready.'

She followed her mum downstairs and into the living room. 'This is my daughter, Rehana.' All eyes turned to look at her. She felt like a specimen in a museum.

'Mashallah,' the older lady said. She must have been the boy's mum. She wore a headscarf, and looked strict.

'Assalamualaikum, Aunty,' Rehana said. There was an awkward moment when Rehana didn't know whether she should hug this lady or not. How familiar was she expected to be? In the end she did some sort of weird curtsey. She turned to look at the dad and greeted him. He smiled at her.

'Salaam, I'm Maryam,' the girl who looked about the same age as Rehana said. 'And this my brother, Asif.'

'I'm Rehana. Nice to meet you,' she said to Maryam. She turned to look at Asif and then realized she had no idea what to say. Future brides were supposed to be demure and ever so slightly shy; she didn't know whether she should be the first to say salaam or not. Would she be considered too forward if she said the first hello? She didn't want to be seen as some sort of Jezebel.

Thankfully, Asif interjected. 'Hi, I'm Asif.' His voice was gloriously deep. Rehana felt a pang of excitement in her tummy.

'Hi,' she said, her throat dry.

'Rehana, sit down,' her mum said. Rehana suddenly realized she was gormlessly standing in the middle of the room.

'Come, sit here,' Maryam said, shuffling up so there was space between her and the Aunty. Rehana didn't want to sit there, it was the farthest seat away from Asif, but she had no choice. Maryam patted the very slim space on the sofa. *Oh God*, Rehana thought as she tried to squeeze herself in between the two women. She could see her mother giving her a disapproving look and Yousef smirking. The aunty shuffled along to the very edge of the sofa so she was wedged between Rehana and the armrest.

'So, your mum tells us you are training to become a teacher?' Maryam asked. 'Are you enjoying it?'

'You know, I didn't think I would, but it's actually really good fun,' Rehana replied. 'The kids are great, and the other teachers have been so kind.'

'That's good. What subject do you teach?' Maryam asked.

'English. I studied it at university.' Rehana thought it should perhaps be Asif asking the questions rather than his sister.

'Which university did you go to?' the aunty asked, turning as best she could, given the space, to look at her. She looked deeply uncomfortable.

'Leeds.'

'Atcha, so you lived away from home?' the aunty said sharply. 'My two stayed with their parents whilst they studied.'

'Well, I think it's important for young people to get a sense of independence. Living away from home taught me so much,' Rehana replied.

Her mother gave a high-pitched laugh. 'Kids today, too modern for their own good.' She gave Rehana a stern look. 'Rehana has been back at home for a year now and she can cook full Pakistani dinner. Very respectful of our traditions.'

There was an awkward silence.

'So, what is it you do?' Yousef asked Asif.

'I recruit people for jobs in IT,' Asif said. Rehana looked at her brother. Poor Yousef didn't know what to ask next. To be fair, neither did she. Recruiting for IT jobs sounded like the most boring job in history. It didn't matter, though, Asif was fit and he had such a sexy voice.

There was another awkward silence.

'Oh, I think you're bleeding,' Asif said, sounding alarmed.

'Who, me?' Rehana said, confused.

'Yes, your feet, there is blood on them.' He gestured towards her feet. Everyone looked. Somehow her freshly applied red nail varnish had smudged across three of her toes. It must have happened whilst she had manoeuvred herself into the tight sofa space. She was horrified.

'Are you okay?' he asked. 'Isn't your brother a doctor or something?'

'Oh no, no, it's okay. It's just nail varnish,' Rehana said, curling her toes so nobody could see. 'I just put it on. Obviously not very well.' The curling of the toes streaked the nail varnish over the carpet.

'Oh, right,' Asif said, but the hint of horror was still in his voice. To be fair, her toes did look disgusting smeared red.

'Beta, you know you can't pray namaaz whilst wearing nail

polish, don't you?' the aunty said. 'You should think about taking it off.'

Bloody hell, Rehana thought. This was not going well.

'Don't worry, she always takes it off before praying namaaz,' her mother cut in. 'Rehana prays five times a day. Don't you, beta?' Rehana decided it was best not to say anything.

'Really? It must be such a faff to have to take off your nail polish just a few hours after you put it on,' Maryam said, sounding genuinely concerned. 'Isn't it easier to just not put any on at all?'

'Erm, it's not too bad. I'm better at taking it off than putting it on.' Rehana wanted to die. Why the fuck would they not stop talking about her toes?

'I find it easier not to put any on at all,' Maryam continued. 'An imaam told me you could wear clear nail varnish and still pray namaaz, maybe try that? But to be honest, I wouldn't risk it. Clean feet are the way forward.'

'Thanks,' Rehana mumbled. 'I'll give it a try.' She was horrified that Maryam now thought her feet were dirty.

Before anyone could say anything else, her mother asked her to accompany her to the kitchen to help with the food.

'All my life, I have never seen you wear nail polish on your toes, and you choose today to put it on?' her mother hissed as soon as she closed the kitchen door.

'Mum, why are you telling everybody I pray five times a day?' Rehana hissed back.

'You should pray five times a day, because you need a miracle for this boy to say "yes" now.' Her mother turned her attention to the food she had laid out on the worktop. 'Take this tray in, and when you offer the food, start with the parents.'

Rehana stared at the tray. 'Why do I have to give the food out?' she said. 'I told you, I don't want them to get the wrong impression of me.'

'Rehana, please, for once do as I say.'

She sighed. 'Fine, but you can do the drinks.'

Rehana's hands trembled at the weight of the tray. She should really go to the gym more, she thought. The clinking of plates and cutlery made everyone stare at her. She handed the aunty and the uncle a plate, then asked them what they would like. Now Rehana was confused: should she next offer her parents a plate and food as they were classed as elders, or should she prioritize the guests and offer Maryam and Asif something first?

She grabbed two plates and gave one to Maryam and one to Asif. They were guests, after all. Maryam took a seekh kebab like her mum. She turned to Asif. 'Would you like anything?' He flashed her a smile. Rehana's tummy fluttered.

'I'll try one of the pakoras,' he said. 'Did you make them? They look delicious.'

Is he flirting?

'Yes, she made all the food today,' her mum said from over her shoulder. 'I don't have to do anything around the house any more, Rehana takes care of everything.'

'Mashallah,' the aunty said, sounding impressed. 'How do you manage that with all your work?'

'Oh, I'm very good at time management,' Rehana said, going along with the lie. She wanted to impress Asif. She caught Yousef's eye, who was trying hard to contain himself. She took a kebab for herself; all this drama was making her hungry.

They ate in silence for a while.

'Is there another room you two could go to so you can, I don't know, maybe talk?' Maryam said suddenly. Rehana looked at her mum, who was looking at the aunty. Some invisible communication took place between the two of them and an approval was made.

'Why don't you go into the other room, Rehana?' her mum said.

Asif immediately stood up. Something told Rehana this wasn't his first rodeo. She grabbed her plate – she wasn't going to let her kebab get cold – and gestured for him to follow. 'It's just through here.'

The 'other' room was a snug. They had not been expecting any guests and it was a mess.

'Sorry, guests don't normally see this room,' Rehana said, picking up a pile of Yousef's books so Asif could sit down. 'So, this is awkward,' she said.

'Is it your first time?' Asif replied, smirking.

'Is it that obvious?' She gave a nervous laugh.

'Kind of, it's just that people put on a big spread of food like you guys did when it's their first time. After a while, you get fed up with all the effort and just give out cups of tea.' Asif looked at the picture of Yousef on his graduation day hung on the wall. 'No picture of your graduation?'

'It's in a different room,' Rehana lied. Her mum had decided not to hang up a picture of Rehana on her graduation day, saying there was not enough wall space.

'Cool.' Then silence again.

Even though he wasn't very tall, there was something appealing about Asif. He held himself with confidence and had swagger, and that voice. Rehana had met boys like this before and usually they were twats. She was really hoping Asif wouldn't be like one of them.

'Have you met many girls in this way?' she asked.

'A few. I don't think you can be too choosy when it comes to looking for your life partner. None of them have been right . . . yet.' He gave her one of his smiles again.

Even though Rehana knew he had said something completely twatty, she had already forgiven him the minute he smiled at her.

'What do you do in your spare time?' she asked. *God*, she thought, annoyed with herself, *could you think of a more boring question?*

'I love travelling, like you. I went to Belize last summer. Have you been?'

'Erm, no, not yet. It's on my bucket list, though.' Rehana had never thought about going to Belize. Wasn't it known for being a bit of a drug den?

'You should go. I'm off to Argentina in a few weeks. I just love South America.' He was becoming more animated. 'What's your favourite place to travel to?'

Shit, she wished she hadn't lied on the application form now. She had only been to Pakistan, and that was mainly to buy clothes.

'Oh, you know, Europe,' she said vaguely. She took a bite of her kebab.

'Where in Europe?' Asif enquired.

Why is he being so nosy?

'Anywhere historical,' Rehana replied. She didn't want to name a city in case he asked her more specific questions.

'You like cities then? Which is your favourite?' he asked.

What is this, some sort of interrogation?

'Erm, I kind of like Italian food,' Rehana said, trying to avoid the question.

'Oh, so Italy then? I love Italy. Rome is incredible,' he said, looking at her for confirmation. 'It's like walking through a huge museum. Naples is amazing too.'

'Yes, it is,' she replied. 'Love Rome, love Italy.' She had never even heard of Naples. Desperate, she changed the topic. 'Your sister seems nice.'

'Maryam? She has the perfect life. Two kids, own house, hubby has a great job. She doesn't have to work, just looks after the kids all day,' Asif said.

'Doesn't she want to work?' Rehana asked. 'What did she do?'

'She was a lawyer, but things change when you have kids,' Asif replied.

'Do they?'

'Yeah, women have to prioritize their families.' He gave her another smile. This time her stomach didn't do a backflip.

'Why do the women have to give up their jobs? Why can't both parents share responsibility?'

Asif laughed. 'What, have the men stay at home and look after the kids?'

'Is that such a crazy idea?' Rehana asked.

'Yes, it is,' Asif said.

Asif was becoming less and less attractive. Rehana could forgive these archaic views in the older Asian generation, but she had hoped her generation would have moved on. Asif sensed she was getting pissed off.

'Your pakoras are delicious, you have skills.' He took a bite.

Rehana didn't feel the need to impress him any more.

'Actually, my mum made them. I don't have time with all the homework I have to mark.'

'But didn't your mum say—'

'I helped, but she did the bulk of the work.' Rehana had had enough. 'Actually, shall we go back in the other room?'

She got up and opened the door. Her mum nearly fell on top of her.

'Oh, sorry, I was just checking to see if you wanted any more food?' she said, straightening out her kameez.

'Mum!' Rehana whispered. 'Were you listening?'

'Don't be silly, Rehana,' her mum said, simultaneously smiling at Asif whilst giving her evils.

'No, that's okay, Aunty, we were just coming back to join you guys.'

The three of them went back to the other room.

'All done?' the aunty said. Asif nodded. 'Okay, well, thank you so much for everything. It has been so nice to meet you all.'

'You must come again,' her dad said. *Please don't*, Rehana thought.

After they left, Rehana and her mum cleared up the dishes. She could tell her mum was itching to ask her what she thought of Asif and his family.

'They didn't eat much, did they?' Rehana said as she brought in the plates of food to the kitchen.

'They were all so slim, probably on a diet,' her mum said. 'A bit rude, though. I made all this food, and nobody ate it.'

'I'm sure Yous and Dad will finish it off later,' Rehana said, loading the dishwasher.

'Hmm, that lady was not very nice, too bossy,' her mum said. 'I don't think she will make a nice mother-in-law for you.'

Rehana looked at her mother. Was she being supportive? She thought her mum would be ready to palm her off to the first man who would take her.

'She was a bit bossy, I guess,' Rehana said. 'And too religious. What was all that nail polish nonsense?'

'I lived with your dad's mum before moving to England. It was very hard,' her mum continued. 'It was her house and I had to do things her way.'

'I always thought you got on well with Daadi Maa?' Rehana asked.

'I do now, but not at first. She would tell me what to wear, how to do my hair and even what I should be eating so I could get pregnant quickly.' Her mum laughed. 'I think she wanted me to have seven children, like her.'

Rehana felt a bit awkward. They never spoke about things like pregnancy. It was a topic far too close to sex and that was strictly forbidden.

'And these days houses are so expensive, you will probably have to live with your in-laws until you can afford to move out. Or they die.' Her mum smiled.

'Mum!' Rehana laughed. 'I think you might be right; she was a bit strict for me. And besides, Asif said I should give up my career to have kids. What century is he living in?'

'Maybe you could go part time when you have children?' her mum said, trying to compromise.

'Whatever I do, Mum, it will be my decision, not my husband's.' Rehana put the tablet in the dishwasher and switched it on.

'Well, I will ring Aunty Henna and tell her it is a "no" from us,' her mum said. 'Let's hope her next rishta is better.'

'I bloody hope so,' Rehana replied.

Chapter Sixteen

Rohit

IT WAS HIS THIRD attempt to get his mum's approval. His first two shirts had failed to impress. Rohit was hoping the cream shirt with the brown buttons would do the trick.

'That's much better,' his mum said as he entered the kitchen. 'Come here, let me have a closer look.' She straightened out his collar and fastened his top button. 'There, very smart.'

'Looking the part, bro. Now all you need is to bring the banter.' Amit smirked. 'Let's hope it isn't another "no" this time.'

'Amit, don't tease your brother,' their mum scolded. 'Those girls were silly to say no to my boy.'

Rohit could feel the heat of his embarrassment rise. He and his family had gone to three prospective girls' houses after his mum had put the feelers out in the community. Each meeting was followed by an anxious wait to hear from the girls' families. Eventually his mum had got fed up and rung the parents herself. All had declined. The worst thing was there was no proper feedback, all Rohit got was an awkward conversation with his mother about how the family didn't think he was the right fit for their daughter. Nothing that Rohit could work with to help improve his chances for the next time.

Rohit had initially been pleased when his mum decided it was time for him to think about getting married. He had never

had much success with members of the opposite sex. He had
spent most of his university years pretending he had a girlfriend
back at home so nobody would see him crash and burn with
any of the girls there. Having an arranged marriage seemed like
the ideal solution. His mother would do all the work and he
would get the prize, a beautiful bride. Although he wasn't a
doctor or a dentist, being an accountant still ranked high up
on the eligibility score card, meaning he should be able to get
a bride who was far more attractive than him.

But things hadn't turned out how he had hoped. Even being
an accountant didn't make up for his lack of charm. He felt a
bit cheated. All his life he had been led to believe that an
arranged marriage meant he would simply have his pick of a
harem of girls offered to him. After the third rejection, Amit
had said he needed a different approach.

'I think it's too much pressure, meeting a whole new family,'
he had said. 'I mean, it's not for everyone.'

'Well, three rejections isn't that bad, I only need to find one
girl,' Rohit said.

'Yes, and perhaps we need to widen the net a bit,' Amit
replied, scrolling through his phone.

'What do you mean? Mum's already got every aunty we know
looking for someone.'

'There's this event on tonight, it's for single Hindus.' Amit
showed him the poster on his phone. 'They're opening this
new restaurant in town and have decided to host a speed dating
event to kick it all off.'

'Speed dating?' Rohit said. That sounded like his worst nightmare. 'No thanks.'

'Rohit, be real. It could take ages for you to find the right
girl going from house to house.' Amit came to sit next to him.
'This way we can get through several girls in one night and
have a better chance of finding the one.'

'Look, I'm not like you, Amit, I'm no good at talking to any girls, let alone several in one night.' Rohit could feel his anxiety level rising. Being forced to talk to a room full of people he had never met before was his worst nightmare. Just breathe, he told himself.

'That's the beauty of it – if you mess it up with one girl, you're on to the next before you know it. Easy.'

'That sounds like the death of feminism right there.' Rohit groaned.

'Don't be silly, the girls have the final say on all of these things. If they don't like you, they'll make it very clear,' Amit replied.

'That's what I'm afraid of. Look, it's easy for you to say. Priya said "yes" to you after your first few dates.'

'No, she didn't!' Amit protested. 'She played hard to get. After Aunty Kajol set us up, Priya told me she had other options she was considering. I had to woo her with flowers and fancy restaurants before she agreed to date me, let alone marry me.'

'Really?' Rohit said. He had always thought his brother had the gift of the gab when it came to the ladies.

'Yes, really. Now will you please come to this event?'

'Absolutely not.' Rohit stood up. 'I'm not going.'

But he had agreed and now he was finally wearing a shirt everyone approved of. Amit said he would come with him for moral support. Rohit didn't know if that was a good or a bad thing.

The restaurant was called Garam Masala and the price for a ticket was £40. *The food better be good for that price*, Rohit thought.

The tables had been cleared, so everyone was forced to stand in the hope this might encourage mingling. All it did was ensure the girls stood on one side of the hall and the boys on the other. Rohit was glad that Amit was with him, otherwise he would be standing alone.

'The key is to look interested but not too interested,' Amit said.

'Thanks, that's really helpful.' Rohit sighed. He couldn't even bring himself to look at the gaggle of girls on the far side of the room. Instead, he was assessing the boys for competition. Some of them looked like they shouldn't need any help finding themselves a wife, but others looked more desperate than even him. He felt he had come too smart; most of the other lads were in jeans or chinos with tight T-shirts on, showing off their muscles. Rohit was hoping the shirt he had on was loose enough to hide his gut.

'Catch the eye of one you like, and then after they serve the food, go and say hello.' Amit was talking as if saying hello to a random girl was the easiest thing in the world. Rohit tried to surreptitiously assess the girls. Most of them were making no secret of goggling the group of lads in the skinny jeans and deep V-necked tees. He dismissed the ones that were clearly out of his league and focused on the ones he felt he had a chance with. He spotted one who was standing on her own, looking a bit lost. She had a glass of prosecco in one hand and was pretending to look at her phone, which was in the other. He stared at her, hoping she would look up. She must have felt his stare as she eventually did. He smiled, hoping she would reciprocate. She looked more alarmed than pleased. Perhaps he was smiling too much. He lessened his grin, continuing to stare. She now looked positively frightened and moved away from his line of vision, into a corner of the hall. Well, that had not gone well.

'Stop freaking them out, dude,' Amit said, laughing. 'That was just embarrassing.'

'You said catch their eye!' Rohit protested.

'Yes, but not in a psycho killer kind of way,' Amit said. 'Tone it down.'

He tried to find another girl. Perhaps he should lower his

expectations. This time he picked one that was part of a trio. The other two were clearly more attractive and had their hearts and eyes focused on the Muscle Boys. He caught her eye and gave her a flicker of a smile, very toned down. She didn't look like she wanted to vomit, which was a bonus. She rather endearingly tucked her hair behind her ear and gave him the faintest of smiles back.

'And we have lift-off!' Amit whispered, punching his brother's arm.

'Amit, stop it! You're making it weird.' But Rohit was thrilled. That was as far as he had got with a girl in a long time. Now all he had to do was not bugger it up.

The buffet was served on a long table at the back of the room. Huge silver trays of tandoori chicken legs, samosas that looked like they had come out of a supermarket freezer and lamb chops were carried out by teenage boys barely old enough to be out of school.

Eventually they were allowed to eat. Amit hurried them to the buffet, saying it would be a free-for-all and the chicken would be gone if they so much as hesitated. He was right, people were shoving and pushing to the front. If there was ever an advert for Asian people not being respectful of the British queuing system, this was it. Even the girls lost all sense of decorum as they leaned over each other to grab the last piece of chicken. Soon all that was left were a few scraps of meat and half-empty bowls of yoghurt sauce.

'Go and talk to her now,' Amit whispered to his brother, mouth full of chicken.

'I don't know what to say,' Rohit said. It was true, he wouldn't even know how to start up a conversation with a random girl. At university it was usually Yousef or Steve who did such things and he would eventually join in from the sides. He never made the first move.

'Go and ask her what she thinks of the food. Quick, look,

her friends have left her, she's on her own.' Amit shoved Rohit forward, causing the bones left over from his chicken drumsticks to spill onto the floor. Rohit was horrified. A few people stopped talking to look at what had happened. Amit turned away from him, not wanting to be implicated. He bent down to pick up the chicken bones, which looked especially disgusting strewn across the floor.

'So, you like your chicken then?' a voice from above said as he was still bent over. He looked up; it was her. He quickly straightened himself out.

'Oh, yeah, love a bit of chicken,' he said, giving an awkward laugh. 'Actually, my brother told me to fill my boots because it would all be gone fairly quickly.'

'Buffets at these events are always carnage,' she said, giving him that flicker of a smile again.

Rohit didn't know what to say next. 'So, do you like chicken?' he said. What a stupid question, he thought.

'Actually, I'm a strict Hindu. No meat.' Rohit noticed she wasn't holding a plate. He wondered if she had eaten any of the food.

'Right, well, I only eat meat on special occasions,' he lied. 'You know, the planet and all that.'

'Yeah, I do it more for religious reasons. Animals being sacred and all that.'

'Yeah, of course animals are sacred. I love cows,' Rohit said. This was why he hated talking to girls; he always said the wrong thing. 'Sorry, I'm Rohit by the way.'

'Shivani,' the girl said. 'What is it you do, Rohit?'

'I'm an accountant,' he said, hoping to impress her.

'God, I'm terrible with money. Maybe you could help me.' She laughed.

Rohit tried to think of something witty to say. 'I'm pretty good with a spreadsheet and budgeting, so . . .'

That was neither witty nor funny. Shivani was now looking

as if she wanted to get away from him. He needed to rescue the situation. 'Well, if you can't eat meat, at least there's a bar.'

'I don't drink alcohol either,' Shivani replied.

Shit. He needed to say something to rescue this conversation.

'My dad died last year, so I now live with my mum.' *What the actual fuck?*

'Oh, right. Okay, well, I'm sorry to hear about your dad,' Shivani said. She was now looking to see if she could spot the girls she had been talking to before.

'I never asked what it is you do?' he said, trying to get her attention again.

'I'm an interior designer,' she replied, still looking for her friends.

'That's cool. You don't meet many Indian interior designers. We're either doctors, dentists or accountants,' he said, trying to be ironic. It didn't work.

'Yeah, I broke the mould.' She looked at him again. 'I think you have a bit of chicken grease on your face.' She gestured to his mouth. He wiped the left side. 'Sorry, it's still there, other side.' He wiped again. 'You've just smudged it across your face, perhaps try a napkin?' She looked disgusted. He used the back of his hand to wipe it again.

'Is it gone?' he asked.

'No, it's still there.' She handed him her napkin. 'Here, use this.'

He wiped away furiously at his face. 'Gone?' he asked. She nodded.

'Sorry about that,' he said, handing the napkin back to her without thinking. She looked even more disgusted, but took it anyway out of politeness.

'So that bloke you were with earlier,' she asked. 'You said he was your brother?'

'Yep, it was his idea that we come here,' Rohit said, relieved not to be talking about chicken juice on his face.

'I was wondering, can you introduce me to him?' she asked.

'Why?' Rohit asked, confused.

'Well, I just want to talk to him, you know, get to know him.' She looked at him for an answer. He said nothing. 'To see if he's my type!' she said finally.

Wait, what? Rohit thought. This girl was only talking to him to get to his brother?

'Well, unless your type is married men with kids, then I'm guessing he's probably not,' he said angrily, finally managing something clever and witty.

'Oh.' Shivani looked hurt. 'Sorry, I just thought he was here for the same thing as the rest of us.'

'He isn't. But I am.' Rohit was willing to give Shivani another chance. How was she to know that Amit was married? 'Maybe you can get to know me, see if I'm your type?'

'Oh, that's cute,' Shivani said. 'Wait, you're serious? Oh, sweet. I'm sure there's a wonderful girl out there for you some-where, but I'm sorry, it's not me.'

Rohit was suddenly back in his old familiar territory of rejection. One would think that the pain would lessen with frequency, but each time cut that little bit deeper. He had never been passed over for his brother before, that was new. He felt deeply embarrassed.

'I think I'm going to go and find my friends now,' Shivani said. 'Good luck.' She turned on her heel and trotted off, leaving him standing alone. He went to throw his paper plate in the black bin liners that were being brought out. He wanted to go home.

'So, did you get her number?' Amit asked, sneaking up from behind him.

'Erm, no. She wasn't the right girl for me,' Rohit replied.

'You can't tell that from one meeting!' Amit said. 'You've got to get to know her. Take her out on a date. Come on, bro!'

'There just wasn't that spark, okay?' Rohit tried to push past his brother.

'Well, okay, no problem. Let's find another girl for you to talk to,' Amit said, looking around. Rohit knew that he was trying to help, but everything he was saying was just annoying him.

'I want to go home,' he said flatly.

'Now? Rohit, we've paid all this money to be here, let's stick around for a bit longer.'

'I've had enough, I want to go home,' Rohit repeated. 'You stay if you want, I'm going.'

'Well, I'm hardly going to stay on without you,' Amit said, following him towards the exit.

They were silent as they got into the car. How could Rohit suck at the whole arranged marriage thing? He had seen men far less attractive than him get hitched to beautiful women, all because the system valued job security and coming from a good family over looks. Why wasn't it working for him? He wondered if he had been born too late and missed the golden age of the arranged marriage. Now it was a minefield where those involved had too much choice and freedom to decline good solid marriage offers.

'There's another event like this next week, shall I get us tickets?' Amit finally said.

'No thanks,' Rohit replied.

'Bro, you can't just give up,' Amit said, sounding exasperated. 'I don't know what happened back there, but it can't have been that bad.'

'I don't want to talk about it,' Rohit said.

'Look, I get it,' Amit said soothingly. 'You get awkward around girls, lots of lads do. But unless you practise, you won't get any better.'

'I don't want to practise being humiliated.' Rohit could feel himself getting angry.

'Okay, okay. Calm down,' Amit said.

They drove in silence for a while.

'You know, there is a way you could get to know a girl without having to speak to her,' Amit eventually said.

'Amit, I said I didn't want to talk about this any more.'

'I'm being serious. It's the perfect solution.' Amit sounded pleased with himself.

Rohit had no idea what he was talking about. How on earth could you get to know someone without talking to them? 'Okay, go on.'

'Online marriage websites!' Amit burst out excitedly. 'Everyone is doing it. It's how Hardeep found his wife and how Devi found Pritesh.'

'Online dating? No thanks.'

'Not online dating, online marriages!' he said. 'There are loads of Hindu marriage websites for people looking for marriage. You can weed out the people who aren't serious fairly quickly.'

'I don't know . . . Isn't it a little bit desperate?' Rohit was not keen.

'Not at all. It's the modern way people are doing arranged marriages these days,' Amit said. 'Parents even get involved and manage the profile of their kids. It's all above board.'

Rohit pondered the idea. Was this really the modern-day arranged marriage? The idea of having the time to come up with well-thought-out questions and quick-witted replies did appeal to him, and it would mean he'd never have to go to another one of these godawful dating events again.

'Okay, Amit, I'm willing to give it a go,' he said, a little apprehensive.

'Brilliant. We'll create an online profile for you tomorrow!'

Rohit lay on his bed scrolling through Instagram. He was convinced his phone was now listening to his conversations. Instagram was suggesting he follow lots of happy-looking couples and after each post was an advert for a dating app. Sighing, he switched it off and tossed it aside, staring at the ceiling. His phone buzzed. It was Yousef calling.

'Hi, Yous,' he answered.

'Hey, you free to chat?'

'I'm contemplating the thought of online dating, which is a horrific prospect, so yes, totally free.'

'How was the speed dating thing?'

'A bust. Amit says I'll have more luck online so he's making me a profile tomorrow. How are things with the matchmaker?'

'I've just had to hand over all my personal data and a collection of photographs of me at various weddings. They call it biodata. Mum has now made it her life's work to get me and Rehana hitched. Shame you aren't Muslim, you and Rehana could have got married and we would have killed two birds with one stone,' Yousef said.

'I think I'm destined to stay single for ever. What's the male equivalent of a spinster?' Rohit sighed.

'A bachelor, I think. Doesn't sound as desperate as a spinster.'

'And you're still going to go ahead with all of this?' Rohit asked quietly.

'What do you mean?'

'You know what I mean,' Rohit said. 'Marry some poor unsuspecting woman, when you could just be with Jess and actually, you know, be happy?'

'Rohit, don't start. I've already had this from Rehana. It's easier for everyone if I just forget about Jess and move on.'

'Filling in forms for a matchmaker, meeting women based on your biodata, agreeing to marry someone because your mum likes her doesn't sound easier than being with Jess to me.'

'Leave it out, Ro, you're doing the same thing, just online.'

'I don't have any other options!' Rohit almost shouted. He really wanted to shake some sense into his friend. There was an awkward pause.

'This whole arranged marriage thing has got us arguing with each other now,' Yousef murmured.

'Yeah, sorry, bro,' Rohit said.

'I actually rang to say Steve has got engaged to his girlfriend, the physiotherapist. He sent me a text earlier.'

'Oh, that's cool,' Rohit replied, genuinely happy for their old flatmate. 'I'll drop him a text.'

'I told Mum and all she said was look, everyone is getting married but my children.' Yousef laughed.

'Typical mum reaction,' Rohit said, laughing too. 'Listen, let's try to meet up sometime. It's been too long.'

'I agree, we need to make more of an effort,' Yousef said. 'I have a week off after my next set of nights, maybe then?'

'Text me the dates.'

'Will do. Catch you later.'

'Okay, bye.'

Chapter Seventeen

Jessica

JESSICA'S SECOND DATE WITH Jonathan yesterday had gone well. The good feeling was still there when she woke up this morning. The first date, after their football match, had been much better than she'd expected. It had helped that they had thrashed the other team and everybody was in a good mood. There was none of the awkwardness she had been worried about and conversation had flowed. He looked nice in his white linen shirt and had complimented her on her dress. Jonathan had been the perfect gentleman all night and even offered to drive her home afterwards. She had declined, not wanting to have to go through a weird moment where he might try to kiss her. It wasn't that she didn't fancy him, she just wasn't ready for *that* yet. She knew Kate would kill her. She had sent her a picture of Jonathan earlier that week after she told her they were going on a date. Kate had been more excited than her.

'It's about bloody time,' she had said.

He texted her as soon as she got into the taxi home, telling her how much of a good time he'd had and how he was hoping they could do it again soon. She texted back saying she had enjoyed herself too.

The following day he asked if he could take her to a local food festival. She liked how direct he was, and it made a change that it wasn't her initiating everything. Jess read the text over and over. She was flattered that Jonathan was showing interest, but something was bothering her. She remembered when she had first met Yousef, her heart racing, the butterflies, not wanting to be away from him for a second. She didn't have that when she thought of Jonathan. He was good-looking and polite and just a bit too nice. She was hoping her feelings might change in time, so agreed to the second date. The sun had been shining and they walked to the festival holding cups of coffee. They ate halloumi wraps and laughed as they watched a live band butcher classic Nineties pop songs. She'd had too many Pimm's but didn't care. Jonathan had matched it with beers and they had danced to a bad version of Cher's 'Believe' behind the food truck, where nobody could see them. Jonathan had taken her hand and spun her around, the combination of the Pimm's and spinning making her dizzy, and she'd felt herself stumble. Jonathan, sensing what was about to happen, tightened his grip on her hand, but it was too late. She fell over, pulling Jonathan with her. They lay on the floor laughing.

'Are you hurt?' he asked.

'No, sorry, I took you down with me,' she said, laughing again.

'It's no bother.' He rolled onto his side to face her, then moved a stray strand of hair from her face and tucked it behind her ear. He looked at her for a few seconds. She parted her lips in anticipation. She watched his eyes as they scanned hers and then darted towards her lips. He held her hand, fingers interlocked, then moved in closer, finally kissing her. His lips felt warm and he tasted of beer. She let his tongue find hers as he moved closer towards her, pressing his body up against hers. It felt good. He eventually pulled away.

'I've been wanting to do that ever since I saw you,' he said, grinning.

'Really?' she asked.

'Jess, I've thought of nothing else.' He locked eyes with her again. She smiled and looked away, getting up.

He walked her home and they kissed again as they said goodbye. Jess flopped down on the sofa, trying to figure things out. No, Jonathan didn't give her the exact same feelings as Yousef had, but she had felt something and it had been pleasant. Plus, she had promised herself she wouldn't think about Yousef. Settling into Birmingham was proving a challenge; a new man was exactly what she needed. The effects of the Pimm's were starting to wear off, but the warm feelings from the kiss remained well into the next morning and were still there when she arrived for work.

This was a good thing as Jessica was not enjoying her new post in respiratory medicine. The ward was extremely busy and two of the other junior doctors on her team were off long term, one with an illness and the other on maternity leave. As with anywhere in the NHS, those left behind were simply expected to get on with the job. She regularly left late. She had complained to the ward manager, who had taken it up with the consultant, who had said she would look into the matter and get her some help. Jess didn't hold her breath. The entire hospital was struggling with staffing issues, and she couldn't imagine anyone being freed up to help her. She was wrong.

'Dr Palmer has managed to get another junior doctor to come and help us today,' Fiona, the ward clerk, said as Jess arrived for work.

'Really?' Jess said, surprised.

'Yeah, from the ophthalmology department,' Fiona continued. 'Apparently it's not too busy down there.'

Jessica's heart stopped. The ophthalmology department? Surely not?

'Did you say ophthalmology?' she asked.

'Yeah.' Fiona gave her wink. 'And according to Sue in HR, he's quite dishy!' She giggled and walked off.

Shit, shit, shit. Jess stood still. There was only one junior doctor currently attached to the ophthalmology team – Yousef. She had managed to avoid him for an entire year and had gone out of her way to continue to avoid him these last three weeks after they had started work at the same hospital. She would rather do all the work herself than have him help her. She rushed over to Fiona.

'You know, Fiona,' she said. 'I was thinking, I don't need any help with the ward jobs any more. I've got so used to doing them myself, someone else will only mess up my system.'

'What?' Fiona stopped typing and looked at her. 'Jessica, you have done nothing but complain about your workload for the last fortnight.'

'I know, but I didn't expect anyone to take me seriously.' Jess laughed. 'I just wanted everyone to know how hard I was working.'

Fiona looked at her and shook her head. 'I tell you what, if I was told that someone was coming to help me type up these discharge summaries, I wouldn't turn it down. Count yourself lucky.' She turned back towards her computer and began typing, signalling that the conversation was over. Jessica groaned and went to put her things in the staffroom. She could handle this, she was a professional. This would be a working relationship. Who was she kidding? This was going to be a nightmare. Her consultant arrived on the ward.

'Morning, Jess,' Dr Palmer said brightly. 'Ready for the ward round?' Jess nodded. There was not a single ounce of the fluttery good feeling she'd had when she arrived at work left inside of her, just dread.

'Morning, Dr Palmer. I'll grab the computer and we can get started.'

Monica, the lead nurse, joined them as they went round the ward reviewing each patient. At the end of the ward round each patient had an agreed plan of action: some needed blood tests or scans ordering and a few could be discharged home. Jessica had made a list of all the jobs she needed to do to ensure every patient got what had been agreed. She sat at the nurses' station with Monica putting the jobs in priority order.

'Bet you're glad Dr Palmer got you some help, that's a lot of jobs,' Monica said, eyeing up her list. 'Really we should always have two doctors on the ward, but all this sickness means everybody is stretched.'

Jessica looked at her list. She would be here well into the evening completing it on her own. 'I don't think this list is that bad,' she said. 'If everybody is stretched, perhaps this helper could go to a different ward where he's really needed?'

Monica frowned. 'Jess, what's wrong?'

'Nothing, I just know these patients and this ward so well, I don't think we need anybody else to interfere.'

Monica stared at her.

Jessica liked Monica. She was one of those nurses who had been around such a long time that she had a sixth sense which told her that a patient was going to get sick before they even displayed any symptoms. She had helped Jessica out a number of times this last fortnight with advice about patients and what was best for them. Jess wondered if she was as good at life advice.

'Monica, can I tell you something?' she said. 'In confidence?'

Monica nodded, looking solemn.

'This doctor that Dr Palmer has got coming onto the ward to help us, he's my ex.' Jess waited for Monica to respond. To her disappointment, there was no shocked face or audible gasp. Kate would have been far more dramatic.

'And that's a problem?' Monica said slowly.

'Of course it's a problem!' Jess blurted out. 'Monica, can you think of anything worse than working with your ex?'

'I take it that it didn't end well?' Monica said.

'No, it didn't. Let's just say he was a royal prick.' Even though she thought about it a lot, Jessica hadn't spoken out loud about her relationship with Yousef in such a long time, she was surprised at how much it still hurt. She felt a lump in her throat and her eyes were suddenly wet with tears. She looked away quickly, trying to dry her tears by counting how many cannulas she needed to insert that morning. Monica didn't say anything for a while.

Jess eventually felt she had to say something. 'You're going to tell me that I need to grow up, aren't you? That this is work, and I have to act professional.'

'No,' Monica said gently. 'I was going to ask if you wanted a cup of tea.'

Jessica felt bad about her accusatory tone. 'I'd prefer a vodka and Coke.' Although Monica was trying to be helpful, Jess really wanted someone who would agree with how awful working with Yousef was going to be. She didn't want the mature approach right now.

Monica returned with two cups of tea, placing them down on the station desk. 'Not quite a vodka, but I got you a biscuit. It's never too early.' They ate their biscuits in silence. 'How long were you together for?' Monica asked.

'Five years, almost,' Jess said. 'We got together at the start of university. It ended just before graduation.'

'Those are some pretty important years of your life,' Monica said. 'A lot of growing up happens at university, a lot of memories.' Jess nodded, her mouth dry from the biscuit. She reached for her tea. 'Do you still have feelings for him?'

'No,' Jess said quickly. 'Yes, maybe, I don't know.'

Monica did her usual thing and stayed silent, making Jess feel as though she had to fill the gap. She needed Kate. Kate would be talking non-stop about how much better she was than Yousef.

'The thing is, Monica, he humiliated me,' Jess said. 'He told me he loved me for five years, made me believe we were going to have this amazing life together and then one day, poof, he says we can't be together any more.'

'And his reason for this was?' Monica pushed.

'Culture, religion, parents. Always stupid religion,' Jess spat out. 'But to be honest, I think he was embarrassed of me, ashamed of what his family might think of me.'

'Sounds complicated,' Monica said. 'I'm not surprised you don't know how you feel about him.'

'What's crazy is I want to hate him, but I can't.' Jess was trying to verbalize her feelings. 'He's trapped by his family and their culture. I thought I could help him, but it turns out I couldn't.'

'Well, he'll be here soon. I could always ask the nurses to make life hell for him on the ward.' She winked at Jess.

Jess smiled. 'You know what? That would be really helpful.'

'Jess, I was kidding.' Monica smirked.

'I know, but it would be fun to see him squirm. Thanks for the tea. I suppose I should get back to work.'

'If you need any more biscuits, I know where they're hidden.' Monica stood up. 'Speak of the devil.' She nodded towards the door. Yousef had just entered.

Okay, look busy, Jessica thought. *Don't stare at him.* Yousef's familiar scent wafted through, taking her back to those nights when they lay in bed together and her head had been fuzzy with the heat of their attraction. She could feel him standing at the end of the nurses' station. She waited for him to say something. He didn't. Typical bloody Yousef, always waiting for her to make the first move.

'You must be Dr Ahmed,' Monica said.

'Yousef, please,' he said.

Fuck off, trying to suck up to the nurses, Jess thought. *They're on my side.* She tried to make herself look busy by writing up a drug chart she had already done earlier.

'Well, Yousef, thank you for coming to help us,' Monica

continued. 'It's very much appreciated. Why don't I show you around?'

'That would be lovely, thank you,' Yousef said. Jess rolled her eyes. 'Hi, Jess,' he said.

Shit, he was talking to her. *Act cool*. She put her pen down, looked up and flashed him a confident smile. 'Oh, hi, Yous. I didn't know it was you that was coming to help.' She wanted to throw her pen at his stupid face.

He looked at her, chewing on his bottom lip. He always did that when he was nervous. Good, she was glad she was making him nervous.

'Do you two know each other?' Monica cut in. 'Jess didn't say. Anyway, no time for catch-ups now, there's lots of work to be done. Follow me, please.' Jess loved Monica; her tone left no room for Yousef to argue, and he obediently followed.

Jess could feel her heart beating. Seeing Yousef had brought back all the hurt that was still left between them but also the memories of the good times they had shared. And he still looked so fucking good. She wished somebody had told her sooner that he would be making an appearance today, she would have made more of an effort. She didn't even have any lipstick on, for goodness' sake. She rushed to the staffroom to inspect herself in the mirror. Her hair didn't look too bad; she had washed it yesterday for her date with Jonathan. She had bags under her eyes from working nights the week before. She took out some concealer from her handbag and did her best to hide them, then a quick application of lip balm, a spritz of perfume and she was back on the ward.

Yousef was talking to Fiona, the ward clerk. Jess could tell by Fiona's body language that she was flirting. To her horror, she beckoned her over.

'Hi, Fiona,' Jess said as she approached them.

'Yousef here was telling me you two went to university

together in London,' Fiona said. 'What a coincidence that you both ended up working here.'

'Yep, total coincidence,' Jess replied, trying to look in any direction but at Yousef. 'Look, I really need to get started on the ward jobs.'

'What a good idea.' Fiona beamed. 'Yousef was asking which jobs he should start with. Jess, you have the list; why don't you divide them between you?' She looked intently at Yousef. 'And Yousef, if you need anything, anything at all, just come and ask me.' She gave him a lingering look before turning back to her computer.

Yuck, could she make it any more obvious?

'Where do you want me to start?' Yousef said, turning to Jess.

'Follow me,' she replied, leading him to the staffroom. *Just be professional*, she thought to herself. 'I've made a list of the jobs Dr Palmer wants doing before the end of the day. I'll order the scans and investigations.' She handed him a piece of paper. 'These are the patients that need cannulas and blood gases doing, if you could make a start on those.'

'No problem,' he said, taking the piece of paper from her. 'Sorry, I know this is weird,' he said quietly.

She was about to tell him to stick it up his arse, but stopped herself. 'Why don't we just concentrate on our work, then it doesn't have to be weird.'

'You look . . . good,' he said. A hint of a smile appeared on his face. Jess felt her heart dance. *What is wrong with me?*

'Don't, Yous. Just don't,' she whispered.

'I'm sorry, it's just that . . .' he said, taking a step closer towards her. *What the fuck is he doing?*

She was furious: how dare Yousef waltz in and tell her she looked good? He had no right to say that to her any more. She was even more angry that she liked that he had said it, and the feeling of the two of them alone was too much to bear. His smell, the shape of his body, the thought of the stubble on his face scratching hers as they kissed overwhelmed her. She had to get out of there. She thought she had put this all behind her, that she was moving on with Jonathan. They'd had such a good time together; he was so uncomplicated. That was what she needed right now.

'I need to get back to work.' She wanted to move, but felt frozen to the spot. Those eyes. 'Yousef, if you don't mind.' She gestured for him to move out of her way so she could leave. He paused for a beat then stepped aside.

Monica was walking quickly, heading their way.

'Geoffrey Harris in bed fourteen is struggling with his breathing,' she said, sounding worried. 'Would you mind taking a look at him?'

Jess nodded.

'I'll come too,' Yousef said, following them down the corridor.

Geoffrey had brittle emphysema from years of smoking. He had come in with a low temperature and feeling short of breath and was subsequently diagnosed with pneumonia in both of his lungs. He was on antibiotics and oxygen, but his improvement was slower than they had anticipated.

'How are you feeling, Mr Harris?' Jess asked as she drew the curtain round his bed.

Mr Harris pulled off his oxygen mask. 'Shit,' he panted. 'But that's not new.'

'It might have something to do with him sneaking out for a cigarette earlier,' Monica said firmly.

'Mr Harris!' Jess exclaimed.

'Sorry, love, old habits die hard,' he said, trying to muster up a smile.

'Oxygen levels are at eighty-six per cent,' Yousef said. 'Heart rate one hundred and forty. Shall we take the oxygen off and put him on a nebulizer?'

Jess nodded. 'I'll do some blood gases. Monica, can you get the aminophylline infusion ready?'

'No need to make a fuss, love,' Mr Harris said between breaths. 'I'll be okay.'

'You just concentrate on breathing, Mr Harris,' Jess called out.

'Oxygen levels dropping to eighty-two per cent,' Yousef said.

Jessica checked Mr Harris's temperature. It was low, a sign of infection in older adults. 'What's his blood pressure?'

'Low,' said Yousef. 'Ninety over fifty-five.'

'We need fluids putting up,' Jess replied. Monica heard and immediately began setting up a fluid drip. 'Mr Harris, I'm just going to take some blood from your wrist. We need to check your oxygen and carbon dioxide levels.'

Mr Harris mumbled something incoherent. Jess looked up. He was becoming drowsy. 'Get the crash trolley ready!' she shouted. Another nurse arrived with the emergency trolley. 'Can you get some steroids too?' The nurse nodded and went to the drug cupboard.

'I've given him a double dose in his nebulizer,' Yousef said. 'Jess, his blood pressure is really dropping. Heart rate is irregular, looks like atrial fibrillation. Call the crash team!'

'Agreed,' Jess said, having finally got the blood from his wrist. 'Monica, bleep the crash team.'

Monica called in Fiona. 'Fiona, crash team NOW!'

Fiona nodded and disappeared.

The monitor began beeping. Geoffrey Harris had gone into cardiac arrest.

'Lie him flat!' Jess called out. Yousef obeyed, adjusting the bed. 'Yousef, you do the oxygen bag, I'll do the chest compressions. Monica, prepare the adrenaline.'

Jess counted the compressions out loud. When she got to thirty, Yousef delivered the oxygen breaths. The emergency crash team, a team of doctors and nurses, arrived. The consultant anaesthetist took over from Yousef.

'I'm going to insert a tube,' Jenny, the anaesthetist, said. She skilfully intubated Mr Harris. Jess continued the chest compressions, but was getting tired.

'Let me assess the heart rhythm!' Jenny shouted. They all stopped. 'Asystole, keep going with the compressions.' Jess got into position.

'Shall I take over?' Yousef asked, seeing she was tiring. She moved aside.

'Okay, get the adrenaline in,' Jenny said. They looked at the heart monitor. 'Is someone keeping time?' Jenny asked.

'I am,' Monica said, holding up her watch.

Yousef continued with chest compressions, until another doctor asked if he wanted a break. He nodded and moved out of the way.

After nearly twenty minutes of attempted resuscitation, Jenny stopped everything. 'We've tried our best, folks,' she said to the team. 'Time of death, eleven thirty-five. Thank you all for your work today.'

The team began clearing up.

Jess felt numb. She had been looking after Mr Harris for the past three weeks, and he had been getting better, albeit slowly. She had only spoken to his daughter about his improvement last night. She had sounded so relieved and had promised to get him to stop smoking the minute he came out.

'I'm sorry, Jess,' Yousef said, touching her arm. 'Are you okay?' She pulled away.

'I just need a minute,' she said.

'Of course,' he said gently. 'I'll document everything. Take all the time you need.' He headed back to the nurses' station.

She needed air, but there was still so much work to be done, and somebody had to tell Mr Harris's family. Jenny came over to her.

'Are you the doctor on the ward?' she asked. Jess nodded. 'You did well. I've just had a look through his notes, his lungs were knackered. There wasn't much else we could have done.'

'I know,' Jess said. 'He's a regular on this ward, with his chest being so bad. He was really nice to me on my first day here, told me I was the only person to get a cannula into his arm on the first attempt.'

'Why don't you go to the doctors' mess and make yourself a cup of tea?' Jenny gave her arm a squeeze. 'Everything will still be here in ten minutes.'

Jess felt relieved. She needed to get off the ward. Between Yousef and what had happened with Mr Harris, it was all a bit too much. 'Thanks,' she said to Jenny.

She passed the nurses' station as she left. Yousef was busy writing in Mr Harris's notes. He looked up and gave her a whisper of a smile. She didn't reciprocate. Focus on the work, she told herself. Plus, she had Jonathan.

'I'll be back in a few minutes,' she told him. 'I'll ring Mr Harris's family when I get back.'

'I can do that if you like?' he said.

'No, I know them. It's better coming from me.'

Yousef nodded, and went back to his writing.

Working with Yousef was going to be a challenge. Jess needed a plan. She decided she would split the ward into two halves: Yousef would be responsible for one and she the other. She knew it wasn't ideal, but the only way to keep him out of her thoughts was to stay as far away from him as possible. And if he tried to come anywhere near her again, she would knee him in the nuts.

Chapter Eighteen

Feroza

FEROZA SAT IN THE car becoming increasingly irritated. Why did it feel like she was the only one who was excited about their trip? Abdul was barely speaking to her – Pakistan were playing some sort of cricket match and he wanted to be at home for it. It was tough. Their children came first, and where were his priorities? Rehana had begged not to come and, after Feroza's insistence on the matter, was now sulking in the back of the car and Yousef had been acting strange for the last few days. What was wrong with him? Feroza's favourite part of the day was Yousef coming home and telling her all the details of his day, but now he wasn't interested in doing that and just skulked off to his room, ate his dinner and went to bed. When she had shown him the photo of the girl they were going to meet, he'd just shrugged and nodded his head in agreement. He had barely even looked.

'Whatever you say, Ma,' he said before disappearing into his room and slamming the door.

It didn't matter, though. Feroza had already approved this girl. Aunty Henna had sent her four profiles over the last two weeks and she had rejected the first three without even showing them to Yousef. She knew what was good for him and those girls certainly were not. One of them was wearing a very low-cut dress in her photos – did she have no shame? Just when she was about to ring Henna and tell her to up her game, she came through with a trainee GP in Shropshire called Seema. She was pretty, petite and her profile said she was fluent in several languages. That would come in handy when Feroza took her to functions to show her off to her friends. They would all converse in Urdu. It also said both her parents were doctors, which meant they were a well-to-do family. If things worked out, Feroza hoped some of their status in the community would rub off onto her by association.

'I think this is the place,' Abdul said glumly, turning into a long driveway.

Feroza stared out of her window, eyes wide as they approached the house. Everything was so green, she thought. Not like their road, where anyone who had a front garden had paved over it to make room for their cars. Abdul parked up in front of an impressive doorway.

'Right, everyone,' Feroza said, turning so she could look at them all, 'I want you all on your best behaviour. And for goodness' sake, we are not attending a funeral, cheer up!' She got out of the car and adjusted her dupatta. Abdul rang the doorbell. As much as Feroza favoured the old traditions, arriving at a strange family's house for the first time with the sole intention of seeking marriage for her son felt awkward, even for her. At least this time she didn't have to do any cooking.

The door was opened by a lady who was wearing a blouse and trousers. Feroza paused, taken aback by her clothing and hair, which was cut short into a sleek bob.

'Hello there,' the lady said. 'Come in. I'm Aleena, Seema's mum. We spoke on the phone.'

Feroza quickly recovered. 'Assalamualaikum.' They entered the impressive hallway. 'Should we take our shoes off?'

'Oh no, it's fine, just come straight in. The dogs always drag mud in, so we've given up trying to keep the floors clean.'

Aleena didn't even have the hint of an accent, Feroza noted. She sounded as if she could have been white. She was immediately intimidated. Also, what Pakistani family had dogs? Cats, yes, but dogs?

'Dogs?' Rehana said, suddenly awake. 'I'm allergic to dogs.'

'Don't worry, they're at the groomer's.'

'You have a beautiful house,' Feroza said, trying to sound posh. Rehana gave her a funny look. 'How long have you lived here?'

'Oh, we had it built about seven years ago. My husband loves that kind of thing.' Aleena sat down and gestured for them to do the same. 'You know what it's like with men, they always need a project.'

'Oh yes, Abdul is the same. Always building something. Last week he put up some shelves for all of Yousef's books,' Feroza said proudly.

There was a pause.

'Lovely.' Aleena smiled. 'I will just go and let my Kamran know you've arrived.'

'Mum, why are you talking in that weird voice?' Rehana hissed, when Aleena had left the room.

'I don't know what you are talking about, this is my normal voice. And besides, nobody else was saying anything.' She looked at Yousef. 'Yousef, could you at least look like you want to be here.'

Aleena returned with her husband, Kamran. He looked a lot younger than Abdul.

'Sorry, I was watching the cricket,' he said.

Abdul immediately perked up. 'How are Pakistan doing?' he asked.

'Losing, thankfully,' Kamran replied. 'England are giving them a right thrashing.'

'You support England?' Abdul asked, sounding horrified.

'Of course I do. It's our home.' Kamran looked at Abdul.

'Pakistan is our home,' Abdul countered.

'I'm sorry, I thought you lived in Birmingham?' Kamran said, smiling. 'That's in England, isn't it?'

Feroza let out a high-pitched laugh. 'Men, always arguing about sport.' She smoothed out her kameez. 'I find cricket so boring. What kind of game goes on for days?' She looked around the room to see if anyone agreed with her. Nobody said anything.

'Yousef,' Aleena said, breaking the silence, 'tell me, how's work?'

Feroza looked at Yousef, willing him to say something engaging.

'Work is fine. I'm covering two wards at the moment due to staff sickness so it's really busy.'

'I remember what it was like being a junior doctor.' Aleena smiled at him. 'But it won't be long before you have to apply for speciality training now. Do you know what kind of doctor you want to be?'

Feroza knew this strategy. Aleena was gently assessing Yousef's plans and eligibility for her daughter.

'He wants to be a heart surgeon,' Feroza answered for him. 'Ever since he was a little boy, it's all he has ever wanted.' She beamed proudly.

'I'm actually not sure if I want to be a surgeon,' Yousef said quietly, looking at the floor.

Feroza looked at her son, confused. 'What do you mean, Yousef?' Then remembering where she was, she looked around the room, smiling. 'Kids today, they are always changing their minds.'

'I'm not sure I want to be a surgeon and I am not a kid,' Yousef said, firmly this time.

Feroza's smile faltered. 'Perhaps this is a discussion for home,' Abdul cut in.

'Why don't I go and see where Seema is?' Aleena said gently.

'Kamran, come with me.' She gave her husband a sideways look. He obeyed. Great, Feroza thought, they would be talking about them upstairs. She was furious with Yousef. How could he embarrass her like that?

'Well, that was awkward,' Rehana chimed in. 'Don't get me wrong, I'm glad it's not me causing the problems this time, but Dad, who cares about the cricket? And Yousef, what is wrong with you?'

'Quiet,' Feroza whispered. 'They are coming back.'

Aleena and Kamran entered the room, followed by Seema. Feroza took a breath. She was beautiful. She wore a floral kurta and a pair of skinny jeans. Feroza wasn't sure about the jeans but she decided to give her the benefit of the doubt. Her hair tumbled down to her shoulders, controlled only by a headband. She smiled at her as she came in. Her teeth were perfect and she had a dimple on her left side.

'Salaam, Aunty,' Seema said confidently to Feroza. 'Salaam, Uncle.' She turned to Abdul.

'Walaikum salam,' Feroza said. 'Mashallah, such a pretty girl.'

Seema smiled at her and gave a faint nod. She greeted Rehana next and then turned to Yousef. 'Hi,' she said casually. Yousef suddenly looked more interested. He sat up straight, his jaw slack.

'Hi, I'm Yousef,' he said, sounding slightly bewildered.

'Come and sit next to me,' Feroza said to Seema. 'Tell me, Seema, beta, you are training to be a GP?'

'Yes, I'm in my first year of training,' Seema replied. Feroza noted she had good eye contact. 'It's a three-year programme, so quite some way to go before I finish.'

'Three years?' Feroza pondered. 'Do they let you relocate halfway through training, should your circumstances . . . change?'

'Mum!' Rehana said.

'No, it's okay,' Seema said, smiling. 'Yes, Aunty, in certain circumstances trainees are allowed to transfer to another GP training programme.'

'Oh, that is good news.' Feroza beamed. 'And do you have any hobbies?'

'Oh, you know, the usual stuff. Hanging out with my friends, going to the cinema, shopping.' Seema looked at Rehana for what Feroza assumed was girly moral support, but Rehana hardly ever went out so Feroza moved the conversation on.

'Do you have any brothers or sisters?' she asked.

'Seema is an only child,' Kamran said. 'Our little princess.'

'Dad, stop embarrassing me.' Seema laughed. Feroza caught Rehana giving Yousef a sideways eye-roll.

'Shall we go into the dining room to eat?' Aleena said, standing up.

'I hope you haven't gone to too much trouble,' Feroza said. 'A cup of tea would have been more than enough.' She lied; a cup of tea would have been an insult.

'Nonsense, you have come from so far and it is no trouble at all.' Aleena led them to the dining room. Feroza gasped for the second time; they had put on a banquet. There were large bowls of pasta, couscous, a whole salmon and an array of vegetables. 'Just something we rustled up,' Aleena said.

Feroza took a seat. She was feeling conflicted: where was the Pakistani food? It all looked spectacular, if a little too English, but she had no idea how she would be able to compete with this should the need arise, and most of her relationships with other women centred around either gossip or competition. But what if Yousef married into this family? She could join forces with Aleena and Kamran and really blow the other ladies out of the water. Musarat would be so envious.

'Are these fish kebabs?' she asked, eyeing up a plate.

'No, they are fishcakes,' Aleena replied. 'Jamie Oliver's recipe.'

'Is he your cook?' Feroza asked. Now it made sense. Aleena couldn't possibly have time to cook all of this food and work as a doctor.

'No, no. I got the recipe from his book,' Aleena said, smiling.

Feroza took a bite of the fishcake. 'Do you have any chilli sauce?' The food was so bland.

The conversation seemed to flow better when it was peppered with people passing around plates of food. Even Yousef seemed to have perked up a bit, probably after seeing Seema, Feroza thought. After dinner Aleena suggested Yousef and Seema talk in the other room.

'Feroza, why don't you come with me to the kitchen whilst I prepare dessert?' Aleena said. 'We can leave the boys to talk about the cricket some more. Rehana, you come too, just us girls.'

The kitchen was exactly how Feroza imagined it would be – huge. She had seen kitchen islands on television but nobody she knew had one. After making a half-hearted gesture of helping to clean up, Feroza perched on a bar stool watching Aleena make a pot of tea.

'Where in Pakistan were you born?' Feroza asked.

'I wasn't. My parents are from there, but I was born here in England,' Aleena replied. That explained the accent, Feroza thought. 'Kamran is the same. Might explain why he supports England in every sport.'

Feroza nodded. 'Do you speak Urdu?'

'Barely. My parents were really keen on us fitting in, so we only spoke English at home. I'm so envious of those who can speak it.' Aleena took out four teacups from one of the cupboards. 'Rehana, will you be having tea?'

'No thanks,' Rehana said. She didn't even bother looking up from her phone.

'What about Seema? It said in her biodata that she was fluent in several languages,' Feroza enquired.

'French and Italian. She's fluent in both, so helpful when we go abroad.' Aleena laughed.

'And Urdu or maybe Punjabi?'

Aleena shook her head. 'Neither. I know it's different in Birmingham, but there really aren't that many people who speak those languages around here.'

'Do you mean not many Pakistani people?' Feroza enquired. She was beginning to wonder whether this family had lost all their cultural identity.

'Pakistani, Indians, Bangladeshi. There just aren't many Asian people around this area. And to be honest, I quite like it.' Aleena loaded the teapot and teacups onto a tray. 'Less gossip. I always feel like I am being judged whenever I have to go an Asian event for not being Asian enough.'

Feroza was judging her right now for not being Asian enough. Before she had the chance to ask another question, Rehana joined in the conversation.

'If you are not particularly traditional, why are you doing the whole arranged marriage thing? Seems a bit counterintuitive.'

Feroza hated it when Rehana used long words she didn't understand. She hoped it wasn't offensive.

'Kamran's father suggested it. Seema wasn't opposed to it, so we thought, why not? Seema will make the final decision on who she marries anyway.' She put the tray down in front of Rehana. 'Could you take this in? I have a cake in the fridge, I'll bring that.'

Feroza was quiet on the way home. This family were so different from hers. She had been so caught up in the impressive house, the food, the kitchen and what Musarat would think, she hadn't stopped to think whether *she* liked them. Yes, she had been the subject of many racist comments in the past, but that hadn't made her stop wanting to be Pakistani; she just wanted others to be more accepting of it. 'Fitting in', as Aleena had referred to it, had to be a two-way street, with compromise on both sides.

'So, son, don't keep us in suspense,' Abdul asked as they drove home. 'What did you think of the girl?'

'She was nice,' Yousef said. 'Very easy to talk to.'

'And she was bloody gorgeous,' Rehana cut in. 'I saw your eyes nearly pop out of your head when she walked in.'

'Rehana, don't be so vulgar,' Feroza scolded. 'Yousef is not that type of boy.'

'They are all that type of boy, Mum,' Rehana said.

'It's hard to tell from just one meeting,' Yousef said quietly. 'What did you think of her, Mum?'

'I didn't get much chance to speak with her,' Feroza said. 'I am not sure this is the right family for you.'

'Yousef liked her and that's the most important thing,' Abdul said cheerily. 'Let's hope you impressed her as much she impressed you.'

They hadn't impressed her, Feroza thought, and that was the most important thing.

Chapter Nineteen

Seema

SEEMA LAY ON HER bed grinning like a Cheshire cat. She had always been sceptical when people had told her that she would know instantly when she met 'the one', but today it had happened. The second she saw Yousef she just *knew*. She was beginning to lose hope with the whole arranged marriage thing. The boys that had been to see her had all been complete weirdos. One of them had a *moustache* – that was an instant 'no' – and another had been far too close to his cat. It was creepy. But Yousef seemed genuinely nice and he was so easy to talk to, it all felt so natural. Of course, it didn't hurt that he was incredibly good-looking and, my God, *those hands*, they were *huge*.

He asked her a lot of questions, which was good. She wanted a man that was interested in her. He was less forthcoming when she was asking the questions, especially about his university life, but that didn't matter, she could find out more about that later. She didn't even mind that his parents were much more traditional than what she was used to. She could win them over.

She could hear her parents talking in the kitchen. She made her way downstairs. They went quiet as soon as she entered.

'Did I interrupt something?' Seema asked.

'No, darling, come and sit down,' her dad said, gesturing at one of the stools. 'We were just saying how we didn't think this family were the right fit for us.'

Her mum laughed. 'I think we are a little bit too modern for them. Too anglicized.'

'Actually, I quite liked them,' Seema said. 'Yousef was really sweet.'

'Seema, tell me you're joking,' her mum said. 'He barely said two words to us.'

'No, Mum, I'm not, I really liked him.' Seema looked at her parents. 'And his parents being traditional didn't bother me.'

'Seema, you've turned down so many more suitable boys,' her dad said in that soothing tone he only used when he was trying to make her do something she didn't want to do. 'Why don't we arrange another meeting with that anaesthetist fellow? He seemed like a good match.'

'No thanks, Dad,' Seema continued. 'You both said if I agreed with Grandad and did this whole arranged marriage thing, I would be in charge.'

'So what are you saying, that you want to marry this boy?' Her mum's lip curled in disgust.

'God, Mum, you're so dramatic.' Seema sighed. 'What I'm saying is that I want to meet with him again and get to know him.'

'Why not meet with some more boys before you make up your mind?' her dad said again.

'I don't want to meet with any more boys, Dad. Don't you understand how tiring it is preparing for these meetings and constantly being left disappointed?' Seema replied. 'I like Yousef and I want to meet with him again, so either you ring his mum and arrange it, or I will.'

'Ha, I'd like to see you ring her,' her mum said. 'She'd think all her Pakistani traditions have been turned on their head.'

'Mum, please,' Seema said firmly.

'Seema, you do know how far Birmingham is from us and that it's very different from Shropshire?' her dad said. 'Are you sure about this?'

'I'm sure, thanks, Dad.' Seema was resolute.

'Fine.' Her mum sighed. 'If that's what you want, I'll ring his mum tomorrow and arrange another meeting.'

'Thank you.' Seema left her parents to it and returned to her bedroom, her tummy alive with butterflies.

Chapter Twenty

Rehana

FOR THE FIRST TIME in for ever, Rehana felt like a boss. She was finally going to be living the life she had dreamed of. Well, at least for the next twenty-four hours anyway. Her mother had somehow wrangled her a date with *two* boys in one day. And to make the whole day seem even more like an episode of *Emily in Paris*, she was meeting both boys in a coffee shop without her parents being present, one at lunchtime and the second at three p.m. Granted, it was just a Costa Coffee in town rather than some fancy artisan one tucked away in *gai Paris*, but it was better than nothing.

It had all happened by accident. Aunty Henna had sent them the profile of a software engineer who used to live here in Birmingham but now worked in Dubai (probably to avoid paying taxes, Rehana had thought). He was visiting his parents for two weeks and only had a narrow window in which he could meet. Rehana's mum had agreed to the meeting assuming it would be the usual family visit, but this boy's mum had phoned back later and said he wanted to meet with Rehana alone first to see if they got on, and if they did, the families could meet. Before her mother had agreed to it she had phoned Aunty Musarat, who told her this was quite normal these days and as long it was in a public place with lots of people, it would still be considered halal.

The second date had been a surprise for everyone. Aunty Rubina had phoned to say that her Lubna's husband had a friend who she thought would be a suitable match for Rehana, and he was a dentist. That was top-tier stuff. He also wanted to meet with Rehana on his own first. Getting help in the form of Aunty Rubina had put her mum into some kind of state of shock, and she had agreed. It might also have had a little to do with Rehana's mum not wanting to let a dentist slip through her fingers.

Both meetings came with one caveat: Rehana's mum had insisted that a mehram be present. This was the Muslim equivalent of a chaperone and ensured that there would be no funny business. Yousef was working this weekend, which ruled him out, so Rehana had asked Emma to come with her on both dates. She could sit on another table and if the date was going horribly wrong, or either one turned out to be a potential murderer, Rehana would send her a sign which meant a fake emergency phone call was needed. Rehana's mum was not too keen on Emma being the mehram, as traditionally it was supposed to be a man, but given she had no other viable alternative, she had agreed. Plus, Emma could drive, which meant Rehana didn't have to look like a complete loser turning up on the bus.

Rehana had been in text conversation with the Dubai boy, Nadeem, over the last week and, much to her surprise, he seemed normal, which she was discovering was a rare trait these days. He had told her that he found the traditional family meetings too much pressure and that a one-to-one meeting where they got to know each other was far more favourable before others became invested in the pairing. This was music to Rehana's ears – no more having to get tarted up and hide in her bedroom until summoned. She'd asked what it was that made him agree to go on a date with her.

You have kind eyes, he had texted back. That had made her blush. Thank God for Sean's eye make-up tutorials.

Thanks, that's really sweet, she had replied.

Look, I'm a straightforward guy. I don't play games. If I like you, I will tell you, he had messaged her. **If it's clear we aren't going to get on, let's just be honest from the get-go.**

Rehana liked his no-nonsense approach. Neither had any time to waste.

'Check you out, you *slut!*' Sean said as he did Rehana's nails. She had just told him about her double date. 'Two boys in one day. You're giving me a run for my money.'

Rehana blushed. 'It's all very above board,' she explained. 'We're meeting in a coffee shop and will only be talking.'

'That's how it starts.' Sean narrowed his eyes. 'Next thing you know you're exchanging steamy messages, making out in dark alleyways and having to book yourself in for an STI check.'

'Sean, I think you have the wrong idea of what this arranged marriage business involves.' Rehana laughed. 'I don't even think there will be making out in dark alleyways after the wedding!'

'How boring,' he retorted. 'There, your nails are done, go break some hearts.'

'Oh, before I forget, Mum sent you these.' She took out a Tupperware box from her bag. 'Pakoras, made this morning.'

Sean took the box. 'I'm supposed to be on no carbs this month.' He removed the lid and took in the aroma. 'Jesus, no carbs will have to wait until next month.'

Rehana paid him and left to catch the bus. She didn't want to be late.

'Don't you think it's a bit risky meeting both of these fellas in the same place?' Emma asked as they drove to Costa Coffee.

'Nah, they're three hours apart. Not even the best first dates can last that long,' Rehana replied. 'Are you're sure you're going to be okay waiting all that time?'

'I have a ton of marking to do, it makes no difference whether I do it at Costa or at home. At least this way I can drink lattes and eat cake.' Emma parked up. 'So how does this work? Do I come in with you, or do we arrive separately and pretend we don't know each other?'

Rehana hadn't thought that far ahead. She didn't want the boys to think she was a slag coming in on her own without a mehram, but at the same time she didn't want them to think she couldn't go anywhere without a chaperone either. She quickly weighed out the merits of both scenarios in her head and decided being thought of as a slag was the worse of the two options.

'Come in with me, Em,' Rehana said. 'That way they know someone is around should they think about having their wicked way with me!'

'Well, you do look irresistible, darling! I am kind of tempted myself.' Emma laughed, linking arms with Rehana as they went inside.

Costa was busy and there was a queue of people waiting to be served. They were ten minutes late, so with any luck, Boy Number One, Nadeem, would be there by now. Rehana scanned the room looking for anyone who matched the photo her mum had shown her. There he was, on a table pretending to look busy on his phone.

'There,' Rehana whispered to Emma. 'What do you think?'

'Hmm, not bad. Looks tall, good eyebrows,' Emma said.

'Good eyebrows? How is that helpful?' Rehana hissed. Nadeem looked up from his phone and caught them staring at him. 'Shit, he's seen us.'

'I didn't know we were hiding from him,' Emma said. 'Why don't you go over and say hello? Do you want me to get you a drink?'

'No thanks. With any luck, he'll buy me a drink.' Rehana was back to pretending she was the star of her own movie and walked confidently over to Nadeem. 'Hi,' she said. 'I'm Rehana.'

'Hello, I'm Nadeem. Thanks for coming,' he replied. 'It's always a bit nerve-wracking being the first to arrive. You never know if the other person will show.' He stood up and pulled out the chair for her.

What a gentleman. He was definitely tall (which meant she could wear heels) and he had a kind face (to match her kind eyes). Not drop-dead gorgeous, but certainly not a straight-up 'no'.

'Can I get you a drink?' he asked. 'Maybe some cake? The raspberry and white chocolate slices looked pretty epic.'

'Just a chai latte,' Rehana said. She desperately wanted cake, but didn't want him to think she was a greedy pig. 'Skinny, sugar free. No cake, thanks.'

'No problem.' He made his way to the counter. Rehana caught Emma's eye and gave her a thumbs up. Emma winked back.

Nadeem returned with their drinks and a slice of cake. 'I couldn't resist the cake,' he said, setting the tray down. 'And I got two forks in case you change your mind.'

'Sharing cake on your first date? That's very forward,' Rehana joked.

'Oh God, is it too forward? I didn't mean it to be, I don't really know the rules in these situations.' He looked mortified.

'No, I was just joking,' Rehana said, laughing. 'Thank you for the latte.'

'Sorry, I haven't had much luck in the past on these dates. I'm a bit nervous.' He took a sip of his coffee. 'That's why I thought we should meet on our own first.'

'Have you been on many dates?' Rehana raised an eyebrow.

'No, no, that's not what I meant. This really isn't going well, is it?' He looked at her and smiled. 'I'm only here for a couple

of weeks. You don't get many holidays when you work in l̶
My parents are on a mission to get me hitched.'

'So, are they packing the girls in for you then?' Rehana was genuinely interested but immediately realized her comment sounded bitchy.

'If it was up to them, I'd be seeing two or three girls a day until we found a match.' He shook his head. 'Imagine being such an arrogant prick that you would think it was okay to date more than one person in a day.'

'Yeah, imagine that.' Rehana let out a nervous laugh. Fuck, now she felt really guilty.

'I'd rather put all my effort into getting to know one person at a time, this isn't *Celebs Go Dating*.'

Rehana wasn't allowed to watch *Celebs Go Dating*, it was considered filth by her mum. 'So, you work in Dubai? That's interesting.' She was keen to change the subject.

'Yeah, I've been there for three years, working for an IT company. Pretty boring stuff but it pays well and I get free accommodation.' He picked up his fork and broke off a piece of cake. 'My contract is due to end next year. I've saved up enough money to buy a house, so I'll be coming home.'

'Wow, sounds like you have it all figured out.' Rehana was most impressed with him buying his own house. That meant no living with the in-laws.

'I think it's important to have a plan.' He wiped the corners of his mouth with a napkin; very well mannered, Rehana thought.

He asked her about her work and family, then got her another drink. He was one of four boys and came second in the line-up. They laughed some more as he recounted some of the horrific arranged marriage family dates he had been on which led to him telling his parents he would now be meeting any future girls on their own first.

'It's just more relaxed, and this whole arranged marriage

thing has got to keep up with the times,' he said. 'I saved that last piece of cake for you. Honestly, it's lush.'

That was cute, Rehana thought. She picked up her fork and took the cake. It really was delicious. In fact, she had enjoyed the entire date and it was much easier without the additional family pressure. 'You have good taste in cake,' she said.

'It's my superpower,' he whispered, leaning in. 'Hey, listen, I don't suppose you fancy going for a walk? There's a park nearby.'

Rehana looked at her watch. Her next date was due in half an hour. The time had gone so fast. 'I would love to, but my friend is here as a chaperone.' She waved in Emma's direction. 'My mum insisted on it.' She rolled her eyes. 'I don't want to leave her.'

'Sure, of course. I understand.' He looked embarrassed.

'No, seriously, I had a great time and it's just, you know, I live around here and can't be seen walking the streets with strange boys.' She tried to give him her best innocent girl look. 'What would the aunties think?' She really did want to go on the walk. The truth was, she didn't want the date to end either. She hadn't enjoyed herself this much in ages.

'I get it,' he said. 'Maybe next time, after I've met your family?'

'Yeah, that would be nice.' She played with a loose strand of hair. Nadeem was so good at eye contact, it was disarming.

'Okay, well, I'd best go then,' he said, not sounding keen to leave at all. 'Is it weird if I follow you on Instagram?'

'No, not at all.' She gave him her handle. 'I have to warn you, it's just pictures of quotes from my favourite authors. Very boring.'

'I would say more cerebral than boring.' That eye-contact again. 'Okay, then . . . bye.'

She stood up, not knowing what to do. 'See you later.' He gave her one last smile and turned to leave. Rehana was about to make her way over to Emma when Nadeem suddenly turned around.

'Listen, remember I told you I was a straightforward guy in one of my messages?'

Rehana nodded.

'Well, I just want you to know, I had a really good time hanging out with you.'

Rehana smiled. 'Yeah, me too.'

'So do you think we could perhaps, I don't know . . . meet again? All above board, of course. Maybe go for that walk before I head back to Dubai?' he said, suddenly shy.

'That would be nice,' Rehana said, playing with that loose strand of hair again. 'And maybe I'll follow you back on Instagram. If you're lucky.'

He smiled. 'Okay, well then . . . I suppose . . . this is . . . bye,' he stuttered.

'See you soon,' Rehana replied.

'Yeah, soon. Definitely.' Nadeem smiled. His gaze lingered. 'I'd better go.' Rehana nodded. He gave her one last smile and left.

Emma came rushing over.

'Tell me everything!' she said, parking herself in Nadeem's seat.

'Oh my God, Emma. It was such a good date!' Rehana exclaimed. 'He asked me questions about me and my family, he was really interested, you know? He has a five-year plan like a proper grown-up, he paid for my drinks and he doesn't want to live with his family after he gets married!'

'Bloody hell, Rehana. I think you've hit the jackpot,' Emma said excitedly.

'And I think I kind of fancy him. I didn't at first, but he grew on me as time went on,' Rehana said, pondering.

'Isn't that what you said arranged marriages were all about? People growing on you over time.'

'Yeah. I meant, like, over months and years, not a few hours!' They both laughed. 'Right, Boy Number Two is coming in twenty minutes. I need to reapply my make-up and have a quick pee then I'll be good to go.'

'Rehana, I'm so jealous of your life right now,' Emma replied as Rehana disappeared into the ladies' room.

Rehana inspected herself in the mirror. She hadn't felt this good since returning from university. Her date with Nadeem had gone well and he had pretty much confirmed that he wanted to see her again, which bolstered her confidence further. She was buzzing. Her hair looked good, she had finally mastered the art of eyeshadow and her lips were fully glossed. She was ready to take on the next bloke.

'This is the boy we are looking out for; he's called Jameel,' she said to Emma, showing her the image on the phone.

'You mean that guy over there.' Emma pointed to a man looking a bit lost by the entrance. 'He arrived a couple of minutes ago.'

'Shit, he's early!' Rehana said, then looked down at the table, which still held the cups and plate from her first date. 'Quick, help me move these cups.' All the movement caught the attention of Jameel, who waved at her. She placed the cup down on the next table and waved back.

'Hi, you like to arrive early too,' Jameel said. 'I love that, I'm always early wherever I go.'

It took a second for Rehana to understand what he meant. 'Oh yes, I'm always early,' she lied. She was usually the last at most events. 'I'm Rehana.'

'Jameel,' he said, holding out his hand. How very formal, Rehana thought as they shook hands.

'This is my friend Emma, we work at the same school. She just popped over to say hello. These are her cups mostly and she ordered the cake.' *Rehana, stop talking*, she said to herself. Why was she spouting nonsense?

'Hi, I'm just on that table over there. I'll leave you guys to it.' Emma gave her a *what the fuck was that about?* look before heading back to her table.

'Shall we get a drink?' Rehana asked.

'Great, I'll have an Americano,' Jameel said, sitting down. He looked at her expectantly.

'Right then, I'll go get that,' Rehana said slowly.

'Oh, and can you ask for oat milk? I'm lactose intolerant.' Jameel got out his phone. 'I just need to reply to this message.'

Rehana joined the queue for coffees. She caught Emma's eye and mouthed for her to check her phone as she texted her.

> *Rehana:* He's making me buy his bloody coffee!
> *Emma:* Red Flag!! 🚩 Run!
> *Rehana:* I can't run, he's a dentist. Mum will kill me ☠
> *Emma:* Fine, but I'm here if you need a fake emergency call 🔊

Rehana returned to the table with the coffees. Jameel was still texting.

'Oat milk Americano,' she said, handing him his coffee. He didn't look up from his phone but held out a hand to hush her. *Okay, that's just rude*, Rehana thought. 'Am I keeping you from something?' she asked.

He continued to text, then after a few seconds, 'Sorry, work. Had to send an urgent email. Thanks for the coffee.' He took a slurp. 'Boy, do I need caffeine.'

'Glad I could be of service,' Rehana retorted.

'I'm just about to buy my own dental practice, so much to do. That's what the email was about.' He looked at her expectantly. 'Can you believe it? I'm only twenty-six and about to own my own business. That's called bossing it in life.'

Rehana didn't know what to say. Was she supposed to be impressed?

'Congratulations, I suppose,' she said.

'Yeah, I decided it was time. I couldn't take orders from anyone else, I need to be my own boss, you know?' He took another slurp of coffee. 'Is this definitely oat milk?'

Rehana nodded.

'Good, I know I'm allergic to lactose, but all the tests have come back negative. It's the same with wheat, makes me bloated. But the stupid specialist at the hospital tells me I'm not.' He laughed. 'What do they know?'

'I imagine quite a lot, being a specialist,' Rehana replied.

'Yeah, well, I'm a specialist in my own body, so they can fuck off.'

Rehana recoiled. She wasn't averse to swearing, but surely that was second or third date kind of language?

'Anyway, I was telling you about my practice. It's in Sutton Coldfield, very exclusive.' He kept looking at her for a reaction. She gave none. 'Private, of course. No money in NHS dentistry any more.'

'Sounds posh,' Rehana said, trying to convey her disinterest.

'Posh? It's Sutton Coldfield, it's like Brummie royalty. And the best thing is I'll have minions working for me.' He looked at her proudly.

Rehana let her mind drift off as Jameel rattled on about his practice, how he next planned to buy a large detached property which he would move his 'wifey' (she hated that word) into and how he planned to buy his dad a new car. How on earth did Lubna think this guy would be a good match for her? She was just about to text Emma for her emergency 'out' when a voice broke through her thoughts.

'Rehana, did I leave my keys here?' It was Nadeem; he was back! Without thinking, Rehana bolted out of her chair.

'Hi, Nadeem,' she said loudly.

'Sorry to interrupt your . . .' He looked at Jameel. 'I went for that walk in the park and realized I didn't have my keys. Have you seen them?'

Rehana made an exaggerated effort to look for Nadeem's keys, hoping it would distract him from the fact she was on a date with Jameel.

'Hi, who are you?' Jameel asked, also standing up.

Fuck! Rehana thought.

'I'm Nadeem, who are you?'

'Jameel. How do you two know each other?'

'Found them!' Rehana said, appearing from under the table. 'They must have fallen out of your pocket. Here you go.' She handed the keys to Nadeem. 'Okay, well, get home safely.' She stood looking at Nadeem, willing him to leave.

'Rehana, who is this guy?' he asked. Rehana felt a pit opening up in her stomach.

'Who am I? Who the fuck are you?' Jameel said, taking a step forward.

'Easy, mate, calm down,' Nadeem said. 'I met Rehana for a drink at this table a couple of hours ago.'

'Nah, man, I'm meeting her for a drink now. That's messed up.' They both looked at Rehana.

'I can explain . . .' She stared at them both. She really couldn't explain.

Jameel folded his arms and turned to Nadeem. 'I think you should clear off, bro, I'm pretty sure the lady wants me to stay.'

Nadeem continued to stare at Rehana. He looked so hurt her heart ached. She hadn't realized just how much she liked him, even after one meeting. She had really messed up.

'I only came back for my keys,' he said to Jameel. 'Good luck.' He left.

Rehana turned to look at Emma, who was watching, mouth open. She knew what she had to do.

'I'm sorry, Jameel, I don't think this is going to work,' she said, gathering her things.

'What, you're turning me down? You're having a laugh, aren't you?' He looked at her. 'Fine, I wasn't interested anyway.'

Rehana ran after Nadeem. She saw him turn down one of the side roads. 'Nadeem, wait!' she cried out. He looked back at her and continued to walk. 'Nadeem, please, hear me out.'

He stopped. 'Look, you don't have to say anything. It was only one date, no big deal.' He paused. 'You have every right to keep your options open. No need to explain anything.' He began walking again. Rehana ran in front of him, blocking his path.

'I'm sorry, okay?' she said, slightly out of breath. 'I didn't expect our date to go so well. You kind of caught me off guard.'

'Rehana, I don't like games or those who play them.' He tried to get past her, but she wasn't giving in that easily. 'I've had women mess me around before, I thought you might be different. It's my fault really.'

'I am different,' Rehana said. 'Honestly, I've never done anything like this before. I know it sounds like an excuse, there is just so much pressure to get married as a single Pakistani girl.' She sighed. 'I guess I just didn't think about anyone else's feelings. I'm sorry.'

Nadeem looked at her, not saying much. 'Can I go home now?' he eventually asked. Rehana's heart sank. She stepped aside.

'Yes, of course.'

He didn't look at her as he walked past her.

'Nadeem?' she said. He stopped. 'I really did have a good time on our date, that wasn't me playing a game.'

'Me too. I'm sorry,' he said, without looking back. He headed back to his car.

Rehana didn't feel like talking much on the journey home. The whole day had been a disaster. Emma, unfortunately, had other plans.

'Babe, I don't think you have anything to feel bad about,' she said. 'You didn't do anything wrong. You're a single girl looking for a husband. You can go on as many dates as you like until you find the right bloke.'

'I know it was only one coffee date, but we had a connection. And it's an unwritten rule that when it comes to arranged marriages, you shouldn't really consider more than one person at a time.' She focused on the rain that had just started to come down. 'Usually it's men screwing me over, not the other way round.'

'You didn't screw anyone over. It was just coffee, after all. And you're only taking control of the situation you're in.' Emma turned into Rehana's street.

'I know, but one date in Muslim arranged marriage land is the equivalent of twenty dates in normal dating land. We only have a limited number of dates we can go on until decisions have to be made,' Rehana said miserably.

'Look, if you feel that bad, just text him.'

'Don't you think it's too soon?' Rehana turned to look at her.

'Well, you said yourself he doesn't like games, so just text him if that's what you want to do.' Emma parked up; Rehana took out her phone. 'What's the worst that can happen?'

'What should I text?' she asked.

'Tell him how you're feeling.'

Rehana thought for a moment.

Nadeem, I'm sorry about what happened today. Can we meet up before you go back to Dubai and start over?

She pressed send. She received confirmation of him reading the message immediately.

She waited. The app told her Nadeem was typing.

'He's about to reply,' she said to Emma, strangely excited.

They both waited.

Nothing. The app suddenly changed his status to 'offline'. Rehana sighed. 'I fucked it.'

'Sorry, babe,' Emma said, giving her a hug. 'Let's hope your Aunty Henna has another ace up her sleeve.'

Rehana got out of the car feeling deflated. She didn't want Aunty Henna to produce another ace. She wanted a time machine so she could start the day over and go for that walk in the park with Nadeem. But it was too late now, and she was back at square one.

Chapter Twenty-One

Yousef

YOUSEF WAS GLAD TO escape the confines of his house. His mother was driving him insane. Ever since she had been to meet that meddling Aunty Henna, she had done nothing but talk about him getting married. Work used to be his one respite, but now he was working with Jess, it was even worse than being at home. Everyone said time would ease his feelings for her, but it had been a year and all he could think about was how his family had persuaded him to make a terrible mistake, and the worst thing was they did it without uttering a single word. The anger was eating him up. He knew Jess deserved better than him, but he wanted her nonetheless.

He was meeting Rohit and Steve for dinner in Manchester. They were celebrating Steve's engagement. He was up from London visiting his sister and it was a rare opportunity for them all to get together, something they hadn't managed to do since leaving university. Yousef needed to take his mind off of the shitshow that was his life right now, and this was perfect.

Both Steve and Rohit were already at the bar having a beer. They hugged him hello.

'It's been too long, mate,' Steve said. 'We ordered you a Coke. How have you been?'

'Yeah, good, working mostly,' Yousef replied. It was good to see his friends. 'Forget about me, congratulations on your engagement! That's huge.'

'Thanks. The beast has finely been tamed.' Steve laughed. 'She's a good girl, I can't complain. We'll be sending out the save the dates soon, so keep your diaries free.'

'Wouldn't miss it, mate,' Yousef said, taking his coat off.

'Rohit was just telling me he's about to hit the internet dating scene, desperate times and all that,' Steve said, taking a sip of his beer.

Yousef turned to his best friend. 'Rohit, mate, good to see you – sorry it's been so long.'

'Water under the bridge, mate. Let's have a good time tonight, eh?' Rohit said. 'Looks like our table is ready.' He nodded to the waitress who had come over to take them to where they would be eating.

They laughed as they recalled their antics at university, then Steve told them about his wedding plans. Steve usually played his relationships with women down, not wanting to ever commit, but now he seemed utterly smitten. Rohit told them about his disastrous attempts at trying to find a wife.

'Wait, you gave her back the tissue after you wiped the chicken juice off your face?' Steve said, laughing. Rohit nodded. 'Mate, that is a mad move.'

'And she was only interested in my brother.' Rohit was laughing now too. 'So now I'm resigned to the world of internet arranged marriages.'

'How does that work then?' Steve enquired. 'Instead of sending each other pics of your bits, you send wedding proposals?'

'Kind of. My brother has set me up an online profile. It's exactly like Tinder but there are additional questions like where in India your parents are from, what religion you are, whether you're a permanent resident of the UK, what your annual income is . . .' Rohit trailed off. 'Loads of inappropriate stuff really.'

'They call it biodata. They even want to know what shade of brown you are,' Yousef explained. 'It's all the stuff Asian parents prioritize, but us guys have no interest in.'

'You can even narrow down who you're looking for by occupation,' Rohit continued. 'My brother says it's best I keep my options open and has put "any" in that category.'

'Lucky you. My mum says I have to marry a GP or dermatologist,' Yousef said, taking a bite of his non-halal steak.

'That's because you've got options,' Rohit said. 'Us beggars can't be choosers.'

Yousef decided to ignore that remark. Rohit always assumed Yousef's life was rosy. He had no idea.

'You know, Yous,' Steve said, 'I always assumed you and Jess would end up back together. I know it ended badly, but you guys were the real deal.'

Rohit nodded. 'Yeah, I agree. Do you see much of her now?'

Yousef paused. He didn't fancy talking about Jess tonight, but they had asked. 'We had managed to avoid each other this past year, but we're at the same hospital now. In fact, we're working on the same ward for the next two weeks.'

Rohit and Steve looked at each other.

'Fuck, mate, the same ward? Like, together?' Steve asked. Yousef nodded. 'Isn't that awkward?'

'Very,' Yousef said. 'We spend the entire time trying to avoid each other.'

'Are you still into her?' Rohit asked.

'I don't know, maybe,' Yousef said miserably. He definitely was.

'Does she know how you feel?' Steve enquired.

'It doesn't matter, nothing has changed, and my mother is hellbent on finding me a nice Muslim wife.'

The three of them sat in silence for a few seconds before Steve changed the subject.

'Ro, do you remember when we went to that party in drag?' He laughed.

'Yes! We had to put balloons in our dresses for boobs!' Rohit said.

'Rohit, you had the best drag name!' Yousef was almost crying with laughter.

Rohit sat up and cupped his chest. 'Dixie,' he said, trying to look serious. 'Dixie Normos, pleased to meet you.'

The three of them fell about laughing.

Yousef was late for work the next morning. The night with the boys had gone on later than expected and he had slept in. Jess was waiting at the nurses' station looking thoroughly pissed off.

'I've already divided the jobs up for today,' she said curtly. 'Here's your list.' She handed him a sheet of paper and walked off. Yousef was too tired to reply. He scanned the list. Shit, he had to get blood from Mrs Greenberry. She had impossible veins. He went to the utility room to collect the equipment he needed. Jess was in there. Great.

'I, er, just need to get some things,' he said. The utility room was small. 'I can come back, if that's easier?'

Jess sighed. 'No, it's okay. I'm nearly done.' He stepped inside, letting the door close behind him. She was rummaging around in a drawer, taking some things out and putting them in a kidney dish.

'Are you . . . are you well?' he said, trying to fill the awkward silence.

'Fine, thank you,' she replied.

'I saw Rohit and Steve yesterday, they said hello,' he said. 'That's why I was late this morning.' Jess nodded, not saying anything. 'Do you see many people from uni?'

'Yousef, please let's not do this,' Jess said, not even looking at him. Yousef nodded. She closed the drawer and turned to leave. They both realized she would have to get past him to get to the door; there wasn't enough room for him to move out of the way completely. He pressed himself up against the wall, but despite his best efforts she still had to brush past. He caught her scent as she got closer. She still wore the same perfume she had done whilst they were at university, her hair gave off the floral notes of the same shampoo she always used, her lips looked just as soft as they had done on the first day he saw her. He moved his hand deliberately so it would brush against hers as she went to open the door. The skin-to-skin contact made his breath catch. She stopped but still didn't look at him. He gently brushed his fingers against hers; she didn't move hers out of the way. Her breathing quickened, and he could see the tiny flicker of the pulse in her neck. He felt it, the same electricity they had all those months ago. He just needed her to look at him, to look into his eyes.

'Jess,' he whispered. She closed her eyes. 'I need you to know—'

She jerked her hand away from his. 'I'm seeing someone, Yousef,' she said abruptly.

Yousef recoiled as if hit by a bullet. 'What?'

'His name is Jonathan, and he's a really decent bloke.' She pulled the door open. 'We both know there's no future in . . . this.' She slipped through the door, leaving Yousef alone.

He knew he had no right to be angry with Jess, but Yousef couldn't help it. How had she managed to move on from them whilst he felt he was stuck in a pit of darkness? Despite his mother's best efforts, Yousef couldn't move on so easily. He hadn't imagined the moment that had just passed between them. She had felt it too, that's why she was desperate to get away. He realized that no amount of time was going to dampen his feelings for her. He was miserable and she was the only person who could save him.

He gathered what he needed from the supply closet and headed back to the nurses' station to get Mrs Greenberry's notes.

'You spent an awfully long time in that utility room,' a voice from behind him said. He turned around. It was Monica, the ward sister.

'Just collecting my things,' he said, not interested in talking to her.

'Dr Ahmed, a word of caution, if I may,' Monica said. 'Most of us can forgive someone for breaking a girl's heart once. These things happen. But breaking it twice?' She looked him dead in the eyes. 'That's unforgivable.'

'Thanks for the advice, Sister. Perhaps we can keep things professional whilst at work?' Yousef's tone was harsher than he had meant it to be. He headed towards Mrs Greenberry, determined her veins wouldn't beat him this time.

'Love, you look dreadful,' Mrs Greenberry said, direct as always.

Yousef smiled at her. Mrs Greenberry had been on the ward for nearly a month following a fall where she had broken her hip. They had replaced the broken hip the next day and had been close to getting her home, but she had caught pneumonia, which had subsequently caused her kidneys to malfunction. She was now waiting for her kidney function to improve before she could go home, hence the blood tests.

'I'm not sure you want to be insulting someone who is about to take your blood, Mrs Greenberry,' Yousef replied, putting on his gloves.

'You're talking with the confidence of someone who didn't fail at getting it the last two times,' Mrs Greenberry said, cocking her head. 'Let's hope third time is a charm.' She held out her arm in anticipation. Yousef tied the tourniquet around it, waiting for a vein to declare itself.

'We'll just give it a few seconds,' he said, getting his needle and blood bottles ready.

'Don't worry, love, I'm not going anywhere,' Mrs Greenberry replied, clenching her fist.

He felt her antecubital fossa for any signs of a vein. When he thought he felt one he carefully angled his needle and guided it in. Bingo! Red liquid flowed back into the bottle. He sighed in relief.

'Success!' he said. 'Oh ye of little faith.'

Mrs Greenberry looked at him and smiled. 'I'm glad I'm not going to be your pin cushion today, well done.'

'Let's hope we get some good results, then we can get you home,' he replied.

'You know, Dr Ahmed, when you spend all day in bed in this hospital you become an expert in watching people.'

'Oh yeah?' Yousef replied, pressing a piece of cotton wool over where he had taken blood. 'What have you seen?'

'That ward clerk over there,' she said, nodding in the direction of Fiona, 'she flirts with anything with a pulse.'

Yousef laughed. Mrs Greenberry was right. 'Very astute.'

'That's not the only thing I've seen,' she said. 'I've noticed the way you look at Dr Pritchard. I don't blame you, she's a beautiful girl. You should ask her out.'

'Thanks, Mrs Greenberry, it's a little more complicated than that,' Yousef said.

'Whatever it is, I'm sure you'll find a way to sort it out. Take it from an old bird, life is much shorter than you think.'

Yousef managed to finish the rest of his jobs without having to speak to Jess. He sat at the nurses' station writing up the last of his notes, thinking about getting an early night, when Fiona cornered him.

'Hi, Yousef,' she said, leaning over the bench.

'Oh, hey, Fiona,' he replied, edging away slightly.

'What are you doing after work?' she asked seductively.

'Going home, why?'

'Don't suppose you're seeing Jess, are you?' She spoke slowly, letting her eyes linger.

He looked at her, startled. Why was everyone suddenly interested in him and Jess? 'No, why would I be seeing Jess?'

'Keep yer knickers on, she left her phone on the ward. Thought if you were seeing her, you could give it to her.' Fiona held up Jess's phone. It still had her old green phone cover on.

Yousef wondered if it had any messages from Jonathan on it.

'I'll just put it in my drawer and give it to her in the morning,' Fiona said.

'Wait, Jess lives in the doctors' accommodation across the road, right?' Yousef said. Fiona nodded. 'Well, I guess I could pop over once I've finished here and give it to her.'

Fiona gave him a smile. 'I thought you might want to do that.'

'I just don't want her to be without her phone all night,' Yousef said to Fiona.

'I'm sure you don't,' Fiona replied, giving him the phone. 'She's in flat forty-three.'

You're just going to give her the phone and leave, he said to himself. *It's a nice gesture, that's all.* He knocked on the door; there was no answer. He knocked again, harder this time. He heard footsteps from inside. He took a step backwards.

Jess opened the door. 'Yousef, what are you doing here?'

'I just . . . you left this on the ward.' He held up her phone. 'I thought you'd want it back.'

She took the phone from him. 'Thanks,' she said. 'I guess I'll see you tomorrow.' She went to close the door but Yousef pushed it back.

'Jess, wait,' he said.

'Yousef, I don't have time,' she said, trying to close the door again. 'Thanks for bringing my phone over.'

It was now or never. 'I still love you!' he blurted out.

Her eyes widened.

'I know you're seeing someone, and I have no right to tell you this after everything that has happened, but I needed you to know.' His confession had caught even him by surprise. He had had no intention of saying any of this to her, but the second he saw her, he'd realized she had to know.

'Yousef, why are you telling me this?' Jess replied. 'You're the one who ended things with me.'

'I know, and it's not that I think we should get back together again but keeping this inside, seeing you every day, it's been driving me crazy.' Yousef was panting between words. 'I just thought you should know.'

'Why, Yousef, why do you think I should know?' Jess turned and walked into her flat. Yousef followed her. 'What the hell do you expect me to say? What do you want me to do?'

'I don't know, I don't know,' Yousef said, his mind racing. He could feel the beginnings of electricity between them again. He wanted her. He took a step towards her. She didn't move away. 'You feel it too,' he whispered.

Jess looked at him. 'Yousef, I'm with someone.'

He touched her cheek with his thumb. His whole body filled with yearning. It all felt so familiar. He took her hand in his, fingers interlocked. He was lost in her. He slowly moved his head towards hers and she closed her eyes as he brought his lips to hers, softly first, just brushing up against hers, tasting her. A sudden wave of desire took hold as he pressed his lips harder against hers. Her mouth opened as their tongues collided passionately. Her breathing became louder as he kissed her neck.

'Yousef, we shouldn't,' she whispered, holding on to him tighter.

'Do you want me to stop?' he said, finding his favourite spot on her neck and gently working it with his mouth. She grabbed his face, looking him in his eyes. She kissed him again, harder, unbuttoning his shirt. He closed his eyes as she kissed his chest and unbuckled his belt. He pulled her up, leading her to the bedroom. He pulled her silk blouse over her head and unhooked her bra. Her skin on his felt good when he pressed up against her as they fell on the bed. She felt exquisite. There was a hunger between them, a sense of urgency. He made love to her in a way that felt better than any of their previous times. He wanted to feel every bit of it, wanted her to remember how good they still were together and he needed her to know how much he wanted her.

They lay on the bed afterwards and he traced his fingers down her body.

'Yousef, you need to go,' she said suddenly, pulling away.

'What?' he asked, confused.

'Jonathan is coming over; you can't be here,' she said, sitting up. She looked around for her underwear.

'Your new boyfriend?' Yousef said, jealousy creeping in. 'Are you going to tell him you slept with another man?'

'And are you going to tell your mother you just had sex with a white girl?' Jess replied. Yousef flinched. 'No, I didn't think so. Leave, please.'

'What if I do tell her, Jess?' Yousef said. He didn't want to leave. 'Will that change things for us?'

'Yousef, I can't do this again. I'm not here to coach you through becoming a fucking man.' Jess pulled on her skirt. 'For God's sake, you should stand up for yourself for you, not for me.'

Yousef put on his clothes.

'Jess, I need to know, can we make this work?' he pleaded as she ushered him out of the flat.

'No, Yousef, this is not going to work. This was a mistake, I'm sorry.' She closed the door, leaving him in the corridor alone.

★

He drove home. His mother would be wondering why he was late, but he didn't care. He was determined to tell her about Jess. Maybe then Jess would see he was serious. His parents would scream and shout, they might even chuck him out of the house, but would that be such a bad thing? He could afford to live on his own, and then he would have a place where Jess could come around. He pulled up to his house, fire running through his veins.

His family were all in the living room watching *Catchphrase*. They didn't notice him come in.

'In for a penny, in for a pound!' Rehana shouted at the television. 'God, all the contestants are stupid this week,' she said, 'I should really go on this show, I would win a fortune.'

They looked like any normal family watching TV, Yousef thought.

Rehana looked up. 'Oh, hey, bro,' she said, then turned back to the television.

'Yousef, I've made aloo keema, there is roti in the kitchen, I'll warm it up for you.' His mother got up. She looked at him as she got close. 'You are late. Is everything okay, beta?' she asked.

No, everything is not okay, he wanted to scream. *Everything is totally fucked up and it's all your fault.*

'Everything's fine, Mum,' he said. 'Just tired, that's all.'

'Well, have some dinner and get an early night.' She kissed him on the cheek before disappearing into the kitchen to prepare him a plate.

Yousef stood in the hallway, alone.

Chapter Twenty-Two

Rohit

ROHIT LOGGED ON TO the Apna Shaadis website and clicked on his profile. The tagline for the dating site was set in bold across the home screen:

MARRIAGES ARE MADE IN HEAVEN.

INTRODUCTIONS ARE MADE ONLINE.

It had never made sense to Rohit. He quickly skipped past it so he could check his inbox. No messages. That was the third day in a row. He sat back in his chair. The first few days on the website had been exciting, he'd had a flurry of messages from girls. He immediately found out why so many people had reservations about online marriage websites.

The first message he got was from Preetu273: **Hey babes, how much do accountants earn then?**

He hit delete. He wasn't prepared to be anyone's cash cow, and besides, he didn't actually earn that much yet.

MarriageMaterial21 sent: **You look hot, wanna chat?**

She was very attractive, so he immediately replied with a yes. She told him how much she fancied him and even offered to send him a few naughty pictures. It was exciting. Rohit couldn't quite believe someone like her could be interested in someone like him. Turned out he was being catfished. MarriageMaterial21 had eventually asked him to transfer £1,800 into her account to help her pay for some alleged emergency medical treatment she needed. When he declined, she became very aggressive. He blocked her.

Poonam34 had seemed more promising. She was a solicitor from York, not too far away. Like him, she lived at home with her parents and enjoyed going to the cinema, something he played up a little bit to impress her. She was looking for someone 'normal' and Rohit thought he fit that bill. But it turned out she was divorced with two kids. Rohit didn't mind, but his mother did. It was a strong 'no' from his family so he stopped messaging her.

He tried chatting to other girls, but they either ignored him or after a few polite messages disappeared. This was way more common than Rohit had anticipated. Maybe they had been chatting to other guys and decided to go with one of them. Whatever the reason, Rohit came to learn that being ghosted online was just as painful as being ghosted in real life.

Eventually the messages in his inbox had dried up. The problem was, online marriage websites were even more shallow than traditional arranged marriages. At least when parents were involved, he would be given the opportunity of a meeting. In the Wild West that was online dating, first impressions (looks) were everything, and sadly Rohit just didn't make a good first impression.

After hearing about Yousef's matchmaker lady, he had subtly tried to quiz his mum about the possibility of enlisting one for him.

'You know, Mum, Yousef's parents have got an aunty who calls herself a matchmaker involved to help him find a wife,' he had told her.

'Matchmaker?' his mum had scoffed. 'These people, they

profit off the desperation of parents. Nobody should be charging money to do God's work.'

'It's no different to paying for a subscription on a matrimonial website,' he countered.

'Beta, don't worry. We will find you a wife, and she will be lucky to have you.' She gave his cheek a squeeze, dashing any hopes Rohit had of getting the help of a matchmaker.

Amit was coming over tonight and would expect a progress update. Rohit had spent last night sending 'likes' to several different girls, hoping that the sheer volume would yield at least one response. Not one of them had sent him a 'like' back.

He was desperate. He perused the profiles of the girls who were currently online. He reluctantly dismissed the ones that were too pretty – he had stopped entertaining that fantasy. He also dismissed girls who were the wrong religion. He knew that was kind of racist but, once again, time was of the essence and he could do without the drama that would inevitably unfold if he tried to introduce his family to a non-Hindu girl. He found a profile of a girl named Kavita which had been recently added to the website and he hadn't yet managed to scare off. He sent her a 'hello'. He waited. Nothing. He was being too eager. He went downstairs to make himself a cup of tea, then when he felt enough time had passed he returned to the computer. The website told him she had seen his message, but she was no longer online. Great, he thought, she'd taken one look at his profile and it had been enough to make her log off. He switched off his computer. That was enough embarrassment for one day.

What if he never found a wife? He had tried every possible way and all he was left with was humiliation. Was he destined to live with his mother as a sad singleton for ever? He wondered if he should ask Yousef more about the matchmaker his family had employed but it didn't seem that his friend was having any more luck with that approach in any case.

The arrival of Amit and Priya with the kids sent his mother

into her usual spiral of excitement. Rohit really didn't want to see any of them – he knew there would only be one topic of conversation.

'Rohit, your brother is here,' his mum called from the bottom of the stairs. 'Come down!'

His nephews jumped on him the minute he appeared. It was a nice feeling. He scooped them both up and spun them around, making them laugh.

'Aw, you'll make such a good dad someday,' Priya said, watching them. 'You just need to get on with it.'

'How's it going, bro?' Amit enquired. 'Any luck with Apna Shaadis?'

Amit, Priya and his mother looked at him expectantly. He put the boys down and shook his head. 'Not yet, but there are a few girls I'm chatting with.'

'Don't do too much chatting, they'll friendzone you,' Priya said. 'Trust me, get on with meeting them.'

'It's not that easy,' he snapped back.

'Rohit, don't get cross,' his mother said. 'You know, he never talks about these things with me. I have to wait until you all come over to find out what's going on in my son's life.'

'That's because there's nothing to tell, Mum,' Rohit said.

'Bro, be honest, are you chatting with anyone who has serious potential?' Amit asked. Rohit shook his head. 'Not even seeing anyone for a bit of fun?'

'Amit!' Priya scolded. 'Is that the example you want to set for the twins?' She looked at the boys, who were busy playing with Lego.

'What?' Amit shrugged. 'I just want to know if we need to start exploring other avenues.'

Rohit frowned. 'What other avenues?'

The three of them looked at each other. 'Go on, Mum,' Amit said. 'Tell him.'

'Tell me what?' Rohit said, looking at his mother.

She looked a bit sheepish. 'I got a call from Uncle Anand last week. You know him, he's a friend of your Uncle Sunil, Roshni's dad.'

'Uncle Sunil in India?' Rohit asked.

'Yes, that's him.' His mother paused. 'Well, Uncle Sunil says Uncle Anand has a daughter, Anjali. They are looking for a husband for her.' She paused again.

'And where does Anjali live?' Rohit already knew the answer to this, but needed confirmation.

'Also India,' his mum said.

'So what, you want me to marry some freshie from India?' Rohit wanted to laugh. They couldn't be serious.

'What is *freshie*?' his mum said, looking confused.

'It means fresh off the banana boat,' Priya said. 'You know, like fresh off the boat from India, arriving here in the UK.'

'What banana boat?' his mum said. 'We didn't come on banana boat, we came on aeroplane.'

'It's just a saying, Mum,' Amit explained. 'Don't worry about it. Rohit, I had my reservations when Mum first told me about Anjali, but the more I think about it, the more I'm coming round to the idea.'

'Good, I'm glad you're over your reservations. Maybe you should marry her,' Rohit said.

'Rohit, don't be rude,' his mum scolded. 'We are only trying to help. You want to be single all of your life?'

He didn't.

'And the best thing is, she's a doctor, and has already applied for a work visa to come here,' Priya said. 'She seems really nice.'

Amit gave Priya a look. She had said too much.

'Wait, how do you know she's nice?' Rohit eyed up his sister-in-law. 'In fact, why is everyone in on this except me?'

'Rohit, I just wanted to see what your family thought of her first before coming to you,' his mum said. 'Everybody agrees, she seems like a good girl.'

'It sounds like you've already made up your mind. Shall I book the temple?' He was pissed off that he had only been brought in at this stage.

'At least look at her picture, talk to her on the FaceTime, will that do you any harm?' His mother got up and took out an envelope from her handbag. 'See, she is beautiful.' Rohit really did want to take a look but he wasn't giving in that easily. He folded his arms in protest.

'Rohit, be honest, it's not like you have any better offers,' Amit said, sounding like he was fed up of the entire conversation. 'Mum's worried about you. I'm worried about you. Having a family, it gives you a whole new purpose.' He nodded towards the twins.

Stupid Amit and his perfect family, Rohit thought.

He considered what was being proposed. If he put his prejudice against freshies to one side, was this really any different to what he had imagined the arranged marriage process would be like? As far as he could tell, there was no girl in the UK willing to give him the time of day, so maybe he did need to cast his net wider. He picked up the envelope his mum had placed down on the sofa next to him and pulled out the photo. It was a picture of Anjali at a restaurant. She was far prettier than the girls he dared to approach here. And a doctor? He had no chance of bagging one of those in the UK. Okay, he would give this a go.

'Has she seen my picture?' he asked. He didn't want to say yes at this stage only to be rejected at the first hurdle.

'She has and she wants to chat to you,' his brother replied.

That surprised him. 'Okay, then I'm prepared to talk to her,' Rohit said.

'Fantastic, I will tell Uncle Anand to let Uncle Sunil know,' his mum said, clasping her hands.

Chapter Twenty-Three

Feroza

FEROZA WAS FEELING VERY smug. She had just finished a call with Aunty Henna. That stuck-up family from Shropshire had rung to say their daughter, Seema, was interested and wanted to come to Birmingham to visit them. That was certainly unexpected. She had thought Aleena was perceptive enough to know it would never work out between their children. Of course, she had told Henna she would think about it, but she already knew she was going to decline them. They were not the right family for her son. She would ring Henna in a couple of days, pretend she had spoken with Abdul and Yousef and tell her that they weren't interested.

Finding Rehana a match was proving trickier; she had refused to talk about what had happened on her coffee dates and the new match Henna had sent her was not up to standard. She knew she shouldn't have let her meet those boys alone.

One thing both of her children would certainly have to learn before they got married was how to clean up after themselves. Since Rehana had started at the school, Feroza was back to making dinner for the family. Not only that, she was always left clearing up after they had finished eating. Rehana said she had marking to do and Yousef sloped up to his room without saying much. She assumed it was because he was working so hard at the hospital. She collected their dinner plates and placed them in the sink. She let the tap run so the water could warm up. A buzzing sound from the kitchen counter caught her attention. It was Yousef's phone. He had left it downstairs.

She dried her hands on the towel and picked up the phone, 'Yousef!' she shouted. She wasn't going upstairs. If he wanted his phone, he could come down and get it himself.

'He's in the shower!' Rehana's voice shouted back.

Feroza went to put the phone down on the counter, looking at the screen.

One new message: Jessica

Feroza hadn't heard Yousef mention anyone by that name before. She wondered if she was someone from work. She placed the phone down on the counter and headed back to the sink. Who was Jessica? She looked back at the phone. Feroza knew that even for the most meddling of Pakistani mums, looking through your child's messages was a step too far. She couldn't resist. She went into the hallway – the sound of running water told her Yousef was still in the shower. She picked the phone up. It was locked. *There should be no secrets between a mother and her son*, she thought. She thought for a moment and typed in 1, 2 ,3, 4.

Incorrect password, you have two more attempts.

She quickly wracked her brain for other combinations. Yousef's year of birth! She pressed it in.

Incorrect password. You have one more attempt.

Allah, help me! She thought desperately again. What could it be? Then it came to her. Whenever they travelled to Pakistan, she insisted they put padlocks on their suitcases. Abdul told her it was pointless. If anybody wanted to steal their suitcase, a tiny padlock would be easy to break. Nevertheless, it gave Feroza the sense of an extra layer of security with the padlocks on. They all had the same combination, the first four digits of their landline number. She pressed it in.

The phone unlocked, revealing the message.

Jessica: Yousef, we need to talk about what happened the other night. I know I'll probably regret saying this, but I still have feelings for you too. Can you talk?

Feroza tightened her grip on Yousef's phone, reading the message over and over again. Who was this Jessica? What feelings was she talking about? And what had happened the other night? Whatever was going on between this girl and her son, it didn't sound good. She realized she had been holding her breath. She sat down on one of the chairs and breathed out. She had to think fast. She scrolled upwards to see if there were any other messages from this girl. The last one had been sent over a year ago.

Jessica: Don't ever contact me again.

Above that

Yousef: Jess, I'm so sorry, I really didn't mean to hurt you.

She scrolled up further. There were some messages about exam results and meetings, then:

Yousef: I love you, can't wait until you're in my bed tonight.
Jess: Love you too, I'm on my way!

She kept scrolling, more and more messages going back years. Some of them obscene. And pictures. A picture of her Yousef holding hands with a girl, laughing with her. Others where the two of them were with groups of friends. She recognized Rohit and Steve in some of the pictures. Then a picture of her Yousef kissing the same girl. On the lips.

Letting out a cry of anguish, she threw the phone onto the kitchen table as if it had turned white hot. She felt sick. Yousef couldn't possibly have sent all those filthy messages, not her Yousef. He was a good boy. Clearly this girl had corrupted him in some way. Yes, that is what had happened, this girl had somehow got her claws into her Yousef and made him think these horrible things.

She wouldn't stand by and let some gori lead her son astray, not when she had worked so hard to get him to this point. She heard Yousef come out of the shower. She grabbed the phone, scrolled down to the message that had just come in and deleted it. There, he would never see it. She carefully placed the phone back on the kitchen counter it had been on.

Feroza knew deleting the message wouldn't be enough, she needed to free Yousef from the grips of the devil. She retrieved her own mobile and dialled Henna's number.

'Salaam, Henna, it's Feroza,' she said when she heard Henna's voice.

'Feroza, I didn't expect you to call so quickly. Is everything okay?'

'Yes, fine, thank you.' Feroza didn't want to waste time. 'I have spoken with both my son and husband, and we would really like it if Aleena, Kamran and Seema came over this weekend for dinner.'

'That is wonderful news,' Henna said. 'I can hear the wedding dohl now! I am never wrong about these things.'

'So, you will let them know? Saturday four o'clock,' Feroza asked. She wasn't in the mood for chit-chat.

'Yes, I'll phone them now,' Henna replied. 'You sure you're okay? You sound . . . different.'

'Fine, just excited about this rishta, that's all,' Feroza said.

She hung up the phone. Seema and her family might be the whitest Asian family Feroza had ever met, but at least they weren't actually white.

Feroza wondered where she had gone wrong. She had worked so hard to instil her religion and traditions in her children. She knew there would be compromises bringing them up here in the UK, but this was too much. She thought about telling Abdul, but decided against it in case he said they should ask Yousef about Jessica. She didn't want to have any kind of conversation about that girl. No, she would sort this out herself.

Yousef appeared in the doorway.

'Mum, were you calling me before?' he asked.

She stared at him. He still looked like her little boy. What had that girl done to him?

'You left your phone downstairs,' she said.

'Right, thanks.' He picked it up and headed towards the door.

'Yousef?' she called.

'Yes?'

'That family from Shropshire, with the daughter, Seema. They rang, they want to come over to see us on Saturday.' She looked at him for a reaction.

'Fine,' he said, not giving anything away. When had he become so good at lying?

'I've changed my mind about her, I like her,' Feroza continued. 'I think the two of you are a good match.' Yousef nodded and went upstairs.

Feroza wanted to cry, but she had to stay strong. She pressed down her emotions. She had made too many sacrifices to fall apart now. She had work to do. There was no time for Yousef to start again with other girls, Seema would have to do. She would do everything in her power to ensure this marriage went ahead.

Chapter Twenty-Four

Rehana

REHANA STARED AT THE picture her mum had given her. 'No thanks, Mum, this one's not for me.' The man had a full beard, and not one of those trendy lumberjack ones that come with a set of full arm tattoos, but a patchy religious one *and* he was wearing an Islamic skull cap. His profile said he had gone to Mecca and completed the holy pilgrimage of Hajj, prayed five times a day and worked in the 'charity sector' (whatever that meant). 'He'll want me to wear a hijab and cover up head to toe, and you know I can't do that, I get far too hot.'

'Rehana, don't make assumptions. But I agree, you do sweat a lot,' her mother said, but Rehana could tell that even her heart wasn't in this match. 'I wish you would tell me what happened with those coffee shop boys,' her mum said for the millionth time. 'I really had high hopes for you there.'

'Nothing happened, Mum,' she replied. 'They just weren't right for me.'

'That's because you are being too choosy,' her mum retorted. 'Next time I will accompany you on all meetings. The sooner I get you and your brother married, the sooner I will be free of this stress.'

It had been four days and Nadeem still hadn't replied to her message. She found him on Instagram, but his account was private and he hadn't accepted her follow request. It was the same on Facebook. She was beginning to feel a bit stalkerish. The temptation to message him again grew stronger every day. She just wanted him to know that she wasn't this 'player' he had her down as. After another talk with Emma, she decided she had nothing to lose by texting him one last time:

> *Rehana:* Hi Nadeem, how are you? I wonder if we could start over? No games.

She pressed send, then immediately threw her phone on the sofa opposite. She didn't want to keep staring at it, waiting for him to message her back. It buzzed almost straight away.

> *Nadeem:* Hi. Okay, no more games, family meeting?

Rehana couldn't believe it. Religious Guy was no longer her only hope.

> *Rehana:* Sure, shall I get my mum to call your mum?

You'd think, as a grown woman, she would feel silly sending such a message, but she had fallen so far down the arranged marriage rabbit hole, it seemed completely normal.

> *Nadeem:* Perfect, I leave next week so the sooner the better.
> *Rehana:* 👍

'Mum!' Rehana said excitedly. 'Coffee shop guy has texted me, he wants to bring his family over.'

'Which coffee shop guy?' her mum asked. 'The dentist?'

Rehana had forgotten there were two. 'Nadeem, from Dubai.' Her mum still looked confused. 'The software engineer, Mum, keep up!'

Her dad came in. 'What's going on?'

'One of Rehana's coffee shop boys wants to come over with his family,' her mum said.

'The dentist?' her dad said, sounding interested.

'No, Dad, the software engineer and can we please stop referring to people by their occupation? His name is Nadeem,' Rehana replied.

'You like this boy?' Her dad looked at her.

'I don't know, maybe,' she said, suddenly embarrassed to be talking about boys with her dad.

'Then we must invite them over!' He looked at his wife. 'Feroza?'

'We have Seema and her family coming on Saturday, I suppose we could do Sunday,' her mum replied, pretending to look exasperated.

'Great, Sunday is perfect!' Rehana said. 'Ring Aunty Henna now, I don't want them to book something else in on the Sunday.'

'What does a software engineer do exactly?' her mum asked.

The three of them looked at each other blankly.

'It's something to do with computers?' Rehana said, not entirely sure.

'Will he have a good salary?' her mum replied.

'He's almost saved up enough money to buy a house,' Rehana said.

'Mashallah,' her dad muttered.

'I'll phone Aunty Henna now,' her mum replied, 'before he gets snapped up by someone else.'

Rehana's stomach was doing cartwheels. She ran upstairs and flopped on her bed, picking up her phone.

Rehana: Looks like Sunday afternoon for our family meeting.
Nadeem: Great, looking forward to it.

Rehana let out an excited yelp. She had three days to decide what to wear. This Sunday she was going to look on point.

Chapter Twenty-Five

Jessica

JESS LAY ON HER bed plagued with guilt. It had only been a couple of months since she had been seeing Jonathan, and they were yet to have the boyfriend/girlfriend chat, but he was completely devoted to her. He would send her messages in the morning telling her to have a good day, pictures of the funny things he saw on his way to work and he even sent a surprise bunch of flowers to the ward on her birthday. Plus, there was no drama, no weird secrets and, most importantly, no family to contend with.

So why then was Yousef lying naked in her bed, again? She turned to watch him sleep, rage and lust battling for dominance in her head. This was complicated and messy. She should run a mile but she didn't feel like this when she was with Jonathan. She had history with Yousef, not all of it good, but there was comfort in being around him.

She had been mad at Yousef earlier that day for not responding to her message. Their shift on the ward had come to an end, and since he wasn't going to bring it up, she decided to confront him.

'I suppose you think the other day was a mistake then?' she said as she ran to catch up with him leaving the ward.

'What? No, of course not,' he replied. 'I thought you thought it was a mistake. You kicked me out of your place so quickly, I assumed you didn't want anything to do with me.'

'Really? Then why didn't you reply to my message?' She couldn't be arsed with his bullshit.

'What message? I didn't get a message from you.' He looked confused.

She pulled out her phone from her bag and brought up the message. 'This message.' He looked at her phone and then took his out.

'I didn't get it, look.' He showed her, the message wasn't there.

'That's weird,' she said quietly.

'Can we talk now?' he asked. She nodded.

Jess had a clear plan in her head. She needed some honesty. If there was a serious future with Yousef, she needed to know and she would end it with Jonathan.

They sat on opposite sides of the sofa.

'Jess, the other day when we . . . Well, I just want you to know it's not about just that for me. I haven't been happy since we split up,' Yousef started. 'Seeing you again, it confirmed what I already knew.'

'And what's that?' Jess replied.

'That I love you,' he whispered. Jess felt her heart rate quicken. She looked at him. She knew he found it hard to talk about his feelings. It was one of the things that had frustrated her about him. She wasn't prepared to say she loved him back; she wasn't sure yet. 'I've really missed you,' he said.

'What about your family?' she asked. 'What about your mother?'

'It will be hard, but they will have to accept it,' he replied. He moved closer to her. 'This last year I have done everything my family have wanted, and it's left me feeling . . . angry, just constantly angry.'

His hand brushed up against hers. Electric shocks pulsed

through her body. She had missed him too; not just the sex, but their conversations. She missed talking to him about random things from politics to movies. They used to talk all night, often disagreeing with each other. She missed that passion.

'So, you'll tell them?' she said.

He nodded, his face so close she could taste his breath. He kissed her. Well, that was it. They had fallen into bed again, and here she was staring at him whilst he slept.

He must have sensed her staring at him, as he opened one eye and smiled. 'Hi,' he said. 'I must have dozed off. What time is it?'

'Almost ten o'clock.'

He bolted up. 'Shit, my mother will be wondering where I am. Have you seen my phone?'

Jess felt a coldness pass through her. Why was his first thought his mother and not her? 'It's on the table, over there.' He got up and began frantically typing.

'What are you doing, Yous?' she asked.

'Telling my mum that I've had to cover part of the night shift,' he said, pressing send on his phone.

'So, you're lying? Again,' she said flatly.

'No, not lying, just trying to . . . I don't know, keep the peace or whatever.'

'Keep the fucking peace?' God, she had been so stupid. 'Why can't you just tell her the truth? I'm not some sort of dirty secret.'

'No, it's not like that, Jess,' he said, coming to sit next to her. 'I am going to tell her, but the time has to be right, and it can't be via a bloody text message.'

She paused. It was so confusing having him here. Was she overreacting? She couldn't expect him to tell his mother on the phone right now, but the fact that he was so quick to lie spooked her.

'I promise, when the time is right, I'll tell her.' He kissed her. She felt heady with his scent. They made love again. After he left, she texted Jonathan. She couldn't string him along any further.

Jess: Can I can come over?

He texted back almost immediately.

Jonathan: Out with the boys, catch up on the weekend?

She had forgotten he was out tonight; it was a relief, if she was being honest. Telling Jonathan would have to wait.

Chapter Twenty-Six

Yousef

THERE WAS A HIVE of activity going on in the kitchen when Yousef arrived home. His mum was supervising Rehana frying pakoras whilst his dad was slicing up mangoes on the table.

'Hey, Yous,' Rehana said, smiling at her brother. 'Have some pakoras, they're fresh. Mum says they need more salt, but I think they taste pretty good.'

'Thanks,' Yousef said, taking one.

'Did the night shift doctor get his car fixed?' his mum asked.

Yousef nodded. 'Yeah, they got a taxi in the end.' His mum gave him a funny look, then turned her attention back to Rehana. He looked around the kitchen. They had been busy. There were platters of samosas, kebabs, cholay and roasted chicken drumsticks. 'What's going on? Why is there so much food?' he asked.

'Look, he has forgotten already!' his dad said, laughing. 'Seema and her family are coming over tomorrow. Your mum wanted to make a good impression.'

'Is that tomorrow?' he said, slightly thrown by how quickly it had come around. He caught his mum looking at him again. Why was she looking at him like that?

'You sure you're okay, beta?' his dad asked. 'Maybe you have been working too hard?'

'Yeah, fine,' he said to his dad. 'Mum, can I talk to you for a minute?' He had to tell her first, then he would break it to his dad and Rehana.

'Yousef, I can't talk now, I am very busy,' his mother replied. 'You saw the spread they put out for us. I won't be outdone.'

'But Mum, I really need to speak to you. It's urgent,' he said. He was beginning to feel anxious. He just needed to get it done, like ripping off a plaster.

He saw his mum tense up. 'No, Yousef!' she said sharply. 'Whatever it is will have to wait. We have a busy weekend ahead of us. First Seema is coming tomorrow and then Nadeem and his family are coming to see Rehana on Sunday.' She gave him another pointed look. 'It's an important weekend for your sister too, nothing can spoil it.'

'Mum, but I really need to talk,' he pleaded.

'No, I have said no and that is that,' his mother snapped. 'Can't you see I'm busy?'

'Yousef, are you okay?' his dad asked. 'Whatever it is, I am sure you can tell all of us?'

Yousef stayed silent.

'Bro, less chat and more help, please. We're cooking all this stuff for you and this girl,' Rehana said. 'Put your surgical skills to good use and chop those onions over there.'

Perhaps he should just tell his dad instead. He caught his mother watching him. She quickly manoeuvred herself between him and his father. 'Here, drink this,' she said, handing him a glass of water.

'What is it?' he replied, taking the glass from her.

'I rang the Islam channel today. There was a special scholar on, he was taking calls from viewers. I rang up and asked for a prayer that would help you find a good Muslim wife.' She gave him that strange look again. 'Someone who will help you.'

'Help me with what?' he asked. What was she talking about?

'Help you in life, show you the right path,' his mother replied, returning to supervising Rehana.

'How come he gets all the prayers and not me?' Rehana asked.

'Because he needs them more,' his mother said curtly.

What was she on about? Yousef watched as his family busied themselves with preparing the food. He felt the heat of anger beginning to rise in his stomach again. His grip tightened on the glass. He tried to take deep breaths to calm himself down, but it didn't work. He threw the glass against the wall; the sound of it shattering brought everyone to a stop. The water dripped down the tiles onto the floor.

'I HATE THIS FAMILY!' he shouted, slamming the door as he left and went up to his room. He could hear his dad calling after him.

Then his mother, 'Leave him, let him calm down.'

He shut his bedroom door. There would never be a good time to tell them; he just had to get it over with. He couldn't live in this house any longer, he needed to be with Jess. His family were beginning to feel like a noose around his neck. The more he did to appease them, the more they expected, all the while the noose got tighter and tighter. He closed his eyes, head pounding. If he didn't tell his family now, then he would once again be the villain in his and Jess's story. He couldn't be without Jess, but could he be without his family?

He picked up his phone and texted Rohit:

Yousef: Just tried to tell Mum about Jess. She shut it down, told me to pray instead. What shall I do?

He waited, seeing Rohit was typing.

Rohit: Just pull the plaster off, no matter when or how you do it, it's going to sting like a motherfucker. JUST DO IT.

There was a knock at the door. He didn't respond.

'Yousef?' Rehana's voice said, sounding tentative. 'Can I come in?'

Yousef got up to open the door. 'What do you want?'

'Are you okay?' she asked, following him in. 'Did something happen at work?'

Yousef lay down on the bed. 'I suppose you could say that.' He closed his eyes. He just wanted to sleep and make the whole thing disappear.

'What is it, Yous?' she asked. 'Did something bad happen to one of your patients?'

'No, no, it's nothing like that.' Yousef wondered whether he should just tell Rehana. He had planned to tell his mum first but she clearly wasn't interested. Perhaps Rehana could help him break it gently to his parents. 'It's Jess.'

'Jess?' Rehana frowned. 'Your old girlfriend Jess?'

He nodded. 'We're working on the same ward together.'

'So, what, is it awkward? Is she making it difficult for you?' his sister asked.

'In a way, yes,' he replied. 'It's complicated . . . well, actually, it's not. We still like each other, like really like each other. We want to be together.'

Rehana remained silent.

'Say something then,' he said.

'Is that why you wanted to talk to Mum just now?' she eventually said.

'Yes, I have to tell her. I know it's going to be shitty, but I need to do it.' He sat up, assessing his sister for a reaction. She got up and began pacing the room. 'Rehana, I love her,' he said quietly. She stopped.

'You can't tell them,' she said resolutely. 'Not right now anyway.'

'What?' he said, taken aback.

'You cannot tell Mum and Dad about Jessica,' she said slowly.

'What do you mean?' he replied. He was confused. 'Didn't you hear what I just said? I love her, it's driving me crazy.'

'I heard it, Yousef!' she snapped. 'And you cannot tell them.'

'Rehana, what are you saying? Aren't you on my side?'

'On your side?' she said, looking at him. 'Yousef, I told you years ago that you needed to come clean to Mum and Dad about your relationship with Jess, but oh no, you wanted to play the martyr, saying they would never understand.' She began pacing again. 'But the truth is, you never gave them a fucking chance to understand.'

He didn't understand why Rehana was being like this. 'But I want to tell them now,' he insisted.

'Oh, you want to tell them now, do you?' She gave a cynical laugh. 'Honestly, Yousef, you're such a selfish prick.'

'Rehana, what the hell are you on about?'

'I have spent my entire life on the sidelines of this family, watching Mum laud praise over you all the while throwing me the odd crumb.' She looked at him, lips curled in disgust. 'I've even learned to cook a full fucking Pakistani dinner to impress her, but still all she cares about is how your day at work was.'

'What does any of this have to do with me and Jess?' Yousef asked.

'Because I have finally found a guy that I actually like and for once in my life, he likes me back, and you pick the weekend he's coming over to drop your bombshell and ruin the entire thing.' Her words were coming out quickly now.

'But this has nothing to do with that,' Yousef said. He didn't understand.

'That's because you're only interested in what's happening in your life,' she replied.

He continued to look confused.

'Look, Yousef, if you tell Mum and Dad about Jess tonight, then it's going to fuck up the entire weekend,' Rehana explained. 'Do you think you can say all of that stuff and then expect us to return to playing happy families? No, it will devastate the pair of them, and then they will be in no shape to meet Nadeem and his family on Sunday.'

'Nadeem, that's the guy you like?' Yousef asked.

'Yes,' Rehana said, suddenly sounding shy. 'Like you, Yousef, I just want a life of my own too. I love Mum and Dad but living in this house is like living in the world's worst house share. I need an out.'

'And what about this girl coming on Saturday for me? Am I supposed to just go along with the pretence?' he asked.

'Bro, you have been going along with it up until now, what difference does an extra few days make?' she challenged him. 'I'm not like you, Yousef, I don't have matches throwing themselves at me. This may be the only chance I get.'

'So what? I just wait until you get your happily ever after before I can get mine?' He still couldn't believe Rehana was being so unsupportive.

'Don't you get it?' Rehana said. 'I have nothing against you and Jess, but news travels fast in this bloody Pakistani community. The darling doctor son running off with a white girl is the kind of thing the aunties will be salivating over. Nadeem's family will find out and then that'll be it for me.'

'Rehana, what am I supposed to do?'

'Yousef, you had your time to tell Mum about Jess, and you didn't. That's on you,' she said, heading towards the door. 'Now it's my turn. Don't ruin it for me. At least not this weekend. Not until things are settled.' She left.

Yousef thought about what his sister had said. Was he being selfish by telling his parents about Jess? He hadn't thought about his sister's feelings in any of this. It didn't matter what the reasons were, he knew Jess wouldn't understand if he delayed things further. Yousef checked his phone. No new messages from Jess. She had been strangely quiet since he had last seen her. He was tired of feeling caught between a rock and a hard place. He just wanted to stop having to think about everyone else and do what he wanted to do. But that was the very definition of selfish. Rehana was right. He fell into a restless sleep.

Chapter Twenty-Seven

Seema

IT WAS THE THIRD time Seema's dad had driven up Yousef's street; there was nowhere to park. Cars were parked bumper to bumper all along the road. 'It doesn't matter how many times you circle, Dad, a space isn't going to magically appear,' she said. 'Just park on the next road, there were plenty of spaces there.'

'And then what, walk?' her mum scoffed. She was peering out of the window. 'Who knew I had to bring my walking shoes for inner-city Birmingham.'

Seema ignored her. She wasn't going to let her mother or this sad-looking street bring her down. It didn't matter where Yousef lived now. After they were married, they could live out in the suburbs somewhere. Birmingham must have some nice places, she thought. Seema was surprised at how much time she had spent thinking of Yousef. She thought of what life would be like with him, what her first name would sound like with his last name. Everyone in her friend circle was getting married and there was nothing sadder than being the only single person at a wedding. Besides, Yousef wasn't like the other boys she had dated at university who had been cocky and confident; there was something quietly vulnerable about him and she wanted to get underneath it. She never really thought she would go for the silent, mysterious type but here she was, standing outside his door feeling nervous about seeing him again.

Her parents remained apprehensive and suggested she keep her options open. They even showed her a photograph of a paediatrician from Cardiff, but she wasn't interested. She preferred to focus her attention on the one boy she actually liked and see where that took her.

She was usually a confident girl, the one the boys chased and were desperate to impress, but today she felt she had to make a good impression on Yousef and his family. Yousef's mum opened the door and greeted them all. Seema had brought brownies from their village bakery. She had transferred them to a plate to make it look like she had baked them herself. She handed them over to Yousef's mum.

'Oh, you shouldn't have,' Yousef's mum said, inspecting the brownies. 'Are they homemade?' Seema nodded. *It's not as bad if you didn't actually say yes*, she thought.

Her mother was looking around the hallway, unable to hide her disdain. 'Do you mind if we keep our shoes on?' her mother asked of Yousef's mum. 'It's just that I'm not wearing any socks.'

Yousef's mum hesitated; she wasn't wearing any socks either. To be honest, the carpet did look a little grubby. Yousef's mum smiled. 'Of course,' she said. 'Whatever is more comfortable for you.' They followed her into the living room. Yousef and his dad were already in there. They got up as everyone greeted each other.

'Please, sit down.' Yousef's dad gestured to the sofas. Seema took a seat next to her mum; she could feel a spring from the worn-out sofas jabbing her in the backside.

'How was your week?' she asked.

Strangely, Yousef looked immediately uncomfortable. It was a simple enough question. 'Okay, I guess.' He ran his hand through his hair. 'Busy. I'm glad it's the weekend.'

'Yeah, mine too, my consultant is a real slave driver.' She laughed. 'He always leaves me with a huge list of jobs.' There was an awkward moment of silence. Seema looked at the pictures on the wall. They were all of Yousef. He had even been gorgeous as a teenager. 'Is that you dressed as a Roman?' she asked, pointing at one of the pictures.

'Doesn't he look handsome?' Yousef's mum said proudly. 'Yousef got the lead as Julius Caesar in the school drama production. First Pakistani boy to play the lead in the school's history. It wiped the smile off that Jason's face, I can tell you.'

'Who's Jason?' Seema's mum asked.

'Jason got the lead in all of the school plays,' Yousef's mum explained. 'Thought he was bloody Shah Rukh Khan.'

'Who's Shah Rukh Khan?' Seema's mum asked, looking bewildered.

Yousef's mum let out a gasp, 'Who is Shah Rukh Khan?'

Seema rolled her eyes. 'Mum, even I know who that is, he's like a huge Bollywood actor.'

'We don't watch Bollywood in our house,' Seema's dad said. 'Far too dramatic.'

Seema decided to change the subject. 'It smells delicious in here, Aunty,' she said, putting on her best smile. 'I hope you didn't go to too much trouble.'

'Not too much trouble at all. I hope you enjoy what we have prepared, it is all very traditional. Do you cook?' she asked.

'Erm, well . . .' Seema did not cook. 'I can make a great tuna pasta bake,' she said. It was all she had eaten at university.

'We don't really believe in gender stereotypes in our family,' Seema's mum cut in. 'Seema can, of course, learn to cook if that is what she chooses, but we don't force her to do so.'

Seema could see that Yousef's mum was put out by the remark. She looked at her husband for support, who sat there silently.

'Well, I enjoy cooking dinner for my family,' she said. 'I don't think that is a gender stereotype, I like to think of it as being a good mother.'

Shit, this conversation was not going well. Seema knew her mum had strong feelings on sexism in Pakistani culture. It was one of the reasons they had no Pakistani friends. She tried to intercept. 'You know, Aunty, I would love to learn how to cook traditional Pakistani food,' she said. 'I think it's a lost art in my generation.'

'That is wonderful. Who knows, I could even be your teacher! I taught Rehana to cook.' Yousef's mum gave her a smile. Seema looked at Yousef, who was looking more uncomfortable by the minute. 'Why don't you and Yousef go and talk in the other room?' his mum said. 'I will prepare the food.'

Yes! Getting Yousef to herself was what she'd been hoping for. She followed him into a small snug-like room. Seema wasn't the type of girl to act coy. She liked Yousef, but wasn't used to being the one doing the chasing. It was about time he showed some interest too.

'Yousef, are you okay?' she asked, hoping to catch him off guard.

It worked. He bristled at the question. 'Yeah, sorry, just a lot going on . . . at work.'

'I'm going to be straight with you,' she said. 'I didn't think much of this arranged marriage malarky, I just went along with it for my grandad. He has cancer, and this was one of his requests.'

'I'm sorry about your grandad,' he said, looking at his hands.

'It's shit, but it does give him the leverage to use it as emotional blackmail.' She laughed and Yousef did too. The tension in the room evaporated.

'Asian families are world-class experts in emotional blackmail,' he said.

'Even us, the least Asian of Asian families,' she replied. Good, she had his attention now. Seema wasn't stupid; she knew she was an attractive girl. She just needed Yousef to keep looking at her and she could take care of the rest. She played with a loose strand of hair. 'Anyway, my family turned to one of those matchmakers, same as yours did.'

'The ones that charge an arm and a leg,' Yousef confirmed.

'Yep, turns out you can put a price on love,' she replied. 'Anyway, here we are and if this is going to go . . . I don't know, anywhere, we have to get to know each other and see if we are compatible. I don't like wasting my time.' She held his eye contact.

'Okay,' he said. 'What does that involve?'

'Well, first you have to actually do some talking,' she said, trying to sound jovial. 'The strong silent type might work in movies, but not for arranged marriages. Time is limited, decisions need to be made. Talk to me.'

'What do you want to know?'

'I don't know, your favourite movie, the best place you've ever been on holiday. Do you see yourself leaving the family home after you get married? Do you want kids? If so, how many?'

'Wow, that's a broad range of questions,' Yousef replied. 'I'm going to need some time to think about the answers.'

'My point is, this whole process doesn't allow us to get to know each other in the same way other English couples might, so we have to cut to the chase.' She knew she was being bossy, but someone had to take control of this situation, and in her experience, men rarely took charge when they needed to.

'My favourite movie is *Jurassic Park*. I've only ever been to Pakistan on holiday and that wasn't really a holiday, it was to attend my cousin's wedding. I really do want to move out from here and, yes, I think I do want children, but not straight away,' Yousef said, sitting back in his chair.

'That's a start,' Seema replied. 'I've never seen *Jurassic Park*.'

'Whoa, you've never seen the greatest movie of all time!' Yousef cried, jolting up from his chair.

'No, it's about dinosaurs, why would I want to see that?'

'It's about so much more than dinosaurs!' Yousef was getting animated. Seema loved it. 'It's about man's fascination with playing God, it's about boundaries that need to be put down when facing the frontiers of science, it's about men putting profit before everything else!'

'Okay, but isn't it about people running away from terrifying dinosaurs?'

'Well, yes, there's a lot of that too, but that's a symptom of everything else I just said.' He sat down in his chair again. 'You're going to have to watch it.'

'Maybe we could watch it together?' Seema said softly. Yousef looked away. There was a knock on the door. Rehana poked her head in.

'Hi, Seema,' she said. 'You look lovely.' She came in and they hugged. 'Mum said dinner's ready.'

The food was so good that even her mother, who hated spicy foods, didn't complain. The dads seemed to be hitting it off, talking about the usual cricket and politics. It was a shame there was still an air of coolness between her mum and Yousef's, but she didn't have time to deal with that now, she wanted to make a good impression on her future mother-in-law.

'Aunty, you sit down,' she said when they had finished eating. 'Rehana and I will tidy up, you did all this cooking.'

'Well, actually, I helped too,' Rehana said. 'In fact, the only person who didn't help was Yousef, so maybe he can do the tidying up with you.'

'Rehana!' Yousef's mum said sharply. 'We don't allow our guests to clean up. Get up and start taking the dishes in.'

'Does Yousef not do any cooking or cleaning?' Seema's mum asked. 'Let me guess, it's a woman's job.'

Yousef stood up. 'Not at all, I'm happy to pitch in.' He grabbed some of the platters and took them into the kitchen. Seema smiled at her mother, who gave her evils.

'Aunty, I'm happy to help.' She followed Yousef into the kitchen carrying a pile of plates. 'That was a ballsy move, standing up to my mum.'

'She's kind of right, there are a lot of gender stereotypes going on in this house. In fact, there are so many traditional stereotypes going on in this house, sometimes it's hard to breathe.'

'What do you mean?' Seema asked.

Yousef turned to look at her. 'Seema, there's something you should know.' He looked to make sure there was nobody in the hallway listening. 'About this whole you and me thing, I really want to be honest with you—'

'Yousef!' Rehana's voice cut in loudly. 'There are more plates to come in. If you want to play the modern man, you have to finish the job.'

Yousef looked at Seema a beat longer and then left.

'Pay no attention to him,' Rehana said. 'He gets a bit awkward around girls he likes.' She opened up the dishwasher and began loading the plates.

'You think he likes me?' Seema asked, trying not to sound too desperate.

'Seema, have you seen you?' Rehana said. 'Any boy would be lucky to have you.'

'Yes, but do you think Yousef likes me?' she asked again. She didn't care about any of the other boys.

'Sure he does, he would be silly not to,' Rehana replied. Seema couldn't help smiling. Yousef was such a closed book, but if his sister said he liked her, then it must be true. 'Come on,' Rehana said, 'it's time for dessert. Mum's ras malai is literally to die for.'

✱

Seema was positively giddy on the way home. The conversation with Rehana played over and over in her head. It totally explained the awkwardness she felt when she was around Yousef. He simply didn't know *how* to act around a girl he liked. Poor boy, his family were so traditional, he had probably never even had a girlfriend before. She could cope with that. Being a bit socially awkward wasn't the worst trait in a husband; it was better than marrying a rabid flirt. She had been with boys who had cheated on her, boys who had the chat and the banter, and she knew how those relationships ended. Yousef would be different.

Chapter Twenty-Eight

Rehana

NADEEM WAS LOOKING ESPECIALLY fit in his navy jumper and dark jeans. Rehana tried her best not to stare too hard. She didn't want his mum thinking she was some sort of pervert. Each time she caught his eye, he gave her one of his mischievous grins.

'So, Nadeem, beta,' her mum said. 'What do you do for work?'

'I'm a software engineer, Aunty. Rehana has probably told you already, I'm in Dubai at the moment, but I'm planning to come back to the UK next year.' He gave Rehana a wink.

Rehana felt the heat rise in her face. Thankfully neither of the mums saw.

'We all want him back home,' Nadeem's mum said. 'He has been away long enough now.'

'Yes, children should be at home with their parents,' Rehana's mum said. 'Tell me, Nadeem, what does a software engineer do? Do you build computers?'

'Kind of,' he said, flashing one of his dazzling smiles. 'I use mathematics and engineering principles to design programmes that can be installed onto computers depending on what the user wants.'

There was a pause. Rehana's mum looked confused.

'Oh, so clever!' she finally said. 'I can't work computers, Rehana does all of that for me. See, you two have so much in common.'

Rehana cringed, but Nadeem took it all in his stride. 'You're so right, Aunty. It's important for a husband and wife to find common ground, that's the foundation of any good relationship.'

Normally Rehana would be vomiting at the creepiness of this conversation, but not today. Nadeem was making a cracking impression on her mother.

Now, it was her father's turn.

'So many people have degrees in computing these days,' he said. 'Will you be able to find a job when you come back?'

'Actually, the company I'm working for now in Dubai has offices in the UK, so it will simply be a case of transferring me across,' Nadeem replied.

'With the same salary?' her dad queried. Rehana nearly died. Why did Asian parents always ask about salaries? Didn't they know it was vulgar to talk about money?

'Well, I'll be paying tax when I return, which I haven't done whilst I've been in Dubai, but it will be a similar level,' Nadeem answered. Rehana was impressed at how at ease he seemed with this line of questioning.

'How much do you earn?' her dad asked. Rehana watched as Nadeem's dad shifted in his seat. She knew her father was trying his best to look out for her, but he was having the opposite effect.

'Let's just say it's enough to support myself and my family,' Nadeem continued confidently.

'Good. You know it's a husband's job to look after his wife, both emotionally and financially,' her dad said. *When the fuck did my dad become such a misogynist?*

'Absolutely,' Nadeem said.

Her dad gave him a nod, signalling he was happy with the

outcome of the conversation. Now it was Nadeem's mum's turn to interrogate Rehana.

'Rehana, how is your teaching job going?' she asked politely.

'Oh, good. I have a few months left, but I'll be qualified in time for the next academic year,' Rehana said proudly. 'I have assignments, of course. But once they're done, I'll be applying for teaching jobs.'

'I must say, I know nothing of the teaching profession. Do you enjoy it?' his mum asked.

'I love it. It's challenging, and I wish the pay was better.' She smiled. 'It's just a shame we aren't allowed to smack the naughty kids any more.' She laughed at her own joke. Nobody else did. Nadeem snorted. Her mum tried to brush over it.

'I hear they are short of teachers everywhere in the country,' Rehana's mum said. 'They are practically crying out for them, so Rehana can work anywhere should the need arise.' She looked at her daughter. 'Rehana, is there a shortage of teachers in, I don't know, somewhere like London?'

Rehana had no clue. 'Probably,' she said.

'See, she could even work in London if that's where she ends up.' Her mum gave her a stern look.

Subtle, Mum. Nadeem's family lived in London.

'Some girls worry about leaving their family home after marriage. Is this something that concerns you?' his mum questioned. 'It can be hard.'

Was she kidding? Rehana thought. She couldn't wait to move out of this house.

'I will miss my family,' she said sweetly. 'But I'll be gaining a new family, that of my husband.'

Even Rehana felt sick at this answer but needs must.

'Won't you miss your friends?' his mum continued.

What friends? Rehana thought. There was only really Emma. 'They can always visit.' Rehana smiled.

'Rehana knows that a girl's home is with her husband,' Feroza interjected. 'We parents only really play guardians to our daughters until they meet their husbands.'

Rehana wanted to make a good impression, but this was too much. She wasn't some kind of possession that people could pass on to each other when they felt it was appropriate. Fuck that.

'You know, Aunty, marriage isn't about closing down one chapter of your life and opening another.' She tried to tread carefully. This was potentially her future mother-in-law. 'It's about expanding your life to include other people. I look at it as expanding my family, expanding my experiences and sharing them with someone very special and with whoever is special to them.'

That seemed to satisfy his mother. Interrogation over.

'One more thing,' her mum said suddenly. 'Rehana can make full Pakistani dinner.'

After dinner, Rehana and Nadeem were allowed to go to the snug and have some private time. The snug was fast becoming the Pakistani equivalent of *Love Island's* 'hideaway', Rehana thought. Just more halal, no hanky-panky allowed.

'I think it's all going well, don't you?' she asked eagerly.

'Really well. My mum bloody loves you. Especially after that expanding your family speech.' He laughed.

'Do you think she bought it?'

'Hook, line and sinker,' he said, smiling.

'Thank God for that. It was ninety-nine per cent bullshit,' she said. Then she remembered that Nadeem might not get her sense of humour. 'Well, most of it was true; I do want to share my life with a special someone and take on their family as my own.'

'Yes, but can you cook a full Pakistani dinner?' he said, cocking his head.

'Piss off!' She laughed. 'I can, but this is a modern world. Most of the time we can order a Just Eat.'

'Don't let my mum hear you say that!' he teased.

She looked at him. It surprised her how much she enjoyed talking to him.

'I wish you weren't going back to Dubai.' Rehana's excitement was darkened by his impending departure. They had been texting all week, sometimes late into the night. It had been ages since she had had a connection like this with anyone, let alone a boy.

'I know, but it's just a few months. You could always come out and visit?'

'What, and break every Islamic rule in the book?' Rehana said. 'No thanks. Mum and Dad will never allow it.'

'Rehana, I want you to know something,' he said.

Oh my God, what? she thought.

'I won't be considering any other girls from now on.' He looked serious. 'I mean it, I'll tell my parents tonight.'

'Tell them what exactly?' Rehana wasn't quite sure what he was trying to say.

'Tell them to tell Aunty Henna to close her account on me,' he said. 'I don't know, whatever it takes to get myself off the market!'

Wait, had she really snagged herself a decent bloke after just two dates? This was quick even for an arranged marriage.

Nadeem must have read her mind. 'Look, I know it's quick, normally we would go on more dates, but I live abroad. I want to come back next year ready to start a new life with someone, no more messing around. That is, if that's what you want?'

'Well, Mum did show me a picture of a bloke who looked like Osama Bin Laden's twin brother, so you know, I have options.' She smiled at Nadeem.

'I can see you with someone like that. In fact, I'll marry him if you don't.' He was smiling again. The feeling in her stomach spread out, reaching the tips of her fingers.

'Nadeem, I need to be clear about the conversation we're having. Are you asking me to take myself off the arranged marriage circuit too, in the hope that you won't have changed your mind when you get back next year?' That was a big ask after the short time they had known each other. 'I know you said no games, but how do I know I won't end up being duped? I'll be a whole year older by then and you know what that's like for Pakistani girls. It's different for you boys.'

'I'm serious, Rehana. I can tell my parents like you and, more importantly, I like you. What more do you need?'

How was she going to say this without sounding desperate? Maybe she should just play him Beyonce's 'Single Ladies', hoping he might take the hint. *Put a fucking ring on it*, she wanted to scream at him!

'I need something, I don't know what, something that shows me you're committed.' If that didn't describe an engagement ring, she didn't know what did.

'I'll speak with my mum tonight, get her to phone your mum and tell her of my intentions,' Nadeem said.

His intentions? Rehana thought. *What is this, 1847?*

'That way your parents will know I'm serious about this whole thing.'

It was about as close to a ring as she was going to get. 'Nadeem, won't you come back at all between now and next spring?' Rehana asked. 'Not even for a holiday?'

'I don't get paid holidays in Dubai. The whole point of me going out there was to save up enough money for the future,' he said.

'I was kind of hoping you might now have more of an incentive to come back?' Rehana asked hopefully.

He gave her a lopsided smile. 'I think I might have. And we can always FaceTime – I don't think the Qur'an has put a limit on how much we can do that!'

'No, I suppose not.' Rehana didn't mind FaceTime, but she

craved being taken out for dinner by Nadeem, having summer evening walks in the park (obviously no hand-holding). Besides, she still didn't feel as though she had a firm enough commit-ment from him to take herself completely off the market. It was a gamble and she only had his word for it.

They returned to the room their parents were in. It was clear they were all getting along famously; there was lots of laughter.

'Have you two finished?' his dad asked. 'We were just getting started in here!' They all laughed again.

'Won't you have some more tea?' Rehana's mum asked.

'No, we really must be going, but it's been a pleasure,' Nadeem's mum said, standing up. She came over to Rehana and took her by the shoulders. 'Such a beautiful girl.' She hugged her. Rehana hadn't had a compliment like that from an aunty for a long time. She melted into the hug.

'Thank you, Aunty,' she whispered, hugging her hard.

'And listen,' Nadeem's mum said, 'just because this ladoo isn't here doesn't mean you can't come and visit me. I have already told your parents they are welcome anytime.'

Rehana looked at her mum, who smiled at her. The dads were embracing their goodbyes too. Things could not have gone better. She caught Nadeem's eye, who gave her a knowing nod. Was this really happening?

After they left, Rehana lingered in the kitchen with her mother. Normally she would have run upstairs and rung Emma to replay the day's events, but today she wanted to know what her mother thought.

'So?' Rehana eventually said.

'So what?' her mum replied, deliberately acting annoying.

'What did you think?' Her dad came to join them. 'Dad, what did you think? Mum's being weird.'

'He seems like a very nice boy, Rehana,' her dad said. 'Good job, nice family, good values. I like him.'

As important as that was, Rehana knew this whole thing

couldn't fly without the approval of her mother. She waited expectantly.

'Well?' she said, getting more and more impatient.

'I'm thinking . . .' her mother said.

'Thinking about what?' Rehana pressed.

'Thinking about how empty this house is going to feel without you in it,' her mum said, sounding emotional.

'Mum! Don't cry, it's a happy occasion.'

Her mum wiped her eyes with the hem of her kameez. 'I know, but you're my daughter, I'm allowed to be sad at the thought of you leaving us.' Feroza came and sat next to her.

'I thought you couldn't wait to get rid of me,' Rehana said, leaning into her mum.

'Don't be silly, I just want you to be happy.' They linked arms. 'Will he make you happy?'

Rehana thought about it. 'I think so.'

'That's good.' Her mum looked at her. 'Now don't mess this up!' she said sharply.

There it was. She couldn't stop at being just nice. 'I'm not going to mess things up, Mum!'

'I mean it, Rehana, this is the toughest part of the whole arranged marriage process. The slightest thing can cause upset,' she explained. 'You have to be on your best behaviour and make them think you are a good Muslim girl.'

What did she mean, *make them think*? She was a good Muslim girl. 'Mum, I'm not going to mess this up. How can I? He lives in bloody Dubai!'

'Yes, that is a problem, normally we would move quickly and secure an engagement.' Her mum pondered. 'I will wait until his mum calls with her thoughts and then we can take it forward from there.'

It sounded like her mum was thinking along the same lines as her, and with her mum's cunning on her side, there was no way she could lose.

'And of course, we will need to get Yousef's opinion on him. It's a shame he was working today.'

It definitely was not a shame. Rehana didn't want Yousef around looking miserable whilst Nadeem's family were there. And besides, she had serious doubts he was actually working. He had come into the kitchen this morning to announce the hospital needed him to cover sickness. Meeting up with Jessica, more like, she had thought. Anyway, that was not her problem, she had her own life to sort.

She went upstairs and lay on her bed, feeling suddenly exhausted from the excitement of the day. She did feel bad about telling Yousef to keep his mouth shut about Jessica and she felt even worse for implying to Seema that her brother was interested in her, but the arranged marriage process had brought out a whole different side to her. She usually put 'sisters before misters', but getting married the Pakistani way meant it was every girl for herself. Yousef would have to wait until she had fully locked down Nadeem before he upset the apple cart with his drama, and who knew what might happen by then? Maybe Seema would have used her prowess to lure Yousef away from Jessica. And if she didn't, well . . . She liked Seema, and really didn't want to shit on her, but Seema would bounce back. She was beautiful (and rich), she must have plenty of suitors knocking at her door. Rehana only had one suitor – well, potentially two if you counted Religious Guy. Yes, her actions were justified.

She sat up and dialled Emma's number. Emma answered after the first ring.

'Bloody hell, Emma.' Rehana laughed. 'Give me a chance to stop dialling first!'

'Sorry, I was texting someone when you rang,' Emma said, sounding excited herself.

'Really? Who?'

'I'll tell you in a minute. Tell me about Nadeem first. Did it go well?' she asked.

Rehana replayed the events of the day, including the conversation she'd had with him about being exclusive.

'Things really do move fast in your world,' Emma said. 'What does he mean? Are you, like, boyfriend and girlfriend?'

'Oh my God, no!' Rehana said. 'Those terms are severely frowned upon. Either you're engaged or you're not. There is no middle ground.'

'Am I being dim, or aren't you now treading some sort of middle ground?' Emma asked.

'I suppose I am, but it's all kept very hush-hush. You know what Asian aunties are like, the slightest bit of gossip could derail the whole thing. Anyway, I'm hoping the mums sort it out.' Rehana laughed. 'So who were you texting?'

'I was going to tell you last week, but things had gone so badly on your coffee dates, it didn't seem like the right time,' Emma said, sounding coy.

'Tell me what?'

'Well, hearing about your dating life kind of galvanized me to take action in my own love life.'

'And??' Rehana was getting excited.

'I met someone online. His name's Chris and we've been on a couple of dates.'

'Oh my God!' Rehana screamed.

'I know, it's so exciting! I'm texting you a picture of him now, tell me what you think.'

Rehana's phone buzzed. She opened up the message. 'Bloody hell! He. Is. Fit!' she said. 'Look at those blue eyes! You're so lucky, we never have the option of blue eyes in the Pakistani community, it's just various shades of brown. Hazel if you're lucky.'

'He is hot, but obviously it's not just about looks. He's funny – like, really funny,' Emma explained. 'We didn't stop laughing the entire time we were on our date.'

'You really like him?'

'I really like him,' Emma said.

'Then I'm happy for you. Who knows, by next year we could both have found our for ever loves!' Rehana exclaimed. 'A giant Fuck You to all those haters who thought we'd be single for ever!'

'You can't see but I'm giving them all the finger.' Emma laughed. 'My mum will just be pleased I'm not a lesbian, not that there's anything wrong with being a lesbian.'

'Of course there isn't,' Rehana confirmed. 'It's just that we're not lesbians, we're girls with partners.'

'Partners with penises,' Emma repeated. 'Cheers to that.'

'Cheers to that.' Rehana laughed and hung up the phone.

Rehana and Emma's conversation about their partners with penises carried on into the next day whilst they were at work. She got off the bus still on a high.

Rehana spied Aunty Angie coming out of her house. She too spotted Rehana and visibly shrank, pretending to busy herself by looking at her phone. Rehana felt bad about their last inter-action when she had nearly bitten Angie's head off.

She waved at her. 'Hi, Aunty Angie. How are you?'

Angie looked up from her phone. 'Oh, hi, Rehana, I didn't see you there.'

'Angie, guess what?'

'What?' Angie said, now very interested.

'I've met a boy!' Rehana said excitedly.

'Really? Do your parents know?' Angie whispered. Poor Angie, she probably thought Rehana was confiding in her.

'Yes, Angie, he came over yesterday with his family,' Rehana exclaimed. 'You know, all proper like. Nobody else knows, so this is kind of an exclusive!'

Angie squealed, then looked a bit sheepish. 'Well, I did actually see them arriving. I wasn't spying, of course, just happened to be looking out of the window at the right time. Very handsome, he was.'

'I know, isn't he dreamy?' Rehana cooed. 'Well, he likes me and I like him, so who knows, you might get to come to that Big Fat Asian Wedding after all.'

'Rehana, that's wonderful news, and you gleaned all that from one meeting?' Angie was now fully invested.

'It was our second meeting, and we've been talking on the phone every day. You have to make quick decisions where arranged marriages are concerned, there's none of this try before you buy,' Rehana said. 'But yes, you're right, it is quicker than most, but I guess when you know, you know.'

'I didn't know your Uncle Jim was the one for ages, but then I got pregnant with Lottie, and had no choice.' Angie smiled. 'But he was a real grower, such a good husband and dad.'

'Yeah, I suppose it's different for everyone,' Rehana said. 'In our culture most of the dating takes place after the engagement but before the wedding. Anyway, I'll keep you posted.' She gave Angie a hug and headed inside.

Her mum was waiting for her in the hallway.

'What is it?' Rehana asked.

'They rang!' her mum said. She was shaking.

'Who rang?' Rehana asked. Oh God, was it something awful?

'Nadeem's mum, silly.'

'And?'

'His mum said they all really liked you and want to make it official.' Her mum almost screamed it out.

'Oh my God, Mum, I need to sit down.' Rehana followed her mother into the living room.

'What do they mean, *official*?' Rehana was sick of vague words. She needed hard facts.

'There is only one way to make this official, we have to do a magni.' Her mum was positively salivating.

'An engagement? Nadeem wants us to get engaged?'

Her mum nodded. Rehana stood up and started screaming. Usually, her mum would tell her to calm down, but this time she sat back and watched. 'Okay, okay,' Rehana said, out of breath, 'how does the engagement work?' She had hoped Nadeem would appear magically one evening and get down on one knee, but clearly it was the mums who did the asking and agreeing to marriage around here. An engagement, or magni, was not a private affair between two lovebirds in the Pakistani world; it was a moment to be celebrated with family and friends. The beginning of many celebrations culminating in the wedding.

'His mum said he can come back for a weekend in a month's time, and we can have an engagement party then, here at the house,' Feroza explained. She gripped Rehana's hand tightly. 'It's finally happening! I can't believe it, mashallah.'

'A month?' Rehana exclaimed. 'Mum, I need a new outfit! Who's going to do my hair and make-up? What about the caterers? And how does he know what kind of ring I want?'

'Leave the ring to him, you can always change it after the wedding if you don't like it, but don't tell him until you are married, understood?' Her mum looked at her. Rehana nodded. Neither of them could hide their excitement. 'Right, come with me into the kitchen, we need to make a list. There is a lot of work to do.'

Chapter Twenty-Nine

Rohit

ROHIT WAS DECIDING HOW many pairs of underwear to pack. He was going to be away for three weeks but didn't own twenty-one pairs of underpants. He could always get them washed over there, he thought, but how accessible was a washing machine in India? It had been well over a decade since he had last visited his family in Rajasthan; he could barely remember anything about them or how they lived.

He hoped he was doing the right thing. He had been so taken by the photograph of Anjali and the fact that she was a doctor, he hadn't read the fine print. He couldn't very well fly back and forth to India to meet her, so he'd had a number of Skype meetings instead.

At first, it had been awkward. The conversations were stilted and centred around what they had done that day (which in Rohit's case was very little). He found asking her questions was the best approach as she was far more interesting than he was, so it made sense she did all the talking. Her shifts in the hospitals seemed so eventful compared to his work at the accountancy firm. She was based in obstetrics, so every day there were new dramas about women giving birth to unexpected babies, mothers having to be resuscitated after huge amounts of blood loss after deliveries and all sorts of reasons as to why women needed emergency caesarean sections. Anjali talked passionately about her work and made it clear it was a big part of who she was. She also seemed to have a lot of friends who she went out with. Most of their conversations ended with her saying she had to go meet 'the girls' for dinner or a game of netball.

Getting a girl like Anjali to even talk to him here in the UK had seemed impossible, but somehow the adults in their respective families had swindled a situation where he was talking to this beautiful, successful, intelligent woman almost every night and, strangest of all, she seemed to want to talk to him. Eventually his mum had wanted to know more.

'How are things going with Anjali?' she asked.

'Yeah, good, thanks,' he replied. 'We've been chatting a lot. She seems nice.'

'That's good.' She paused, looking at him.

'What is it, Mum?'

'Uncle Anand rang. He said Uncle Sunil thinks we should go to India so you can meet Anjali.' She took his hand. 'You know, you can't keep talking to the girl for ever, you have to make a decision.'

'It's only been a few weeks, Ma, and it's not like I've been indecisive up until now, is it? I haven't ever got to the point where I have to actually make a decision.' He pulled his hand away and stood up.

'The thing is,' she continued, 'Uncle Anand says that Uncle Sunil thinks Anjali is getting other offers.'

'Really?' Rohit asked. He didn't want that.

'Well, that's what I was told.' His mum nodded. 'And we don't want to let this rishta pass us by. We should go to India and make it clear we like her.'

'Can't we do that over the phone?' Rohit looked bemused. 'India is a long way to go to tell someone I like them. Can't you just tell Uncle Anand to tell Uncle Sunil to tell Anjali, or something?'

'Rohit, it's not that simple,' his mum said. 'If you are serious about Anjali, we need to make it clear by going over there.'

'Ma, you keep saying *make it clear*. What do you mean?'

His mum sighed. 'Anjali is a doctor, no?' she asked.

'Yes,' he replied, confused by the line of questioning.

'Well, if she plans to move here to the UK for, I don't know' – his mum pretended to pluck a reason out of the air – 'let's say marriage reasons . . .'

'Okay,' Rohit said slowly.

'. . . then finding a job takes time.' She looked at him. He stared back blankly. 'Rohit, are you really that dim?'

'Ma, what are you saying?' Rohit said. What was he being dim about?

'We go over there, you spend some time with her and if all goes well, we have a small engagement in their home. Easy,' his mum said, slowly and deliberately so he could follow.

'A small engagement?' he repeated just as slowly. 'For me and Anjali?'

'Yes, then she can come over to England and stay with Uncle Anand, apply for a work visa, and you two can get to know each other. Once she is settled and you are both happy, we can have a big wedding.' She smiled at him. 'We could have you come in on a white horse like your brother did. You will look so smart in your wedding suit.'

'Wait, what?' He furrowed his eyebrows. What was happening right now?

'Rohit, what did you think would happen, huh?' His mum stood up and met his eye. 'That you would just talk to Anjali for ever over the phone?'

'I don't know, I suppose I thought it would take longer than a few weeks.'

'Girls like Anjali don't wait around for long,' his mum said. 'Uncle Anand told Uncle Sunil there is already a lawyer from

Leicester interested in her too. He said he was very tall. We have to move quickly.'

'Ma, I just feel this is a bit sudden.'

'Okay, well, think about it,' his mum said matter-of-factly. 'This has to be your decision, but if you say no, it will be back to the beginning trying to find a girl again.' She left the room.

He tried to ring Anjali but the time difference meant she was already asleep. He thought about what his mum had said. He certainly did not want to go back to the drawing board with his search, that would be a complete disaster.

He rang Yousef. 'So you know this Indian girl, Anjali, I've kind of being getting to know?'

'Yeah,' Yousef said.

'Well, Mum wants me to get engaged to her. Which is weird, right? I haven't even known her for long.'

'Honestly, Ro, I've given up thinking anything is weird when it comes to arranged marriages. Things move at a crazy pace,' Yousef replied.

'I suppose so. But it's marriage, you know. It's all a bit permanent. I was hoping to be at least friends with the girl I marry, I don't even think we're at that stage yet,' Rohit said wistfully.

'My mum says all of that comes after the wedding,' Yousef said, sounding miserable. 'I suppose you need to trust the process. I mean, look at the oldies in our communities. They've been married for, like, for ever, and they all had arranged marriages.'

'That's true, but it's a lot of trust to put into a process we know so little about,' Rohit said.

'Do you like this girl – like, really like her?' Yousef asked.

'I don't know. She's nice,' Rohit answered, uncertain. 'I just think she's a bit out of my league and hasn't figured that out yet.'

'Girls think differently to boys. If you like her, then you should hold on to that feeling.'

'Don't you think it's a bit quick?' Rohit asked.

'It is, but it's the same with my sister and she's over the moon,' Yousef replied. 'Think of it this way, what's the alternative?'

'Back to the hell that was internet dating,' Rohit said miserably. 'I'll probably end up getting catfished again and giving all my money to some middle-aged man in Ghana.'

'There you go. Just go to India. If it turns out you aren't compatible, come home. You'll never have to see her again.'

'Maybe you're right.'

'All I know is, if there's a girl who you like and who likes you, then nothing else really matters,' Yousef said in a solemn voice.

Maybe Yous was right? He had hoped for more time to get to know Anjali, but then again, there was only so much you could get to know about someone virtually. He didn't really believe in love at first Skype. Perhaps going to see her wouldn't be so bad. He could always pull the plug if things went tits up. He would ring Anjali tomorrow and see what her thoughts were.

Anjali seemed more on board with the idea than he had expected. She told him about the visa system and how it could take months before she was allowed to work in the UK, but she could apply for a short-term tourist visa in the meantime. She explained that for her to get a training post in obstetrics and gynaecology she would have to apply soon, otherwise wait a whole year before the jobs came out again. It all felt a bit clinical to him at the time. He hoped it wasn't just the job she was moving for.

'It's a very competitive speciality in the UK,' she had said. 'I don't want to work as a locum. The training posts ensure I am on a pathway to becoming a consultant.'

If Anjali was all for it, who was he to protest? The trip was confirmed.

Amit was coming with them too. He said someone had to oversee the whole affair in the absence of their father. Priya wasn't best pleased at being left to look after the kids so decided to make it a family trip, so now everybody was coming. This had put pressure on Rohit. What if he decided he didn't want to go ahead with the whole thing, and they had spent all that money getting the whole family to India? He couldn't think about that now, he had underwear to pack.

He counted them. Twelve pairs. He would buy some more at the airport.

Rohit rationalized the trip in his head. It was the only way he could keep his anxiety at manageable levels. He was simply going to India to meet a girl he had spoken to online. The purpose of the trip was to ensure they got along well enough to see if they might have a future together. He could change his mind at any point should he wish, as could she. If he did go out there and find he and Anjali didn't get on in real life, he would tell his mum to tell Uncle Anand to tell Uncle Sunil the whole thing was off. Simple.

Chapter Thirty

Jessica

'Do you want jam or marmalade with your toast?' Jess's dad asked as he carefully carried over a pot of coffee and three mugs, placing them on the table.

'Dad, you know I can make my own breakfast,' Jess said, getting up.

'Nonsense,' he replied. 'You deserve to rest after all the work you're putting in at the hospital.'

'Let him do it,' her mum chimed in. 'It's been so long since you've visited, he's missed pampering you.'

'Well, in that case, I'll have marmalade.' Jess sat back down.

It was good to be home. Her mum was right, it had been too long. The familiarity of the surroundings engulfed her like a warm blanket. To be honest, she had been reluctant to leave Yousef now they had rekindled their romance, but she had promised her parents she would be visiting this week and they had really been looking forward to it.

The fresh coffee made a welcome change from the instant stuff she had been drinking back in the doctors' dorms. She savoured each sip. Her dad came over with a jar of marmalade.

'Stephanie across the road made this,' he said, popping it in front of Jess. 'It's got lime peel in too, makes it extra tangy.'

She loved her dad. He would have saved that especially for her. She scooped out a generous dollop and spread it on her toast. It was delicious.

'Yummy,' she said, her mouth full of warm toast and tangy marmalade. The look of satisfaction on his face made her smile.

'Did you know Stephanie is seeing Daniel now?' her mum asked.

'Who's Daniel?' Jess frowned.

'You know Daniel, works at the garage. He fixed your car last winter.'

'I thought Daniel was married?' Jess asked, helping herself to another piece of toast.

'He was, but he left his wife for Stephanie. He's even moved in with her.' Her mum was loving sharing this news.

'Scandalous!' Jess exclaimed.

'How's work at the hospital?' her dad asked, clearly trying to steer the conversation away from local love affairs.

'Oh, you know, good mainly,' Jess replied. She hadn't told them about Yousef. They had been so supportive after she had broken up with him, she didn't want them to feel all of that had been in vain.

'And how is that gorgeous boyfriend of yours, Jonathan?' her mum said, squeezing her arm.

'We kind of broke up,' Jess said. Her mum looked horrified. 'Nothing bad, Mum. With my work schedule we were hardly seeing each other, and it just fizzled out.'

'That's a shame, love,' her dad said. 'Are you okay?'

'Fine, Dad, thanks. It was a mutual thing.'

Jess was lying. The break-up had been awful. She had caught Jonathan after a training session at the pitches, when they had been planning to go back to his flat for dinner. She started off saying she wouldn't be coming over and that perhaps they needed to re-evaluate their relationship. He hadn't taken this well and told her that he was really into her and didn't feel the need to re-evaluate anything. She then said she really needed to concentrate on her job, and would be applying for speciality training next year, and was thinking of applying for jobs closer to home in Somerset, and finally that she didn't want to be in a long-distance relationship. Jonathan had replied by telling her that neither of them knew what the future held in store for them, and that they could just see where things went and, if needed, he could work anywhere. Eventually she confessed that she'd met someone else and watching his face crumple when she delivered that blow had hurt. She had been so caught up in her feelings for Yousef she hadn't stopped to consider just how much Jonathan cared for her. She felt terrible, but she had to break up with him. It was the right thing to do.

'Plenty more fish in the sea,' her mum said. 'I hear James Robinson is single again. Maybe you can text him while you're here and meet up for a drink?'

James Robinson had been her college boyfriend. They had ended things when going off to different universities. She'd followed him on Instagram and knew he was back working as a financial analyst in Bridgewater. He had slid into her DMs a few times asking when she might be visiting her parents.

'No thanks, Mum,' Jess replied. 'I think I just need some time to myself for now.'

'Wise girl,' her dad chimed in. 'There's no rush.'

'I just think a pretty girl like you shouldn't be single, it's such a waste,' her mum added wistfully.

Her dad refilled the coffee pot as Jess recounted stories of patients she had seen in hospital. Her parents, fascinated by all the gory details, wanted to know everything about the surgeries she was allowed to assist with and all the people she had been able to help resuscitate.

Jess looked at her watch. 'Shoot, is that the time? I need to get ready to meet Kate for lunch.'

'You should have told her to come here for lunch,' her mum

said. 'You know we love Kate, it would have been nice
her.'

'Mum, I haven't seen her in ages, we have so much to catch
up on,' Jess replied. 'We need some private time.'

'Let her go, Jackie,' her dad cooed. 'We can't hog all of her
time.'

Jess gave them both a hug and went upstairs for a shower.

She was meeting Kate at a small Italian cafe. She was the
first to arrive and ordered two glasses of Pinot, knowing Kate
would approve. She saw Kate approaching and waved at her.
Kate squealed with excitement. Although they called and texted
regularly, it had been over a year since they had last actually
seen each other. Kate's squeal got louder as she got closer. Jess
stood up and hugged her friend.

'Sorry I'm late, babes,' Kate said, taking a seat. 'I couldn't
find my bloody phone.'

'Don't worry. I ordered us wine, hope you don't mind.' Jess
raised her glass.

'Course I don't bloody mind.' Kate lifted her glass too and
took a glug. 'Cheers to old friends.'

'To old friends.' Jess took a large sip. It felt immediately
comfortable to be with Kate. They had shared so much time
together at university, a few months apart couldn't shake their
bond.

'How's Alex?' Jess asked.

'Still a pain in the arse, but I love him. The heart wants what
the heart wants,' Kate replied. 'I must be a glutton for punish-
ment.' The waiter came over and took their order.

'You two must have the longest-lasting relationship of our
entire medical school,' Jess said.

'Nearly five years now,' Kate said. 'That title would have
belonged to you and Yousef if he hadn't been such a twat.'

Jess pursed her lips. She hadn't told Kate she was sort of
back together with Yousef. Well, sleeping with him at least.

She played with the glass of wine, twirling the glass back and forth.

'What is it?' Kate asked. Jess didn't say anything. Kate studied her face and then a look of horror came over her. 'Oh God, Jess, no!' she said. Jess winced. 'Jesus, I'm going to need more wine.' She beckoned the waiter over.

'Yes, miss?'

'A bottle of whatever this is, please.' She tapped her glass. He nodded and disappeared. 'Right, tell me everything.'

Jess didn't know where to start. 'You know Yous and I were working on the same ward?' Kate nodded, rolling her eyes. 'Well, obviously I made it clear I wanted nothing to do with him after what happened last year.'

'Good,' Kate interrupted. 'But I'm assuming that didn't last for long.'

'Honestly, Kate, I tried. I had Jonathan and things were going well,' Jess explained, 'but there is a certain . . . magnetism between me and Yousef, I can't resist it.'

'Try, Jess,' Kate said firmly, 'because when he left you broken-hearted, it was me who was left to pick up the pieces.'

'I know,' Jess replied, slightly annoyed that Kate would throw that in her face. 'Five years of history is just really hard to erase and when you're working on a ward with someone, you're really close to them all the time.'

'I work on a ward too, Jess, and you don't see me shagging half the staff,' Kate replied.

'Forget it, Kate, you're not going to understand, I don't know why I'm bothering.' Jess took a piece of bread from the bread basket, as the waiter appeared with the bottle of wine.

'Would you like to try it first?' he said, looking at Kate.

'Just crack it open and leave it there,' Kate said, pointing at the table. 'Look, Jess, I'm sorry, it's just a lot to take in.'

Her feelings for Yousef were hard to explain to anyone, but most of all Kate, who had always been suspicious of how reluctant he'd been to tell his family about their relationship. Hell, even Jess found their relationship hard to understand. On the surface of it, she should run a mile, but Yousef was tender, he was kind and thoughtful and the situation with his family was not of his making. She had always thought that if she could offer him a safe and loving alternative to his family, it would give him the strength to be honest with them. Despite what he said, she still held visions of them accepting her once they realized how good she was for Yousef, even welcoming her into the family.

'I'm sorry, Jess, go on, tell me. I won't interrupt this time,' Kate said.

'This thing with me and Yousef, it's too hard to ignore or brush away under the carpet.' Jess felt a little out of breath just talking about Yousef. 'Let's say if you and Alex broke up for a reason out of the control of the pair of you, and then he came back, changed and more grown-up, wouldn't you take him back?'

Kate pondered the question. 'I'd probably kick him in the bollocks first.' She smiled. 'Then maybe, just maybe, I'd give him a second chance.'

'See, it's the same for me and Yousef.'

'But what about his family? Is he going to tell them this time?'

'He says he has already told Rehana, his sister, that we're back together,' Jess said. 'So that's a start, and he was going to tell his parents but Rehana has an engagement party coming up and he doesn't want to spoil it.'

Kate rolled her eyes again. 'This is all starting to sound very familiar.'

'No, it's different this time. I'm going into this with my eyes open, more guarded,' Jess lied.

'But you still love him? Despite everything?'

Jess nodded. She did and that was the most painful part.

She knew this was a gamble, that her heart could be broken again, but if things went the right way, it would all be worth it. She could have Yousef and she could have the life she wanted with him, with or without his family.

'I do,' she said.

'Well then, I'm with you. Whatever you need, I'm here,' Kate replied, giving Jess's hand a squeeze. 'But I will fuck him up if he messes with you again.'

'You have my full permission,' Jess laughed.

'So have you told your parents yet?'

'No, I've decided I'm not telling them until Yousef tells his.' Jess had thought about this on the drive home. 'They were so invested in our relationship last time, especially Dad. I don't want to get their hopes up.'

'Hmm, you don't sound so sure yourself,' Kate quizzed.

'I think the best way to describe how I'm feeling right now is cautiously optimistic.'

'Cautiously optimistic,' Kate repeated, 'what a bloody great way to start off a relationship.' She topped up her glass.

Chapter Thirty-One

Yousef

YOUSEF TOOK A SIP of his espresso. It was strong. He wished he had asked for a vanilla latte now – he could do with the sugar rush. Seema sat opposite him; she was talking about how busy her week had been in general practice.

'I had to wait with the patient until the ambulance arrived,' he heard her say as he zoned back into the conversation. She had been telling him about a home visit to a sick old man. 'He was really short of breath, and all the while the patients on my list back at the surgery were waiting.'

He zoned back out. Having coffee with Seema was the last place he wanted to be. His mother had arranged it without any input from him, and as Rehana's engagement party was next week he decided it was better to go than create a fuss. And besides, Jess was visiting her family this weekend and Rohit had flown to India, so he had very little else to do. He needed to get out of the house. His family were doing his head in with all the preparations for the big party next Saturday. There were cheap plastic decorations up on the wall, food was being prepped and frozen and there had been numerous trips to the shopping centre to get gifts for all of Nadeem's family. Worst of all, his mother had invited Seema and her family to the engagement, presumably to give them a taste of what they could expect should things progress between Yousef and Seema, which once he had spoken to his parents, they wouldn't. He planned to tell them both about Jessica first thing Sunday morning. He couldn't wait a minute longer.

Seema looked at him expectantly. She must have asked him a question he hadn't heard.

'Sorry, what was that?' he asked.

A flicker of annoyance passed over Seema's face. 'I asked what colour Rehana is wearing at her engagement party on Saturday. I don't want to clash with her.'

'I have no idea,' Yousef said. He had paid no attention to what was going on with the engagement.

'Typical bloke.' Seema laughed. 'I hope you're going to be involved when it's your turn.'

He gave her a feeble smile. He really did not want to be here.

'So have you given any thought to what speciality you will be applying for next year?' Seema asked, sipping her frappe. 'You know we could always do with more GPs.'

He knew she was trying to be nice, but she had only been training to be a GP for a year and Seema talked as though she represented the entire GP profession.

'I know you want the more glamorous job of being a surgeon, and as much as I hate to admit it, it is a sexy profession. All the jocks of the medical world head that way. Did you play any sports at university?'

God, does she ever stop talking?

'Hockey mainly,' he replied. He had only played hockey a couple of times because he heard they had the best socials.

'I loved hockey. The hockey team always had the best socials. I played netball and was the captain of the Outdoor Pursuits Club for two years,' Seema said proudly.

'Of course you were,' Yousef muttered under his breath.

'Sorry?'

'I said, I knew you would be.' Yousef backtracked. 'It's just you're so . . . outdoorsy.' He thought of the days watching Jess play football all afternoon. He missed it.

'I know, strange for a Pakistani girl, right?' Seema beamed. 'But Mum and Dad are keen hikers and always used to take me with them. We were the only brown people on the Mendip Hills one time. I think my mum prefers it that way.' She gave a nervous laugh. 'Do you think your mum likes me?' she asked suddenly.

'What?' He was taken aback by the sudden change in topic.

'Your mum, do you think she likes me?' She looked at Yousef. 'It's just that, I know sometimes I can be a bit full on. I hope she doesn't think that.'

Yousef felt sorry for her. It was no fault of Seema's she had walked into this complicated situation. He couldn't be angry at her, it was his family who had forced this whole thing.

'Seema, my mum loves you. I wouldn't be here if she didn't,' he said gently.

'Oh, that's good.' She looked relieved. 'I know there's a bit of awkwardness between her and my mum, but I'm sure that will get resolved in time.' She tucked her hair behind her ear. Yousef had noticed she did this when flirting. 'I know your sister likes me. We had a bit of a girly chat in the kitchen when we came over the other week.'

'Rehana?' Yousef said, surprised. He couldn't imagine her having a girly chat with anyone. 'What did she say?'

'Never you mind, it's between us girls!' Seema said playfully. 'Anyway, I'm looking forward to getting to know her better. She seems nice.'

'Are we still talking about my sister?' Yousef said. He thought he'd better try to be civil.

'Yes!' Seema cried. 'You're so lucky, I have always wanted a sister.'

This conversation was beginning to make Yousef uncomfortable. 'I should probably get home. Long drive ahead and my parents need me to help with the engagement.' He summoned the waiter over and asked for the bill.

'I'll get this. You've driven all this way, it's the least I can do,' Seema said, taking out her purse.

'No, absolutely not, I'm paying.' Yousef wasn't about to let Seema pay for the privilege of having her time completely wasted.

The waiter placed the bill on the table. They both went for it at the same time. Seema's hand brushed against his. He heard her gasp slightly. He quickly grabbed the bill and pulled his hand away.

'I'll pay,' he said to the waiter who was standing by oblivious to what was going on.

'Nice to know chivalry isn't dead,' Seema smiled.

Yousef drove home, fists clenched tight on the steering wheel. He should have told her. It didn't matter that Rehana's engagement was next week; leading Seema on felt shit. It was a familiar feeling. He had grown accustomed to it back at university when he'd planned to tell Jess about his family, but never did. This was different, though, he reasoned. He was now protecting his sister against family shame. There was a real risk that if he ran off with a white girl, Nadeem's family might call off his sister's wedding in fear of being associated with such a scandal. At least, that's what Rehana had implied. He wanted to believe he was the victim, but something told him it was the opposite. How was he the bad guy in a scenario where all he was trying to do was protect his family? Was Yousef really the villain in his own story?

He arrived home to find his mum in the living room trying to adjust Rehana's dress.

'I want it tighter around here,' Rehana said, pointing to her waist area. 'And this should be lower.' She pulled the lengha in at the waist and down at the bosom area.

'You want to look like a prostitute at your engagement then get someone else to adjust your lengha, I won't do it,' her mum said crossly.

'Feroza!' his dad scolded from behind his paper. 'Don't talk to her like that.'

'Abdul, stay out of it, this is women's business. I will make the waist tighter, but that's all,' Feroza said. Rehana seemed satisfied at the compromise. She looked up and saw Yousef.

'Hi, bro, how was your date with Seema?' she asked, as if she was not the architect of his nightmare.

He nodded. 'Fine.'

'Just fine?' his mum said. 'Such a beautiful girl and you say your date was just fine. I don't understand boys today.'

'We left you some Chicken Cottage over there if you want. Chips will be soggy by now, but the chicken wings should still be good,' Rehana said.

'I've already eaten.'

Rehana shrugged. 'Suit yourself.'

'I'm going upstairs,' Yousef said. Nobody heard him.

Yousef opened his laptop and logged into his job application form. Jess had already told him she would be applying for a training post in emergency medicine and would be putting the Somerset deanery as her first choice of location. She had always wanted to be an A&E doctor. If she got it, it would mean a seven-year rotational post that would eventually lead to her becoming a consultant. Seven years was a long time. After dragging her to the West Midlands for her foundation year training, he couldn't ask her to stay any longer. She, too, had the right to be close to her family. Yousef now had to decide where he wanted to train to be a consultant and, equally important, what he wanted to do. His mother had made it clear she wanted him to be a heart surgeon and had assumed he would be staying at home. There had been no open conversations about it recently, but the assumptions still stood.

He looked down the list of specialities. He had always enjoyed respiratory medicine when he was at medical school and this interest had been further established during his foundation years. He would have to do core medical training in order to progress down the respiratory route. His mouse hovered over the option. He thought about what his mother would say if he told her he didn't want to be a surgeon. He didn't care. He clicked and confirmed the core medical training option.

Do you want to save this option? the pop-up box asked.

He clicked yes.

Are you sure? You won't be able to edit this if you click confirm, the box threatened. Without needing to think, he clicked confirm.

The next box asked for his preference of location. Yousef opened up the drop-down box and scrolled down the list until he reached the Somerset deanery. His mouse hovered over the option.

Chapter Thirty-Two

Feroza

FEROZA WAS HAVING DIFFICULTY attaching a zip to one of her client's dresses. It was lace on a background of velvet and getting the metal zip to sit straight against the fabric was a challenge. But Feroza relished a challenge, and was yet to be defeated by any of her sewing jobs. She wasn't about to start now.

Her mind was on other things. To her surprise, of her two children it was Rehana who was proving the least problematic when it came to getting married. She had chosen wisely. Nadeem was a good boy from a decent family, everything was going according to plan and, inshallah, by next summer she would be married and in her own house, with Feroza relinquishing responsibility for her. Yousef, however, was proving to be a thorn in her side. Her darling boy who was so perfect in every way had been taken advantage of by some girl. Feroza couldn't stand the idea of it. She thought about this girl, Jessica, a lot. She didn't hate her. She was after all someone's daughter and they too would want what was best for her, but Yousef was not what was best for her and she was definitely not what was best for Yousef.

Feroza's plans for her son didn't stop at him becoming a surgeon. He would be responsible for carrying on the family traditions, their culture, their name. She had already made enough compromises – her children did not pray as often as she would have liked, their Urdu was fragmented at best and they hardly ever wore traditional Pakistani clothes – she couldn't let what little culture they had left in them get diluted by the introduction of some girl from an entirely different background. She wanted Yousef's children to look like him, she wanted to be able to take them to Pakistan to meet her parents. What if Yousef did marry this girl? Then they'd have children who would be mixed, who would grow up and perhaps marry other white people and soon there would be nothing left of Feroza and Abdul in their own family. Her mind raced. She needed to act fast.

She manoeuvred the zip again. There, perfect. She stitched it in place and went upstairs. Abdul was having one of his afternoon naps. She gave him a nudge.

'What is it?' he said sleepily.

'Wake up, I have something I want to talk to you about.' She sat on the bed next to him.

'I'm awake,' he said, sitting up.

'Have you spoken to Yousef lately?' she asked.

'About what?' He looked confused.

Sometimes he infuriated Feroza. He went out to work but she did the heavy lifting when it came to this family. 'About Seema, what else?'

'Well, he said the meeting they had by themselves went well,' Abdul replied. 'She is a nice girl. I am not sure about her family, but I suppose he won't be marrying them.'

'Good. I like her too. I do not think we will find a better match for our son,' Feroza said. 'She has a good job, one which means she can work around the responsibility of children, and she has already said it would be easy for her to move.'

'Have you spoken to Yousef about this?' Abdul asked her.

Feroza still hadn't told Abdul about Jessica. He was soft when it came to their children and there was a real possibility he might be supportive of the relationship. 'Yes, I've spoken with him,' she lied. 'He is happy too.'

'Mashallah,' Abdul said. 'And he is sure?'

Feroza nodded. 'I think we should ring her parents and confirm our intentions. Maybe in a few months we will have another engagement.'

'If he is sure, then we should go ahead,' Abdul confirmed.

'Good, I will ring Seema's mum today.' She got up to leave.

'Feroza?' Abdul called. She turned around. 'Did we ever find out why he was so angry the other day in the kitchen?'

'Oh, that.' Feroza smiled. 'Just a bad day at work.' She left before he could ask any more questions.

Normally Feroza would never entertain the idea of Yousef marrying a girl with such abrasive parents. She had hoped for a close relationship with the families her children chose to marry into, but she just couldn't find any common ground with Aleena. She would have to settle for only having a good relationship with Rehana's in-laws. Her conversation with Aleena had gone as expected.

'Abdul and I have spoken with Yousef and we really want to make this rishta pakka,' Feroza explained.

'Rishta pakka?' Aleena replied, sounding more annoyed than confused. 'What does that mean?'

Did this woman really not speak a word of Urdu? She thought about how to put it in plain English. 'It means we would like our son to get to know your daughter and who knows? If they like each other, they can marry,' Feroza said, trying to sound as English as possible.

'Oh, I see,' Aleena said.

Is that all she could say? Did she not know what a good catch Yousef was?

'Well?' Feroza pressed.

'I mean, that's lovely of you to call,' Aleena said. 'This is all new to me, so I will discuss it with my husband and, of course, my husband's father. But to be honest, Seema will have the final say and she has been talking non-stop about Yousef for the last two months so I can imagine her answer.'

Well, at least Seema recognized Yousef's value. 'Take your time, we will wait for your phone call.'

Now that was done, there was one last thing Feroza had to take care of.

It was the morning before Rehana's engagement. Feroza had lots of things she needed to do but she couldn't focus. Yousef was on nights and had just returned home. She made him his breakfast and watched him eat. He might be as tall as his father, but he was still her little boy. A pang of guilt hit her gut as she thought about what she was about to do. She pushed it down. She was a mother who was just looking out for her son. If he no longer knew what was best for him, it was her job to step in and take over.

Rehana came in. 'Mum, I'm going for my hair appointment, then I'm meeting Emma and we're having our nails done. Should be back by lunchtime.'

Feroza nodded. 'Enjoy yourself,' she said, not taking her eyes off Yousef.

'Don't forget to pick up the flowers, Mum,' Rehana continued. 'And remember the fresh rose petal confetti. I ordered it and it should be ready to collect today.'

Feroza nodded again. She knew her jobs for the day, she didn't need Rehana reminding her. Yousef finished his eggs and put his plate in the sink. 'What are your plans for today?' she asked him.

'Sleep. I've been working all night,' he grunted.

'Yousef, do you know what the Qur'an says about mothers

and sons?' she asked him. He looked at her, confused, and shook his head. 'That paradise lies at the feet of your mother. There is nothing like the love of a mother. Remember that.'

'Mum, what are you talking about?' he asked.

'Nothing, it's just important you know, nobody will love you like I do.'

'Right, well, I'm going to bed,' he said.

She waited for Rehana to leave and for Yousef to go upstairs before she put on her coat and headed out of the front door. She walked to the bus stop, looking back at the house to make sure nobody was watching her.

Getting to the hospital meant catching two buses. The hospital foyer had a big board which set out all the wards and which floor they were on. Ward thirty-eight was on the third floor. She took the lift. The door was locked and she needed to press a buzzer so that someone could let her in. She checked the time as she pressed. It was outside visiting hours.

'Can I help you?' came a voice through the intercom.

'Yes, I'm here to see Jessica,' Feroza said.

'Jessica who?' the voice replied.

Feroza had no idea what Jessica's last name was, or what job she did. She did a quick calculation. The messages she had seen on Yousef's phone spanned back at least a year which meant he must have known her at university, which meant she was probably a doctor.

'Doctor Jessica,' Feroza said.

'Are you a relative of a patient? Visiting hours start in an hour,' the voice replied.

Feroza was beginning to get annoyed. 'I am not a relative of a patient, I am Dr Yousef Ahmed's mother.'

There was silence on the other end. She pressed the buzzer again.

'Yousef isn't working today,' the voice came back.

'I know, he is on nights. I have just made him his breakfast and put him to bed. I am here to see Jessica!' Her voice went up an octave.

Another pause, then the door clicked open. 'Come in,' the voice said.

Feroza walked down to the nurses' station. The voice that had been coming through the intercom belonged to a skinny lady with short red hair. 'Can I help you?' she asked again.

'I am here to speak to Dr Jessica. Can you tell her Yousef's mum is here.'

The woman looked apprehensive. Feroza could tell she wasn't sure what to do. Feroza had come prepared for this. 'Yousef really enjoys working on this ward,' she said, smiling at the woman. 'He says the staff are so supportive. He tells me about his work every night. I bet you are Fiona.'

The woman blushed and smiled. 'Did he really tell you about me?'

Feroza nodded. 'Says you always make him a good strong cup of tea whenever he needs it. He said the ward would not function without you.'

'That is true. He's a good lad.' The woman got up. 'Why don't you wait in the relatives' room and I'll go and find Jessica for you.'

Feroza thanked her and took a seat in a tiny room at the end of the ward. She waited half an hour before she heard the sound of footsteps approaching the room. She stood up. A tall girl came in. Her eyes looked kind. She smiled at Feroza.

'Hi, Mrs Ahmed, I'm Jessica.' She held out her hand. Feroza didn't take it.

'Jessica, I am Yousef's mother,' Feroza said curtly. Jess withdrew her hand. 'Shall we sit down?' Jess nodded and they both took a seat.

'Look, I won't waste your time,' Feroza continued. 'I know there is something going on between you and my son.'

A look of hopefulness flashed across Jessica's face. 'Has he told you about us?'

Feroza shook her head. 'No, he has not. I found a message from you on his phone. I want to know how serious it is.'

Jessica looked deflated. She moved to get up. 'Maybe you should be speaking with him about this.'

'Please sit down, we need to talk,' Feroza said. The girl looked at her, eventually sitting down. 'How long has . . . this been going on?'

'You know, I feel really uncomfortable talking about this without Yousef. Perhaps I can call him?' The girl took out her phone.

'Do you not want to speak with me?' Feroza asked. 'I am just here for the truth, is that not what we both deserve?'

The girl didn't say anything.

'How long?' Feroza repeated.

The girl shifted in her seat. 'Not long, maybe three months, but we were together for five years during medical school.'

Feroza felt sick. Five years? How could she not have known? 'And what are your feelings towards my son?' she eventually said.

'I love him,' the girl said quietly.

'You mean, you think you love him?' Feroza said.

'No, I mean, I do love him, and he loves me,' Jessica said, louder this time. 'He's been so worried about what you would say about us he broke off the relationship when we were at university, but now you know, we can move past all of that.'

'Yousef does not know that I know,' Feroza said quickly. 'And he is not to find out either.'

'Aren't you going to tell him now that you've spoken to me?' Jessica looked confused. 'Isn't that why you're here?'

Feroza shook her head. 'Look, I am sorry to have to tell you this, but my son does not love you.'

She waited for Jessica to take this in.

'What do you mean?' Jess replied.

'I mean, he is not serious about whatever this relationship is. Actually, he has been seeing someone else.'

The girl shook her head. 'You're lying.'

'I am sorry, but I am not,' Feroza continued; she hated doing this but it had to be done. 'We confirmed his engagement to this girl just yesterday. Yousef is going to marry her.'

Feroza watched as the girl's eyes filled with tears. 'Why are you saying all of this?' she asked.

'Because I want you to stay away from my son,' Feroza said firmly. Watching this girl's heartbreak was harder than she had imagined. 'He has found a more . . . appropriate girl, one we all approve of.'

She watched as the girl wiped away a tear that had fallen onto her cheek and composed herself. 'I think you should leave. This is my place of work.'

Feroza stood up. 'I am sorry to deliver this news to you, but I did not want you wasting your time with my son. I need you to stop seeing Yousef, stop calling, stop texting, stop everything.' She picked up her handbag. 'Can you do that?'

The girl looked at her. 'You know, you really are as bad as Yousef said you would be.'

'I am just trying to protect my family.' Feroza left.

She was angry. For the first time she was angry at her son for putting her in such a position. Now that the girl was no longer an anonymous sender of text messages, Feroza felt bad. Her son had led that poor girl on, her son had probably made her promises he knew he couldn't keep, her son had made her cry today. For the first time since she could remember, Feroza was disappointed in Yousef.

She calmed herself as she waited for the bus. Her daughter was getting engaged tomorrow, she had to stay focused on that.

Chapter Thirty-Three

Yousef

YOUSEF'S ALARM WENT OFF, jolting him out of his sleep. He checked the time – four p.m. He should get up. He had worked his last night shift for the week so didn't want to sleep so much or he wouldn't be able to sleep again tonight. He checked his messages.

One new message from Jessica. He opened it up.

> Yousef, I will be blocking your number after I have sent this message, please do not try to contact me again. I see you now for who you are, a liar. I wonder if you will ever know how much you have hurt me? I can't believe I fell for it again, that's on me. I have told the ward manager there is no longer enough work for the two of us, so you will be deployed back to your own ward. Don't try to come and see me, it will only be embarrassing for you. I don't ever want to see or speak to you again. Please respect my feelings.

Yousef read the message twice and then immediately dialled Jessica's number. It didn't connect. He tried again: same. He thought about replying to her message, but then if he was blocked, would she even see it? He had to try.

Jess, call me please. I don't know what this is about. Please just call.

His mind was going into a panic. What had happened? He wracked his brain. It must have been Rehana, she must have spoken to her. He got out of bed and barged into Rehana's room. She was in there with Emma, trying on bangles for tomorrow.

'Have you spoken to Jess?' he demanded.

'What?' Rehana said, looking confused.

'Answer the question. Have you spoken with Jessica?' he repeated.

'Of course I haven't,' Rehana said, 'Also, Emma is here so stop acting weird.'

'I don't give a FUCK who's here, I need to know if anyone has spoken with Jessica?'

'Maybe I should go . . .' Emma said, getting up.

'No, stay,' Rehana said. 'Yousef, I have not spoken with Jessica, and I would keep your voice down if I were you,' she said through gritted teeth. 'We have guests downstairs.'

'Guests?' It was Yousef's turn to look confused.

'Yes, Mum's been telling everyone about the engagement, and they're here to help kick off the celebrations,' Rehana said through a false smile.

'Are you sure you haven't spoken to Jess?'

'Stop asking me the same thing. How could I even contact her? I don't know where she lives, I don't even have her number. Now if you don't mind, I have lots to do.' Rehana returned to showing Emma her collection of bangles.

Yousef went back to his room. What was he going to do? He thought about going to see her at the hospital accommodation, but she had been clear about not wanting to see him. He needed to find out what had happened so he could straighten things out. Clearly this was just some big misunderstanding.

He thought about ringing Rohit for advice, but he would be busy with his family in India. Maybe Steve could help? He dialled his number, but it went straight to voicemail. He left him a message asking him to phone him back.

He scrolled through the list of contacts on his phone. Kate! He pressed dial.

Before he could say hello, she cut him off, 'Fuck off trying to call me, Yousef. In fact, fuck off and then when you get there, fuck off some more.' She hung up.

He dialled her again. No answer. He was panicking. He could feel his heart racing. A sense of dread engulfed him. He closed his eyes. What was going on? He tried Jess's number again. Nothing. He lay back down on his bed. Maybe this was all just a bad dream, he just needed to find a way of waking up. He opened his eyes. Nothing had changed. He wanted to cry, scream, punch something. It felt as though his entire world was caving in on him.

Chapter Thirty-Four

Everyone

REHANA LOOKED AT HERSELF in the mirror. The jewels on her blue and gold engagement gharara shimmered with her every movement. Her eyebrows had been perfectly threaded. Sean at John Lewis had agreed to a home visit (with a fee, of course) and had even managed to get rid of the soft hair of her sideburns which had always plagued her. For once, she was happy with her make-up. She gave in to Sean's expertise and it had paid dividends, though she had to say no when he'd suggested waxing her forearms. She wore a silver ankle bracelet which Nadeem had sent in the post to her, along with one hundred red roses. Her mum complained they didn't have enough vases, but Rehana didn't care. Nobody had sent her roses before. They were the posh ones without any thorns on. Her dad had got teary when he saw Rehana in her engagement outfit. She told him he had to leave because her mascara would start running if she cried and she couldn't afford Sean's fees a second time. She was ready, most of the guests had already arrived, and she had got a text from Nadeem a few minutes ago to say they were half an hour away. Rehana would be making a dramatic entrance later, looking like the delicate bride-to-be she was. She could not wait.

★

Jessica rang her parents to ask them if it would be okay for her to move back home if she got her training post in A&E in Somerset next year. They were so supportive it made her cry. Her dad kept asking her if everything was okay, which, of course, she said it was. She hated it here in Birmingham now. The loneliness she thought she had said goodbye to was back and had slowly taken over her like a cancer. She was too embarrassed to see Jonathan, so had stopped going to football. Kate was on her way over. She said she would stay for the weekend, just until Jess was feeling better. That encounter with Yousef's mother had been one of the most humiliating experiences of her life, but at least it had happened on a Friday, which meant she had the weekend to pull herself together. She still couldn't believe Yousef was engaged; how could he say all those things about telling his family about the two of them when all the while he had been seeing someone else? She didn't want to give him the opportunity to lie his way out of this. She wanted nothing more to do with him.

Rohit sat cross-legged on the floor of a room that was packed full of his relatives. He hardly knew any of them, but they were all there to see him. They fussed over what he wanted to eat, whose house he should visit next and why he was so skinny, wasn't his mother feeding him at home? He had just returned from seeing a jyotishi, who had studied his face and, after matching them with the planets, told him that Anjali was a good match for him. Rohit hadn't ever given much notice to some of the more traditional parts of his religion, but his Indian relatives were keen to make sure their religious leaders were in favour of his and Anjali's union, which was odd because he hadn't decided if *he* was yet. An astrologer sat in the middle of the room with scrolls of paper laid out in front of him. He was advising the parents on when a good time for the engagement would be. Sitting on the far side of the room was Anjali. He kept giving her furtive looks. It was almost impossible to spend any time alone together, but he had managed to steal her away the night before for a walk. His mum was right, meeting up in real life was different to meeting online. They didn't have a great deal in common, but she was definitely a nice girl. Most of their conversation revolved around what life was like in the UK. Rohit did his best to sell it to Anjali as positively as he could. There seemed to be an assumption by all in this room that Rohit and Anjali were a done deal. It made him feel uneasy. He liked her, but could he marry her?

For as long as she could remember, Anjali had dreamed about working as a doctor in the UK. There was a certain level of respect commanded by those working in Great Britain. She hadn't been short of offers of a rishta here in Delhi, but she wanted a fresh start, a new adventure. When Uncle Anand had suggested Rohit, she hadn't been too impressed with his photo but speaking to him had slowly changed her mind. He asked lots of questions about her, something the boys here didn't do. He didn't mind when she got passionate about her work. She liked that. He wasn't vegetarian, nor was he as religious as she was, but that could change. She would go to England, get to know him and get to know what life in the UK would be like. And if she was being honest, he wasn't that bad looking in real life.

Yousef watched as Rehana was accompanied down the stairs by her father. Even Aunty Musarat clasped her hands together at the sight of her. He had to admit she looked stunning. But it was resentment he felt now. If only he hadn't listened to her, if only he had told his family about Jessica when he wanted to, perhaps then he wouldn't be in this situation? He felt numb to the celebrations that were going on around him. He watched Seema try to get as involved as possible, fussing around his mother, asking if there was anything she could do to help? A few of the aunties had asked him when his turn to get married would be. He must have scowled at them as they made a hasty retreat. His mind raced. If he didn't have Jessica, it would mean being stuck attending an endless array of events such as this one, having meaningless conversations with people he barely knew and probably marrying a woman he didn't love. People began to clamber to get a photograph with Rehana and Nadeem so he used the opportunity to go out for a walk. He needed air.

Seema knew how to impress an Asian family. She had donned her peach gharara and had her hair and make-up done enough to impress Yousef and his mother, but not too much as to outshine the bride-to-be. As soon as she arrived, she made a beeline for Yousef's mum, asking what help she needed. She then headed upstairs to play the dutiful sister-in-law to Rehana, helping her adjust her dupatta and get into her shoes. Once she had completed this she went downstairs. Yousef looked a bit miserable, but she assumed this was because he was coming to terms with his sister moving out soon. He would probably miss her. Plus, he had just finished a set of night shifts, which would make anyone grumpy. Her parents had told her that Yousef was keen on her and wanted to get to know her more. Her mind was almost made up about him, but she didn't want to make it too easy. A girl had to play just a little bit hard to get.

Feroza watched proudly as her friends ogled Nadeem and his family. She could tell they were jealous. She had told them all he had a six-figure salary (she had come to that conclusion on her own) and owned his house. The look on Musarat's face was a picture. She wished she'd had a camera. Both of her children happily married, that was her dream and it was about to become a reality. Yousef would thank her in the long run. He was far better suited to Seema and, in time, he would love her in a way that just wasn't possible with Jessica. That was the way with arranged marriages: you found a suitable person and then love followed naturally. She could see the future for her family in her mind's eye. She would be living in a big house with Yousef, Seema and, of course, Abdul. She would split her time between looking after Yousef's children and travelling down to see Rehana so she could do the same for her. It would be a busy life, but one *so fulfilling*, her heart was bursting just thinking about it.

Part Three

Eight months later

Chapter Thirty-Five

Rehana

REHANA STEPPED OUT FROM the dressing room and looked earnestly at her mum and Emma. She was beginning to feel the pressure. Time was running out and they were yet to find the perfect wedding lengha. They had been to bridal boutiques in Birmingham, Southall, Manchester and they were now in Bradford. Every lengha, sari, gharara or kameez she had tried on had not been right. They had spent two days in Southall trawling through every bridalwear shop. She almost settled for a cream and peach number just to put an end to the search, but after she burst into tears at the chai cafe, Emma had convinced her she mustn't settle. Her mum was panicking. If she didn't find a dress today, she wouldn't have time to adjust it for her wedding.

My wedding. She loved how that sounded.

Emma gasped. 'Wow, you look stunning.' She took a sip of the mango lassi they had been given when they arrived. 'I love it. How do you feel?'

'It feels very glamorous,' Rehana said, turning to her mum. 'Mum, what do you think?'

'No, too much midriff showing. You are not Kareena Kapoor, what will everyone think?' Her mum shook her head. 'No, definitely not. Take it off.'

Rehana had picked this one out precisely because it did show off her midriff. She wanted Nadeem to get excited when he saw her walking down the aisle. Their relationship had been very much PG up until now and she was beginning to get frustrated.

'Madam, we can adjust the length of the choli, no problem,' Mustafa, the owner of the bridal shop, said. 'The colour really suits you.'

Rehana wasn't sure she wanted this particular dress if she couldn't show off her waist; she didn't like it that much. 'No, I've changed my mind. Show me that one again.' Rehana pointed to the crimson lengha that Mustafa suggested she try on first.

Mustafa nodded. 'Red, a beautiful colour for any bride.'

'Don't you think it's a bit too traditional?' Rehana asked. Holding the dress against her and looking in the mirror, it did look nice.

'No, madam, red has come full circle,' Mustafa explained. 'Girls always want something different. Over the last few years we sold lots of golds, creams, purples, greens, nobody wanted red. But now nobody is wearing red, everybody wants it again. You should try it on. That one has been hand-stitched in Karachi.'

Rehana scooped up the lengha and disappeared into the changing room. Her wedding was only two months away, she still had so much to do. Nadeem was back from Dubai now and working at his new job in London. They were seeing a lot more of each other in the guise of 'sorting out the wedding'. It was wonderful. She got excited each time. Last weekend he had come up so they could make a final decision on the flowers for the tables.

Whilst they were having two of all the other ceremonies that made up a Pakistani wedding, it was proving expensive, so they had decided to join forces for the big day and combine the wedding and walima into one event. Most people were doing that now, so Rehana's parents had agreed. Thankfully she had found her mehndi dress relatively quickly in Birmingham, but finding the perfect wedding dress was proving much harder.

She pulled up the skirt and adjusted the dupatta. She liked it but didn't love it.

'What do you reckon?' she asked, waddling out of the dressing room. The suits were so laden with jewels it made it hard to walk.

'Beautiful,' Emma said. It was her reaction to everything Pakistani. Rehana really should have brought someone who knew the difference between a sari and a shevani.

'It makes you look dark,' her mum said. 'And I do not like how it is backless.'

The last thing Rehana wanted on her wedding was all the aunties whispering about how dark she looked. 'Not this one, then.' She was beginning to think she was never going to find her wedding dress.

'Well, you have seen our entire spring collection,' Mustafa said, sounding deflated. 'Maybe madam is being a little too . . . picky?'

Spring collection? Rehana thought. Where did Mustafa think he worked, the offices of *Vogue*? This was Bradford, not Paris.

'You call that a collection? It was four dresses!' her mum retorted. 'I knew we should have just gone to Pakistan and had a dress made.' She paused to finish the last of her mango lassi. 'Come on, girls, let's go.'

They walked down White Abbey Road. It was wall-to-wall Asian clothes shops. It was clear wedding season was coming up. Families with harassed-looking daughters and frazzled mums walked with urgency in and out of shops. 'When is our next appointment?' Rehana asked.

'In about an hour,' Emma replied, looking at her watch.

'Great, let's have some lunch. I'm starving,' Rehana suggested. They all nodded in agreement.

The good thing about Bradford is that you are never far from a decent curry house. They were sat down immediately and presented with menus.

'Rehana, maybe that man is correct. You need to stop being so choosy and pick a dress,' her mother said. 'We have so many other things to sort out as well.'

'Mum, don't you think I know that?' Rehana exclaimed. 'Me and Nads were arguing over what to put inside of the wedding favour bags last night. Maybe if you hadn't insisted on inviting every Tom, Dick and Harry to my wedding, it wouldn't be so stressful.'

'Look, now she is blaming me,' her mum said dramatically to Emma. 'The first wedding in our house, of course I will invite everyone,' she continued. 'My daughter is finally getting married, I need everyone to witness it. Don't you agree, Emma?'

Emma looked scared. She looked at Rehana for help.

'All I'm saying is there was no need to invite the bloody Shekars to the wedding. We haven't seen or spoken to them in years.'

'The Shekars invited us to their son's wedding, it is bezati if we do not do the same.' Her mum rolled her eyes at her. 'Besides, what can I do? You have said only five hundred guests! People will think we are poor.'

'Mum, that is the maximum number of guests the venue would allow,' Rehana almost shouted.

'Weddings are about the community, Rehana,' her mum said. 'Everybody just wants to see how happy you are and wish you well.'

'More like they're coming for the free food and a good old gossip,' Rehana muttered.

'I think I'm going to order the samosa chaat,' Emma said. Rehana could tell she was keen to change the subject. 'It looks delicious, and don't worry, Aunty, I am sure we are going to find Rehana's dress today, I can feel it.'

Her mum nodded. Rehana loved Emma. She was the only person that her mum didn't seem to want to argue with. Since the disastrous coffee date, Emma had become fully invested in her relationship with Nadeem and had impressed her family by coming to the engagement party in a sari and pulling off some bhangra moves she had learned from YouTube. She had also become an integral part of the wedding preparations over the last few months, driving Rehana and her mum to the caterers and offering her opinions on what kind of stage decor they should go for. She had even jokingly asked her mum if Aunty Henna could find her a man if she supplied her with her biodata, if her relationship with Chris didn't work out.

Once they had finished eating, they headed to their next appointment. They rang the bell at the door and waited.

'Is it the right time?' her mum asked Emma.

Emma looked at her printed timetable. 'Yes, I booked for two o'clock.'

'See, that is another thing, when did we have to start making appointments to look at clothes?' her mum said. It was Rehana's turn to roll her eyes. She had heard this speech before and knew her mum was only doing it for Emma's benefit. 'It used to be you just walked into clothes shops and they were happy for your custom. Now they make you feel grateful to them for giving you the time.'

'It's the same in English bridal shops,' Emma replied, nodding. Why was she colluding with her mother?

A lady appeared at the door. 'Rehana Ahmed?' she asked. Rehana nodded. 'Come in, we have prepared some beautiful gowns for you.'

Rehana entered the plush-looking boutique. There were none of the usual racks of clothing she had seen at the other shops, just a few elegant-looking mannequins dotted around wearing the most exquisite dresses.

'You don't seem to have much choice,' Rehana's mum said, clearly not as impressed as she was.

'The bridalwear is in a private room in the back. We don't want the pieces to get damaged.' The woman gave Rehana's mum a smile. 'People like to touch things and our gowns are precious.'

'I am a seamstress, I know how precious gowns are.' Her mum nodded, not wanting to be outdone.

They were led to the back of the store and invited to sit down on a large chaise longue. 'Can I offer you some alcohol-free champagne?' the lady asked. She looked at Emma. 'Or maybe some regular champagne?'

'Champagne? Sherab?' Rehana's mum exclaimed. 'Thoba, thoba. No thank you, I will take a cup of tea. Milk, two sugars.'

'I'll take the champagne,' Emma said eagerly. Poor Emma, Rehana thought, she probably needed the alcohol.

'I'll have a tea as well, please,' Rehana said, knowing no champagne would be alcohol-free enough for her mum's approval.

'My name is Divya, I will be showcasing your gowns today.' Divya had a soothing voice. It reminded Rehana of the bedtime stories on telly that parents put on when they couldn't be bothered to read to their kids themselves. She was thin with long, glossy hair which only added to her ethereal appeal. 'Thank you for sending in your photo. We have selected five gowns we thought would suit you.'

Was that another dig at her complexion? Rehana wondered. She couldn't decide whether she liked the snootiness of this store or hated it. She waited to see what gowns they had for her before she would decide. Divya explained the gowns were kept behind a curtain and she would be bringing them out one at a time. She put on a pair of white gloves before she handled the gowns. *A bit dramatic*, Rehana thought.

'I thought, because you have such beautiful eyes and gorgeous dark hair, you might consider wearing this gold and green gown.' She held up an elegant lengha that had only a modest amount of embroidery and jewellery sewn into it. 'It's more muted than our other pieces, but I am sure you will agree it is beautiful.'

Her mum nearly choked on her tea. 'It is so plain. People will think she is one of the guests at the wedding, not the bride. Absolutely not. Emma, maybe you can wear it?'

'I already have my dress, thank you, Aunty,' Emma replied.

Rehana quite liked it, but daren't say.

'Perhaps something with a bit more work on it then. This green gharara just came in yesterday,' Divya said from behind the curtain. 'It has silver and black gemstones along the hem, and intricate silver threadwork on the sleeves.' She came carrying the dress like it was a precious baby. 'We had a bride-to-be in this morning who was keen on this one, so if you like it, you will have to be quick!'

'Green?' Rehana's mum exclaimed. 'Green is for the mehndi ceremony, not for the wedding day. No, no, not green. Rehana, what do you think?'

'It's beautiful, but I have to agree with Mum, I'm wearing green on my mehndi so can't duplicate it for the wedding.' She was trying to be as diplomatic as possible.

Her mum nodded. 'Next, please.'

'Okay,' Divya continued, keeping her professional cool, 'might you consider wearing turquoise? Not many brides can pull it off but I think it matches your skin tone perfectly.' She pulled out a dazzling gown from behind the curtain. It was the most enchanting shade of turquoise Rehana had ever seen, decorated with navy embroidery and green jewels that caught the light as Divya showed it off. 'The stones are from Rajasthan, in India. The dress itself was handmade in Delhi.'

'I love it,' Rehana whispered. She stared wide-eyed. She hadn't had an emotional connection to a dress before now. It called to her. 'Mum, Emma, what do you think?'

'It's nice,' Rehana's mum replied. 'I don't know, is it a wedding colour?'

'I think it's stunning, the way the turquoise turns to that dark blue on the edges, it's just flawless,' Emma said. 'Rehana, you have to try it on.'

'May I?' Rehana asked Divya. She was worried the shop might be too posh to let people actually try on the dresses. Divya smiled and nodded.

'I will help you get into it.' She gestured for Rehana to follow her. Rehana shot Emma a look. She really hoped this dress looked as enchanting on her as it did whilst Divya handled it. She followed Divya to the dressing room, which was huge and decorated with more chaise longues and giant urns.

'You can undress here,' Divya said. 'Then we can put the gown on.'

Rehana wasn't used to having anyone present when she took her clothes off. At home everyone went into the bathroom fully dressed, had a shower and emerged fully dressed. There was no half-naked wandering around at the Ahmed house.

'Erm, here?' Rehana said timidly. Divya nodded. Rehana pulled her T-shirt over her head and unbuttoned her jeans. As soon as they were off, Divya got to work, instructing Rehana to step into the skirt so she could pull it up. Then she pulled on the choli top. Divya began pulling at the strings behind the choli, tightening it around Rehana's ribs. 'Steady on, Divya,' she said. 'I want to be able to breathe at my wedding.'

'To make this dress pop in the way it should, we need to make sure it's as tight as can be,' Divya replied, rather aggressively. 'If you choose this dress, you may need to let it out a bit at the bosom area.'

What happened to that gentle woman who had been floating around earlier?

'There, perfect,' Divya announced. She stood back to admire her work. 'You look . . . bewitching, winsome even.' She smiled. She was back to her usual tones.

Rehana had never been described as 'bewitching' before;

frumpy and plain, yes, but never bewitching or winsome. Those words were reserved for other girls. She looked at herself in the mirror. Her breath caught. She could hardly believe it was her. She looked like the brides in the magazines she had collected over the last year. This was the dress. She stepped out from behind the curtain.

There was silence from both her mum and Emma. *They hate it*, she thought.

'Oh, Rehana,' Emma said eventually. 'You look absolutely perfect.'

Rehana smiled. She could feel herself getting emotional. She wasn't the type of girl to get emotional over a dress. What the hell had Divya put in that tea?

'Mum?' She looked at her mum.

To her surprise, her mum was becoming tearful. 'This is it,' her mum said, trying to calm herself. 'This is the one, Rehana.'

Rehana nodded. They were all in agreement.

'How much is it?' Rehana's mum asked.

'That is a one-off piece. As I said, designed in Rajasthan, handmade in Delhi. But even still, it's very reasonably priced,' Divya said.

'How much?' her mum repeated.

'I can give it to you for five thousand pounds,' Divya said.

The three of them gasped.

'Five thousand pounds! Are you mad? Itna mahenga?!' Rehana's mum shrieked. 'Is it made up of real diamonds and gold?'

'The gemstones are amber and some of them are made of jade,' Divya replied. 'There has been a lot of interest in this dress with wedding season coming. We do have some more modestly priced ones, if you would like me to show you those?'

'There is no need for that, we would just like a reasonable price for this one,' her mum said, indignant. 'What is your best price?'

'Five thousand. It's a fixed price,' Divya replied calmly.

'No such thing as a fixed price in an Indian shop. What discount can you give?' her mum countered. She was just getting started. Rehana had seen all of this before. Her mum always haggled no matter where they went. She even tried to haggle in Asda once. Rehana had been deeply embarrassed by it when she was younger and would scurry off to a different part of the store, but now she watched, fascinated.

'I could maybe take off a hundred pounds, but that is my best offer,' Divya countered.

'Don't insult me,' her mum scoffed. 'I want a proper discount.'

Emma leaned forward. 'Rehana, what's going on?' she whispered. She sounded stressed. 'What's your mum doing?'

'Bartering. Don't worry, it's normal,' Rehana whispered back. 'Trust me, they'll both put on performances like they're gunning for an Oscar.'

'You tell me a realistic price,' Divya said to Rehana's mum.

'Well, I would have to make several adjustments to the gown to make it perfect for my daughter, that will take a lot of time,' her mum mused. 'And one or two of the gemstones look as though they might need stitching back on . . .'

'Go on, tell me a price,' Divya said, looking amused.

'Three thousand, and that's being generous,' her mum said flatly.

'Now you are insulting me, Aunty.' Divya laughed. 'How about four thousand five hundred? I am being fair here.'

'You know Mustafa down the street, he has a similar dress for two thousand,' her mum replied. 'Rehana, come on, let's go. We will buy that dress.' Her mum got up and made a show of slinging her handbag over her shoulder. Emma got up too.

'Please, sit down, Aunty. I am sure we can come to some sort of arrangement,' Divya said gently.

Emma looked at Rehana. 'Are we staying or going?' she asked.

'Staying,' Rehana hissed. 'Sit down.'

Emma sat down, looking equal parts uncomfortable and confused.

'Perhaps you can have a talk with the shop owner and get a more realistic price?' Rehana's mum said rather patronizingly.

Divya smiled. 'My husband and I own the store. I can give you the dress for four thousand, and that really is the best I can do.'

'Three thousand five hundred,' her mum challenged immediately.

Divya shot her look of disdain. 'Aunty, come on. I need to make some money on this sale,' Divya said.

'Okay, three thousand six hundred, and remember I work in the business, I know what these dresses are worth,' her mum said.

Her mum was overselling herself, Rehana thought. She made adjustments and repaired other people's clothing, it was hardly the same as creating something as beautiful as this.

'Let's meet halfway and say three thousand, seven hundred and fifty,' Divya replied, holding out her hand to signal the bartering was over.

Her mum nodded. 'Challo, I'll take it, but I still think we are overpaying.' She shook Divya's hand. Rehana wanted to jump for joy. She had finally found the perfect dress, she couldn't believe it. She texted Nadeem.

Rehana: Dress found, you are going to die when you see me in it.

He replied almost immediately.

Nadeem: Send me a pic.
Rehana: It's bad luck, you'll have to wait for the big day.
Nadeem: Not fair ☹

The three of them walked out of the shop. The stress Rehana had felt driving into Bradford evaporated as they emerged.

'Aunty, you were pretty awesome in there,' Emma said, linking arms with Rehana's mum.

'We haggle all the time in Pakistan, it's part of the fun of shopping,' her mum replied. 'You goray should try it.'

'Are you kidding? I can't imagine my parents trying to haggle in shops. They would die of embarrassment,' Emma said. 'I can't believe how much money you saved.'

'Not my money,' Rehana's mum said. 'Nadeem's family are paying for the dress, they saved money.'

Emma looked at Rehana, even more in awe of her mother. Rehana nodded.

Chapter Thirty-Six

Feroza

SAMOSAS, SPRING ROLLS, POTATO cutlets, paneer tikka and a token salad. Feroza assessed her spread proudly. Her friends were coming round for afternoon tea and she wanted them to be just as envious of the food as they were of the news that both of her children were well on their way to being married and settled. She had gone to the local mithai shop and bought packets of ras malai. With all of the preparations for Rehana's wedding, she didn't have time to make a dessert as well.

She took her best teacups out of the cupboard and placed them on a tray, ready for when everyone arrived. Abdul and Yousef were at work and Rehana was out with Nadeem; the less Feroza knew about that, the better. The doorbell went. Feroza grabbed her dupatta and gave herself a quick once-over in the mirror.

Musarat stood on the doorstep. Feroza could see her assessing their tiny front garden. Luckily the hydrangeas she had recently bought to impress Seema's family were in bloom. Musarat handed her a small bunch of flowers which she took with a smile. Pinky and Rubina arrived a few minutes later. Feroza took their coats and they all sat down at the table.

'You have gone to so much trouble, Feroza,' Rubina said,

looking at the food. 'I thought we were having afternoon tea? I was expecting scones and jam.' They all laughed.

'Don't be silly, Rubina. This is Pakistani afternoon tea, much nicer,' Feroza replied. 'Try the cutlets, they are a new recipe I got from the Islam channel cooking show.' Feroza passed around the plate, insisting everyone take one. 'I added paprika to them.'

'So how are the wedding plans going?' Pinky asked.

'Oh, very well,' Feroza replied. 'There is so much to organize when it comes to weddings, you know what it is like, and being the mother of the bride, I have to do everything. I wanted a big wedding, but you know children today, so modern, they all want small weddings.'

The four of them nodded in agreement.

'Youngsters today don't realize that their community is their family also,' Pinky said. 'When we came to this country we left our families behind and we became each other's family. That is being lost with this new generation.'

They all nodded again.

'We invited eight hundred to Zara's wedding,' Musarat said. 'Then people brought their relatives and friends and there were nearly nine hundred in the end. Thank God we ordered enough food.'

'People have no shame,' Pinky said, her mouth full of cutlet.

'I hope you haven't invited Mariam and her family to the wedding. At Zara's she brought her entire family who were visiting from Pakistan. The waiters had to get extra chairs out from the back,' Rubina replied.

'Has Zara settled in her new home?' Feroza queried.

Musarat looked slightly uncomfortable. 'Yes,' she said. 'She is enjoying married life.'

'That's good. It's just that she is spending a lot of time at your house, no?' Feroza said in her most innocent voice. The truth was, Rubina had told her that Zara and her husband were having issues. She just wasn't getting on with his mother and had come up to stay with Musarat to get away from it all. Of course, Feroza didn't wish anything ill on Zara and her marriage, but Musarat had been so smug when she had announced the wedding. 'I just wondered if everything was okay?'

'She just missed her dad.' Musarat smiled. 'She will be going back next week.'

'Well, my Lubna is happily settled,' Rubina announced. 'She and her husband have just bought their own house in Luton – detached, of course.' Feroza went through the motions of marvelling at this news, but she was bristling inside. This afternoon was not about Rubina's good news, it was about hers.

'And what about you, Pinky?' Feroza asked. 'Have you found anyone for your Yasmine yet?'

Pinky shook her head. 'Not yet,' she replied, the sadness audible in her voice. 'It is so hard to find decent families these days, no?' They all nodded. 'We show her boys, she says no, what can I do?'

'Children today are so fussy,' Musarat said. 'They spend too much time on Tickety Tock. They all want good looks, good job, funny, tall, nice family – it's impossible to find all of that in one person.'

'So true,' Rubina said. 'You should tell Yasmine to compromise, then she will find someone.'

Pinky nodded. It felt as though she had already had this conversation with her daughter. 'Inshallah, she will find someone when the time is right.'

'And how about your son, Dawood?' Musarat asked Pinky. 'How old is he now?'

'Almost thirty,' Pinky said, 'Still, we cannot find someone for him.'

Nobody said anything for a moment.

'It is so nice to know both my children have found good partners,' Feroza said, after she felt there had been a long enough pause. 'It will be such a relief to see them married, Rehana in her own home, Yousef and his wife living here.'

'When are you doing Yousef's engagement?' Musarat asked, always the first to want any gossip.

'Not long now. Seema is such a wonderful girl. You know, she keeps sending me flowers.' She pointed to a ginormous bouquet of lilies on the mantelpiece. She had placed the rather pathetic bunch Musarat had brought her next to them to highlight the fact they were not up to her new standards. 'I keep telling her not to waste her money on me, but she won't listen.' Feroza laughed.

'That's nice,' Musarat said. 'Zara's husband has bought me and Asad tickets to Dubai. They are going next month and wanted us to come with them, isn't that nice?'

Feroza smiled politely. 'How lovely.' She was seething. 'I'm sure when Rehana and Nadeem get married, we will be going on trips with them. Nadeem has a top job in London and travels all over the world.'

'And his family, what are they like?' Pinky asked.

'Perfect, we couldn't have asked for nicer in-laws for our daughter,' Feroza said proudly. 'He has just bought a house off-plan, so Rehana will live with them for a short time before it is ready to live in. But I know Rehana will get on very well with his mum.'

They all nodded. 'It's such a blessing to get good in-laws,' Musarat said. 'What are Seema's family like? We don't hear much about them.'

'They are busy doctors, you know what it's like,' Feroza replied. 'They're always working, no time to visit.' She was lying. She had tried to phone Seema's mum to strike up a relationship with her a couple of times, but each time talking to her was like getting blood from a stone. 'I will go and get the dessert.'

She took the ras malai out of the fridge and placed it on the tray next to the teacups. She was thoroughly enjoying herself. It had been so long since she could gloat about her children, especially to Musarat. She couldn't wait for the wedding day itself when she could glide through the hall, chatting to everyone on the pretence of asking them whether they had eaten enough and whether they needed anything else, when all she wanted them to see was how perfect her family were.

She picked up the tray and made her way back to the room. 'Ras malai,' Musarat marvelled. 'Homemade?'

Feroza nodded. 'Of course. The shop-bought one never tastes the same.' She had added a few pistachios to the dessert to make it look more homemade. 'Have I told you, Rehana and Nadeem are going to the Maldives for their honeymoon? Nadeem has arranged a five-star trip. He is so good.'

'Very nice,' Pinky said.

'And they are stopping in Istanbul on the way back,' Feroza said proudly. 'Rehana has always wanted to go there. She was very excited. Rubina, what's wrong? Don't you like the ras malai?' Rubina hadn't touched her dessert.

'I'm sure it's delicious. I just had some big news to tell you and was waiting for the right moment,' Rubina replied. Feroza did not like the sound of this.

'Tell us, we are always happy to hear exciting news,' she said, smiling as best she could.

'Lubna is expecting!' Rubina exclaimed. 'She is due in three months. I am going to be a naani.'

Musarat and Pinky congratulated her. Feroza held back. Why would Rubina choose her afternoon tea party to make her announcement? She had gone to great effort to make this food. This was about her children and their achievements. Rubina looked at her expectantly. 'Well, I'm very happy for you,' Feroza said. 'Children are a blessing from God.'

'Thank you,' Rubina replied.

'I think I will go and make us some more tea,' Feroza said.

She didn't want to be in the room whilst they all applauded Rubina's daughter for getting pregnant. She slammed the tray down, and took a moment to catch her breath. She was happy for Rubina, she really was, but there was a time and a place. Rehana's wedding was no longer enough to make her friends jealous, she needed something more. She needed to formalize Yousef's engagement.

Chapter Thirty-Seven

Jessica

ONLY SIX WEEKS TO go before her fresh start, Jess told herself. She had got her training post in emergency medicine and was heading home. Most of her things were already packed in boxes, ready for the move. The process had been cathartic for her. The boxes represented an end to this tumultuous chapter of her life.

She had spent the last few months going from trying her best to avoid Yousef to realizing that because they worked in the same hospital, that was impossible. She afforded him only the most professional courtesy when they saw each other. She had told Monica, the ward sister, what had happened. In true Monica fashion she had been super supportive and said she would make sure the staff knew to send Yousef packing should he come looking for her. Jess had been relieved. She didn't want to create a scene in front of everyone, especially Fiona, who would no doubt use it as a source of gossip for weeks to come.

The hardest part was the loneliness. Jess lay on her sofa and swiped through her matches on Tinder. It was slim pickings. Her messages were even worse. Most of the guys just wanted a quick hook-up. One of the doctors at the hospital was on the app and had asked her out. It had been a bit weird as she definitely didn't want to date anyone she worked with – she had already made that mistake once. Her mind kept going back to Yousef and his mother. There were so many things she wished she had said to that woman when she turned up on her ward, but the shock of it all meant her brain wasn't working properly. Part of the pain she was feeling was a result of all her un-answered questions.

Her Instagram pinged, telling her she had a DM.

It was James Robinson, the old college boyfriend her mum was keen for her to get back together with.

Hey you, I hear you're moving back to Somerset?

She looked at the message then scrolled through the pictures on his profile. He had grown his hair and had a bit of facial fuzz. It suited him. Jess thought back to her days with James. They had been so easy. They had grown up in the same village and his parents had already known her. Like with Jonathan, there was no sneaking around, no lying, no sinister family members hiding in the shadows. Plus, her mum would be over the moon.

She reread his message. It would be nice to have an uncom-plicated relationship. She decided to reply.

Moving back next month, new job etc. How are you?

He responded almost immediately.

Yeah, good. We should meet up for a drink when you're back?

Oh shit, that escalated quickly. She was hoping for a text conversation that didn't really commit her to anything, but the question mark at the end meant she had to answer. She wasn't ready for anything new with a boy, but James wouldn't be new, it would be old familiar territory and it felt safe.

Jess: Yeah, that would be nice.

James: Great, let me know when you get here and I'll arrange it ☺

Chapter Thirty-Eight

Rohit

THE TRAIN WAS FULL so Rohit had to stand. There was a time when he would have been incapacitated by one of his panic attacks at the thought of getting on a train with so many people on it, but he was on his way to see Anjali and that made even the busiest of journeys worthwhile. In fact, everything was just better now. Even work didn't feel like such a chore. The lady standing opposite him was giving him a funny look. He had been smiling to himself. He did that a lot these days.

He got off at the next stop and decided to walk over to Uncle Anand's house as it was a nice day.

Uncle Anand was in the front garden, pruning the hedges.

'Namaste, Uncle,' he said as he walked up the path.

'Ah, Rohit. Namaste. Nice to see you, beta.' Uncle Anand smiled. 'Anjali is inside, just go straight in.'

'Thanks, Uncle. Do you need a hand with those hedges?'

'No, no, you go and enjoy yourself.' Uncle Anand winked at him. 'You shouldn't keep a lady waiting.'

Rohit laughed and went in. He could hear Aunty Jennifer in the kitchen.

'Hi, Aunty Jen.' He handed her the bunch of sunflowers he had picked up at the station. 'These are for you.'

'Rohit, you little charmer!' Aunty Jen said in her strong

cockney accent. 'These are bloody lovely, I'll stick them in a vase. Anjali is upstairs. Sit down, she won't be long.'

Rohit took a seat at the breakfast bar and watched Aunty Jen fill up a jug with water and unpack the sunflowers.

'So, what you got planned today, then?' she asked.

'It's a beautiful day outside, so I thought we would go for a walk, and then maybe some lunch. There's a new Spanish place that does tapas dishes the size of normal meals. I thought we could try that.' Rohit was making it sound very casual, but he had it all planned out and had already booked the restaurant.

'Sounds lovely. I can't be doing with those tiny plates at tapas gaffs, so that sounds right up my street. Might have to get Anand to take me there. There, these look gorgeous.' She admired the sunflowers and placed them in the centre of the dining table. 'Things going well with you two, then?'

Rohit nodded. 'I think so.'

'Well, she's always smiling after she gets back from seeing you, so you must be doing something right,' Jen replied. 'You know, I wasn't so sure when your Uncle Anand told me he was setting the two of you up, what with her being from India and you growing up here.' She laughed.

'You and me both, Aunty Jen,' Rohit replied. 'To be honest, I was beginning to think I wasn't going to find anyone.'

'Funny what life throws at you, isn't it?' Aunty Jen said. 'My parents were so dead set against me marrying Anand, they didn't even come to our wedding. It wasn't the done thing in the eighties to marry an Indian fella, but since we had kids, I can't bloody keep them away.'

Rohit thought about Yousef. Times hadn't changed that much. Anjali appeared looking as beautiful as ever. 'Hi,' he said, 'you look . . .' – he wanted to say something brilliant and charming, but words always failed him when Anjali was around – 'nice.'

Anjali smiled. 'Thanks. Do you need a hand with dinner, Aunty Jennifer?' she asked.

'Don't be ridiculous, darling, go and enjoy yourselves.' Aunty Jen ushered them out of the kitchen. 'Go. Be young, have fun.'

Anjali had been in the UK for a few months now. She was working at the local hospital as a doctor in obstetrics and gynaecology. Rohit waited patiently each day for her call so she could tell him about her day. He loved the sound of her voice, the way she got excited if she was able to assist in the delivery of a baby, how she mixed in Hindi words to her English sentences.

The park was stunning, the trees were wearing the thick coats of summer foliage, and the sun felt warm and comforting on Rohit's skin. Anjali was talking about how her parents and sisters had told her they were coming over to visit in a few weeks. She missed them terribly and was looking forward to the visit. Rohit was nervous. He planned to kiss Anjali today but didn't know how to initiate it. He had hoped there would be a natural break in the conversation and flow of walking where they would be looking into each other's eyes so he could make his move, but they had been walking for nearly forty-five minutes and that was looking less and less likely.

'So do you know if the temple is doing anything for holi?' Anjali asked.

Rohit knew how important these religious festivals were to Anjali and he wanted to make more of an effort to get involved with them himself. Before Anjali, he wouldn't have dreamed of allowing himself to get covered in coloured powder and have paint thrown at him in the name of Lord Vishnu and good triumphing over evil, but now with Anjali he wanted to try everything.

'Amit and Priya normally take the kids to the temple for holi. They have a garden at the back where everyone celebrates,' Rohit said. 'We can go with them.'

'Perfect, my parents will love that,' Anjali said. 'What time did you book the restaurant for?'

Rohit looked at his watch. 'In about fifteen minutes. We can walk there, it's not far.' Anjali nodded and carried on walking. Rohit stopped where he was.

'Is something wrong?' she asked, turning to look at him.

He shook his head and moved closer to her. 'Nothing's wrong.' He took her hand in his. 'I just wanted to try something,' he whispered as he moved his face closer to hers. Anjali gave him the hint of a smile. Their lips touched, soft at first. She tasted of minty toothpaste and cherry lip balm. It was enchanting. He closed his eyes, his body going into sensory overdrive. After a few seconds, he pulled himself away. 'I, er, hope that wasn't too . . . forward?'

Anjali shook her head, smiling. 'No, it was perfect. I was beginning to think you didn't like me.'

'Me, not like you?' Rohit said incredulously. 'Anjali, I'm crazy about you.'

Anjali laughed and kissed him again. 'Let's go before they give our table to someone else!'

They walked hand in hand to the restaurant.

Chapter Thirty-Nine

Yousef

YOUSEF DROVE HIS MUM to the Dhumaka Asian Events Store to pick up decorations for the house. His mum was stressing out about how little time they had.

'Yousef, why are you driving so slow, huh?' his mum moaned. 'Normally, you race around like a hooligan.'

'Ma, there is traffic, what do you want me to do?' Yousef said, pointing at the cars in front of them.

'I told you to take the back roads, but nobody listens to me. We have to get back before one o'clock because Nadeem and his brother are coming to put the lights up on the house.'

'Don't you think putting lights up outside the house is a bit over the top?' Yousef replied.

'Nonsense, Aunty Musarat did it for Zara's wedding. How else is everybody going to know there is a shaadi going on in our home?' His mum shook her head at him as she always did when she felt he didn't understand her point.

Musarat was in the back seat. She had become the unofficial wedding planner, her only qualification being she had done it once before for her daughter.

'Yousef, beta,' Musarat cooed, 'decorating your house with lights is a Pakistani tradition.'

'And don't forget you have to pay the deposit for the DJ

today, you can do that on your own.' His mum looked out of the window. 'I wish your father was around to help more.'

His dad had taken up extra shifts at work, probably to pay for the wedding. All his mother seemed to care about was having the biggest and best of everything so she could show off to her mates.

'I don't see why Rehana couldn't drive you to pick up the decorations. After all, it is her wedding,' he muttered.

'Because Rehana has the girls coming round to practise the dances for the mehndi. There is only three weeks left and that bloody Amber can't get the dhandia routine in her head. I told Rehana she should cut her from the dance, but she said it would be rude now.'

Musarat nodded. 'It was the same at Zara's mehndi, Amber kept getting the steps wrong. You can see it on the video. Ruined everything, she did.'

'Park here, the shop is just over there,' his mum said.

'I can't park there, Ma. Double yellow lines,' he said, pointing to the road.

'Never mind, nobody cares. It's Sunday,' his mum stated. 'Hurry, we don't have time.'

Yousef sighed. He knew not to mess with his mother and Aunty Musarat when they were on a mission. His phone buzzed. He took it out from his pocket.

Seema: At your house, dance practice. Hope to see you soon.

He groaned. Seema always seemed to be at his house. Yousef knew what she was doing. His entire family loved her, which made it harder for him to tell her he wasn't interested. He put the phone back.

His mum and Aunty Musarat barged into the events shop like they meant business. He followed. He knew his role was chauffeur and silent bystander.

'Sister, you are back!' the owner exclaimed excitedly. 'The invitations are ready. They look beautiful.'

Yousef smiled to himself. This was typical of Pakistani weddings. Steve, his friend from university, was getting married in just over eighteen months and had sent him a save the date card just last week. Rehana was getting married in three weeks and his parents planned to personally deliver the majority of them by hand this week. That was as organized as Pakistani families were.

'You said they would be ready last week, Rashid,' his mum retorted. 'I expect a discount for the delay.'

'Always the best price for you, sister,' Rashid said, looking sheepish. He brought out the invitations. Each one was packed in an individual box. He opened one up and pulled out a small dark green card with gold writing on. 'This is the mehndi card,' he said, handing it over to Feroza.

'Beautiful,' Aunty Musarat whispered. 'Green is the perfect colour for a mehndi card.'

Rashid nodded in agreement. 'And see,' he said, taking the card back and turning it over, 'we have put this picture of a dhol on it. Beautiful, no?'

'Very nice,' Feroza said. 'Show me the wedding cards.'

He nodded, opening up the individual box again. The wedding card was made from thick textured card and came in an envelope decorated with coloured plastic stones. So much for saving the planet, Yousef thought. Rashid unfolded one and a dusting of glitter and confetti fell out. He looked at them proudly for a reaction.

'You didn't do that for my daughter's wedding cards,' Aunty Musarat said sharply.

'This is a new feature, sister,' the man said. 'Perhaps for your next daughter's wedding?'

Yousef's mum took the card and he peered over her shoulder. It was deep purple with the same gold writing on and the corners were decorated with tiny birds. She passed it to Musarat for inspection. It must have passed the test as they both nodded in agreement.

'Are the house decorations ready?' Feroza asked.

Rashid nodded, getting up. 'All in these boxes for you to take home,' he said, gesturing to a stack of boxes by the door.

'Now I gave you plenty of business for Zara's wedding,' Musarat said, in full wedding planner mode, 'and I have brought my friend here. You give us a good price and I will tell more of my friends about you.'

'And don't forget we are getting the wedding staging from you too,' Yousef's mum added.

Yousef still didn't know why the bride and groom had to sit up on a stage that was mocked up to look like the set of some Pakistani Greek tragedy, complete with pillars and thrones, but he had stopped questioning the excessive nature of this wedding months ago.

'Sisters, I always give best price,' Rashid said, taking out his calculator.

Yousef's phone buzzed again. It was Seema. She had sent him a picture of her and Rehana together on the sofa with the caption:

Getting ready to start rehearsing!

Why did she feel she needed to update him every second? Another message came through:

Hope to see you soon xx

Seema hadn't arranged this visit with him – it had all gone through Rehana – yet she had expected him to be there as well. After everything that happened with Jessica, Yousef had retreated into himself. He tried and tried to get Jess to take his calls, he tried to accidentally bump into her in the canteen and had even gone to her ward a few times, but each attempt was met with a firm rebuttal. He still didn't understand what he had done. He was yet to tell his family about his job application results. He was dreading it. He wanted to tell them all at once, but every time the four of them were together, it was only ever Rehana's wedding that was discussed. This meant poor Seema was stuck at the bottom of his to-do list. He knew he had to do it before she got too attached, but then she had involved herself in his family, sending them gifts, going on spa days with his sister and even taking his mum out for lunch. He didn't know how to tell her without upsetting everyone. He had somehow managed to get himself into another shitty situation, so he did what he did best – buried his head in the sand.

'And for that price, you will do the chocolate fountain too?' Aunty Musarat was asking. 'With fruit and sweet options to dip?'

Rashid nodded. 'All in the price, sister.'

The deal was done. Yousef watched as his mum unzipped her handbag and took out a large brown envelope. His mum was old school; she didn't own a credit or debit card. If she needed money, she would make him or his dad take her to the bank and she would withdraw cash. She began counting the twenty-pound notes. Rashid looked on greedily. Clearly he preferred cash too; probably tax avoidance, Yousef thought.

'Yousef, start loading the boxes into the car,' his mum demanded. She looked at Rashid. 'You help him too.'

Rashid, who had carefully put away the cash, got up immediately. He followed Yousef to the car. His mum was right, he didn't have a parking ticket.

'Your mama says you are next to get married?' Rashid said.

'I'm not sure about that,' Yousef replied. When had his mum said that? It must have been whilst he was checking his messages from Seema.

'She says you have found a nice girl and the wedding is next year,' Rashid said in a tone that implied Yousef was being coy.

'My mother has a very active imagination,' Yousef said, trying to put an end to this conversation.

'Well, remember, I will give you a discount on decorations, invitations, chocolate fountains, whatever you want.' He looked proudly at him. 'We also do prestige cars, Lamborghini, Ferrari, Mercedes, whatever you want to arrive in.'

'I'll keep that in mind,' Yousef said, trying to be as polite as he could.

His mum and Aunty Musarat were chatting about how many gifts were the appropriate number to buy the groom as they arrived home.

'Yousef, once you've put the boxes inside go and pay the DJ. If we don't pay him today, he will give our date to someone else,' his mum instructed.

Yousef lugged the boxes into the hallway. There were shrieks of excitement and laughter coming from the living room. He wanted to make a quick getaway before he got spotted. Just one more box to bring in before he could escape. He went to the car to get it.

'Yousef!' a voice called after him. It was Seema.

Yousef turned around. 'Hi, Seema.'

'We have had such fun, just us girls,' she said. 'Look, I've even had henna applied to my hands. That's so unlike me!' She showed him her hands. They were decorated with intricate dark orange patterns.

'Looks nice,' Yousef said.

'My mum will hate it, but I don't care,' Seema whispered, as if letting Yousef in on a secret.

Yousef didn't know what to say to that.

'Where are you going?' she asked.

'I need to go pay Tariq, the DJ,' he said, kicking a stone on the pavement. 'He must be in demand, Mum thinks he will give our date to someone else if we don't pay today.'

'I'll come with you,' she said excitedly. Before he could answer, she got in the car. 'They're still practising some of the routines, but I know my bit now. They won't miss me. To be honest, there's this one girl, Amber, she's hopeless.'

Yousef smiled. 'Amber's two left feet are world-renowned.'

They carried on in silence for a while. Seema turned on the radio. It blasted out TLC's 'No Scrubs'.

'Oh my God! I love this song!' She began singing it. 'Come on, Yous, everybody knows the words to this old song.'

'Not me,' he said. He was lying but he wasn't in the mood for singing. She ignored him and continued to sing until the song had finished. 'We used to dance to that song all the time when we were out,' she said, turning to look at him. 'You know, I remember you saying you have a vinyl collection. You still haven't shown it to me.'

'It's in storage in the garage,' Yousef replied.

'And don't forget you promised we would watch *Jurassic Park* together and we still haven't done that.' She brushed his arm gently in jest. It lingered for a fraction longer than it should have done.

'I know, sorry.' Yousef tried to think of an excuse. 'It's just been so busy with all the wedding stuff.' He parked the car outside DJ Tariq's house. 'I'll just nip in and pay him then we can get home.'

When he got back in the car, Seema was scrolling through her phone. 'I'm hungry,' she said. 'Fancy getting something to eat?'

Yousef shook his head. 'Mum will be making something, she won't like it if we eat something from outside.'

'Come on, Yous, do you always listen to your mum?' Seema said in a sultry voice. She moved closer to him. 'Let's live dangerously. Take me to these places I hear about: Chicken Cottage or MacMoods. We don't have them where I live.'

'Are you sure? They're pretty gross,' Yousef said.

She got closer and whispered in his ear, 'I fancy something a bit dirty.' She pulled back. Yousef could feel her breath. She wanted him to kiss her.

'We should really be getting back,' he said, putting his seat belt on. 'We don't want the aunties gossiping about us.'

Seema sat back in her chair and didn't say a word for the rest of the journey. Yousef felt like shit. He wasn't into her but he didn't want to hurt her feelings.

'Look, Seema, I didn't mean to upset you back there,' he said.

'What is it then, Yousef? Have I done something wrong?' she demanded. 'Because it's been eight months and we've barely even held hands.'

Yousef wanted to tell her the truth, but there were only three weeks to Rehana's wedding, he couldn't risk it. 'I'm just not that kind of guy. Sorry.'

'What does that even mean?' Seema said, getting out of the car. 'Honestly, Yousef, I wish you would just tell me what's going on inside of your head.' She slammed the door. Her lower lip trembled. 'I'm really trying here. It's not easy with Mum and Dad being so unsupportive and you being so . . . closed off.' She turned and walked back to the house.

'Seema, wait,' he called out.

'Wait for what? Are you going to tell me what's going on?'

He remained silent. She turned and walked off without saying anything. Yousef couldn't bring himself to follow her. He went for a drive instead.

Chapter Forty

Rehana

REHANA FELT LIKE SHE was cheating on Sean, but she was only planning on getting married once and needed to make sure there was nobody better than him to do her wedding make-up. So she had booked a free trial with Sangeeta, who had done both Lubna's and Zara's wedding day make-up. With Sangeeta's prices, Rehana was expecting her to be working out of some plush beauty shop, but instead she was instructed to come to Sangeeta's house in West Bromwich. Rehana wasn't one to judge, but West Bromwich was not exactly a desirable neighbourhood, so she had begged Emma to come with her. Plus, it would be nice to hear how Emma's relationship with Chris was going.

'He's such a dream,' Emma said. 'I went to his for dinner the other night and he cooked a proper three-course meal. It was lush.'

'A man who cooks, lock that down immediately,' Rehana said, checking the satnav to make sure she was still heading in the right direction.

'Plus, my mum and nan love him, so that's a bonus.' Emma smiled.

'Look at you, all loved up!' Rehana said, gently brushing Emma's arm. 'Seriously, though, I'm really happy for you.'

'Thanks,' Emma said. 'I was thinking, do you think I could bring him to your wedding as my plus one? I know numbers are tight, so feel free to say no—'

'Of course you can, silly! As my maid of honour, you can bring anyone you want!'

'Rehana, have you just asked me to be your maid of honour?' Emma asked.

'Now, don't get too excited, it's different in Pakistani weddings. There's no raucous hen do, definitely no inflatable penises, no strippers and no naughty games,' Rehana explained.

'What's the point then?' Emma replied.

'We can go out for a nice girly meal if you want, but our hen do is the mehndi. That's when all the ladies get together to sing and dance.' Rehana tried to appease her. 'But your main job will be to manage the aunties and uncles on the wedding day.'

'What do you mean, "manage" the aunties and uncles?'

'Well, after the wedding dinner, or what you guys call the wedding breakfast – I still don't understand that by the way, you never eat it in the morning.'

'Stick to the point, Rehana!' Emma almost shouted.

'Sorry, yes,' Rehana continued. 'Basically, Pakistani people come to weddings for two reasons. Number one, the food. It has to be good and it has to be hot. If you don't serve piping hot food and plenty of it, it is wedding suicide. You might as well not show your face ever again.'

'Bit harsh, no?'

'Just the way it is. Anyway, the second reason they come is to get a family photo with the bride and groom. I think it's just to prove they attended.' Rehana checked the satnav again. They were close. 'So, after dinner, everybody suddenly makes a mad dash for the stage to get their photo taken and it becomes a crazy free-for-all.' She gave Emma a pointed look. 'Pakistani people don't understand the meaning of an orderly queue, so that's where you come in.'

'I see,' Emma said, nodding. 'You want me to boss them about and create some order.'

'Exactly.' Rehana winked at her.

'Well, I am a schoolteacher. If I can organize teenagers, I can organize some Pakistani aunties and uncles,' Emma replied.

'Plus, I think the fact that you're white may confuse them into complying.' They both laughed. 'I think we've arrived.'

'Bit rough round here, don't you think?' Emma said.

'Yeah, but Lubna and Zara both looked amazing on their wedding day, so it's worth running the risk of getting mugged.' Rehana got out of the car.

Sangeeta lived in a semi-detached house. The door had a sign on it saying 'Beware of the Dog'. Rehana shivered. She wasn't really a dog person, or a cat person for that matter. In fact, she just wasn't an animal person. Sangeeta, a small woman in her thirties, opened the door and ushered them in.

'Do you have a dog?' Rehana asked nervously. 'It's just that I'm allergic.' She wasn't, but she knew dog owners found that more acceptable than 'I'm scared of dogs.'

'A dog?' Sangeeta looked confused.

'The sign on the door,' Rehana said.

'Oh, that.' Sangeeta laughed. 'That's just to scare off any would-be burglars. We don't actually have a dog!'

Rehana breathed a sigh of relief.

'Now which one of you two is getting married?' Sangeeta asked, hands on hips. Emma pointed at Rehana. 'Okay, let's get you into the living room, there's better light in there.'

They followed Sangeeta into a room that had two small sofas and a massive flatscreen television on the wall. Sangeeta pulled out a ring light and shone it on Rehana's face.

'Hmm, lots of clogged-up pores,' she said to herself. 'Do you wax or thread?' she asked.

Rehana shook her head. 'Neither. Only my eyebrows . . . once,' she replied, slightly embarrassed.

'And how do you feel about bleaching your skin?' Sangeeta asked.

'Absolutely not!' Emma cut in. 'Her skin is beautiful the way it is.'

'Okay, I was only asking. Some girls want to be a shade or two lighter on their wedding day,' Sangeeta said, non-plussed. 'We will have to do something about your facial hair. But you do have very good lips, I can work with them.'

Why were Asian beauticians so brutal? Didn't they have any training in customer services?

'Have you got a photo of the wedding gown?' she asked. Rehana nodded and took out her phone, showing her the photo. 'Good choice.' Sangeeta approved. 'Okay, let's see what we can do.'

She got to work, opening up a giant case of make-up and brushes. The threading was like torture, but now that more than one person had mentioned her facial fuzz, Rehana thought she should quietly bear the pain. Similarly, Sangeeta was a bit harsh on the eyebrow pluck. Eventually, when she felt she had a canvas she could work on, Sangeeta started applying the make-up.

An hour later, Rehana was finally allowed to look in the mirror.

'Now remember, this is only a quick trial, a taster of what I can really do,' Sangeeta said as she held up the mirror so Rehana could see.

Rehana barely recognized herself. Sean had done a decent job in the past, but this was a whole new level. She had cheek-bones for the first time, her foundation was the perfect colour and her lips looked lustrous. This was what she had imagined she'd look like on her wedding day. She could feel herself tearing up. 'What do you think, Emma?'

'You look gorgeous, babes,' Emma said, smiling. 'Just perfect.'

Rehana turned round to Sangeeta. 'I love it.'

Sangeeta smiled. 'You just needed someone to show you.'

Now the big question: 'How much for you to do both my mehndi and wedding make-up?'

'Both days?' Sangeeta pondered. 'Three hundred pounds.'

Emma suddenly sat up. 'No, that's way too expensive! What's your best price?'

Oh no, what was she doing? Rehana thought. This was not the place to barter.

'That is my best price,' Sangeeta said, sounding offended. 'I'm sure you'll find it's very competitive.'

'We'll give you one hundred pounds,' Emma said resolutely. 'We have another person who could do it for that price.'

'Emma, what are you—' Rehana started.

'Maybe you should book them then,' Sangeeta said sharply. 'And next time, don't waste my time.'

'No, no, Sangeeta, please. Wait,' Rehana said.

'Come on, Rehana, let's go,' Emma said loudly, winking at Rehana. 'We'll get Sean to do your make-up.' Emma walked slowly to the door. Rehana did not follow. After a few seconds, Emma turned around. 'Aren't you going to stop me?' she asked Sangeeta.

'Stop you?' Sangeeta said. 'I'll be slamming the door behind you.'

'But that's all part of the act, right?' Emma wasn't sounding so sure of herself any more. 'I say a low price, you pretend to be offended, we find a middle ground and everyone is happy.'

'This isn't a bazaar, love,' Sangeeta said in her broad Brummie accent. 'There's no haggling here.'

'Oh, I see,' Emma said quietly. 'Okay, well, I'll just stop talking then, shall I?'

'Good idea,' Rehana hissed. 'Three hundred pounds sounds perfectly reasonable, Sangeeta. And I'm sorry about my friend, she was only trying to help.'

Sangeeta gave Emma a look of disgust and then said, 'Fine, I'll book you in, but only because you're a friend of Lubna's.'

'Thank you, thank you,' Rehana said, relieved.

'Sangeeta?' Emma said from the doorway.

'What?' Sangeeta said, turning to look at her.

'Would there be a discount if we booked you for both the bride and the maid of honour?'

Rehana went to see Sean when they got home to tell him he had been relieved of make-up duties. As expected, he had not taken it well.

'Suit yourself,' he had said sullenly.

'Sean, if it wasn't for you showing me how to apply make-up, Nadeem probably wouldn't have agreed to marry me,' she said, trying to appease him.

'That's true,' he said, looking at the floor. 'You were the only girl in Birmingham who couldn't do a smoky eye.'

'No, I couldn't,' she agreed. 'That's why I have something for you.'

He perked up, looking interested. 'What is it? Not more pakoras? I really am trying to be good.'

Rehana smiled. 'No, this.' She took out an envelope from her bag. 'An invitation to my wedding.'

Sean snatched it from her. 'Really? I can come?'

Rehana nodded.

'I've never been to an Asian wedding before.' He paused to think. 'Can I bring my boyfriend?'

Rehana thought about it and nodded. 'I suppose so.'

'Won't your family mind? Are they, like, strict Muslims?'

'Yeah, they are,' Rehana said. 'But as long as it's not their children who are gay, they seem to look the other way.'

Sean looked slightly deflated.

Rehana took his hand. 'But I would like you to come, as my friend. With your boyfriend.'

Sean smiled. 'Then we'll come.'

'Sean, one more thing,' she said. He looked at her. 'Wear

something appropriate. Do not upstage me. It's my wedding, I want to be the centre of attention.'

Sean laughed. 'I'll try my best, but I can't promise anything.'

Now that was taken care of, she had one more invitation to deliver. Rehana nipped across the street and knocked on Aunty Angie's door. Angie's husband opened the door.

'Hello, love,' he said.

'Hi, Uncle Jim.' Rehana smiled. 'Is Aunty Angie in?'

He nodded and went to fetch her.

'Hello, love,' Angie said, coming to the door. She was in her dressing gown despite it only being five o'clock. 'What are you doing here?'

'I came to give you this.' Rehana handed her the wedding card.

'What is it?'

'Come on, Aunty Angie, don't tell me you haven't figured out there's a wedding going on in our house.'

Angie smiled. 'Well, maybe, yes.'

'This is your invite to my wedding,' Rehana said proudly.

'Oh, love, really?' Angie said.

'Yeah, bring Uncle Jim and Lottie too.' Rehana beamed. 'It's that Big Fat Asian wedding you always wanted to come to.'

'We wouldn't miss it,' Angie said. 'Come here.' She pulled Rehana in and gave her a hug. 'Whoever you're marrying is a very lucky man.'

Rehana felt a bit emotional. 'Thanks, Aunty Angie. You're the first person to tell me that. Everybody's been saying how lucky I am.' Rehana pulled away. 'Right, I'd better go. This very lucky man is waiting to meet me, and I can't be late!'

The big advantage of combining the wedding and walima in one event was spending more time with Nadeem. Plus, the venue was in Birmingham, so whenever anything did need to be organized, he would come up and see her. They met in the Jungle Cafe for a quick coffee before going to see the photographer.

'Less than three weeks until we're hitched,' Nadeem said. 'I can't believe how quickly it's come around.'

To Rehana, it couldn't come soon enough, but she played along. 'I know, where has the time gone?'

'So, are you feeling okay about the whole thing?' he asked.

'What whole thing?'

'Well, it's a big deal, moving down to London, new job, new family,' he mulled. 'I want you to know, you can visit your family anytime. I know it'll be hard to adjust at first. You know we have to live with my parents until our house is ready.'

'I'll be all right, Nads,' Rehana said. 'Besides, it's not like I'm moving to another planet, it's less than two hours away.'

'We need to choose the fixtures and fittings soon. They'll be installing the bathrooms and kitchen next,' Nadeem said proudly. 'And we need to choose a dishwasher.'

'Yes, because I'm not big on washing up,' Rehana said. As well as preparing for the wedding, Nadeem had been buying a house for them to move into, a new build, near his family. She had passed her initial teacher's training course and was now on a summer break until her new job in September at a school within walking distance from their new home.

'Seriously, Rehana, I can't wait to be married to you,' Nadeem said, giving her one of his grins that made her go weak at the knees.

Rehana couldn't believe how her life had turned around. A couple of years ago she'd had no job prospects, no friends and no love life. But now, she had all three and she also had a much better relationship with her mother, something she'd never thought she would have. 'I can't wait either.'

Nadeem looked at his watch. 'We'd better get moving, or we'll be late for the photographer.'

'I don't know why everyone is calling him "the photographer". It's just Majid who works in Aldi,' Rehana scoffed. 'He bought himself a snazzy camera and a drone, and suddenly he's Steven Spielberg.'

'Majid who works in Aldi is cheap,' Nadeem replied. 'And when you're paying for a wedding and a new house, cheap is good.'

'As long as he doesn't do the Pakistani classic of filming everyone whilst they're eating, I don't mind,' Rehana laughed.

To be honest, there wasn't a lot Rehana minded when she was with Nadeem. Even Majid who worked in Aldi couldn't put a downer on her mood these days.

Chapter Forty-One

Jessica

JESS HAD TAKEN THE last two weeks of her job in Birmingham as annual leave to help with her move to Somerset. Her last day on the ward had been emotional. The nurses had all clubbed together and bought her a bottle of nice wine and Monica gave a little speech in the staffroom. Jess had brought in some cupcakes from a cute bakery she had discovered in town and they'd had them with a cup of tea.

Her parents had come up to help her move.

'We're so pleased you're coming home,' her dad said, loading her boxes into the car. 'We've got your bedroom ready for you and your mum has cleaned out the spare room for you to keep anything extra in.'

'Thanks, Dad,' Jess said, putting her arm around him. 'I'll be glad to be home too.'

'Jess, I hope you don't mind me asking?' her dad said. 'Did something happen? It's just that you haven't been the same these last few months.'

Jess wanted to tell him everything, but what was the point? Yousef was in the past, she was closing the door on that phase of her life, why upset her father when there was nothing he could do? 'I think I've been working too hard,' Jess replied.

'Right,' her mum said, appearing from her room with the

last of the boxes, 'that's everything, I think. Jess, you'd better do one last check before we leave.'

'Thanks, Mum.' Jess returned to the flat to make sure she hadn't forgotten anything. The place was empty, it was time to move on. She left the key on the kitchen counter and closed the door one last time.

Chapter Forty-Two

Feroza

FEROZA WASN'T AN EMOTIONAL woman, she didn't have time for those people who cried at the slightest thing, but seeing Rehana in her mehndi dress made her heart burst with pride. Not just for her daughter, but for herself also. She had been the one to convince Rehana to go down the arranged marriage route and apply to become a teacher. Had she not, her daughter would still probably be spending her days in bed, glued to her computer. It would be the same for Yousef. He didn't know it yet, but she had done what was best for him in the long run.

Feroza's mother and father had come over from Pakistan for the wedding. It was always her going over to see them, but the wedding of their only granddaughter had been a temptation too much to resist. Having them there was the icing on the cake. She could show them how much she had achieved as a mother.

She adjusted Rehana's dupatta. 'You look beautiful,' she said, taking her daughter's hand.

'Thanks, Mum. I think it's Sangeeta's magic make-up, but I'll take it.' Rehana smiled. 'It's a shame Nadeem won't get to see me like this. Maybe I'll send him a photo.'

'Don't you dare,' her mum warned. 'The groom is not allowed

to see his bride on her mehndi, it's bad luck. And besides, this event is just for us girls.'

'Fine,' Rehana said sullenly. 'When can I make my entrance?'

'After the boy's side arrive,' her mum said. 'Then you can come in and we can start the dancing.'

'Oh God, Emma, have you got the paper I gave you, the one which tells you which order the dances have to go in?' Rehana asked Emma.

'I have it here,' Emma said, looking over the sheet of paper. 'The dhandia dance first, then the rumaal dance, then Nida's solo number followed by Ruby and Farah's Jennifer Lopez routine.'

'Good,' Feroza said. 'And don't forget, we only have the hall until eleven o'clock so everything has to be done by then.'

'Yes, Aunty,' Emma replied obediently.

Majid from Aldi knocked at the door. 'All right, ladies?' he said. Feroza rolled her eyes. Why they had got Majid was beyond her. There were always rumours flying around about him and different girls.

'You should have been here an hour ago,' Rehana said sharply.

'Sorry, had to extend my shift at Aldi, they were short-staffed.' He shrugged. 'A quick photo of the three of you?'

They huddled together. 'Be quick!' Feroza snapped.

'Aunty, if you put your arm around Rehana,' Majid instructed. 'Rehana, put your left hand on your neck to show off your henna, and . . . sorry, what's your name, love?'

'Emma.'

'Emma, you look beautiful in that outfit. Just turn to the side a bit.'

Feroza turned to Emma and whispered, 'Be careful of this one, he likes to flirt.'

Majid began snapping photos of them. 'Hurry up, Majid,' she said impatiently. 'I have things to do.' Eventually satisfied, Majid said he was going to take 'action shots' of guests arriving.

'Okay, Rehana, I will come and get you when it's time.' Feroza left her daughter with Emma in the back room of the church hall so she could go and greet the guests.

Although the invitation stated a five o'clock start time, the only people who had arrived at that time were Angie and Lottie, plus Yousef's friend Steve with his girlfriend, all of whom were waiting patiently for the festivities to begin. Everyone else, knowing what Pakistani timing was like, began to trickle in around six thirty. Feroza had placed Abdul and Yousef at the door to welcome the guests, usher them towards the welcome drinks stand, where she had poured 7Up and Lilt into plastic cups, and then encourage them to take a seat.

The caterers were setting up the buffet on the far side of the room and the DJ was playing music a bit too loud for Feroza's liking, but she let it go. Things were going well. She saw Seema and her family arrive and went to meet them.

'Assalamualaikum,' she said to Aleena, giving her a hug. 'Seema, you look lovely, doesn't she, Yousef?'

'Yeah, lovely,' Yousef muttered.

Seema's smile faltered at Yousef's lacklustre greeting, but she found it again. 'The hall looks great, Aunty,' she said. 'I can't wait for the dholki and singing to begin.' She took out her phone. 'I didn't know any of the traditional mehndi songs, so I looked them up on YouTube and have downloaded the words onto my phone.'

'Yes, she is really throwing herself into this whole Pakistani wedding thing,' Aleena said flatly. 'She even wants to start taking Urdu lessons.'

'I just want to learn more about my culture, Mum,' Seema stated.

'Why don't you have a drink and find a seat?' Feroza said, smiling politely. 'Nadeem's family will be arriving soon.'

'Plastic cups?' Feroza heard Aleena say to Seema. 'Why am I not surprised?'

She decided to ignore her. This wasn't the time to make a scene. Musarat arrived with the dhol.

'Good, you're here,' Feroza whispered. 'I've put a rug down at the front of the hall. Gather a few of the women and start the singing over there.'

Musarat nodded and delegated the job to Pinky, who rounded up some of the girls and sat them down on the rug. Now it was starting to feel like a proper mehndi, Feroza thought as the singing began. She went to check on her parents, who were sitting with some of the older aunties near the front. They seemed to be enjoying themselves. She spotted Yousef's friend Rohit arrive with a very pretty girl she didn't know. She couldn't let that pass her by.

'Hello, Rohit,' she said, 'so nice you came all this way. And don't you look smart?'

'Hi, Aunty. Well, I couldn't miss my best friend's sister's mehndi. Plus, Yousef said you might need some help.' Rohit gave her a hug.

'You're a good boy, and who is this?' Feroza turned to look at the pretty girl who stood next to Rohit.

'Hello, Aunty, I'm Anjali,' the girl said.

'How do you two know each other?' Feroza quizzed.

'Mum, leave it out,' Yousef moaned. 'Guys, why don't you go and sit down?'

'I was only asking!' Feroza said. 'Okay, Rohit, if you want to help, can you arrange those fruit baskets and trays of sweets nicely on the front table? There is a roll of tablecloth in the kitchen.'

Rohit nodded and got to work, taking Anjali with him.

Abdul came up to her. 'Feroza, Nadeem's family are here.'

Feroza quickly gathered the guests together into a welcoming committee, shoving her mum and dad to the front and arming them with tiny bags of confetti. As the women of Nadeem's family walked in they were showered with tiny pieces of rose petal. Feroza stood at the front making sure everybody could see her. She gave Nadeem's mum and sisters a big hug. In return they had brought more cellophane-wrapped fruit baskets and a cake from Kareem's Bakery. She had reserved the front three rows of chairs for them. After they were all seated, she grabbed Abdul, Yousef and her parents and went to get Rehana.

'Are you ready, beta?' she asked.

Rehana nodded. 'Emma, go tell the DJ to play my entrance song.' Emma disappeared out the door.

'Abu, Amee, you go first. Abdul, you stand on Rehana's right side, link arms. Yousef and I will walk behind you. I want everybody to see us all together. One big happy family.' Feroza couldn't hide the joy in her voice. This was everything she could have hoped for. Once they heard the song start, she lined up her family and slowly walked them down the middle of the hall, taking in all the stares, smiling at all the camera phones that went up, listening to the whispers of how wonderful they all looked together. She savoured every sight and sound.

Nadeem's mum got up and embraced Rehana, and told her she looked beautiful.

The evening was a success, despite Amber getting almost every step in the dhandia dance wrong. Feroza made a mental note not to let her dance at Yousef's wedding. The food was delicious and the DJ got all the aunties up dancing. It was the perfect mehndi. Now it was only a week to the wedding, and then, Feroza would focus all of her attention on getting her son married.

Chapter Forty-Three

Anjali

WORKING IN THE NHS was very different from anything Anjali had experienced back home. She had expected a sleek modern service where patients were offered tests and treatments that weren't available in India. She was wrong. In many ways things were worse here. Of course, not having to ensure her patients had appropriate funds or insurance before giving them medicines was a good thing. Anjali recalled having to watch the faces of some young parents crumble when she told them they couldn't have the test that might help diagnose their baby's health problems if they couldn't pay the bill. There also seemed to be a severe lack of respect for doctors here. She had been shouted at by her patients numerous times simply because she had been busy with another sick person and so they had been made to wait.

Her friends kept sending her messages on Facebook telling her how cool it was her working in England, and how they wished they were too. If she was being honest with herself, it didn't feel that cool. Her lifestyle had changed dramatically; people lived differently here. At home she had a maasi come in and clean the house, do her ironing and put away her clothes. It sounded extravagant when she described it to some of her colleagues, but it was standard practice in India. You didn't have to be rich to have a maasi. Here most people would do those things for themselves. She had thought England was a wealthier country than India, but most people seemed worse off than back home. And the weather . . . She couldn't believe what Brits classed as summer. She still wore her sweaters in the middle of July.

Despite all of this, she had Rohit. Kind, sweet Rohit. Anjali had been worried he would be too reserved for her, but had soon realized this was what she needed. She grew fonder of him each time they met. He was so patient with her, always happy to explain the things she didn't quite understand, like the time she asked one of the nurses if she'd enjoyed a movie Anjali had recommended, and the nurse had replied, 'No, yeah, it was good.'

'What does "no, yeah" mean?' she had asked Rohit.

'It means yes,' Rohit had explained.

'Why say both no and yes then?' She was perplexed.

He had shrugged. 'Not sure, haven't really thought about it. But you might hear people say "Yeah, no" as well if they don't like something, so my advice is always go for the last one of the two they say.'

'So weird,' Anjali replied.

When she was especially homesick, he would listen to her for hours talking about her family and what she missed about India. One time she told him she missed proper desi chai and paratha for breakfast and he had taken her to a place in Manchester which made both of them just like at home in Delhi. They had shared their first kiss a few days ago and it had been magical. She could tell he was nervous; so was she. But it felt right.

And now her parents were coming. She had overheard her dad talking to Uncle Anand on the phone, quizzing him on how she and Rohit had been getting on. Her sister had told her that her parents had been to see the astrologer again and he had advised a summer engagement would bring them good luck.

'Do you think you are ready to get engaged to Rohit?' her sister asked. 'It would mean staying in the UK for ever.'

Anjali pondered this question. There was so much she missed about India.

'I don't know,' she said. 'It's a lot to take in.'

But after that kiss, she did know. She hadn't felt like this before. She wanted to be with Rohit all the time; she wanted to hear his voice, feel his touch. She was in love. And although her job in the NHS was different to what she had envisaged, she enjoyed it and wanted to progress.

So, when her parents asked her if she wanted to marry Rohit, she said yes.

Chapter Forty-Four

Yousef

YOUSEF WAS GLAD TO be leaving for work. With Rehana's wedding tomorrow the house had become a bit of a circus with people coming and going. It was good to get away. He was sharing his room with his grandad, so had to be quiet so as not to wake him.

'Are you going to work?' a voice called from behind him. It was his grandad. 'You look smart.'

Yousef turned around. 'Sorry, I just needed to get my bag. Yes, last day today before the wedding. I'll be home for dinner. Do you need me to get you anything?'

'No, I need to get up to pray namaaz.' He sat up. 'Yousef . . . Are you okay, beta?'

'Yeah, course I am, Naanu, why?'

'You are different to what I remember,' his grandad said. 'When you came to Pakistan last time, you were full of energy, you never stopped talking, always asking questions.' He paused. 'And now, you are quiet, like the energy has left you.'

'I'm fine, Naanu. I think it's just the wedding and work. It's a lot.' Yousef slung his bag over his shoulder.

'No good to work too hard,' his grandad said. 'As for Rehana's wedding, it will be over soon, but something tells me that won't bring back your energy.'

'Honestly, Naanu. My energy is fine. I've got plenty of energy,' Yousef said.

'You can't lie to me, beta. You are of my blood.' His grandad got up. 'This Seema girl, she is a good girl, beautiful and a doctor like you.'

Yousef rolled his eyes. Not another person telling him he needed to marry Seema.

'But just because someone is good doesn't mean they are right for you,' his grandad said.

'Naanu?' Yousef wasn't sure what he was getting at.

'Go to work, we will talk another time.' His grandad made his way to the bathroom.

That was strangely cryptic, Yousef thought. Now he was late for work.

When he arrived at the hospital, he was informed by the ward manager that the doctor on call for the day had rung in sick, so she asked him if he would cover until five p.m. It wasn't really a question, Yousef had no choice. He took the on-call bleep and got to work on the list of jobs handed over to him by the night team.

The third item on the list was to carry out arterial blood gases on an elderly lady on ward thirty-eight. That was Jess's ward. Shit, he didn't want to go there. Each time he had tried in the past, he was met with a wall of silence and death stares. He wondered why Jess couldn't do the gases herself. Yousef sighed and made his way over there. Yousef was already living with a low level of anxiety; this was the last thing he needed. He still hadn't told his parents about the outcome of his job application form, and now with the wedding going on they were even more distracted than ever. He swiped his card against the entry system and gained entry to the ward.

Monica was standing at the nurses' station glaring at him.

'I'm here to do some blood gases on Nora Bradley,' he said.

'She's in bed fourteen,' Monica said curtly. 'You know where the equipment is.'

Yousef went to gather his things. Thankfully, Nora had good

arteries, which made getting the blood easy. He wanted to get off this ward as quickly as possible. He made his way into the dirty utility room so he could throw away the used equipment. Shit, Monica was in there.

'Oh, hey, Monica,' he said sheepishly. She clearly knew about him and Jess. She gave him the faintest of nods. 'No Jessica today then?'

'No,' Monica said, not making eye contact with him.

'Is she sick or something?' he asked.

'Not that I know of,' she answered.

'What's happened then?' Her vagueness was making him concerned. 'Is she okay?'

'She's left, Yousef,' Monica replied, 'She's gone home.'

'Home?'

'Yes, back to her parents in Somerset.' Monica picked up her tray and left.

Jess was gone. He had never found out what happened between the two of them and now she had left. He felt a sadness deep in the pit of his stomach. It was more than sadness – he felt hopeless.

He made his way out and down the corridor.

'Yousef!' a voice called after him. 'Yoo-hoo, Yousef!'

It was Fiona, the ward clerk. He really wasn't in the mood for her gossip now.

'Fiona, hi,' he said quickly. 'Look, I'm in a rush, lots of jobs to do.'

'You doctors are always in a rush,' Fiona said, smiling at him. 'You never have time for a break.'

'Sorry, Fiona, I'm on call and—'

'How about I make you one of my famous cups of tea? I know you like them,' she said, twirling her pen around.

'I really don't have time,' Yousef protested.

'Now come on, I know you've told your mum about how good my cups of tea are,' she continued.

'My mum?' Yousef said, looking puzzled.

'Yeah, your mum. She said you told her I make the best cups of tea.' She squeezed Yousef's arm. 'You little charmer.'

'When did you see my mum?' Yousef was becoming more confused by the second.

'She came onto the ward a few months ago looking for Jessica.' Fiona smiled. 'She said they had something to discuss.'

'What? When?'

'I don't know, maybe eight or nine months ago.' Fiona was no longer smiling. 'Didn't she tell you?'

'No, no, she didn't,' Yousef said quietly. What was his mother doing talking to Jess? 'Fiona, do you know what they spoke about?'

Fiona shook her head. 'No, Jess wouldn't tell me, but she did seem awfully quiet afterwards.' She looked at Yousef. 'How about that cup of tea?'

Yousef's bleep went off. 'I have to go,' he said, walking as fast as he could down the corridor. What had just happened? His mother had spoken with Jess? He went through the time-line in his head. Eight months ago would coincide with when Jess had sent him that message. But how did his mum even know about Jessica? Rehana was adamant she hadn't blabbed. No, she must have found out about her some other way. What had his mother said to Jess to make her close the door on him so firmly? He wished she was here so he could ask her. But Jess was gone and continued to block his number. Surely if his mother knew anything about his and Jess's relationship, she would have confronted him about it and not Jess? Nothing made any sense. Fuck! This was too much, his head hurt.

His bleep went off again. He answered it. A patient was short of breath on ward thirty-four. He had to focus. The last thing he needed was to get into trouble at work, especially when he only had a week left to complete. He would talk to his mother tonight.

Chapter Forty-Five

Rehana

IT WAS THE DAY before her wedding. People were coming over later, but before all of that, Rehana had an important job to do. Emma had been summoned for moral support. They were sitting in the waiting room at the beautician's, waiting for their appointments. Rehana wanted to double-check she was getting the right thing.

'You've never waxed *down there* before?' Emma asked again, eyes wide.

Rehana shook her head. 'I've always shaved. But then I get a weird spotty rash afterwards and I don't want that for my wedding night.'

'And you really want the whole lot off?' Emma was now repeating questions they had already been over.

'Emma, I told you before. It's a Muslim thing – no pubic hair allowed. I want to be fully waxed and hairless.'

'Like a dolphin?' Emma said, confirming she understood.

'Like a human who doesn't have a shaving rash,' Rehana replied.

'Well then, you want to ask for the Hollywood.' Emma pointed it out on the brochure.

A Hollywood wax is where all pubic hair is removed from the whole intimate area, the brochure read.

'Why is it called the Hollywood?' Rehana asked.

Emma shrugged. 'Dunno, maybe because there are a lot of paedos in Hollywood who like a fully waxed bush?' They both laughed. 'I'm getting a Brazilian.' Emma turned to look at her friend. 'Rehana, didn't you say you had boyfriends when you were at university?'

Rehana nodded. 'Yeah, I did.'

'Didn't you keep a tidy shop for them for, you know . . . ?'

Rehana looked simultaneously horrified and embarrassed. 'I always keep a tidy shop Emma, just through shaving not waxing. And none of those boys got that far. They were all very much above-the-clothes kind of relationships.'

'Oh, I see!' Emma said. They sat in silence. 'Are you worried about your first time with Nadeem?' she eventually asked.

Rehana shook her head. 'No, it will be his first time too.'

They sat in silence again. The beautician emerged from the back and called Rehana in.

'Are you sure it's the Hollywood I want?' Rehana whispered. Emma nodded. 'Right, okay. Wish me luck.'

The waxing room looked quite comfortable: there was a bed in the middle with a folded-up towel on the end of it. iHeart Radio was playing in the background.

'Says here, you've booked in for the Hollywood,' the beautician said.

'Yes, that's right.' Rehana gulped.

'Knickers or no knickers?' the beautician almost barked.

'Sorry?'

'Do you want to wear knickers or not, love?' she asked again, sounding a bit pissed off.

'I think I'll keep my knickers on please,' Rehana replied. There was no way she was going to be completely naked in front of a total stranger.

'You'll have to put these on.' The beautician handed her a piece of folded-up paper.

'What's this?' Rehana asked, unfolding it.

'Knickers, disposable ones. Stick them on and lie down on the table. I can step out if you want, whilst you get changed.'

The knickers were made of paper, and were practically see-through. 'Erm, yeah. If you don't mind giving me a moment.' The woman sighed and left the room. Rehana unbuttoned her jeans and put the paper knickers on. She felt like she was about to undergo a major surgical procedure. She sat at the end of the bed, and the beautician came back in.

'Right, what are we doing?' she asked.

'The Hollywood, I thought we agreed on that?'

'No, love. I mean is it just the front, or the perineum and anus as well?'

Rehana hadn't really given her anus any thought, but since she was here she felt she might as well get her money's worth. 'In for a penny, in for a pound.' She laughed nervously.

'What does that mean, you want your whole tuppence done or not?'

'I want it all done, front and back,' Rehana said, ensuring there was no room for error. 'I'm getting married, you see.'

'Good stuff,' the lady said, not interested at all. 'Lie back, make yourself comfortable.'

Rehana did as she was told. 'Sorry, it's a bit messy down there. I let things grow because I knew I was coming here.'

'Don't worry love, I'm used to all sorts,' the beautician replied. Rehana wasn't sure if that was reassuring or not. She felt the woman move the knickers out of the way and apply the wax. It wasn't as hot as she was expecting. So far, so good. 'Right, here we go.' The woman pulled off the wax in one smooth movement. Rehana nearly jumped off the bed; the pain burned through her.

'Jeez!' she exclaimed. 'Wow, that hurt.' She waited for the stars in her vision to settle. 'Are we done?' she asked, trying to get up.

The lady pushed her back down. 'That was just one side. We have the other side and your anus to do.'

Rehana lay back down. Why hadn't she just stuck to shaving? Nadeem was marrying her for better or worse, surely he could deal with a little shaving rash? She braced herself as more wax was applied. Why did women put themselves through such pain for men, she wondered as the next strip was torn off.

Rehana sat cross-legged on the floor trying not to make eye contact with anyone. She was still sore from her waxing but was doing her best to be the sharmeeli bride, all shy and coy. It was hard with all these people around her. Nadeem's family had come round for the gift-giving ceremony. They had brought a huge tray of Pakistani sweets which had been wrapped in clear plastic and decorated with ribbon. There were numerous gift bags packed with exciting-looking boxes, a whole suitcase filled with new clothes all in Rehana's size and, most importantly, they had an extravagantly wrapped parcel which had Rehana's wedding lengha inside of it. Her mother had only just finished adjusting it last week, then once that was done, they had to return it to Nadeem's family, so that they could bring it over today as part of the big giving of gifts ceremony. Her family had also bought new clothes for Nadeem's family members. She had gone to Marks and Spencer last week to buy his dad and brothers new shirts, and her mum had forked out for a posh watch for Nadeem himself.

Rehana never thought she would enjoy playing the role of the traditional Pakistani dhulan, but here she was loving every moment.

Aunty Henna, who had been responsible for setting Rehana and Nadeem up, had prime position on the main sofa and was being treated like a deity. A garland of flowers was placed around her neck on arrival and both sets of parents had bestowed upon her gifts (annoyingly before Rehana). Once everybody was happy they had appeased Aunty Henna, it was Rehana's turn.

Nadeem's mum opened up a red velvet case. Inside was the most exquisite gold necklace and matching earrings Rehana had ever seen. There was an audible gasp in the room as it caught the light.

'Bloody hell!' Auntie Angie exclaimed, standing up to take a closer look. 'They're like the crown jewels!'

'These were given to me by my grandmother,' Nadeem's mum said. 'Nadeem was her favourite grandson. She made me promise to give them to his wife on his wedding day.'

'You lucky girl, Rehana,' Angie said loudly. 'All I got from my mother-in-law was a few dirty looks and a broken food processor.'

Rehana's mum gave Angie a look which said *Shut up and sit down*. Angie obeyed.

Rehana didn't know what to say. She was pretty sure you weren't supposed to have a favourite grandchild as a grand-parent, but she didn't have time to think about that now. 'Wow, Aunty,' she said, taking her future mother-in-law's hand. 'They are so beautiful. I promise to look after them.'

'Now you don't call me Aunty any more,' Nadeem's mum said. 'I am your second mother now, beta.'

Rehana smiled. She did feel connected to Nadeem's mum in a way she didn't with her own mother. She didn't seem to have as many hard edges. 'Thank you,' she whispered. They embraced.

Once the gift exchange was over, the ladies rubbed upton into her face, neck and arms so that she would have soft skin on her wedding night. Rehana hated the earthy smell of upton, but she took it all with a smile, and when she was finally dismissed, she ran herself a bath. It was late, she was tired. It suddenly occurred to her that this was her last night in the house she had grown up in. As much as she was ready for this new chapter in her life, she would miss being at home. She'd miss hearing her parents' conversations with each other every morning. She'd miss her dad reminding her to pack her lunch before she set off to work. She'd definitely miss her mum's cooking. And as much as she hated to admit it, she would miss the banter she had with her brother, although there hadn't been much of that lately.

Her phone buzzed.

Nadeem: Only one more day to go and then you become Mrs Nadeem Hafeez.

She smiled.

Rehana: I'm a modern girl, I'm thinking Mrs Rehana Ahmed-Hafeez.
Nadeem: Whatever you say, as long as you still marry me.
Rehana: Always ♥

Chapter Forty-Six

Feroza

FEROZA WAS PUTTING AWAY the dishes that had been used earlier. Most of the guests had left, she had insisted her mother go to bed, and Abdul and her father were still up talking in the living room. She heard someone come in through the front door, and recognized the sound of Yousef's keys. She was used to him coming home late after work. She took out one of the plates she had just put away and began preparing food for him. He entered the kitchen.

'Yousef, you must be tired, beta,' she said. 'Sit down, I've made your favourite, palak paneer.'

Yousef didn't sit.

'Shall I get you a drink?' she asked. He was looking at her strangely.

He stared at her, not saying anything.

'Is everything okay, beta?' she asked. 'Did something happen at work?'

Yousef didn't shift his gaze. Something was wrong. She could see anger in his eyes.

'Yousef?'

'Mother, I am only going to ask you this once, and I want you to listen very carefully and then I want you to tell me the truth.' Yousef was spitting his words out, his upper lip curled up in anger. 'Do you understand?'

'What are you talking about, Yousef?' Why was he talking to her like that?

'Do you understand?' he repeated.

'Yousef, I am your mother.' She hadn't heard Yousef like this before. 'You can't speak to me—'

'I SAID, DO YOU UNDERSTAND?' he shouted.

She jumped, nodding.

'Good, then listen. Why did you come to see Jessica at the hospital last year?' he asked, deliberately and slowly.

Feroza's stomach lurched. 'Jessica?' she said. Perhaps denying it would be best. 'Who is Jessica?'

'DON'T LIE TO ME!' he shouted again.

'Yousef, calm down, I don't know who you have spoken to, but you have it all wrong,' Feroza stuttered.

'Explain it to me then,' he replied.

Feroza looked away from him. That was so long ago; surely he must have forgotten about that silly girl by now, especially with him having Seema?

'I went to talk to her,' she said.

'About what?' he demanded.

'About you and her!' Now Feroza raised her voice. 'What? You thought you could keep it from me, your mother?' She was angry now. She had kept it in all this time, but he had lied to her, he had deceived her time and time again. 'I know you were together for years, I saw her messages. You and her, you and her . . .' She could barely get her words out. 'You slept together,' she spat out.

'What did you say to her, Mum?' he asked again.

'Yousef, listen to me,' she said, trying to soften her voice. 'We all make mistakes. Young people, you like to test bound-aries. I've seen it on television, you . . . experiment.'

'Jess wasn't an experiment, Mum,' he said. 'I am asking you one last time, what did you say to her?'

'You really want to know?' she asked, her voice hard again. He nodded.

'I told her the truth.'

'What truth?'

'That I am your mother, I know you best. She can't compete with that, she can't compete with your family, your culture, everything we stand for,' Feroza hissed. 'You think you love her, but you don't, beta. Trust me, in years to come you will thank me.'

'Thank you?' Yousef said. 'Thank you? You have been telling me what to do since the day I was born, and I had this one thing, this one thing that I loved, that was mine and you took it from me!' Yousef was becoming tearful. It was okay, Feroza told herself, he just needed to get it out of his system. He would be fine.

'Beta, listen to me.' Feroza took a step towards him. 'That girl, she doesn't understand you. You are both better off without each other.' She took another step towards him. 'You will forget all about it when you are married to Seema.'

'I'm not marrying Seema, Mum,' Yousef said quietly.

Feroza stared at her boy. Had someone put nazar on him? That was the only explanation. Some jealous person saw how happy her family was and cursed them with the evil eye.

'Now, Yousef. Don't say that, that girl adores you.' Feroza was panicking. If Yousef broke off his relationship with Seema, how would she explain it to everyone? 'You can't just throw that away.'

'Mum, I'm not marrying Seema. You want that, not me,' he said. 'My God, this will never end, will it? You'll be dictating my life for ever.'

'No, Yousef, just do this one thing for me, for your mother?' Feroza pleaded. 'I promise, I won't ask you to do another thing.'

'You want me to marry a girl I don't love?' he asked incredulously.

'Love comes later. She is a good girl, she will make you happy.'

'But I won't make her happy, Mum. Doesn't that matter to you?' He looked at her.

It did matter to Feroza. She didn't want to see anyone's daughter upset, but she knew Yousef was wrong. He just had to marry her, they would be fine once that was done. That was how arranged marriages worked. Parents always knew best.

Yousef now took a step towards Feroza. 'Wait, Mum, did you tell Jessica about Seema?'

Feroza didn't say anything.

'Mum?'

She turned away, putting the rest of the dishes away in the cupboard. 'Yousef, go to bed, your sister is getting married tomorrow. We can talk about this later.'

'No, Mum, we are talking about it now.' He marched over to her, slamming the cupboard door shut. 'Did you tell Jess about Seema?'

'Fine!' Feroza snapped. 'Yes, I did. She needed to understand that you and her were just a fantasy, that you had had your fun at university but now it was time to get back to real life.' She tried to cup his face.

'GET YOUR HANDS OFF ME!' he shouted.

'Yousef, remember what the Qur'an says, paradise lies at the feet of your mother,' Feroza said desperately.

'Mum, don't. You twist our religion to suit yourself.'

The kitchen door opened. Abdul and her father came in.

'Yousef, why are you shouting at your mother?' Abdul asked. 'Feroza, is everything okay?'

'Did you know about all of this, Dad?' Yousef asked.

Feroza felt a pang of panic. 'It's nothing, Abdul. You and Abu go back to the living room.'

'So, he doesn't know then?' Yousef said, turning back to her. 'Maybe I should fill him in.'

'Yousef, stop!' Feroza shouted. 'Just stop! Tonight is supposed to be a happy occasion, the first wedding in our family, and you choose now to bring all of this up.'

'No, Mum, I'm not letting you do this. I have put so much off because the timing hasn't been right, but not any more. I don't care who knows.' Yousef was almost hysterical now. 'CALL EVERYONE WHO WANTS TO HEAR!' he screamed. 'Yousef, your precious fucking son, is in love with a white girl.'

He collapsed onto one of the kitchen chairs.

'Yousef, what's going on?' Rehana entered the kitchen. She was wearing pyjamas, her hair still wet from the bath.

'Rehana, I'm glad you're here, you can listen to this too.' Yousef laughed. 'It's funny really. Remember when you told me not to tell Mum and Dad about Jessica? Well, guess what? Mum knew all along.'

'Feroza,' Abdul asked, 'what is he talking about? Yousef, what has got into you?'

'Oh Dad! Now you're interested, huh?' Yousef stood up and faced his father. 'So many times you just let Mum do whatever she wanted, no questions asked. Of course you don't want to get your hands dirty with us. Leave it to Mum, isn't that your mantra?'

'Yousef, please,' Abdul said, clearly embarrassed this was all unfolding in front of his father-in-law. 'What has got into you?'

'I'll tell you. I've been in love with a girl for almost seven years. Mum found out about it and made her leave, so she could force me to marry Seema.' Yousef sat back down on the chair, tears streaming.

'Feroza?' Abdul was looking at her in a way that broke her heart.

'Abdul, she was a white girl.' She came up to her husband. 'White. What would everyone think?'

'You knew and you didn't tell me?' Abdul looked at his wife in disgust.

'I handled it, like I do everything. You didn't need to know,' Feroza said.

'Yousef, it's my wedding tomorrow.' Rehana came to sit next to him. 'Please can all of this wait?'

'I should never have listened to you,' he said to his sister. 'When you told me not to tell Mum and Dad, I should never have listened to you. Maybe then Jess and I would still be together.'

'Yousef, please, I'm begging you to stop this . . .' Rehana said.

'Rehana, you knew as well?' Abdul said.

'Rehana, I'm happy for you, I really am, but I'm not coming to your wedding,' Yousef said to his sister.

'Bro . . . don't,' Rehana pleaded.

'I've taken a new job,' he said, turning to them all. 'I know you wanted me to be some kind of surgeon, but guess what? That's not what I want.'

'Yousef, what are you talking about? What job?' Abdul asked.

'I'm leaving, Dad,' Yousef replied. 'I've accepted a training job in Somerset. It's a three-year position. I leave next week.'

Feroza didn't understand what was happening. What was Yousef talking about? And had Rehana known all along about Yousef's relationship and not told her?

'Yousef, stop all of this now!' Feroza said firmly. 'Nobody is moving to Somerset, you will be attending Rehana's wedding tomorrow and we are all going to bed and will discuss this after the wedding.'

Yousef smiled at his mum and took her hand. 'Here's the thing, Mum. You don't tell me what to do any more.'

He let go of her hand. It fell by her side, and Yousef walked out of the kitchen. Feroza knew in that moment she had lost her son. The way he let go of her hand, she felt it. The connection they'd had for all those years had been severed. An emptiness engulfed her. She couldn't focus.

'Mum, what are we going to do?' Rehana asked.

Feroza couldn't answer her.

'Dad, you talk to him,' Rehana continued. 'He can't miss the wedding. Dad, do something.'

Abdul nodded and headed upstairs after Yousef.

'Mum?' Rehana said, shaking her. 'Mum? Are you okay?'

Feroza didn't respond.

'MUM!' Rehana shook her more forcefully.

Feroza jolted up. 'Yes, yes. I'm here.'

'Mum, I'm getting married tomorrow. Whatever is going on right now needs to be put to one side until after my wedding.'

Feroza nodded.

'Rehana, make two cups of tea.' It was the soothing voice of Feroza's father. 'Feroza, listen to me. Parents and children fight all the time. Yousef will come around.'

'Abu,' Feroza cried. Having her dad there took her back to being a child. 'I did the right thing, didn't I? Yousef couldn't have married a white girl.'

Rehana put down the cups of tea on the table. Feroza's dad asked her to leave so the two of them could be alone.

'Why didn't you want Yousef to marry this girl?' he asked.

Feroza looked at him. Surely he understood? 'Abu, why are you asking me this?' she asked. 'So much of our culture has already been lost just by us bringing up our children here. This would erase whatever was left.'

Her dad shook his head. 'Beta, time changes all cultures.' He smiled at her. 'Do you think Pakistan is the same as how you left it? No, it has changed, become more modern.'

'What are you talking about, Abu?'

'I've been watching you and your friends. You are trying so hard to hold on to the past. Things change, we've changed.' He looked at his daughter. 'We used to worry so much about things like caste and whether or not people come from a good family, but in truth, all that matters is whether the girl and boy like each other.'

'Abu, you are saying this? After what happened with me? After what you did?' Feroza looked her dad in the eyes. He turned away from her gaze.

'That is all in the past. We learn to live with our regrets,' he said quietly.

Feroza ignored him. 'What about our heritage? Who will carry that on?'

'What use is heritage if your son is unhappy, huh?' her dad said. 'And maybe he will be spreading his heritage and culture, not erasing it.'

Feroza wanted to remind him of what he had done to her all those years ago, but didn't have the energy. It was easy for people to say things that sounded understanding when it wasn't their child who was straying, she thought. Maybe he had some form of dementia? No, this wouldn't do. Yousef was her son and only she knew what was best for him. She stood up.

'Abu, leave these family matters to us, we will sort it.' She opened the door. 'I think you should get some sleep.'

Her dad took one last look at her, shook his head and left.

Chapter Forty-Seven

Abdul

ABDUL WATCHED AS HIS son threw clothes into an open suitcase. How had he been so blind to what was happening in his own house?

'Yousef, can we talk?' he asked gently.

'No, Dad, I've done all the talking I want to do,' Yousef said resolutely. 'Ask Mum, if you want to know any more.'

'Yousef, sit down!' Abdul said firmly. Yousef looked at him, startled. Abdul rarely raised his voice. 'I want to talk.'

Yousef sat on the end of the bed. 'What?' he said sullenly.

'Tell me about this girl,' Abdul asked. He realized he didn't really know his son. He had been working hard to ensure they had enough money and food, and somewhere along the way he had lost touch with his family.

Yousef's lips trembled as he talked. 'Jessica? She's everything, Dad,' he said. 'Funny, clever, beautiful. She plays football, and she's really good. She loves politics and talking about things like saving the planet, but most of all she's kind and she put up with me for so long, and I wasn't kind to her, Dad.'

His son looked lost.

'How long have you been together for?' Abdul still couldn't believe all of this had been going on right under his nose.

'Since the first month at university.'

'Why didn't you tell us about her?' Abdul asked.

'Because I knew you and Mum wanted me to marry a Muslim girl, someone you could be proud of,' Yousef replied.

'You don't give us enough credit.'

'Well, look at Mum, see how she reacted when she found out? I think I'm giving you more than enough credit,' Yousef said.

'That is because you didn't come to us, you were not honest with us,' Abdul said. He was sad that the bond he'd thought he had with his son was so feeble that Yousef couldn't come to him with something so important.

'It doesn't matter now,' Yousef said. 'She's gone.'

'Gone where?'

'Back home, to Somerset,' Yousef said miserably.

'Where your new job is?' Now it was all starting to make sense. Yousef nodded. 'And what about Seema?' Abdul asked.

'I don't want Seema, Dad,' Yousef said. 'I can't just make myself want her.'

'Then you have to tell her.'

'Tell her how?'

'At Rehana's wedding tomorrow, you will tell her the truth, and then we will sort all of this out,' Abdul said. It was time he took charge.

'Dad, I told you, I'm not going to Rehana's wedding,' Yousef repeated. 'I need to get away from all of this, I need time to think.'

'Yousef, listen to me,' Abdul said. 'If you don't come to Rehana's wedding, you will regret it for the rest of your life. Is that how you want your sister to start married life, without her family?'

'Dad, no,' Yousef said. 'I need to start thinking of myself for once.'

'And Seema, who is thinking of her?'

'That's not my fault,' Yousef replied.

'Whose fault is it, then?' Abdul said. He thought he had raised his son better than this. 'That girl deserves an explanation, from you.'

Yousef stayed quiet.

'Yousef, I'm asking you as your father. Please come to your sister's wedding.' Abdul got up and left.

Chapter Forty-Eight

Rehana

R EHANA WAS WOKEN UP on the day of her wedding by a text. It was Nadeem. She quickly checked to see if the ping had woken up her grandmother, who was sleeping on the main bed while Rehana slept on a mattress on the floor. She was safe, Naani was still asleep.

> *Nadeem:* Hi, wife (to be). Hope you're not getting cold feet, that would be embarrassing. Anyway, can't wait to see you later. My family are super excited to welcome you into our family too. See you soon xx

Rehana smiled, then recalled the events of last night. She shot out of bed and into Yousef's room. He was lying on his makeshift bed too. He hadn't left. Good. One less thing to worry about, she thought as she turned to leave.

'Hey,' his voice whispered.

She turned around. 'Hey.'

'So, I'm still coming to your wedding.'

'I'm glad,' she replied.

'But then I'm leaving,' he said solemnly.

She nodded. 'Okay.' She had so much more she wanted to say to him but today was her wedding day and it would have to wait.

Sangeeta would be arriving soon to do her make-up and she was bringing her friend, Jasmine, who was going to do her hair. She went into the living room to find her mum making final adjustments to her wedding gown.

'Hey, Ma,' she said. Her mum looked up and smiled.

'Have you packed all of your things?' her mum asked, looking up at her. Rehana thought she looked like she had been crying.

'Are you okay, Ma?' she asked, coming to sit next to her.

'Fine, just trying to get this choli right for you. Are your suitcases ready?'

Rehana nodded. She had spent the week slowly packing her belongings into four large suitcases. After today this would no longer be her home.

'Good. When your dad comes back from the mosque, tell him to put them in the car,' her mum said. 'We need to make sure everything is ready for tonight.'

'Ma?' Rehana said gently. Her mum looked at her. 'I'm going to miss you.'

Her mum shook her head. 'Don't be silly, Rehana. You can come and visit anytime.'

Rehana knew her mum wasn't very good at these conversations. 'Ma, stop. Listen to me.' She gently took her arm. 'I know we haven't always seen eye to eye on things, but you're a good mum, and I'll miss you and Dad and even stupid Yousef.'

Her mum smiled. 'I am going to miss you too. Who will I shout at now you have gone?'

'Dad, probably.' Rehana laughed. 'I'm a bit scared, Mum.'

'Beta, it's normal to be scared a little,' her mum said. 'But I wouldn't let you marry just anybody. Nadeem is a kind boy, he will look after you and you will look after him. That is what marriage is about.'

'Were you scared when you married Dad?'

Feroza pondered the question. Her marriage to Abdul had been so quick. 'Yes, I was scared to leave my parents, my home and my country. It was hard. But I wouldn't have you or your brother if I didn't. Things always work out the way they should, even if you think they won't at first. But your dad, he is a good man and your husband will be the same. And if he is not, I will tell him.'

To Rehana's surprise, her mum gave her a kiss on the forehead.

'Thanks, Ma,' Rehana whispered.

Within an hour, Rehana was sat in a chair in her bedroom being fussed over by Sangeeta and Jasmine whilst Emma brought her cups of tea. She felt like a princess, though she didn't quite look like one. She was told she had to put on her wedding lengha top before the hair and make-up but she could keep her pyjama bottoms on for now.

'Are you sure you don't want to go for a lighter foundation?' Sangeeta asked for the twelfth time that morning.

'No thank you, I want my face and body to be the same colour,' Rehana replied, slightly distracted by Jasmine, who, after pulling her hair into a painfully tight bun, was now attaching reams of hair extensions to her scalp.

'I'll need these back after the wedding,' Jasmine said, curling one of the extensions after she had just finished straightening it. She was chewing gum with an open mouth, which would usually piss Rehana off, but she daren't say anything in case she made her look bald.

'How am I supposed to get them back to you? I'm going on honeymoon tomorrow,' Rehana asked.

'Take them out at the end of the night, give them to your mum or something, whatever. Just get them back to me. I have another wedding on Saturday I need them for. Otherwise I'll charge you extra.' Jasmine clearly didn't think extracting hair extensions was a strange thing to do at the end of your wedding

day. It was worth it, though. By the time the two of them had
finished she looked amazing. She was finally allowed to put
on her lengha skirt before Jasmine pinned the dupatta to her
hair and let it cascade down. Rehana inspected herself in the
mirror. Everything was perfect.

There was a knock on the door. It was her dad.

'I've come to get the suitcases.' He stopped and looked at
her. 'Oh Rehana.' He had always been a man of few words, but
she could see the emotion in his face. 'Mashallah.'

'Thanks, Dad.' She felt emotional herself.

'Don't cry!' Emma instructed. 'Think of your make-up! Come
on, Uncle, I'll help with the suitcases.'

Rehana took deep breaths to avert the tears. Majid from Aldi
appeared with his camera. 'I've come to get some "getting ready"
shots,' he said. 'Sorry, I'm a bit late again, they needed me to
do a double shift at Aldi. Couldn't say no to the cash.' Rehana
sighed. It was a good job he was cheap.

The house slowly filled with people. She could hear her Aunty
Musarat shouting instructions at everyone, eventually gathering
them all into the tiny hallway. She told them which cars they
were all in and they left en masse. Rehana and Emma (and,
annoyingly, Majid from Aldi) were being driven by Uncle
Jaswinder. He had a black Mercedes which would look nice in
the photographs. When she arrived at the hall, there was a
covert operation headed up by Aunty Musarat and Aunty Rubina
to get her to a private room in the back without anyone seeing
her. Now all she had to do was wait to be told when it was
time for her to make her entrance.

'Emma, I'm desperate to see the hall,' Rehana said. 'Go and
have a look and tell me if the flowers on the tables look real.
We couldn't afford fresh flowers so went with fake ones.'

Emma nodded and peeked through the door. 'They look

pretty good to me.' She checked her phone. 'Chris is here, can I go meet him?'

Rehana nodded. She didn't really want to be left alone but she couldn't very well keep Emma from seeing Chris. When she was gone, she texted Zara and Lubna and told them to come and wait with her. They came almost immediately.

'Oh wow, you look gorgeous,' Lubna said.

'Isn't this part horrendous?' Zara said. 'I remember on my wedding day, Raheem's family were so late I was practically starving when they arrived.'

'And on mine, half the boy's side got lost on the M6, so we had to delay the nikkah. It was so embarrassing!' Lubna said.

'Really?' Rehana said. 'I thought everything you two did always went perfectly?'

'Are you kidding?' Lubna laughed. 'The caterers brought the wrong food to my wedding. We were supposed to have butter chicken but they brought lamb karahi. Dad was furious.'

'We ran out of cups at our wedding,' Zara chimed in. 'So many aunties were complaining about not getting a cup of tea.'

'The point is,' Lubna said softly, 'it all seems like a big deal at the time, but these things mean nothing really. You'll see.'

Rehana was grateful for the chat. She thought about every time she had sneered when her mum talked about Aunty Musarat, Aunty Rubina, Zara or Lubna. But these people were her friends, her community, her family and when called upon, they were always there and, crucially, always got things done.

The sound of drums and cheering signalled the arrival of Nadeem and his family. Rehana was desperate to see so sent Zara and Lubna out with the promise they would livestream it to her via FaceTime. She watched as a man dressed in traditional shalwar kameez playing a dhol led the procession. Nadeem, who looked incredibly sexy in his sherwani, was surrounded by his brothers and friends, who bhangra'd their way into the hall. Her mum and dad put garlands of flowers, real ones this time, around his parents' neck and welcomed them in. The feed cut at that point. *Bloody Zara*, Rehana thought. Now what was she supposed to do?

She knew he probably wouldn't read it, but she sent Nadeem a text. **You look great, plus your bhangra ain't half bad either.**

'Rehana?' It was Aunty Musarat. She quickly hid her phone. She imagined demure Pakistani brides probably weren't on WhatsApp on their wedding day. 'Almost time to make your entrance. Be ready.'

Aunty Musarat was taking her role of wedding planner extremely seriously. She rounded up Rehana's parents and grand-parents, and even managed to drag Yousef into the room so they could all walk Rehana out together. She then made a no-nonsense announcement that everybody should be seated because the bride was about to enter. She repeated that three times, because as expected, trying to get groups of Pakistani people to do anything is like herding cats.

'Rehana, you and your dad will be at the front this time,' her mum said. 'Ami, Abu, you come in next. Yousef and I will come in last.'

'I'll come in with Naani this time,' Yousef said, taking his grandmother's arm.

Sensing an argument, Rehana cut in. 'I think it will be nice to mix it up,' she said to her mum.

Aunty Musarat poked her head around the door. 'Ready?' she asked.

Rehana's mum nodded. The DJ began playing Rehana's requested entrance song from her favourite Bollywood movie, *Kabhi Khushi Kabhie Gham*. It was time.

The six of them walked slowly down the hallway, trying their best not to bump into rogue children who were still running around. Every so often they had to stop so Majid from Aldi could take a photo. Rehana wasn't sure where to look. She wanted to focus on Nadeem – he was her comfort blanket – but she was also desperate to soak in the moment. She looked around the room. Emma gave her a wave, then the thumbs up and pointed at Chris, who was sitting next to her. Aunty Angie and Uncle Jim were there, looking very excited; their daughter, Lottie, less so. Sean and his boyfriend were on their feet, smart-phones in hand, recording everything. Aunty Henna was there, looking especially proud of herself. Zara and Lubna smiled as she walked past them. Then she looked at Nadeem. This was it, she was getting married to a man she loved. And Zara and Lubna were right, nothing else mattered.

Chapter Forty-Nine

Seema

SEEMA CHECKED HERSELF IN the bathroom mirror. She quickly re-applied her lipstick. *Better.* She had driven to Manchester the week before and bought a cream sari. Despite the shop owner showing her how to put it on, she had struggled to get it on this morning. And her mum was of no help. In the end, she had resorted to a YouTube tutorial.

The wedding was a bit of a bore. She didn't know anyone apart from the girls who had been in the dance routines at the mehndi, but they were now on tables with their families and she was stuck sitting next to her mum, who just complained about everything. Rehana had looked gorgeous walking down the aisle. She imagined herself doing the same thing. The problem was, it was getting harder and harder to imagine it happening with Yousef. Even today, he had a face like a slapped arse. Did she really see her future with someone so miserable? Seema didn't know what else she could do. She had totally immersed herself in his family and tried her best to get to know him. He hadn't even been to see her parents once in the last few months. She decided that today would be his last chance. If he didn't get his act together and show her some attention, she would have to reconsider the whole thing. She sat back down. She saw him giving her an intense stare. Thank God, she thought, he has noticed me. She gave him a hint of a smile. He came over.

'Hi,' she said. 'You okay?'

'Erm, yeah,' he said. Something wasn't right, he was being all fidgety. 'Can we talk?'

'Hello, Yousef,' her dad said. 'It's polite to acknowledge your guests, don't you think?'

'Sorry, Uncle. Salaam. Hi, Aunty.' Her parents gave him a pained smile. 'Can we talk, please?'

'Sure,' Seema said. 'Here?'

'No, let's go for a walk outside,' he replied. She followed him into the grounds of the hall. It was warm. They walked along a small path, her bangles clinking with each step.

'Yousef, what's going on?' she asked. He had been silent for too long.

'Seema, I'm sorry. I don't know how to say this,' he started, then paused.

'Say what?' A feeling of dread came over her. Something did not feel right.

'I don't think this thing we have, you and me, whatever this is, has a future.' His words came out fast. 'I'm really sorry, I should have told you sooner.'

'Wait, what?' Seema stopped walking. 'Have you brought me out here to break up with me?'

'Look, I wish I could explain. Everything is really complicated. My parents wanted this to happen, I kind of went along with it, which I know is awful, and then I found myself in too deep. I'm sorry.'

He was looking at her, waiting for her to say something. She couldn't believe this was happening.

'Your parents wanted this to happen?' she said, staring at the floor. She couldn't even look at him. 'My parents didn't want this to happen, did you know that, Yousef? They were one hundred per cent against it, and you know what I did?'

She was trying not to raise her voice but it was hard. 'I fucking stood up to them, because that's what grown-arse people do.'

'I know, I should have done that from the start,' he said.

From the start? 'Wait, so you never really liked me? From day one?'

'No, it's not like that. You're amazing, clever, witty, beautiful.'

'Yousef, I know I'm all of those things, I don't need you to fucking tell me.' Seema wasn't prepared to let him charm his way out of this.

'I'm in love with someone else!' he blurted out.

Seema reeled. That hurt. She tried to search for the right words. 'All this time, you were in love with someone else. Why did you waste my time?' She couldn't understand why anyone would do that to another person.

'I wish I hadn't. I'm truly sorry,' he said miserably.

'You know what, Yousef? Fuck you.' She wanted to slap him, but couldn't be bothered to lower herself to that level. She had known there was something wrong, but not this. 'I'm going back in now. I'm going to get my parents and leave. Stay out here until we're gone. I don't want to see you.'

Yousef nodded.

Seema walked back to the hall as fast as the sari would allow. She wasn't going to cry. Seema was angry. She had been made a fool of. She marched up to her parents.

'Mum, Dad, can we go, please?'

Her dad looked at her. 'Seema, is everything okay?'

'Please, Dad. Let's just go.' She blinked away tears.

Without any further questions, her parents got up and the three of them walked to the car.

She thought her mum would be full of 'I told you so's' on the drive home, but she surprised Seema.

'Did something happen with Yousef?' she asked.

'I don't want to talk about it, Mum,' she said, eyes fixed

firmly on the window. 'We won't be seeing him or his family again.'

She saw her dad looking at her in the rear-view mirror. 'Whatever you want, Seema,' he said soothingly. 'Whatever you want.'

Chapter Fifty

Yousef

YOUSEF FELT SHITTY ABOUT what he had done to Seema, but he couldn't dwell on it now. He had to move on. He waited until enough time had passed and then he made his way inside of the hall.

The meal was being wrapped up and people were making their way to the stage to have their photo taken with the happy couple. His mum and dad were doing the rounds, making sure everyone had eaten properly. He made his way over to them.

'Mum, Dad,' he said, 'shall we get a family picture before the mad rush starts?'

His mum gave him a strange look. 'Beta, that's a good idea. Thank you. Abdul, challo, let's go.' The three of them bypassed the crowd that was gathering. Yousef watched as Emma tried to make sense of the chaos.

'Family photo, Emma,' he said to her. 'Just us guys.'

She nodded and instructed the next family in the queue to hold on a bit longer.

Majid from Aldi organized them – his parents on the chairs that were either side of the decorative sofa the couple were sitting on, and Yousef squeezed in next to his sister.

'You guys okay?' he asked the two of them.

'Yeah, it's a lot to take in,' Nadeem said, 'but we're enjoying it.'

'That's good.' They all smiled for the photo.

'Sis, look, I'm really happy you found someone,' he said to Rehana. 'You deserve to be happy.'

'You okay, bro?' Rehana asked, furrowing her eyebrows.

'Fine,' he said. 'Nadeem, look after her, she's a keeper.'

'I plan to,' Nadeem replied.

His parents were getting up to exit the stage so other families could have their photos taken.

'Mum, Dad,' he said as they made their way down the steps. They turned to look at him. 'You've done a great job on this wedding, it's really beautiful.'

'Thank you, beta,' his mum said. 'We will do the same for you too.' Yousef smiled at his mother. Despite everything, he really did believe she had done what she thought was best for him, in her own way. It was his fault it had gone so wrong.

He made his way quietly out of the hall and to his car. Most of his things were already packed; he threw the rest into the back seat. Whatever was left would have to stay. He sent an email to the hospital saying he would not be coming in for his last two days of work, mentioning a stress-related issue he needed to deal with urgently, and thanked them for everything. He got in his car and drove.

Chapter Fifty-One

Feroza

THE RUKHSATI HAD BEEN an emotional affair. Letting go of Rehana was harder than Feroza had thought it would be. They had said a tearful goodbye to each other as she got into the car with Nadeem. Abdul had transferred the suitcases over to one of Nadeem's brothers' cars and for Feroza, that was it, her daughter was gone.

She'd always thought she would feel a sense of relief when Rehana was married. People told her it was like relinquishing responsibility for her daughter to another person. It was an old-fashioned view that she now knew not to be true. She was happy for her daughter, but she felt an emptiness in her heart.

Everyone helped pack up what needed to be taken home.

'Has anyone seen Yousef?' she asked. But nobody had. He must have gone home, she would see him there. She gathered her parents and Abdul drove them all back to the house. The house was still lit up with the wedding lights as they made their way inside. After all the excitement of the wedding, it felt strangely quiet.

'Yousef!' She could do with his help getting the things out of the car. No answer.

'Leave him, he'll be asleep,' Abdul said. 'We can get the things out of the car in the morning.'

She went into the kitchen and put the kettle on. They all needed a good cup of tea, it had been a long day. Her mum came in saying she was tired. She needed help getting up the stairs so Feroza went up with her. She helped her out of her shoes and into her nightclothes. Rehana's room seemed so empty, almost everything was gone. She put her mum to bed and switched the light off.

Something caught her eye as she headed towards the stairs. Yousef's bedroom door was open. That was strange; he would never leave it open when he was asleep. She went in. Yousef wasn't there. She looked around. His things were not there either. The cupboard was almost empty, his computer was gone. Her heart started to thump inside of her chest. Where was he?

There was a piece of paper folded in half placed on the desk. It was from her son.

Dear Mum and Dad,
   First of all, I love you. You guys have been good parents. I couldn't have achieved what I have done so far in my life without your love and support.
   Dad, you were a great role model. Always working, putting your family's needs ahead of your own, showing me what a good man looks like.
   Mum, where do I start? You are the definition of a Mama Bear. Your one goal in life has been to make sure Rehana and I would always be the best versions of ourselves, no matter what that took. You spoiled me growing up. I wanted for nothing and I thank you for that. I know money isn't something we have lots of in our house, but you never made us feel poor in any way.
   I tried to do things your way, believe me, I did. I fought the feelings I had, I prayed to God to make them

change. I even drank our holy water, hoping it would
make a difference. But none of that worked. I still love
Jess and I hope she still loves me.

So, I'm leaving. I'm going to be with Jess, however
long that might take. Please don't try to convince me to
come back. I won't. I need to do this.

I will always be your son, always be here when you
need me, always be your Yousef.

Feroza let out a wail of anguish. Yousef had left her. She
screwed the note up and threw it against the wall. How could
he do this to her? Her breathing quickened. 'Abdul!' she
screamed. He came rushing up the stairs.

'What is it?' He looked at her.

'He is gone,' she said in a whisper. She could barely believe
it. 'Yousef. He has left us.'

'What are you talking about? He was just at the wedding,'
Abdul said. Feroza pointed to the piece of paper that lay on
the floor. Abdul read it. He got his phone out and pressed it
against his ear. 'His phone is switched off.'

'He's gone,' Feroza repeated.

'I'll ring Rohit,' Abdul said, 'he'll know where he is.'

Feroza didn't need to ring Rohit. A mother knew. Yousef
was gone. Rehana had left. Tears fell from her face onto her
new shalwar kameez. Someone sat next to her. It was her
dad.

'Beta?' he asked, his eyes soft with kindness.

'Abu, Yousef has gone,' she said tearfully. 'He has left us for
this girl.'

'I'm sorry,' her dad said.

'He has chosen some girl over his own mother,' Feroza said.
She couldn't believe he had done this to her.

'Beta, perhaps you should—'

'No, Abu,' she said. 'Don't try to make excuses for him.'

'You have to let him be happy. Sometimes children need to find their own paths in life.'

She looked at him. She couldn't believe he was saying this to her. After what he had done. 'Like you did with me?' He stared at her. 'Abu, you think I didn't know what you and Ami did to me all those years ago?'

Her looked confused. 'Beta, what are you talking about?'

'I'm talking about Azeem,' she said, looking her father in the eye. It was the first time she had said his name out loud in nearly thirty years. The boy she'd once liked who had walked her home from school.

He looked away. 'Feroza, I am sorry about that. We were . . . wrong.'

Feroza wiped away her tears. She was done crying over the actions of men.

She stared at her father now, old emotions resurfacing. 'You knew I liked him, you were friends with his father.'

'Feroza, stop,' her dad pleaded.

But there was no stopping Feroza tonight. 'You must have seen us walking home from school.'

'The whole street saw you! I had to do something!' Abdul said, his voice full of anguish.

'So you made arrangements for me to marry Abdul instead?' she whispered, voice breaking.

Her dad shook his head. 'Things were different back then. He was the son of a market stall worker. We believed you deserved better. It was a different time, I am sorry.'

'And you stopped talking to his father as well,' she said. 'You made sure I would never see Azeem again.'

Her father simply shook his head. 'I am sorry, beta. I am an old man, I have regrets. But learn from my mistakes, don't do the same thing with Yousef.'

'You have no right to tell me how to raise my son,' she hissed at her father.

Abdul came back in. 'Rohit doesn't know anything. I'll try Steve.'

'No!' Feroza shouted. Abdul startled. 'Let him go.'

'What do you mean?'

'If he wants to go, let him go,' she said, wiping her face. 'We have done everything for that boy. Everything. And this is how he repays us. Let him go. Let's see how long he can last without his family.'

'Feroza, no. He is our son,' Abdul said.

'I said, let him go,' she said again. 'I don't want to see him.'

'Feroza . . .' Now her dad tried.

'No, Abu!' she whispered. 'Stay quiet. He thinks he can embarrass me like this? Bring shame on his family? No. I don't want to see him.' She got up and made her way down to the kitchen. She needed that cup of tea. She knew her son would be back, he would see the error of his ways. She knew he couldn't be without her, without his mother.

Feroza went to her bedroom and opened up her cupboard. She unfolded the little stepladder she kept in the back of the cupboard and climbed up so she could reach the top shelf. She found what she was looking for: a box she had brought with her from Pakistan when she first moved over with Abdul. She climbed down and sat on the end of the bed. She hadn't opened this box in over twenty years. She wiped away the dust that had collected on its lid. Even after all of these years, it was painful knowing what was inside. But she had made a promise to herself all of those years ago. No matter what happened when she moved to England, she wouldn't lose her culture, her heritage.

She lifted the lid.

Inside was the book Azeem had given to her on their last walk home from school. She took it out, the pages curled at the edges from age. She remembered what he had said about Pakistan being made up of different people from different cultures. She just wanted her children to know their heritage, to be brought up immersed in it. But she had failed. She had taken her eye off the ball and one of them had strayed. Now she had lost him. But she had to be confident he would find his way home again. All lost children came home. Eventually.

Chapter Fifty-Two

Jessica

JESS COULDN'T SLEEP. THE rain was coming down hard and the noise kept her awake. The same as when she was a child. She went downstairs to fetch a glass of water. A knock on the door startled her as she started to make her way back upstairs. Who would be calling at this time, in this weather? It was nearly three in the morning. She thought about waking her parents, but decided to look out the window first.

It was Yousef. What was he doing here? She thought about ignoring him, but he knocked again and she didn't want him to wake her parents. She still hadn't explained about them getting back together and then breaking up again. She unlocked the door, opening it only a tiny fraction.

'What do you want?'

'Jess, I'm sorry,' he said. 'I know it's too late, but I need you to know the truth. Please hear me out. I don't expect you to take me back, I just need to tell you some things.'

She looked at him. He was wet through. She sighed. 'Come in, but you have to be quiet. My parents are asleep.'

She led him to the kitchen, closing the door behind them.

'Go on then,' she said, folding her arms.

'I know my mum came to talk to you at work,' he said, water dripping onto the floor. 'I'm sorry, she shouldn't have done that.'

'I'm glad she did, otherwise I wouldn't have known the full extent of what a lying bastard you are,' she replied.

'I deserve that,' he said. 'My mum told you I was engaged to some other girl . . . That wasn't true. Yes, there was a girl she wanted me to marry, but I couldn't do it. I couldn't do it to her and I couldn't do it to you. I love you, Jess, I've always loved you.'

'Yousef, I've heard all of this before.' Jess was tired of hearing how much Yousef loved her. 'You say it and then nothing changes.'

'I've left them, Jess, I've left my family,' he said.

'What do you mean, Yousef?' She had never asked him to leave his family.

'I mean, I've taken a training job here in Somerset. I told them I wanted to be with only you.' His words were coming out quick now. 'All my things are in the car.'

Jess tried to take in what he was saying. 'What did your family say? Wait, wasn't your sister getting married today?' She still followed Rehana on Instagram and had kind of stalked the wedding.

'Yes, and that's all done. But I couldn't stay in that house any longer, I needed to see you. I needed you to know that I always planned to tell them about you, things just kept getting in the way, and then my mum found out about us without me knowing and that's why she came to speak to you.' Yousef was crying now. 'I'm sorry, Jess, for everything. I don't expect you to take me back, but I wanted you know I'd done it and that I still love you.'

'Yousef.' This was all a bit much to digest. 'I never wanted to come between you and your family. I just wanted to be a part of that side of your life. Not take it away from you.'

'I know, none of this is on you. It's all me. I needed to get my shit together and it took me longer than it should have done.'

'I don't know what you want me to say, Yousef,' Jess said. 'I'm glad you stood up to your family – you needed to do that for you, not for me. As to where that leaves us, I don't know. You really hurt me. Twice. I'd be an idiot to take you back again.' Plus, Kate would murder her, she thought.

'I understand,' Yousef said. 'I just need to know one thing.'

'What?' she asked.

'Is there even the smallest part of you that might still love me?' He looked at her, the way he had done a million times over, with those eyes that penetrated her soul.

'Maybe. I don't know.' That was the truth. He had hurt her so much, she just didn't know how she felt about him.

'Okay, that's enough for me,' he said. 'That gives me hope. I'll work on that, show you that I'm serious. I'll do whatever it takes to make you love me again.'

What was it about this boy? He made her feel things that nobody ever could.

'I think you should leave now, Yousef,' she said, giving him the faintest of smiles.

'Thank you, Jess. Thank you for listening to me.' He came close to her. She could feel his breath on her face. 'I meant it, I will do whatever it takes.'

'Yousef, it isn't just a case of coming here and apologizing. It's going to take a lot for me to trust you again,' she said, pushing him away. 'And you will have to convince Kate too, with the way she wants to kill you . . .'

'Good,' he replied. 'I like a challenge.'

Part Four

Twelve months later

Chapter Fifty-Three

Rehana

'ARE WE GOING TO sit here all day?' Nadeem asked Rehana as she stared out of the window of the car. 'I mean, I don't mind, but this isn't really what we came here for.'

Rehana pulled herself out of her thoughts. She was building up the courage to go in. It had been nearly a year since she had seen Yousef on her wedding day. She had briefly questioned why he hadn't said goodbye to her when she was leaving, but then other things had taken over and the thought had left her mind. When she learned he'd deserted their parents, she couldn't believe how selfish he had been. Her first few months of marriage were supposed to be the happiest and they were, but there was now a shadow cast over them. She resented Yousef for this.

She had left Yousef angry text messages and voicemails. He didn't reply to any of them. But as the months went on her emotions tempered. It took being with Nadeem to see what Yousef wanted: to be with the person who made him as content as she felt now. Rehana was content. She knew she was lucky, and it was still early days, but she was happy. Their honeymoon in the Maldives had been idyllic. Just the two of them getting to know each other, and nobody telling her off for wearing swimsuits. She fell in love with Nadeem on that trip. She'd always thought she would fall in love with someone before she married them; that was what she had always seen on the television, what she had read in books when she was at university. She had scoffed when her mum told her that in arranged marriages, love comes after the wedding. She thought she might love Nadeem before the wedding, as they got to know each other, but being with him all day and each night while on honeymoon was different. He constantly surprised her with his kindness. She knew she hadn't known love until that trip.

Moving to London and living with Nadeem's family while they waited for their house to be finished was a big adjustment. As much as they told her the house was as much hers as it was theirs, she continually felt like a guest. They had been given the guest room of the house, complete with its own en-suite, which Rehana was grateful for. She wished she could stay in her room all day with Nadeem, but she knew she had to play the dutiful daughter-in-law and make an appearance downstairs. It was tradition that a new bride make herself up each day and wear the extravagant clothes that were gifted to her at the wedding. Her mother had explained all of this to her before the wedding, but still it felt like hard work to Rehana, who was used to lounging about in jogging bottoms and a T-shirt. Each morning, she would wander downstairs looking like she had stepped out of *Asian Bride* magazine. It didn't feel glamorous at all. All of the jewellery she was obliged to wear got in the way of her making snacks and, if she was being honest, the clothing was a right pain in the arse to hike up whenever she needed to go for a wee. She told herself it was only for a short time, while they waited to complete on their new home.

And then there were the dinners. Nadeem's family knew so many people and, as tradition dictated, they all wanted to invite the newlyweds to their homes for dawat as a sign of respect. Rehana wasn't complaining; at each dawat she was presented with a huge Pakistani banquet and even more gifts of clothing or jewellery.

It took a while for Rehana to understand her feelings, but it eventually dawned on her. For the first time in her life, she was being treated like an adult. She wasn't constantly being told off, or shooed into another room whilst the adults talked, and Nadeem and his family asked her opinion on things before a decision was made.

'Honestly, Em, it's a whole new world when you don't have someone judging your every move,' she told her best friend as they sat outside a London cafe drinking coffees.

'And you seriously don't mind living with your mother-in-law?' Emma quizzed as the waitress brought over their lunches.

'Well, it's not easy. No matter how many times Nadeem's mother tells me to call her "Mum", it still feels weird.' Rehana took the peppermill and seasoned her omelette.

'God, Chris's parents would drive me insane if I had to live with them,' Emma said.

'Oooh, how's that going? I loved the pictures of the two of you in Switzerland on your Instagram. Très chic!' Rehana exclaimed.

'Switzerland was gorgeous. Chris is like some sort of semi-professional skier, and I like to après-ski, so we're a match made in heaven really.' They both laughed. 'Plus, my mum and gran love him.'

'That's definitely a bonus. Having family on side makes relationships so much easier.' Rehana nodded.

'Any word from your brother?' Emma asked.

Rehana shook her head. 'No, he isn't responding to my messages. I just wish I'd been more . . . supportive,' she said wistfully.

'He just needs time.' Emma took a bite of her French toast. 'And I am not so sure having family support is the be all and end all in a relationship. My gran keeps telling me I need to get my skates on with Chris, otherwise I'll be too dried up and wrinkly to bear children.'

Rehana didn't say anything.

'What is it?' Emma asked.

Rehana gave her a coy smile.

'No!' Emma squealed.

Rehana nodded.

'Shut up! You are not!' Emma said excitedly.

'I am. About nine weeks now. Nobody knows. Not even our parents, so you can't say anything. Not a word.' Rehana's voice trembled with excitement.

'Rehana, I am so happy for you! Congratulations.' She looked around for the waitress, beckoning her over. 'One glass of champagne and another of orange juice for my friend, please.'

Rehana gave her a look.

'What? Somebody needs to wet the baby's head!' Emma said.

'I thought you only do that after the baby's born?' Rehana replied.

'Rehana, you won't know this, being Muslim and all. But there is never a wrong time to drink champagne.' They clinked their glasses. 'You know what, Rehana, I had my doubts about this whole arranged marriage thing, but you've changed my mind. It kind of works.'

'I'm glad I could be of service.'

After her first scan, she told her parents. Her mum cried and her dad hugged her hard. Even with the news of the pregnancy, there remained a sadness in her family home. Her parents still weren't really talking to each other. She didn't know the details of what had happened the day Yousef left, but it had left a chasm in the relationship between her mum and dad. They avoided being in the same room as each other. Her dad would ask her if she had heard from her brother when her mum left the room. She shook her head. Her mum never asked.

She tried ringing Yousef again, but each time it would go to answerphone. She left messages, asking how he was and saying that she would like to meet with him and, most importantly, that she was sorry. At first, she got nothing back but last week, her phone had pinged with a message from her brother. He wanted to meet with her.

Yousef lived in a place called Frome. Rehana had never heard of it but it was nice. They were parked outside a cafe. Rehana was late, but she still couldn't bring herself to go inside.

'What's wrong?' Nadeem asked.

'Nothing, just thinking of what I'm going to say to him,' Rehana said softly.

'He's your brother, just punch him in the arm and tell him he's a twat. That's how I greet my brothers,' Nadeem said. She was grateful to him for trying to lighten the mood. 'Do you want me to come in with you?'

She shook her head. 'I need to see him on my own first.'

'Then go!' Nadeem replied. 'Our parking ticket runs out in a couple of hours, and it's almost as expensive as London round here.'

She got out and walked towards the cafe. She could see Yousef sitting at a table in the corner. He must have felt her gaze as he looked up and caught her eye. Rehana went in.

'Hi,' she said to him awkwardly.

'Hi, sis,' he said. 'I got you a vanilla latte. You still like them, right?'

'Skinny, sugar free?' she asked.

'Obviously.'

Rehana sat down. She wasn't sure where to start. They both sipped their coffees. 'It's nice round here,' she said. Yousef nodded. 'Bit posh for the likes of you, though.'

He laughed. 'Yeah, I kind of stick out like a sore thumb. You know what they say, you can't polish a turd.' They laughed. It was awkward.

'It's good to see you, Yousef.' She brushed his arm. 'Are you . . . well?'

'Yeah, I'm well. Things are going good.' He spoke softly. 'How about you? How's married life?'

'It's actually pretty good.' She smirked.

'And Nadeem, is he okay?'

'He's good. In fact, he's here. Waiting in the car,' Rehana said.

There was another awkward silence as they both drank their coffees.

'I bet you're driving his parents mad,' Yousef said.

'I'm the model daughter-in-law, actually. You know how charming I can be.'

'I don't remember charm being one of your strong suits.'

They sat in silence again.

'Look, Yousef, I'm sorry,' Rehana blurted out.

He looked up at her. 'Sorry for what?'

'For so many things,' she professed. 'I'm sorry I told you not to tell Mum and Dad about Jessica that night. Maybe if I'd been more of a supportive sister, things might have worked out differently.'

Yousef took his sister's hand. 'You know, Rehana, I was angry with you, Mum and Dad too. I blamed you all for everything.' Rehana felt a pang of guilt in her gut. 'But I've had a lot of time to think about things. It's been good for me being here on my own, away from everything. I know now that I should have told Mum and Dad about Jess sooner and that's on me, nobody else. My decisions, my fault. But I'm trying to rectify all those things now.'

'Yousef, did you digest a self-help book or something?' she asked.

Yousef laughed. 'Maybe, I don't know. The thing is, I've moved on from all of those negative emotions.'

'Now I know you've definitely been reading one of those woo-woo books!' Rehana stated. 'Seriously, though, are you okay?'

He nodded. 'Best I've been in years.'

'And you and Jess, did that work out?'

'We're taking things slowly,' he pondered. 'There's a lot of healing to be done, but we're getting there.'

Rehana nodded her head. 'And Mum and Dad? They ask about you all the time. You should go and see them.'

Yousef cocked his head. 'Mum asks about me?'

Rehana wanted to lie and say yes, but she was done with lying. 'She's still angry, Yousef. You know all she cares about is what people think. She's been having to tell them you have this one in a million job here in Somerset so had to move out.'

Yousef smiled. 'She'll never change.'

'Dad misses you.'

Yousef stared at his coffee. 'He hasn't called. Neither of them have.'

'Pakistani parents are stubborn, Yousef,' Rehana explained. 'They will never admit they're wrong, especially to a younger person, but they're heartbroken. Maybe you should make the first move.'

'I'm all right,' Yousef said. 'I'm good with my decisions and I'm good on my own. Anyway, are you going to tell Nadeem to come in or what? I'd like to know what his secret is.'

'Secret?' she quizzed.

'Yeah, the boy must have the patience of a saint to put up with you,' he said with a smile.

She threw her napkin at him. 'Is work okay? Have you settled in?'

Yousef nodded. 'It's intense but I'm getting there. I have a couple of weeks off at the end of the month. It's Rohit's wedding. In India.'

'Wow, India?' Rehana raised her eyebrows. 'I still can't believe Rohit's getting married. He was always your loser friend.'

'Well, if you can get married, I suppose anyone can. So, are you going to get your husband or not?'

They both laughed. 'I'll go and get him.' She got up.

'Whoa, sis!' Yousef said. 'They've clearly been feeding you well at your new place.'

Rehana threw a menu at her brother. 'I'm pregnant, you idiot!'

'What?' Yousef said. 'Pregnant?'

'I'd hate to be a patient of yours if you can't even tell if a woman is—' Rehana's sentence was cut short as Yousef squeezed her hard in an embrace.

'Congratulations,' he whispered. 'I'm really happy for you.'

Rehana smiled. 'Thanks.'

Chapter Fifty-Four

Rohit

'YOU LOOK SO SMART,' Rohit's mum said to him. 'My Dulhe Raja.'

Rohit was trying on wedding shervanis. 'I'm not sure about the hat,' he said, pointing to the elaborate pagri placed upon his head. 'I look a bit ridiculous. Like that kid in *Indiana Jones and the Temple of Doom*, you know, the one with the voodoo doll?'

'Don't be silly,' Amit called out. 'You can't get married without a pagri on your head. How would anyone know you're the groom?'

Priya nodded in agreement. 'I think you look handsome. And don't forget you're coming in on a horse, so it won't look so out of place.'

Rohit was dreading the horse. He had tried a horse-riding lesson once and failed miserably. The riding hat he had been given smelled of sweat and the horse refused to move, no matter how much he squeezed with his thighs. In the end a twelve-year-old girl had to pull him and the horse around the barn for half an hour so he didn't hold the rest of the group up. But he was quickly coming to realize that his wedding was about everyone else as much as it was about him and Anjali. He was quite happy for his family to take the reins – so to speak.

'Just make a decision, I'm hungry!' his nephew moaned.

'Fine, fine,' he said. 'Let's go with this one.'

'YES!' his nephew cried, fist-pumping the air. 'Mum, now can we go to McDonald's?'

Rohit texted Anjali: **Found my wedding outfit** 😊

They were meeting for dinner later that evening. They had only seen each other two days ago, but he was already itching to talk to her again. He thought about what it would be like to see her every day, to wake up next to her, to have breakfast together. They would be married in less than two months. He didn't have long to wait before those things became a reality.

Amit drove them all to McDonald's. His family chattered away in the car about the wedding. He wished his dad were here to see him get married. Somehow being with Anjali lessened the pain of missing his father. Rohit had never thought he could feel as happy as he did around her. He had resigned himself to a life of mediocrity. But Anjali made him feel differently. Seeing her passion about her work made him want to strive for better. Being stuck in a job he hated was no longer enough, so he had applied to a bigger accountancy firm and got the job. It had only been seven months but he had already been promoted. She had been so proud when the news of the promotion came. He'd never thought he would find someone who supported him in the way she did. He had even joined a gym, in a bid to lose some weight before the wedding.

She was heading to India a fortnight ahead of Rohit and his family to prepare for the wedding. He was going to miss her, but hopefully this would be the last time they would be apart.

'Do they have McDonald's in India?' his nephew asked.

'Yes, but not beef burgers. Cows are sacred there,' Priya replied. 'You can have the fillet-o-fish instead.'

'Yuck,' his nephew replied. 'Do we have to go to India? Why can't Rohit Chacha get married here in Manchester like you and Abu?'

'Because Anjali Chachi is from India and it's tradition to get

married where the girl comes from. You will love Rajasthan. It
has lots of big palaces!' Priya said, handing him a tissue. 'You
have ketchup on your chin. Here, use this.'

'You're almost fifteen kilograms over your weight allowance,'
the lady checking them in at the airport said. 'You'll have to
either pay extra, or remove it.'

Rohit knew this would happen. It happened every time they
went to India. His mum was adamant about packing a gift for
everyone they knew there. 'What will Seeta say, if we give
Shweta something and not her?' she had said. And with all the
additional things they needed for the wedding, it was no surprise
they had surpassed their luggage weight allowance.

Amit came forward. 'Come on, can't you let it go?' He smiled
at the woman. 'It's my brother's wedding, everything in the
luggage is important.'

She shook her head. 'Sorry, if it was just one or two kilos
over, then perhaps I could, but fifteen kilos is just too much.'

'Please?' he pleaded. 'Look, that's my brother over there. He's
getting married to the girl of his dreams in India. It's all mainly
clothing and gifts, essentials really. You don't want to ruin his
wedding by making him leave half his luggage here, do you?'

'Sorry, there is nothing I can do,' the lady replied. She looked
over his shoulder. 'There's a queue of people waiting, what do
you want to do?'

'Just one minute,' Amit replied, turning back to the rest of
them. 'She won't budge, she doesn't care that it's your wedding,'
he said loud enough for everyone to hear.

Rohit was mortified. He didn't want his wedding being
announced in the middle of Manchester Airport.

'What are we going to do?' his mum said, sounding anxious.

'Let's see if we can squeeze more things into our hand luggage,'
Priya suggested.

'My hand luggage is almost empty,' Yousef offered. 'I can take more things.' He had come up from Birmingham last night to travel with them to the wedding. Rohit was glad to have him there.

'Good boy, Yousef,' Rohit's mum said.

Amit took their suitcases off the conveyor belt and began unzipping them.

'You can't do that here,' the lady said. 'You'll have move over to the side, we have people waiting to check in.'

Amit assessed the long line of people. 'It won't take us long, love. Just give us a few minutes.'

The lady glared at him.

'Right, come on, everyone,' Amit said. 'Let's see what we can do.' He unzipped the three large suitcases. 'Who has space in their hand luggage?' Yousef, Rohit and Priya came forward.

His mum began pulling out saris she had bought for Anjali and handed them to Yousef. 'Here, squeeze these into your bag. What about these shoes, can you fit them in?' Yousef nodded, taking the shoes and saris. 'Rohit, you take these.' She handed him three large tubs of Celebrations chocolates.

'Ma, why are you even taking these?' he whined, trying to force the large tubs into his bag.

'Because they love English chocolates over there,' his mum retorted. 'Why can't you just be helpful like Yousef?' Rohit rolled his eyes.

Priya was going through one of her suitcases. 'I'm sure I put them here somewhere,' she said to Amit. 'Ah, here they are.' She pulled out two ginormous bottles of Barcadi. Rohit shot her an inquisitive look. 'What?' she said. 'You can't have an Indian wedding without a Bacardi and Coke.' She unzipped her weekender and carefully placed them inside.

'Can you lot hurry up!' a woman called from behind them. 'We all want to get on this flight.'

'Keep your hair on, love,' Amit replied. 'It's not our fault the airline has such lousy luggage allowances.'

'Right, can anyone fit this toaster into their bag?' He looked up. 'Mum, what about you?'

His mum shrugged and took the toaster. 'I will just carry it under my arm.'

'You can't do that, madam,' the lady from behind the counter said.

'Why not?' his mum replied. 'It's just a toaster.'

'Mum, why do you even have a toaster?' Rohit asked.

'Last time I went to Aunty Chintal's house for breakfast, she made toast in a grill! It took so long. The toaster is for her.' His mum tucked the toaster under her arm. 'See, easy.'

'You are only allowed one piece of hand luggage,' the woman said from behind the counter. 'If you carry that toaster, that makes two items with your bag. Plus your handbag, so it's three really.'

Without taking her eyes off the woman behind the counter, Rohit's mum slowly and deliberately unzipped her bag and forced the toaster in. The bag was now so full it wouldn't zip back up. 'Now only one item of hand luggage,' his mum said to the lady. 'Plus my handbag, but that doesn't count.'

The woman scowled, got up and walked off.

'Mum, who is this for?' Amit asked, pulling out a sizeable metal make-up case.

'Oh, Tanya gave that to me. She wanted to give it to her sister in India. You know how expensive postage is these days, it's easier if we just take it.'

'Maybe we should leave that here,' Priya cut in. 'We can always buy make-up there and give it to Tanya's sister.'

Rohit's mum looked horrified. 'What? No, I promised Tanya I would deliver it myself. What will she think if she finds out we left it at the airport?'

'Priya, can it go in one of the kids' bags?'

Priya nodded and took the make-up box.

'You can't repack suitcases here,' a deep voice said from behind them. 'You need to move to the side.' Rohit turned to look. The woman from behind the counter had returned with a member of the airport security team.

'We've nearly finished,' Amit said, zipping the last of the suitcases back up. 'Right, let's try again, shall we?' he said to the woman. She looked thoroughly pissed off.

Amit lifted the suitcases back onto the conveyor belt to be weighed. They were now six kilograms over their limit. 'Come on, you said if we were just a few kilos over, you would let us through.'

The woman sighed. 'Fine,' she said. 'But only because I don't want to delay the flight.'

His mum clasped her hands together. 'Thank you, beta,' she said. 'I knew you weren't that bad.'

Poor Priya's Bacardi got confiscated from her hand luggage at security, but she bought two even bigger bottles in duty free.

Rohit heard the sound of a distant brass band as he and his family waited for their luggage at Jodhpur Airport.

'That's for you, mate,' Amit said, smiling at his brother.

'What's for me?' Rohit asked, confused.

'Just wait and see.' Amit winked at him. Yousef laughed. They both seemed to know something he didn't.

They piled up their suitcases on a trolley and headed towards the exit. The doors slid open and a cheer erupted from the crowd. It felt as though every member of Anjali's family had come to collect them from the airport. The brass band had apparently been hired by her family for their arrival and was now playing an array of Bollywood wedding classics. Uncle Sunil and Uncle Anand rushed over and placed a haar of flowers around everyone's necks. Rohit's nephews especially liked this part. There were hugs and some of the younger lads insisted on pushing the luggage trolleys. Polite refusal was futile. Rohit's grandmother was also there. His mum burst into tears when she saw her, which set a few other people off. Rohit went to his grandmother to do charan sparsh, the blessed touching of her feet. 'Namaste, Naani,' he said. She patted his head, then signalled for him to stand up and hug her.

'Jaheetai Raho, beta.' She smiled through tears. 'I am so happy you are getting married here in your motherland.'

'Me too, Naani,' Rohit said. 'This is my best friend, Yousef.'

'Namaste,' Yousef said, putting his hands together. Rohit gestured for him to touch her feet. Yousef quickly cottoned on, bending down and doing the charan sparsh.

'Welcome, my son,' his grandmother said, taking Yousef by the shoulders and forcing him into an embrace.

'Right, come on,' Anjali's mum, Aunty Nandani, said. 'No time to waste.'

Rohit nodded and began heading towards the exit.

'Oh no!' Uncle Sunil said, laughing. 'Not like that. We are now a wedding procession and you are our dhula.' He nodded to the trumpet player in the band. They took up their instruments and began playing 'Sajan Ghar Aaye'. All the boys cheered and rushed towards Rohit, lifting him up into the air, carrying him to the car park. 'This is how we leave!' Uncle Sunil shouted over the top of the music.

Anjali's family home was a large open khoti, which had been designed to allow the Rajasthani breeze to flow and naturally cool the building. The outside of the khoti was decorated in thousands of fairy lights that sparkled in the evening light as they approached. The inside was bustling with people preparing for the wedding.

'This is your cousin, Raj,' his mum said, as Rohit hugged yet another stranger. 'And this is Khala Meena. She is married to your dad's uncle.' Rohit greeted her.

'I am just sorry your dad isn't here to share in these happy times,' Aunty Meena said. Rohit's mum immediately welled up and had to be taken away. Rohit looked around for Amit and Priya. Both were talking to yet more relatives. Yousef had been desperate for the loo and had rushed off. A gaggle of aunties and uncles had surrounded poor Yousef. They had found out he was a doctor and had been talking to him about their ailments.

'Do you know where Anjali is?' he asked Raj.

'She will be in her room, but you cannot see her. It's bad luck.' He smiled at him. 'Come with me, I'll show you the mandap. That's where you will be getting married.' Rohit followed Raj to the garden where a huge wooden frame, adorned with fresh flowers, was erected. Raj looked at Rohit for a reaction.

'It's beautiful,' Rohit whispered. The garden opened onto the Rajasthan hills and the desert beyond. Only a few other homes dotted the landscape. He couldn't quite believe this was his wedding venue. This really was the Land of the Kings. He suddenly felt very connected to the land and his ancestors. A tap on his shoulder woke him from his thoughts. It was Anjali's sister, Karishma.

'Why are you hiding out here?' she asked. 'Come on inside – it's time for the Graha Shanti!' she squealed, dragging Rohit back inside. Amit, Priya and Yousef were already there covered in yellow paste. 'Come sit, sit!' Karishma said. Several women surrounded him, rolling up his sleeves and pulling up his trouser legs. Rohit tried to protest against the unbuttoning of his shirt, but his hand was slapped out of the way by Aunty Meena. Yousef wolf-whistled as more buttons came undone. The women covered him in haladi.

'This is a blessing, it will bring you and Anjali peace and prosperity,' his mum, who had clearly known this was going to happen, explained.

'It will protect you from evil spirits,' Aunty Meena said, slathering it over his face as Rohit scrunched his eyes closed.

The Graha Shanti turned into a full-blown party as cocktails and glasses of whisky were passed around. The aunties began singing traditional folk songs and the uncles started to dance. Rohit laughed and clapped along. It all felt surreal. Less than twenty-four hours ago he had been in Manchester preparing for his flight, and now he was surrounded by a family and culture he barely knew existed, but one which had welcomed and embraced him as one of their own. He pulled out his phone to see a text from Anjali.

Anjali: Welcome to the family. They love you.

Rohit: Have you been spying on us? I thought it was bad luck?

Anjali: I may have sneaked a peek. I couldn't resist.

Rohit: I love you.

Anjali: I love you too, now get some sleep. It's a busy day tomorrow.

The following day was the Sangeet. The caterers arrived early to set up food stalls around the garden. The aroma of pani puri, paneer saag and channa chaat wafted through the air. Vans arrived with yet more flowers and boxes of mithai were piled high on tables. Anjali's mum and sister hurried around making sure the preparations for this pre-wedding party were going as planned, occasionally scolding the staff as they did. Yousef seemed to have completely embedded himself in the wedding affairs and was now helping move crates of drinks from the back of the van to the kitchen.

Amit was helping Rohit get ready. Priya came in to check on their progress.

'I brought you this,' she said, holding up a freshly cut lotus flower. She pinned it to the breast of his shirt. 'It's a holy symbol,' she said. 'Your grandma wanted you to wear one.'

Rohit looked at himself in the mirror. Anjali's parents had gifted him a pale pink kurta churidar suit, embroidered with a delicate silvery pattern. Priya placed the scarf around his neck and under his arm.

'There,' she said. 'Ready?'

He nodded.

'Time to make your grand entrance, bro,' Amit said, slapping him on the back.

Rohit was immediately surrounded by drum players and people dancing as he came out of his room and made his way downstairs. The women guided him towards a seat in the centre of the room. There was more singing and dancing, and Rohit was made to eat what felt like his own weight in ladoos and gulab jamuns as the elders fed him.

Eventually the singing quietened down and Anjali was brought downstairs, flanked by her mum and sister. It was the first time Rohit had seen her since he had arrived. She looked exquisite. She wore the traditional Sangeet colour yellow, and her hands and forearms had been covered in henna drawn in the most intricate patterns. Her hair cascaded over her shoulders, intertwined with lotus flowers similar to the one Priya had pinned on him earlier. Anjali caught his eye for a second and gave the faintest of smiles before returning her gaze to the floor.

She was placed on a chair next to him. Rohit couldn't take his eyes off her. Suddenly there was a tugging at his feet. It was Karishma. She slipped off one of his shoes and began jumping up and down; other girls began to join her shouting 'Joote de do Paise le lo!' Anjali laughed and encouraged her sister and friends.

Rohit recognized this from his brother's wedding. He had to

give the girls cash in exchange for his shoe. Amit had given him a wad of Indian rupees earlier for this very reason. But he also knew, this was as much about the show as it was the money or shoe.

'I don't have any money!' he cried, turning his pockets inside out.

'Sister, you are marrying a pauper!' Karishma shouted. 'I say call off the wedding!' The rest of the girls joined her in a rallying cry. 'Call off the wedding!' they chanted.

'Come on, girls, be reasonable!' Amit said, joining his brother's side.

'Yes, come on, girls – he said he doesn't have any money!!' Yousef shouted out above the noise.

'What a kanjoos family!' Meena Khala shot back.

'If you want your shoe back, give us your money!' one of Anjali's school friends countered.

'Okay, okay.' Rohit made a dramatic gesture of reaching into his breast pocket. 'Here's ten rupees, that's all you're getting!' He made a swipe for his shoe.

'Ten rupees!' Karishma said, pulling the shoe out of his reach. 'Sister, you are marrying such a kanjoos stingy man, we should never have agreed to this wedding!'

Anjali laughed. 'You are going to have to do better than that, if you want to marry me,' she said. The girls cheered louder. 'Girls, don't let them off the hook!' she shouted. More cheering.

Rohit pulled out a hundred-rupee note. 'Okay, this should do it.' Karishma snatched the money out of his hand.

'And the rest!' she cried. Rohit's nephews were now trying to take the shoe from Karishma and the girls, but were having no luck.

'Okay, but only because your sister is worth it.' He smiled at Karishma, handing over a five-hundred-rupee note.

That seemed to appease her. She passed the shoe to the next

girl. 'But you have to pay each one of us if you want this shoe back.' She laughed.

Rohit turned to his brother. 'Amit, I'm going to need some more cash.'

The Sangeet went on well into the following morning. The whole town was in attendance, all wanting to see the boy from England who was taking one of their own away. Food, drink and music were in generous supply. Despite sitting next to each other, Rohit and Anjali had little time to converse, but it didn't matter. It was the wedding in a few days' time and then they would have all the time in the world.

Rohit woke on the day of his wedding with a jittery feeling in the pit of his stomach. He was getting married today. It all felt a bit surreal. He turned onto his side. Amit was still asleep on the bed opposite, Yousef was on the floor. He picked up his phone. He had a text from Steve. **Finally making it official! No more shagging around now. Good luck, bro!**

He smiled. Today was the day.

'Amit!' he hissed. His brother didn't stir. 'Amit!' he said, this time louder.

Amit groaned and turned to face him. 'What?'

'I'm getting married today!' Rohit said excitedly.

'What?' Amit sat up, looking bewildered.

'I'm getting married today!' Rohit repeated, this time with even more enthusiasm. 'It feels kind of strange, like it's happening to someone else.'

'I remember that feeling,' Amit said, now fully awake. 'Enjoy it. It'll be over before you know it, and you want to be able to remember every part.'

'Thanks,' Rohit said, staring up at the ceiling.

'You nervous?' Yousef was now awake too. 'It's a pretty epic day.'

'Kind of. There are so many rituals, what if I do or say something wrong?'

'Mum will be there,' Amit said. 'She's like the wedding whisperer, she can sense when things are about to go wrong and will swoop in and sort it.' Amit got out of bed. 'Now are you having a bath first, or am I?'

Rohit got dressed in his wedding shervani and carefully placed the pagri on his head. He was being driven out to the middle of the town and then returning to the house on a horse. Amit, Raj and Yousef accompanied him, with Uncle Sunil driving. This was the thing he was looking forward to the least.

'We are here,' Uncle Sunil said, sounding more excited than was necessary. The four of them got out of the car. Some of the other men from the town were waiting for them, along with the brass band from the airport. 'Where is she?' Uncle Sunil asked one of the men.

'Around the corner, she is ready,' he replied.

Rohit assumed they were talking about the horse. Perhaps naively, he had expected to be riding in on a stallion rather than a mare.

'Come with me,' Uncle Sunil said, beckoning them over. Raj gave Amit a knowing look. What was going on?

Rohit followed them to the end of the road where even more men were waiting.

'Your ride!' cried Uncle Sunil.

Rohit stared slack-jawed. 'That's . . . that's not a horse,' he whispered, mouth suddenly dry.

'No, this is India!' Uncle Sunil said proudly. 'Here our dhulas arrive on elephants.'

As if on cue, the elephant let out a high-pitched trumpet. The men all cheered.

'She is called Shree,' one of the men told him. 'Treat her with respect and she will do the same for you.' He patted Shree on the side. Shree too was decorated with flowers and swirly painted patterns.

'Come on, get on,' Raj said. 'We have a wedding to get to.'

'I'm not so sure . . .' Rohit hesitated. 'Is she tame?'

He looked at his brother, who shrugged, laughing. 'On you get.'

He looked at Yousef, who had quickly made friends with the elephant handler and was now happily feeding the elephant peanuts.

The men pulled out a ladder and helped him get on the elephant. Once he was on, the man shouted 'Challo!' and tapped Shree on the side and she began moving. The band began playing music and the group of men erupted into some sort of bhangra convoy as they walked. The bharat was making its way to the wedding.

As Rohit made his way through the town, some of the locals came out to wish him good luck and children ran out of the houses to join the dancing procession. The house and garden looked even more vibrant than when they left as yet more staff had arrived to help with the wedding. The guests had assembled at the gate to meet the bharat. Rohit could see his mum and grandmother waiting for them. The procession stopped a few yards short of the gate and the dancing continued. The band played 'Didi tera devar deewana', an old wedding classic that even Rohit was familiar with. It seemed to cause a frenzy amongst the guests and more of them joined in with the gaggle of dancing boys ahead of Rohit and the elephant.

Rohit couldn't quite believe all of this was for him. He felt like a prince. He laughed from on top of his perch. The dancing boys gestured for him to join in on the dance. Keeping a tight hold of the reins with one hand, he lifted the other into the air and bounced his shoulders up and down, his version of bhangra. The boys went wild. He felt like a rock star.

Eventually it was time for him to come down. The handler unfolded the ladder and signalled for Rohit to step down from on top of the elephant. Somehow coming down felt harder than climbing up, and now everybody was watching.

'Easy, girl,' he whispered to Shree as he swung his leg around. There was no dignified way to do this. He stumbled as he came down, causing Shree to panic and jolt forward. The ladder lurched; it was either jump or fall. He made a quick decision and jumped, landing on his feet. The crowd cheered again. Yousef and Amit rushed forward, steadying him, and then Raj pulled him into the dance. Rohit didn't remember a time he had been happier.

Anjali's family tossed rice over the bharat, a sign that welcomed him into the family. Anjali's mum hugged him and placed a haar around his neck.

'We are trusting you with our daughter, look after her,' she said, smiling and kissing his forehead.

'I will, Aunty,' he whispered. 'Thank you.'

She handed him an aarati. 'May this light shine on you wherever your marriage takes you,' she said. He could see she was welling up. It was a bit awkward. He felt he should hug her, but she had just handed him a plate with a burning candle in the middle and she looked to be wearing a highly flammable sari, so he opted to smile and nod instead.

She led him to the mandap, where the priest was waiting. A fire burned brightly in the middle of the structure. The noise diminished as everybody quietened down and prayers were recited. Rohit's mum and brother came to sit next to him. They remained silent as the priest continued to pray. Eventually he signalled for the bride to enter. Rohit stood up, turning around.

The band began playing a song Rohit didn't recognize, and there was an audible gasp from the audience as Anjali appeared from the house. She looked incredible. Rohit knew she was the one for him, and nothing else mattered. He had hit the jackpot.

He still wasn't quite sure why she had picked him, an ordinary accountant from Manchester, but he was so glad she had done. He blinked back the tears.

'Steady,' Amit said from behind him.

Anjali was accompanied by her dad, who looked to be bursting with emotion. They walked down the aisle, people snapping photos on their phone. Once she arrived at the mandap, Rohit mouthed 'wow' at her, making her smile. Her dad took her hand and placed it in Rohit's, nodding at him. The kanyadaan was complete.

The priest signalled for them to sit down. Rohit wanted to skip past the prayers and get to the part where he could be alone with Anjali, but the priest had other ideas. A two-hour ceremony ensued, starting with a prayer to Ganesha, the priest explaining to the guests that this would ensure good fortune for the newlyweds. Just when Rohit's bum was going numb, the priest announced the prayer section over and asked the couple to exchange jai malas. Amit handed Rohit an extravagant garland of flowers which Rohit placed around Anjali's neck and she did the same to him. Rohit's mum came forward with the mangalsutra, a dazzling gold beaded necklace which Rohit carefully extracted from the box and put over Anjali's head. It caught in her hair as he tried to place it around her neck. She laughed and helped him untangle it.

Anjali's dad then tied her veil in a knot with Rohit's sash and the couple were instructed to walk seven times around the fire. Rohit's mum had explained this to him earlier: the saptapadi was important in establishing friendship between the newly married couple.

That was it, they were married at last. Rohit's final job was to apply a streak of red powder to the front of Anjali's hair, signifying she was now a married woman. There was applause as he did so. He laughed, still not quite able to believe his luck.

The wedding party continued way into the small hours of

the morning. Rohit couldn't take his eyes off Anjali and was counting down the hours until he could be alone with his new wife. He thought back to the time when he had turned his nose up at marrying a 'freshie' – what a fool he had been. Anjali had saved Rohit from getting up every day and simply existing. He now finally knew what really living was.

Chapter Fifty-Five

Seema

SEEMA PULLED INTO THE car park of the surgery. She had come in early for a meeting with the partners. She wasn't quite sure what it was about. The practice manager, Peta, had been strangely coy about the whole thing. Seema had stayed on as a fully qualified GP at the surgery she trained at. It was coming up to a year and she assumed this was going to be some sort of annual review.

She said hello to the reception staff as she entered and went to the kitchen to make herself a coffee. Her phone buzzed in her handbag – an email she had been waiting for. She slipped the phone back in her bag and headed to her meeting.

Seema worked at a small practice near the centre of Shrewsbury. The three partners who ran it were already sitting waiting for her. One of them saw her waiting at the door and beckoned for her to come in.

'Seema, thank you for coming in,' Sue said, smiling. 'How was your weekend?'

'It was good. I went out for dinner in that new Greek place that's opened up.' Seema leaned in. 'It doesn't live up to the hype.'

'Oh, that's a shame, we were thinking of going there ourselves. Think we'll stick to the local Italian now,' Sue said, sounding disappointed.

Pam, one of the other partners, cleared her throat. 'Seema, we asked you to meet with us today as we have something important to discuss with you.'

Oh shit. Seema hoped a complaint hadn't come in about her. She quickly wracked her brain for any patient she had seen recently who might not have been satisfied at the end of one of her consultations. Nobody came to mind. She was a diligent GP and worked well beyond her hours in order to get the job done.

'Okay,' she said slowly, looking at the three doctors.

'We love having you at the surgery,' Gareth picked up. 'You work really hard, and the patients like you.'

Oh, thank God! Seema thought, sighing. This was no longer sounding like a performance review.

'And we want you to stay with us,' Sue added, beaming. 'You know I'm retiring next year . . .'

Seema nodded.

'So, we want you to come on board as partner!' Pam finished off.

Seema stared at the three of them open-mouthed. She hadn't been expecting that at all.

'Well?' Sue asked.

'Erm, thank you,' Seema said. She was still feeling slightly blindsided by all of this.

'Is that a thank you, you accept?' Gareth asked.

'It's a thank you for the offer. I'm just a bit taken aback. I've only been working here for ten months, I didn't expect to be offered a partnership so soon.'

'You have really proven yourself,' Pam explained, 'even in that short amount of time, and we wouldn't want you going off to another surgery. Good GPs are hard to come by.' She laughed.

'Can I think about it?' Seema said, knowing they would be disappointed with her lack of enthusiasm.

'Think about it?' Gareth said, sounding perplexed.

'Of course you can!' Sue cut in. 'I suppose we caught you by surprise. Take a few days to think about it and let us know, maybe by the end of the week?'

Seema nodded. 'Thanks.' She got up. 'I'd better go, my first patient will be arriving soon.' The meeting felt suddenly awkward. She wanted out of there. She hurried down to her room, unpacked her doctor's bag and slumped in her chair.

A partnership at a practice she liked working at! That was what she had thought she always wanted. She should have been jumping up and down with joy, but instead she felt conflicted. A partnership would tie her to the practice for years. Was that what she really wanted? Had this been a year ago when she thought she'd be marrying that dickhead Yousef, she would have jumped at the chance of a partnership. But ever since he humiliated her at Rehana's wedding, Seema had slowly begun to re-evaluate what she wanted in life. Yes, she still wanted to twat Yousef in the ballsack for being an absolute shit to her. She had hoped that marrying him would be the start of a new adventure in her life. Now, reflecting on things, she realized marrying Yousef wouldn't have been an adventure at all; quite the opposite, in fact. Her mother had been right all along. Yousef, and especially his annoying mother, were so traditional that she would probably have to inform them if she fancied a trip down to the shops. No, he had done her a favour by ending it with her. She just wished she had ended it with him first.

Girls like me don't get dumped, she thought. *We do the dumping.*

She took out her phone and looked at the email that had come in earlier. Seema mulled over her reply. A few months ago, she'd decided she was done waiting to start her life's adventure and had responded to an advert she had seen online. A company in Australia was recruiting GPs for jobs over there.

They boasted better pay and longer appointments with patients. Seema had always found the standard ten-minute GP consultation with a patient difficult. How much could you really sort out in ten minutes? Especially now patients had so many social issues going on as well as medical ones. She wanted to be the best GP she could be, and the current model of general practice didn't really allow for her to do that. Plus, there was the weather. She was fed up with cold winters and damp summers; she wanted real sunshine. Weather she could really get outside in and enjoy, without having to pack extra layers 'just in case'. She had applied on a whim, but the company had emailed her back detailing a job they had found her not far from Melbourne. She scrolled through the photos of the surgery and the surrounding areas. It looked beautiful. It looked like an adventure.

She paused, imagining what her parents might think of her passing up a partnership and leaving the country. *Fuck it.* She hit the reply button.

Dear Sophie,
Thank you for your email. I would be delighted to accept your kind offer of a job . . .

Chapter Fifty-Six

Feroza

FEROZA SAT ON THE phone listening to Rubina rabbit on about her new granddaughter. It was exhausting. She seemed to think everyone needed updates on what the baby had done that week. Had she forgotten that they were all mothers themselves and were well versed in the antics of newborns?

Eventually Rubina moved on to some local gossip.

'Did you hear about Atiya's son?' she asked.

'No, what about him?' Feroza asked.

'He is getting divorced,' Rubina replied. Feroza could tell she relished being the first to break the news. 'It wasn't even a love marriage. Fully arranged through families.'

'That's a shame,' Feroza said half-heartedly. She didn't revel in gossip in the way she once had. 'He and his wife were well matched.'

'The problem with children today is that they want a divorce too quickly,' Rubina mused. 'They don't want to stay and work things out. Always running at the first sign of trouble.'

'True,' Feroza said, thinking about it. 'You didn't hear about divorces in the Pakistani community until this generation came along.'

Any divorce was a scandal, and this was normally the kind of conversation Feroza would have loved to sink her teeth into.

But the truth was, her own marriage was in trouble. Abdul barely spoke to her since she had forbidden him from contacting their son. They were like shadows living in the same house. When he got back from work each night, they would eat their dinner, her in the kitchen, him in the living room, and then he would go to the mosque, not returning until she had gone to bed. He had been furious with her for not telling him what she knew about Yousef and that girl. She couldn't remember a time when he had raised his voice to her, but the nights following Yousef's departure had been dark, and he had shouted.

With both Yousef and Rehana gone, Feroza spent most of her days alone. She wondered what Yousef was doing. Why hadn't he tried to call her? She would forgive him for leaving; he just had to call. But her phone remained as silent as her home felt. Rehana tried to visit as much as she could but she was busy with Nadeem and his family. Feroza missed her family. She missed them being together under one roof. She had worked so hard for them to get married and live their own lives, she hadn't stopped to think of what that might mean for her.

All that time alone gave her space to think. What had she done that was so wrong? She only wanted the best for her children. She had been right about Rehana. Her daughter had just needed some guidance from her and now she was happily married and living with her husband. That was all she wanted for her son. She thought of those last few months with Yousef. He had been so different, quieter. She had expected him to have come back by now. After he realized how important his family was, he should have come home. After he realized what a terrible mistake he had made. But he was still absent, and her home remained empty. The life she'd dreamed of, living with Yousef and his wife, helping them bring up their children, parading them around at community events, had gone with him. And now with Abdul also refusing to attend any functions with her, Feroza was mostly confined to the four walls of her house. Alone.

She heard Abdul come in. She quickly said her goodbyes to Rubina and went to meet him in the hallway.

'Assalamualaikum,' she said.

'Walaikum salam,' he replied, taking off his shoes.

'I've made aloo paratha, they're still warm. Shall I prepare them for you?' she asked.

He looked at her and shook his head. 'I can do it myself.' He pushed past her and headed into the kitchen. She went back to the living room and switched on the television. The scholar on the Islam channel was taking calls from viewers and giving out advice. She had rung him several times over the last few months and asked for prayers to get her family back together. She told him that someone had put the evil eye on them, probably after seeing how happy they all were at Rehana's wedding, and she needed it lifting. He had given her a number of prayers to recite. She did as she was told, praying day and night, but none of it had worked. Whatever jaadu had been placed on her family, she was unable to undo it.

She tried the scholar again. He told her that along with prayer she also had to look at what action she could take to unite her family. Only then would her prayers work. What could she do? She tried to make amends with her husband but his anger seemed impenetrable. She prayed harder. She listened as the scholar gave out advice to other callers. She thought about what he might advise if he knew the true extent of what she had done. She heard the clinking of dishes coming from the kitchen as Abdul prepared his dinner. Somehow having him there but not talking to her made her feel even more alone than when he was at work.

Maybe the scholar was right, prayers alone would not work. She needed to take action.

She switched off the television and headed into the kitchen. She knew what she had to do.

'Abdul,' she said, 'we need to talk.'

Chapter Fifty-Seven

Jessica

BEING AT HOME IN Frome was such a contrast to being in Birmingham. Jess was back playing football with her old club, Kate was only a short drive away and her parents continued to think she was a novelty to be fussed over. She loved it.

Yousef moving here was not something she had planned for, and Jess wasn't going to give him an easy ride. He had to prove to her that this wasn't just him rebelling against his parents, that he was willing to graft for her and show her he was for real this time. It was cute watching him try. Initially he would post her little notes, telling her how much he had been thinking about her. She knew he wasn't very good at talking about his feelings, so these notes, full of emotion, were an impressive change of direction for him. She had eventually unblocked his number and they began exchanging messages. They were flirty at times, but she was clear he hadn't done enough yet.

Persuading Kate had been difficult, but even she was quietly impressed with the fact he had moved to Somerset to be with her. Jess had decided to keep her options open and had even gone on a couple of dates with James, but the spark they had at school wasn't there any more and she found her mind drifting back to Yousef.

Five months ago, she agreed to go for dinner with Yousef.

She hadn't seen him that excited for years. They had talked into the night, and to her relief he hadn't tried to kiss her.

'I want to show you I really mean it this time,' he said. 'I want this to be on your terms.'

It felt as though she had the old Yousef back, the one she had met at university all those years ago, not the capricious one that trudged round the hospital in Birmingham. One time, he had come to watch her play football and they had gone for dinner, and afterwards she had kissed him. It felt right, like coming home. There was none of the trepidation she had felt when they had got back together in her old hospital room. She felt comfortable, so she had told her parents. Her dad was apprehensive at first but was now coming round to the idea. Her mum was just relieved she was seeing someone – anyone would have done.

'Show me the pictures of you at Rohit's wedding again,' she asked him. They had just finished watching a movie.

'Really? Again?' Yousef groaned.

'Yes, you know I love seeing you in traditional clothes,' she replied.

'You know that's a bit weird, like a fetish.' He laughed. He pulled out his phone and began scrolling through the photos.

'You all look fantastic,' Jess said. 'Have you sent any of them to your family?'

'A couple to Rehana.'

'What about your parents?'

Yousef shook his head and put his phone away. She knew Yousef missed his family. He had been close to his mum in particular. Jess had insisted on him telling her everything; there would be no secrets or forbidden conversations this time around. She was glad when Rehana made contact and Yousef had agreed to meet her. She hoped that might spur him on to renew contact with his parents, but he was yet to do so.

'You should call them,' she told him as they lay on the sofa. 'Let them know you're okay.' He didn't say anything. 'Yousef?'

'I can't,' he said. 'I wouldn't know where to start. Mum would just shout. She doesn't listen.'

'But you should at least try, that way you won't have any regrets,' Jess said gently.

'You know, Rehana said Mum doesn't even ask about me. She doesn't even care if I'm okay or not.'

'She probably doesn't know where to start either.'

'I've made my decision; I want to focus on us now.' Yousef lifted his chin and kissed her. 'Focus on you.'

'Don't me get wrong, Yous,' Jess said, propping herself up. 'I have no qualms about you focusing all your attention on me. Trust me, I love that. But I hate thinking that I'm the reason you and your family don't talk.'

He looked at her. 'You're not the reason. They are. I'm here if they want to talk, but not if they want to try to change my mind or make me feel guilty about wanting to be happy. For wanting to live my own life. Well, I've left guilt behind now. That's not an emotion I want anything more to do with.'

Jess didn't push it any more. It had been a year. Everything was going well, but she continued to feel the shadow of his family over their relationship. Yes, of course it was better now that everything was out in the open. She just wanted for Yousef what she had for herself, a family who was happy for her.

'Let's talk about something else,' Yousef said, getting up. 'Shall I cook some of my famous chilli, or shall we order takeaway?'

'Takeaway, please,' Jess laughed. 'The only thing famous about your chilli is how awful it is.'

'Hey!' Yousef said. 'That hurt.' He threw a cushion at her. Jess caught it and tossed it back at him, laughing. He picked her up by her waist and swung her around.

'Yousef, put me down, you're making me dizzy!' Jess tried

to say as the room spun around her. He dropped her on the couch, falling beside her.

'What?' she asked. 'Do I have something on my face?' She began wiping away at her mouth.

'No, no, it's not that.' He smiled.

'What then?'

'Move in with me?' He took her hand.

'What?'

'I'm genuine, move in with me.' He sat up, suddenly looking very serious. 'We spend almost every day together anyway. Move your stuff in, live with me.'

Jess laughed. 'Yousef, we're supposed to be taking it slow.'

'Jess, we've known each other for over eight years. I love you, that's never going to change. Not ever. Move in with me.'

'Yousef, I think the sun must have gone to your head,' Jess said. Was he serious?

'No, Jess. I want us to live together.'

Jess thought about her parents. While her father described himself as 'loosely' Catholic, her mother would never allow them to move in together before being married. Especially not in Frome, around the corner from the church she attended every Sunday. 'Yousef, you know my parents wouldn't allow that,' Jess said. 'Not until we're married.'

Yousef paused. 'Marry me then,' he said suddenly, the biggest smile forming on his face.

'What?!'

'Jess, I don't want to wait any more. I want you. Marry me. Be my wife.'

'Yousef, this is crazy.' Jess laughed, but butterflies were beginning to flutter in her tummy.

Yousef got off the sofa, and down on one knee. 'Jessica Pritchard, will you marry me?'

'Yousef . . .' Jess cupped her hands over her mouth.

'Please?' he said, head cocked to one side.

She thought about everything they had been through. She was supposed to be taking this slow, making him prove himself. But could she see herself with anyone else? The answer was no. The truth was, there was only Yousef for her. There always had been.

'Jess?' Yousef asked.

'Yes . . .' she whispered.

'Yes?' he repeated.

'YES!' she shouted.

Yousef looked lost for words. He stood up, pulling her with him. 'You're serious?'

She nodded. He kissed her.

She pulled away. 'I still want a ring, though.' She looked around. 'And a proper proposal. This doesn't count.'

'Whatever ring you want,' Yousef replied, his voice giddy with excitement.

'And you'll have to ask my dad's permission, pretend none of this happened. He'll need to think he was in charge,' she said, suddenly thinking about how things needed to be done.

'Jeez, I thought my family were the traditional ones!' Yousef said. 'I'll do whatever it takes.'

'We're going to get married?' Jess asked, her voice high pitched.

'We're going to get married,' Yousef whispered. 'I love you.'

Chapter Fifty-Eight

Yousef

YOUSEF RETURNED HOME AFTER watching Jess train. He loved watching her play. She was meeting Kate tonight but said she would come round later. Being at Rohit's wedding had confirmed what he already knew: he wanted the same thing for Jess and himself. He had been going to buy a ring when he got back, planning on a grand proposal, but last week when Jess had come over, the time had just felt right. And she had said *yes*. He still couldn't quite believe it, after all they had been through. It was a strange feeling. Yousef was happier than he had been in a long time, but he wasn't content. Rohit's wedding was good for him in many ways, but at the same time seeing his best friend surrounded by his family, all of them immersed in the wedding preparations, happy for *both* the bride and groom, he hated to admit he felt pangs of jealousy. He thought he had vanquished these feelings months ago. He had known leaving his family would be difficult, but he'd hoped the joy of being free to spend time with Jess would more than compensate for it. And in the most part it had, but there was always a sadness that lurked in the periphery of his new life.

He loved his life in Frome, his job was going well and Jess's family and friends were now his. The darkness that prevented him from being totally satisfied was more than not having his parents' blessing; it was the complete absence of Pakistani culture in his life. He had grown up being able to enjoy the best parts of his heritage whilst straddling his British upbringing, but that connection had been lost when he severed ties with his family. He missed trying to talk in Urdu to his dad's friends, coming home knowing there would be a delicious curry on the table, aunties dropping by unannounced. He missed pretending not to enjoy his mum's Asian dramas on the telly and even missed his dad making him go to the mosque. It was all a part of him, without which Yousef felt incomplete.

But being incomplete was the price he was willing to pay so he could be free to love Jess openly, and it was worth it. He took out a fajita-making kit from the cupboard. Jess would be hungry when she came by later and Mexican food was her favourite. He laid out the peppers and onions ready to chop. He still hadn't quite mastered cooking but was getting better at it. The doorbell rang. Jess must have finished with Kate early. He wiped his hands on a tea towel and opened the door.

It was his parents. He stood in the doorway, unable to move. What were they doing here?

The shock of seeing them gave way to panic that there might be some sort of awful showdown where they tried to persuade him to come home.

'Mum, Dad,' was all he was able to get out. 'You're here?'

The three of them stared at each other, still, as though any movement could shatter the moment.

His dad pushed past his mother and took Yousef by the shoulders. 'My son,' he whispered, enveloping Yousef in a hug. Yousef, rigid at first, sank into the hug, his dad's familiar smell washing over him.

'It's good to see you, beta,' his dad said, emotion overcoming him.

'Dad, I . . .' Yousef still didn't know what to say. They embraced again. His dad stepped aside, so his mum could see him. She didn't move. 'Mum, hi. Do you want to come in?' Yousef said.

His mum didn't make eye contact with him as she entered. She was wrapped in a shawl, despite it being August, and was carrying a plastic bag that looked heavy. She looked around the living room, still silent.

'Are you well, beta?' his dad asked.

'Yes, Dad, how are you?'

'We are missing our children,' his dad replied. 'Life is not the same as it once was.'

Yousef looked at his mother. 'You've come a long way, shall I make you a cup of tea? I was, erm, about to make fajitas. Would you like some?'

She shook her head. 'I have brought you food. Your favourites: paneer saag, aloo gosh and channa rice. Make sure you sprinkle water on the rice before you heat it up in the microwave, otherwise it won't fluff up.' She handed him the plastic bag. 'There are some samosas in there too, homemade.'

'Right. Thanks.' Yousef took the bag. The three of them stared at one another. 'How did you find me?' he asked, not quite sure what to say.

'Your sister,' his dad said, wiping his eyes. 'She said you met at a nearby cafe. We asked around until we met one of your neighbours, Alice. She told us.'

'Right, Alice.' Yousef nodded. 'She lives two doors down.'

Another awkward silence.

His mum was walking around, first looking at the furniture, then stopping at the photos above the fireplace of him and Jess.

'Yousef, you left us,' she said quietly.

'Mum, I—' he started.

'You left us and you didn't phone to see how we were, not even *one* phone call,' she said. Her voice broke. Yousef couldn't remember ever seeing his mum cry.

'Mum, I had no choice.' He hoped she wasn't here to lecture him. He was no longer prepared to stand for it.

'Was life so bad with your family?' she asked. 'With your parents?'

'No, Mum, it wasn't. But I had to do the right thing for me, for my happiness.'

'Why didn't you just talk to us, son?' his dad interjected. 'Be honest with us from the start?'

Yousef looked at the floor. 'I didn't want to embarrass you, I didn't want to bring shame on the family. You have always said that was the worst thing I could ever do.'

'There are worse things,' his dad said. 'A father without his son, that is worse.'

'I'm sorry, Dad.'

His mother picked up the photo of him and Jess at the beach. 'Are you happy here?' she asked, staring at the picture.

'I am happy, Mum. I'm so much happier now.'

She nodded. 'That's good. That is all I wanted for you.'

'Mum, all I want is for you to be happy for me. Happy for me and Jess, *together*.' Yousef took a step closer to his mother.

'I always taught you to be honest with us.' She turned to look at him. 'But you lied to me, you lied to all of us.'

'I'm sorry, Mum. I just didn't know what else to do.'

'It's okay, beta,' his dad said, shooting his mother a look. 'We are not here to argue, we just want you back in our lives.'

'That's all I want too, Dad, but it can't be like it was before. It can't be you both telling me what to do, how to behave, how to **think**.'

His mum turned to look at him. 'Not even a phone call, Yousef? You took the light from our lives, broke our hearts and you didn't even call to see if we were okay?'

'I'm sorry, Ma,' Yousef said. 'I didn't think you'd want to hear from me. Rehana said you couldn't even bring yourself to ask about me.'

'Am I that bad of a mother that you simply stopped caring?'

'No, Mum, it's just you wouldn't *listen*.' Yousef looked at his mother. 'But Mum, what you did, all those things. Going to the hospital to see Jess, encouraging me to marry Seema—'

'I know what I did,' she said, cutting him off. She was crying now. 'I thought it was the right thing when I did those things. Believe me, I really did.'

'Mum, listen, we don't have to bring all that up now,' Yousef said.

'Yes, we do,' she said. 'I have to tell you something, Yousef.'

'Mum . . .' Despite everything, he didn't want to see his mum cry.

'Let me finish,' she said. 'I have paid a heavy price for my actions and I have come here to tell you I am sorry. I am sorry for what I did to you and to . . . Jessica. Can you forgive me?'

Yousef knew his mother never apologized. Never.

'Of course I forgive you, Mum.' He felt the sting of tears in his eyes.

'But you should be sorry too,' she said.

Here was the mum he knew. 'Me?' he said. 'For what?'

'We are your elders, it should be you coming to see us,' she said, pulling him closer to him. 'You should never have left it this long.'

He hugged her. 'I'm sorry too, Mum. You're right, I should never have left it this long.'

'It's okay, beta,' his mum whispered in his ear. 'Elders always forgive.'

'Now we can have a cup of tea,' Abdul announced.

Yousef went to put the kettle on. His mother began unpacking the food she had brought.

'Where is your freezer?' she asked. 'You can have the saag tonight with the rice, and freeze the gosh and eat it another day.'

Yousef showed his mother where the freezer was.

'This is your freezer?' she asked incredulously. 'It is so *small*. How do you fit all your food in there?'

Yousef looked at his dad, who was shaking his head and smiling.

'No, no, this will not do,' his mum continued, 'Abdul, what time is it? Is there a Currys in this village? You need a bigger freezer.'

'Mum, it's fine. I can get one online.'

'*Online!*' his mum exclaimed. 'Look' – she turned to her husband – 'modern children now, getting everything online. Yousef, you need to go and choose a freezer from the store. You need to see how many compartments it has, you need to know whether they are big enough for trays of samosas, you need to—'

There was a knock on the door. They all froze for a second. Yousef went to get it.

'Mum, Dad,' he said, bringing the new arrival into the room. 'This is Jess.'

Yousef's parents stared at Jess.

'Hello, Mr and Mrs Ahmed,' Jess said. 'Nice to meet you.' She paused and looked at his mum. 'Again.'

His parents remained silent.

'Yousef didn't tell me you were coming, did you, Yousef?' she hissed at him. 'I would have worn something more appropriate. I've just come back from football practice. Sorry, I'm still in my kit.'

His dad stepped forward. 'Hi, Jessica, nice to meet you.'

Jess put out her hand, 'You must be Abdul—'

'*Uncle*,' Yousef whispered at her.

'Sorry, *Uncle* Abdul,' Jess quickly corrected.

'Do you *live* here?' his mum asked.

'Oh, God no,' Jess replied, laughing awkwardly. 'My parents would never allow me to move in with someone without marrying them.'

'Sensible parents,' Yousef's mum said.

'I just came round for dinner. Yousef was going to make Mexican food,' Jess continued. 'That's my favourite.'

'Actually,' his mum said, 'I brought some home-cooked Pakistani food. We thought we would eat that instead.'

'Oh wow,' Jess said, with genuine excitement. 'I've heard about your food, Aunty Feroza. Yousef talks about it all the time. I can't believe I'm finally going to taste it.'

'Well, thank you.' His mum sounded slightly disarmed. 'Why don't you get changed and we will get the food ready?'

Jess nodded and headed for the stairs, 'Yousef?' she called from the landing. 'Can I just have a quick word with you, please?'

'Coming!' Yousef headed upstairs. This was not the evening he had been planning. Jess pulled him into the bedroom.

'What the heck's going on, Yous?' she said in an aggressive whisper. 'You didn't tell me your *parents* would be coming.'

'I didn't *know*,' Yousef said. 'Alice told them where I lived and they just turned up.'

'Bloody Alice, she can never keep her nose out of people's business. What do they want?' Jess asked.

'They're not here to cause trouble, Jess. I think they want to make amends.' He looked at Jess. 'Mum even *apologized*.'

Jess paced the bedroom. 'I can't believe that the first time I meet your folks, I'm in shorts and my legs are covered in mud.' She caught a glimpse of herself in the mirror. 'Jesus, look at the state of my *hair*!'

'Jess, you look fine,' he said, trying to calm her down.

'No, I don't. It's no wonder they want you to marry a nice pretty Pakistani girl, when I turn up looking like this.' She headed to the bathroom. 'I need a shower, and some time to think.'

Yousef left her to it, and headed back downstairs. His head was spinning.

'She seems like a nice girl,' his dad said as he came back to the kitchen.

'Does she always wear such *short* shorts?' his mum enquired.

'Mum!' Yousef said firmly.

She put her hands up. 'Sorry, it's cold outside. I am just worried, like any normal mother would be.' She passed him the saag. 'Put this in the microwave for two minutes.'

Yousef did as he was told. His mum emptied the rice into another dish and his dad was searching his cupboards for glasses.

'Mum, Dad, I have something to tell you,' he said. His mum had said that honesty was all they had ever wanted from him, so it was only right that he was honest now.

'What is it, beta?' his dad asked.

'I've asked Jess to marry me. And she's said yes.'

It wasn't as hard as he had expected. The words felt good coming out of his mouth. There was none of that anxiety about keeping something from them, agonizing over the right time, the right phrasing.

'Marriage?' his mum said. 'She's not . . .'

'No, mum, she's not *pregnant!*' Yousef said. 'For God's sake.'

'My son is *engaged*,' his dad said, wide-eyed.

'When are you going to get married?' his mum asked.

'Well, nothing is decided yet, I only asked her last week. I guess we have to plan it.' He looked at his mum and dad. 'But I really want you to be there. By my side.'

His dad looked at his mum. She was still processing this new information. 'What parents wouldn't come to their only son's wedding?' he finally said. 'This is really good news, my son. Isn't it, Feroza?'

'Wait a minute. Nothing is planned?' his mum said slowly.

'Not yet,' Yousef replied, slightly confused at this line of questioning.

'No venue, no dates, no decorations, no *dresses*?' his mum said, more to herself than to either Yousef or his dad.

'Well, it's early days. I haven't even got Jess an engagement ring yet.'

'What kind of wedding are you going to have, English or Pakistani?' his mum asked.

'We hadn't really thought about it.'

'You will have to have a nikkah, you cannot get married without a nikkah,' his mum said firmly.

'I don't know . . .' Yousef cut in.

His mum turned to his dad. 'We can make this work. If we give it our blessing, the rest of the community wouldn't be able to gossip about it. We can tell them how proud we are of our son and new daughter-in-law,' she said. 'A mixed wedding, brown and white. Nobody has done that before.' She paused and thought about it. 'Well, not with their parents' blessing anyway.'

'Feroza, I think you need to *calm down*,' his dad said.

'Musarat will be so *jealous*! She thinks she is so modern, I will show her!' his mum continued, ignoring her husband. 'All the class of a white wedding and the food of a Pakistani wedding. Perhaps instead of hiring a minibus to transport the guests to the venue we can hire a vintage red double-decker bus. I saw that on television. It's very English, no? Our family in Pakistan will think they are going to a royal wedding!' She turned to Yousef. 'Obviously, with her pale complexion she couldn't wear the traditional red dress. But maybe we could get something made up in white, then it would embrace both cultures.'

'Mum!' Yousef tried again.

'Feroza . . .' his dad said.

'She will have to wear green at the *mehndi*, not yellow. Pale people do not suit yellow.'

'Well, I'll need to talk to Jess about that . . .' Yousef tried to say.

'Talk to me about what?' Jess entered the kitchen. 'Sorry about that, just had a quick shower. What can I do to help?' She looked around. They were all staring at her. 'What?'

'My **daughter**!' Yousef's mum cried out, hurrying over to her. 'Yousef just told us the good news!' She put her arm around Jess, pulling her in.

'What good news?' Jess asked.

'That we're engaged,' Yousef said.

'Oh, right.' Jess looked blindsided again. 'Yes, I suppose we are. Though Yousef hasn't officially asked my dad for my hand yet . . . He's quite traditional.'

Feroza nodded appreciatively. 'Traditions are good. But there is no time to waste,' she said. 'We have a wedding to plan.'

'Aunty, we haven't really got to that stage—'

'Don't worry, my child. That is what I am here for.'

Jess looked at Yousef for help. He smiled and shrugged.

'Come, beta, I know we have had our differences but you're family now.' Yousef thought that was the nearest Jess might get to an apology. 'Help me prepare dinner.' Yousef's mum guided Jess to the kitchen area. 'We have lots to talk about. We can speak to your parents and help them plan the wedding. Now, you must tell me how much holiday allowance do you get from work? But first, obviously Yousef cannot simply propose to you, we need to have a small engagement ceremony, only about a hundred of our closest friends . . .'

Glossary

aarati – a Hindu ritual of worship, where light (usually in the form of a candle) is offered up to the gods

Assalamualaikum – Muslim greeting meaning 'Peace be upon you'

beta – 'my child'

bezati – 'shame' or 'humiliation'

bharat – groom's wedding procession

challo – 'let's go'

charan sparsh – bowing down to touch someone's feet in reverence

choli – a short-sleeved bodice worn as part of traditional South Asian clothing

Daadi Maa – Grandmother

dawat – dinner invitation

dhandia – sticks used in traditional dancing

dhol – double-sided barrel drum played in traditional South Asian celebrations

dholki – South Asian drumming

dhula, dhulan – groom, bride

dupatta – scarf

gharara – a pair of loose trousers with pleats below the knee worn by women from South Asia

gol gappay – a crispy fried pastry ball filled with spicy water, chickpeas and onions

goray – white person or people

haar – a garland of flowers

haladi – turmeric, applied before a wedding to the bride or groom

inshallah – 'if God wills'

itna mahenga – 'so expensive'

jaadu – magic

jai malas – the exchange of garlands at a Hindu wedding to signify unity

jyotishi – one with the knowledge of astrology and constellations

kanyadaan – the giving away of the bride

kameez – long tunic worn by people from South Asia

khoti – large open-plan house

kurta – a long, loose collarless shirt

ladoo – an Indian sweet made from sugar and flour

lengha – a full, ankle-length skirt worn by South Asian women

maasi – an affectionate term for a housekeeper

magni – engagement

mandap – a temporary structure constructed for the purpose of a wedding ceremony

mangalsutra – a necklace worn by a Hindu woman to signify she is married

mashallah – 'thanks be to God', or 'what God has willed'

mehram – a family member or friend with whom marriage would be unlawful

mehndi – a night of fun before a wedding with dancing and food

mithai – sweets

namaaz – obligatory prayers for Muslims

nazar – black magic

nikkah – an Islamic-law marriage

pagri – a turban or hat worn by the groom at his wedding

puthar – Punjabi word for 'son' or 'child'

ras malai – an Indian dessert make with cheese, milk and nuts

rishta – confirming an arrangement of a wedding proposal

rukhsati – the end of a wedding, when the bride departs and leaves her family to start a new life with her husband

rumaal – scarf

Sangeet – a Hindu ceremony prior to the wedding for partying, dancing and singing

saptapadi – the seven steps a couple takes together during a Hindu marriage ceremony

shaadi – wedding

shabaash – 'well done'

shalwar kameez – traditional South Asian combination of a long, loose fitted collarless shirt or dress with loose trousers which are narrow at the bottom.

sharmeeli – 'shy'

sherab – alcohol

sherwani shevani – a knee-length coat, buttoning to the neck

thasbi – the Muslim equivalent of a rosary

thoba – 'God forgive me'

upton – the ceremony where turmeric paste is applied to the bride or groom before their wedding

walaikum salam – 'and unto you peace'

walima – a celebration that follows the wedding ceremony, usually organized by the groom and his family

Dr Amir Khan is a full-time GP and bestselling author working in inner-city Bradford.

Amir is a resident doctor for ITV's *Lorraine* and *Good Morning Britain* and has recently been seen hosting *Dr Amir's Sugar Crash* (Channel 5) and *You Are What You Eat* (Channel 5) with Trisha Goddard.

Amir is president of the RSPB, vice president of The Wildlife Trusts and an ambassador for the British Hedgehog Preservation Society and Butterfly Conservation, working closely with them to ensure access to green spaces for inner-city children and spreading the word on how being outside with nature is good for health. When he is not in surgery or on TV, Amir spends his time gardening, baking, running and supporting wildlife conservation.

He is the *Sunday Times* bestselling author of *The Doctor Will See You Now*. *How (Not) to Have an Arranged Marriage* is his first novel.